Irish Eyes...

"Tonight I just want to fill my being with looking and longing." His eyes, livened by hunger, shone like sapphires, hardened to brilliant perfection.

She quivered beneath his gaze, unaware that his hands had stopped touching her. Her soul seemed to burn and cry out its loneliness. Loneliness she did not know existed until this night. A virgin still, she lay before him, a child no longer, threshold crossed and womanhood come. From this point on her life would be a dull aching nothingness unless he was near.

And in that moment she vowed: No man would ever touch her, save Kevin the McErin...

Raven at Sunrise

Claudia McCormick

DIAMOND BOOKS, NEW YORK

RAVEN AT SUNRISE

A Diamond Book / published by arrangement with
the author

PRINTING HISTORY
Diamond edition/April 1991

All rights reserved.
Copyright © 1991 by Claudia McCormick.
This book may not be reproduced in whole or in part, by
mimeograph or any other means, without permission. For
information address: The Berkley Publishing Group, 200
Madison Avenue, New York, New York 10016.

ISBN: 1-55773-489-5

Diamond Books are published by The Berkley Publishing
Group, 200 Madison Avenue, New York, New York 10016.
The name "DIAMOND" and its logo are trademarks
belonging to Charter Communications, Inc.

PRINTED IN THE UNITED STATES OF AMERICA

10 9 8 7 6 5 4 3 2 1

To Mary Dubh

Acknowledgments

I wish to thank Mary Brockway for her sharp eye and sensitivity to "all things Irish"; my colleague, friend and resource librarian, Jack McCormick; Linda Lee, founder of The Edmonds Writing School and Linda Meyer, founder of The Charles Franklin Press, whose encouragement was instrumental in bringing me back to my native northwest, where I subsequently became founding president of The Seattle Chapter of National Writers Club; and those members of The Seattle Chapter, past and present, whose encouragement and support have enriched my life. Thanks also to Richard Curtis, whose workshop for the Chapter brought this manuscript to publication; and Beth Fleisher and Jennifer Enderlin of Berkley, whose editorial skills have brought to light a people whose thinking patterns and belief system are totally different from ours.

Although this work is entirely fiction, I cannot help but be grateful for those legendary heroes, real or imagined, who stubbornly refused to die and to their chroniclers who sparked the flame that brought this story to life.

But most of all, I am grateful to a woman named Madgie, who lived next door to me when I was a child, and night after night gathered the entire neighborhood around her, creating what the Irish call a *ceili*—a telling place—and birthed in me a sense of story.

"To live
one must challenge the gods
and demand life.
If they grant you your wish,
they may allow you to die a hero."

OLDE CELTIC PROVERB

Foreword

Before the coming of Saint Patrick, mighty warriors walked Ireland as young gods. Handpicked, and gruelingly trained, they were known collectively as the Fianna. They so inspired the poets' fancy by near magical feats of daring that they still walk, untouched by mortal hands.

They were chosen from among the nobles when very young, often at the great fairs of Tara, Uisnech, or Taillte, and they were put to fosterage, that is, given to other chieftains for training and to secure tribal alliance. Both families assumed responsibility, for the Fian led a rugged, hazardous life and could not be avenged.

All fathers taught their sons common skills: to ride, hunt, bear arms, and swim. Secondary education was a matter of aptitude and leaned toward math, arts, or sciences. Even then they were watched by the druoai, or druids, as we call them today. Druids were not just representative of the priesthood, as in this tale, but wise and learned men from many walks of life.

The Fian embarked upon an education that embodied the best of all possible learning. Sweet as they were savage, Cealteach were creatures of fierce loyalty and a finely keened sense of justice. Physical beauty, sense of symmetry, the need for balance, passionate love for all things, and deep respect for learning were their gods. The brow was the seat of learning, the skull the temple of the soul.

Since they roamed the wilds from Beltaine to Samhain (May to November) in the name of justice, they had to be well acquainted with brehonic law, both the intricacies and polemics of polity, its origins and history. Storytellers in their own right, they were not creators, but repositories of oral tradition.

They were required to memorize at least twelve books of poetry and were to recite, verbatim, the listener's choice whenever called upon. These stories are equivalent to *Beowulf*, the *Song of Roland, Gilgamesh,* or even this tale, were it set in poetry and not lyrical prose. Ireland was the only place in the world with an official season of storytelling. It began when the cattle were brought back on Samhain (November 1) and ended at their move to summer pasturage on Beltaine (May 1). The longest tale on record in Ireland today takes four nights in the telling.

Because life was sacred, war held different meaning. Often it was fought and won with oratorical skills. The Fian called challenge and bore arms, and great was the hero who could spare his people by the turning of a phrase.

Although they were a deeply religious people, they had no creation cycle. The glories of war were held in high esteem, and in those tales the heroes of today became the gods of tomorrow.

As youths, the Fianna were required to run through the wood, driven into pits deep as their kneecaps, and expected to rise unscathed from the deadly aim of at least ten lances. They could leap as high as they were tall, pick a sliver from an enemy's chest with their toes, and run a field without disturbing a blade. Totally fearless of death, they most often fought naked as battle heat, or furor, overcame them. Yet, in the face of all odds, their weapon must not shake in their hand.

Before becoming Fian, the warrior must agree to uphold the four rules of the geasa, or vows of chivalry, which are:

FOREWORD

- He must never be violent or disrespectful toward any woman.
- He must never refuse any request for help, however costly.
- He must never run from any less than ten men.
- But first and foremost, he must take to himself a good and faithful wife.

Women were the equal of men in all things, for women were not banned from warfare until the late fifth century. There were as many as ten stations of marriage, but only a few of them binding. Marriage among the noble class tended toward both monogamy and permanence.

But Fianna did not live as other men and could not look for a wife as other men did. A Fian could not give thought to wealth or social position, nor think to ease life or increase holdings through marriage.

Instead, he must choose a wife of:

- comely virtue,
- goodly manners, and, most of all,
- agreeable, pleasant, and kindly disposition. . . .

Raven at Sunrise

Chapter 1

Brigianna ni Colym slipped inside her father's meadhall and clung to the outer wall, silent as a shadow. Careful to keep her eyes down, she edged her way through the darkened maze of clansmen eagerly awaiting the feast of Beltaine.

Smoke from the central fire pit funneled toward the flume. But it had been a rainy spring, the thatch was wet, and cough-spitting haze blanketed the room. Parting strands of ravenblack hair that shielded clabber-smooth skin and startling blue eyes, Brigianna watched her father talking with his druid.

Tormaigh McColym was a generous chieftain, offering protection to anyone willing to work; as a result he rarely kept slaves and, with canny wariness, he knew his people well. Most of his clansmen had sparkling blue eyes and dark, unruly hair. The few that didn't, such as the druid, Lochobar, were related to the clan by fealty, not by blood.

Tormaigh sat directly opposite the fire pit. He was behind his bronzed lap table and squatted comfortably on his furs. Next to him sat his wife, Fiona, his mother, Amabel, and his rabble of children. A wide smile graced his beardless face and his wiry body bore the pride of a well-honed hunter. As he turned to look up at Lochobar, his crown slipped to one side and lay buried in a tumble of graying curls. He caught it absentmindedly, then reached for his wife's hand.

She glanced from husband to priest and slowly nodded assent. Something in her look disquieted Brigianna, making her want to disappear into the shadows forever. But too late! Her father had seen her.

"Brigianna!" he called.

Lochobar spun around and a wide smile brightened his bony face. Ceremoniously he took his place near the fire. Knowing she dared not disobey, Brigianna sat down just as ceremoniously by her brothers and little sister, Dierdre.

Even after bearing nine children, Fiona was still lithe and slim. Brushing a strand of graying hair from her face, she gave her daughter a reprimanding glance. "Ye disgrace your father by making us wait. Moodiness at moonset is not a thing well tolerated by men; it makes them nervous, especially on feast days when there are portents to be made. Now push your hair away from your face and listen up."

Stubbornly Brigianna hunched forward. Her raven hair cascaded over her face, shielding her from the disturbed glances of her clansmen and from Lochobar's penetrating gaze. Hers was a world of darkness, and she willed it so. Pulling the cowl of her cloak over her face, she concentrated on darkness until her hackles rose.

She did not understand this moon madness, nor did she understand why she had it and her mother did not. The heavier her flow, the worse her disposition. The worse her disposition, the more susceptible she was to priestpower. Now the flow had subsided but had left her exhausted. And tonight, she promised herself, she would not look up, she would not fall prey to casting games. In deep concentration she stared at the floor.

Tormaigh stood. "Silence," he announced, and the din stopped as if he had sliced it with his knife.

Lochobar held his hand perfectly still.

Beneath it, suspended by a single golden thread, the amber trembled as its life-force wakened. Slowly at first, then gaining momentum, the translucent stone began to circle in a wide arc. Safe in the shadows and away from the glow of the central fire, the clan watched intently as the golden resin, dug deep from the bowels of earth, where all mysteries of time lay safely buried, held them captive.

The stone caught the glow of the central fire to shower withe and wattle dome with a splatter of bright lights. Through this magic window the clan would see sights that rivaled the northern lights; though not one of them would ever speak of this later in the cool, clear light of day.

Lochobar possessed the wide, rounded forehead of priests, wizards, and scholars and eyes that flashed golden fire. His skin hung to his frame in waxy folds, desperately clinging to the last vestiges of life; his long gray beard spilled down his hairless chest in scraggly curls. He wore a loincloth and a massive cloak of mottled wool, into which were sewn hundreds of ravenfeathers. The hem of this cloak was attached to his wrists by wide leather bands so that it moved with him, and when he spread his arms wide, he became the image of that dark and dreadful bird.

He stood perfectly still, hand steady above the amulet. Beneath it a shower of bright lights flashed iridescent green, brilliant blue, and smoldering, hot purple and rained against the withe and wattle dome.

Seeing old Lochobar's eyes turn as golden as their sacred stone, the clan took comfort. Soon secrets would unfold. They stared at their priest like eager children. Their chieftain leaned forward.

Even with her head down and her eyes closed, Brigianna felt the flashing fire in Lochobar's yellow eyes.

"Brigianna!" he hissed like a sword of lightning rending the sky asunder, and his call pierced her inner being.

But like a newly forged blade at its first blooding, she was born to fight. She would not fall prey to the priestpower; she would be in control of her own life! "No!" she cried, willing Lochobar's fiery gaze into darkness.

No word passed between them; that is, no word the clan could hear or understand. But Brigianna's unbending will clashed with Lochobar's bidding, and the force of its fury struck a soul-crunching blow to each of them.

Lochobar flinched and staggered backward in surprise, a quick movement, barely perceptible. Sweat beaded across his forehead.

Exchanging fearful looks, the clan drew back with suspended breath.

Beneath her cloak Brigianna clenched her hands together so tightly her knuckles turned white. She pushed them hard against each other, fiercely battling the power of Lochobar's gleaming yellow eyes. He smoldered with inner rage. "Brigianna? My beloved Brigianna? My spirit-child—you defy me?" he hissed. "How dare you! 'He who obeys not his priest must be banished.' Banished! You know this, and still you defy me?"

Brigianna felt his snapping anger welt her cheek. Trembling, she put her face to the earth, resolved not to look.

Tormaigh leaned forward, frowning. His eyes squinted into half-moons as he tried to fathom the depths of his priest's golden eyes. He saw nothing. Those eyes were like evening sun on water and just as blinding. Quickly he turned away.

Fiona scooted closer to him, but her eyes wandered back, helplessly locked in Lochobar's gaze. Now even men whose swords had drunk blood and whose bones had felt death lowered their eyelids. Sweat beaded their upper lips like mustaches.

Finally Lochobar broke the deadlock. At the sound of his voice Brigianna jerked her head upward, empty eyes veiled in fear.

"Divine for us, chieftain's daughter," he began in a voice like a gentle wind stirring up dry leaves of the forest.

"No!" She trembled, eyes aburn like hot coals. "Please, I beg!"

Lochobar's fury dashed across the hall. Brigianna's dander rose, a sword of ire in front of her. She gripped it with both hands, ready to do battle.

In her mind's eye she leapt high above the clan, brandishing her blade. But in one fleeting moment of self-doubt, she hesitated, and in that split second before courage and determination rallied to the fore, Lochobar, armed with invincible, eternal power, forced her down.

When she looked up, she saw him not as he was, but as a warrior standing duty with his feet braced apart, his blade pointed to the dirt, and his hand resting on the hilt. When he turned the blade and raised it in the air, it turned white hot, with sizzling waves of emerald and cobalt emanating from it. Seeing it, her resolve crumbled to dust and lay beside her, a useless and forgotten dream.

She looked again and realized she was staring into the amulet.

Mesmerized by their sacred stone, the clan saw their withy dome splattered with kaleidoscopic light, brighter than the aurora borealis. It surrounded them, filling them with an inner glow, certain as if they were standing inside a rainbow, and their faith was complete.

As she had done ever since she was a child, too young to question but old enough to trust, Brigianna came to him by silent bidding. She walked through the sparkling haze of lights in the deliberate gait of the bewitched, her cheeks drenched with tears she didn't know she'd shed. Her hair, rich as obsidian, blazed with deep blue and green shadows, just like the ravenfeathers in the old priest's cloak.

Unlike her clanswomen, she walked proudly with chin raised. Wary in her presence for the first time, Lochobar's eyes narrowed.

Obediently Brigianna ni Colym knelt before her priest and bent backward, hands held upward in silent supplication. Slowly she began to sway, following an inner rhythm known only to her. Eyes rolled back into her head till only the whites showed against her delicate ivory skin.

Lochobar smiled slightly, but held his hand steady. Fires within his eyes warmed as the translucent stone continued to shower the dome with blinding, capricious lights, changeable as the unending sky.

"Beltaine's flame burns bright. Our cattle have passed through fire; our wealth is protected," he cawed. "Tell us, chieftain's daughter, what fate awaits. Will our women be fertile? Our men strong? Our lands lie in peace? Portend, Brigianna. The McColyms await."

Lochobar could make his voice rumble like a distant storm, turn shrill as the sidhe, or project it from the farthest corner of the domed hut to become a spirit voice calling from a surprised and innocent body. All this he did, waiting Brigianna's portent. Watching his clansmen, his eyes burned fierce with possessive fire. Soon their breathing deepened and they panted in unison. Their panting became as furtive as the hoofbeats of deer in flight.

Nostrils flared as Brigianna honed in on the pattern of their breathing, swaying to a music beyond call of human ears. Her head fell back; heavy lashes fluttered over white, sightless eyes; lips parted in answer to an ancient call rising deep within.

Like the welling of an ill wind, her keening rose above the steady dip and swell of tranced breathing.

Lochobar's bones creaked as he leaned forward so that his face nearly touched hers. "Tell us our fate!"

As she gazed into Lochobar's yellow eyes, her blank look registered a shadow of surprise. In those eyes she saw two ravens flying the golden sky. Two ravens winging their flight into the hidden world of secrets. She alone saw the ravens. Nestled deep within unfathomable reaches of her druid's eyes, they stirred up deep yearnings.

The vision faded as quickly as it had come, and her body went rigid. When she spoke, her voice came from inside a hollow well and was not her voice at all. When she stopped, she stopped right in the middle of a word.

Perspiration clung to her like dew. Pain flashed through her eyes, and she slumped to the floor.

Time was suspended, caught in the black fishnet of forever.

"Brigianna! Brigianna! Ye portend your own future."

Fiona rushed to her and feverishly pinched her cheeks. Leaning on her haunches, she sighed her relief as Brigianna's color returned.

"Ye are to wed, my fair Brigianna, ye are to wed."

The years had marked Fiona's face and clouded her eyes. Still, to see the mother was to see the daughter's future, and Fiona looked like Brigianna's fetch then, come to warn her.

"But it's an old man she's got, and not a fair and handsome laddie like her heart's been set," Brigianna's lookalike sister cried and skewed her face into a knot. "Oh, Brigianna, more's the sorrow."

"Hush, Dierdre, if it is to be, it is to be. Never do we question the stone, or its priest," Amabel cut in.

Amabel, as kingmother, was everyone's favorite and much fatter than the rest. Even Tormaigh gave her cream and fatlings, sometimes even the chieftain's cut. Always seeking Lochobar's approval, she stole a quick glance his way. Seeing her remark had not gone unnoticed, she smiled sweetly and added. "Ye ken?"

"Aye, Grandmother," Dierdre said, voicing acceptance of ancient ways, which were never questioned.

"That's me darling," Amabel cooed, catching Dierdre's smile. "But what's this? A wedding it is?"

Brigianna moaned and put her hands to her head, trying to bring the sea of smiling faces into focus. "A wedding? Whose?"

"Why, your very own," her mother answered.

From near the fire Balfe raised a grimy fingernail to the gut and strummed a sharp note on his lap harp. Immediately babbling women edged back to their places, leaving Brigianna alone.

Nothing was so terrible in all Ireland as a bard gone sour. Grumpish and crotchety, they blessed or cursed, all in the guise of winsome melody or clever verse. Knowing this, Brigianna quickly sat up and tossed her hair back over her shoulder with a defiant air.

Lochobar's eyes were no longer a brilliant gold. Instead, they had turned a deep and shadowy green. They were like the sapphires of earth: gold green, or midnight blue, depending upon his mood.

She saw nothing in them now, for he had shielded his thoughts from her. Hurt by this, and still angry, she looked away as Tormaigh's bard pronounced her fate. Curling the corners of his mouth into a satisfied sneer, he paused only long enough to make certain he held the clan's rapt attention before he strummed the gut with his grimy fingernail.

She, Brigianna ni Colym, was slated to become a Finucane. Through this union the fertile valley, north to the great oak derries and east to the shining sea, would be made safe for both clans.

Though the valley was fertile, the Finucane in question was an old man with the best of his battles behind him. "Alas, fair maiden, alas," Balfe wailed, "his only trophy, a dinger in a slinger, for by now, certainly, his dong has gone wrong."

Brigianna's eyes snapped with anger as the look on his face told her the obscenity was no accident.

Caught off guard by Balfe's blatant humor, Amabel giggled. Too late she put her hand to her mouth. High-pitched titters burst out among the women, and gut-rumbling laughter erupted from the men.

"No!" Brigianna cried and threw herself at her father's feet. Panic cast aside all semblance of dignity. The clan, horrified by this outburst, drew back, uncertain what their chieftain would do next.

Tormaigh McColym stood up. He had been pleased with this alliance, ever since Lochobar first mentioned it. It could make him a rich man.

"Ye have forecast weddings, birthings, and even deaths at our feast days before, but at your own forecast ye grovel like some common beggar? Daughter, ye shame me."

"No, Father, it's ye who shame me!" she cried with tears streaming down her face. "I'm still a maid ablush, and ye would bed me to an old man ready to eat soft meats and cold soup? Me? Your favorite?"

"I would plant the seeds of kings in ye, bonny darling. I would ye bear seven sons like your mother before ye. I would have ye bring honor and sunshine to me old age."

"No, Father! Oh, hear me, I beg."

She spun around to search the hall for her youngest brother, Doughall. Her heavy cloak caught beneath her knees and plunged her vanishing dignity even further to the ground. Of all her brothers only Doughall possessed her same spit and fire. Surely he would help.

But he was nowhere near.

Choking in despair, she turned back to her father, and as she looked up, her muffled cry was like a trapped rabbit's.

The McColym had spit into his hands, rubbed them together, and raised them in triumph. By the power invested in him as chieftain, he had by his own spit and right sealed his daughter's fate.

Immediately the hall rang with shouts of joy and laughter.

To the McColyms, the deed was good as done.

Brigianna slowly turned to face Lochobar. Haunting those green eyes was the shadow of grief and a look on his face she did not understand.

Then she saw the ravens again, flying deep within blue-green shadows. Through thick forests and over high, treacherous mountains, they coursed to the sea and flew steadily onward, certain of their path and bidding her to come. Then the priest's eyes narrowed, and the ravens were no more.

What happened next happened very quickly.

While the clan was distracted by gossip and busily exchanging opinions over this good news, Lochobar turned to face the fire. His waxy skin gleamed in the golden light, and when he spread his arms wide, his cloak looked like the wings of that dark and dreadful bird. When he whirled around, something fell from his hand into the fire.

The hut became filled with nauseous gas. Hearthfire exploded into a violent shower of hissing sparks, which left black smoke trails behind.

Fiona screamed. She grabbed Dierdre by the hand and ran to the outer wall. Amabel was right behind them, wheezing and panting from the thick smoke. Children screamed and cried at the same time, choking on their own breath. Mothers threw their bodies over them for cover. Tormaigh sprang into action, his knife ready. His men, tight-lipped and wary, hurriedly followed their women to the outer wall.

Lochobar whirled round and round, flapping his cloak like the wings of the mighty raven. His eyes narrowed to yellow slits as he brushed his face close to Brigianna's.

"Go!" he demanded, as surely as if he had given the order out loud.

Brigianna's reaction was instinctive and unreasoned. She bolted through a side door and out into the night.

Darkness blinded her way. In spitless fear she waved her arms, trying to chase it away. Tiny hairs on her forearms prickled up at the sudden chill. She gathered her cloak tightly around her and stumbled on, unable to see. She came to an open area but couldn't tell where she was. Her feet had propelled her onward, but her disoriented mind lagged far behind.

Suddenly she stopped, not even daring to blink. In spite of the warmth from her cloak, the tiny hairs on her forearms prickled up again. Her throat went dry as she realized where she was. Blinded by her own fear she had run, unthinkingly, right into her father's cattle bawns.

She could feel the presence of the huge coppery beasts milling about her, even though she couldn't see them.

Blood pounded her ears. Her breath came in short, uneven

spurts and tore at her throat like hot fire. She wished she could call out, but she dared not. Very slowly she forced her breathing to even out.

Just then the clouds parted to give the moon full reign of the night, and her father's prized bull raised his head. Silvery rays caught the tips of his great horns, a span as wide as Brigianna was tall.

She had often been amongst the cattle with little concern; she had even come close to her father's prize bull, but not like tonight, not alone, not in the dark, where any sudden movement could make him charge. All too well she knew the dangers of aggravating this particular bull.

Willing her breathing to slow down, the acrid scent of fear away, and her blood to cease its furious pounding, she became as silent as a tree standing in the forest. Lochobar had taught her this. With eyes cast down so the moon's reflection against them wouldn't give her away, she watched the bull watching her. Earlier today this prized bull had led the procession of cattle through the two neat fires of Beltaine. Doughall had prodded the herd between the rows of bonfires while she ran happily by his side. The smell of fire was still on the cattle. And as the damp night air settled in, that smell, even more pungent, more acrid, clung to her cloak, masking her scent.

The moon played fickle games by darting naughtily behind dark clouds and then unveiling itself, making the night as bright as day. The herd milled about the pens, unaware of Brigianna's presence. She searched through the darkness, hoping to catch sight of Doughall, knowing she was safe as long as she didn't move. One sudden movement and her life could be over, snuffed out like a rushlight.

At the caprice of the wind the bull lifted his head and snorted. His eyes flashed white in the moonlight. Earth quaked beneath her.

In spite of the danger Brigianna couldn't help but admire his sinuous beauty. He is wonderful, she thought, thinking of her father's love and unabashed pride in his cattle.

But thinking of her priest's wicked game, she stiffened, realizing her father had sold her to the Finucanes as if she were one prized cow.

The bull caught this sudden movement. Nostrils flared as he lowered his head and faced her with flashing eyes. Testing the ground with his hoof, pawing it back and forth, he snorted his warning.

The moon darted behind a cloudbank and dyed the night indigo.

The bull let out a great bellow and charged.

Brigianna stood stone still, judging his speed and distance by the tremors in the ground.

With canny timing, she dived through a hole in the bawns, and the bull missed her by a hairbreadth, veered his course, and with a loud bawl crashed into the willow staves. His cows echoed his confusion as they fell all over themselves. Beneath their weight, the willow fence bowed like barrel staves.

The night wind howled with rage and confusion.

Behind her, Brigianna heard the fence strain and creak against the weight of the animals bumping into one another, and scrambled backward.

Suddenly she slipped and, in a tumble, fell down the hill. Her scream swirled behind her, lost in the maddening howl of the wind.

Chapter 2

Her fall propelled her into a laurel slick, dark as a bucket of pitch. Dank air nearly suffocated her. And even though she knew these boggy backwaters well by day, at night she was no more than a frightened animal with fear blotting out reason as instinct took over.

Jagged roots gouged her legs and tore at her skin. She reached for a branch and tried to pull herself up, but her hands were so wet from the sweat of fear that she slipped and fell. Underbrush stung her face and beat her back, parting willingly at her fall, then snapping back into place to whip her without mercy. Panting, she stopped to gulp air.

The tunneled labyrinth circled backward and had more blind paths than the fretwork on her father's crown. Gingerly she fingered the exposed roots of a large willow and confirmed her suspicion that she had been here before. Fear balled her gut, but she forced herself to ignore it. The sharp cree of a hawk startled her, and she bolted forward. Her scream matched the hawk's. Plunging headlong into a tangle of brush, she cried out again, this time in pain. She held her cloak tightly to her, crawling low to the ground so it wouldn't get caught on the sharp branches. Her head rang from the impact as she slid miserably deeper into the tangle.

The earth was boggy here and the grasses sweet smelling. She sniffed the wind and over the earthy smell of greening saplings caught the unmistakable scent of early spring irises and water lilies. Now she knew where she was. Like an animal nosing its way to fresh air, she made it through the brush and tumbled into the clearing, panting in relief.

The hillock around her father's land lay in the shape of a good drinking horn. Nestled in the hollows behind it, the clan remained hidden. Climbing up, she stopped at its spine to gain her bearings.

Fire glow reddened the night, and sounds of music and laughter whirled in the capricious whip of the wind. "Already they have forgotten me," she lamented and sat down on a rock to contemplate her fate. Shivering, she pulled her cloak, now her one prized possession, around her.

"Lochobar banished me. I defied him and he banished me. Father sold me off like one of his prized cows!" she cried to the great darkness above. "Do they no longer love me?"

The clan was everything. Without it she would become a faceless, nameless, human animal wandering in darkness. A soul without honor, left to the mercy of the gods. Had not Lochobar told her so? And often?

Her heart skipped back to happier times when she and Lochobar laughingly shared each other's thoughts. Even as a child, she clung to him, listening intently as he revealed dark mysteries during quiet walks in the wood. At storytime she ran wind with him, for as his apprentice, it was up to her to make certain he retold the legends correctly.

But when her womanblood came, and she marked moonset by it, her world changed. Her father, delighted, immediately made plans. "I'll not marry a man I do not know, just because ye say so," she announced, and Tormaigh looked at her in astonishment.

"Moonset often makes women stubborn. She'll sweet up like a marsh pea in no time," Fiona twittered nervously. But she didn't. She stood resolute and resolved to choose her own path. Finally Lochobar turned away; finally, he banished her.

Shuddering at her predicament, she cried to the darkness.

Suddenly a hawk plummeted out of the sky with such incredible speed the air behind his fall sang like the air behind the shaft of an arrow. Wings held tight to his body, and head down, he dove for the kill. The rabbit, crouching in the darkness not far from Brigianna, let out its one and only cry as the razor-sharp talons cracked its backbone and severed the spinal chord. Tearing into the warm, juicy meat, the hawk looked up to give Brigianna an indolent glare.

Brigianna felt the sky cave in above her and she screamed in terror. She cut a smart path east before she realized what had happened.

Perfidious May winds beat at her back and marched her on. Tenacious as the morning glory and just as gripping, pride fueled her steps. Well," she announced to the all-encompassing dark when she finally stopped for breath, "there'll be no turning back now."

If it weren't for the fickle turning of the moon, she could have passed through the night unnoticed. Her soft leather boots clung to her feet and muffled her footfalls, making her movements silent as shadows. Her hair, rich as obsidian, cascaded down her back and lost itself in darkness. Even the heavy woolen cloak wrapped tightly around her was as dark as a forest glen. But the scudding clouds picked up speed as the wind changed, and the moon glow bathed Brigianna in gossamer light that heralded her coming to waiting eyes below.

She put her hand to her neck to finger her golden torc as she always did when she needed comfort. It wasn't there. Instead, she traced the imaginary outline with her finger, remembering the necklace's delicately scrolled turnings, the almost silky feel of skillfully hammered gold.

It might have brought a worthy sum and guaranteed her keep, but in the end it might do her harm by announcing her station. Realizing this, she undid her brooch pin, which was shaped like a small sword, and drew it out of the circle of amethysts. The many facets of polished stone and hammered gold reflected the glow of the moon in a stunning paean of brilliance before she slipped it into the inside pocket of her boot. She put it next to the little silver dagger she always carried there, and walked on.

Like the hawk, the man came from nowhere; a hairy arm plunged out of darkness and grabbed her.

The hand caught her mouth and clamped her jaw shut, slicing her scream in two. The man backed her against him and yanked her off the road into the brush. She thrashed her body weight against him in violent struggle and tried to kick his shins. But all she could do was flail the air.

With a grunt, he rammed his thigh forward to butt his way between her legs. He jerked her violently into the air and squeezed his forearm tighter across her stomach, pinning her to him. With all the force her eight-stone weight could muster, she grabbed his arm and tried to push it down, thrashing madly back and forth. Finally she jerked her head free and, before he could get his arm away, gnashed him with her teeth.

With a quick jerk and an angry snarl, he was knocked off balance. Dirt gave way beneath and they fell backward, rolling over and over each other down the skid-slick slope. Her cloak caught between them, flipping her over, and rammed her chin down on hard collarbone to force her face into the hollow of his neck. Now her cloak caught the metal rungs of his belt and pinned them together like they were in a bedroll.

They careened down the hill with such alarming speed that new terror took over. Brigianna let out a wail like the high-pitched cry of the sidhe and turned her eyes inward so that only the whites showed. Long nails dug into his shoulders, and her wild cry shattered into jagged sobs as the metal rungs of his leather gird battered against her and spikes from his shinguards gouged her legs. When her long nails tore into his skin, he jerked violently, nearly knocking the breath out of her.

Mercifully the ground flattened out beneath them, and they skidded to an abrupt halt. The man landed on top of Brigianna with such force that she screamed in bitter surrender.

He quickly clamped her jaw shut, then stared at her with piercing blue eyes and stern brow before dragging her farther into the brush.

"Bedams it all," he cursed as he tore at the cloak still knotted between them. Her eyes widened in alarm, but her brow creased in determination as his hand ran its way up the length of her thigh to grab the firm round of her butt. Spitting mad, she bent her knees to plant her feet squarely on the ground and bucked.

Snarling, he slammed his weight hard against her and dug his fingers into her jaw. Pain shot through her like white fire.

"Lie still," he barked, pulling the cursed cloak free and tossing it aside. But instead of moving away, his hand still clamped her jaw and his body weight pressed heavily against her.

"And now, fair maid, may I be trusting ye not to scream? There's trouble afoot."

She fluttered her eyelids in assent, determined to scream like the sidhe if necessary, and he took his hand away. Instinctively she twisted sideways, edged her right hand down toward the tip of her boot where her knife lay waiting, then lay perfectly still, looking at him.

In the blurry haze of moonlight his firm-set features were outlined in silver-edged shadow like a piece of fine sculpture. His bushy hair was molded by crusty limepaste into a great mane, and his mustache fell in a long golden curl. His eyes were most certainly blue, but right now they gleamed like black coals. Unlike the men she was used to seeing, he had a fine straight nose and firm square jaw. To her surprise, the mouth, set between golden mustache and clean-shaven chin, appeared to be smiling, and his eyes bore no malice. Had they been standing, she wouldn't have come to more than the pit of his arm, for she was dwarfed beneath him. This close he smelled of leather, sweat, and dirt, and, she chuckled inwardly, too much woodland garlic.

"Listen," he said before she could speak. The toss of his head made Brigianna turn over quickly and look back toward the road.

Tremors rumbled the earth, reverberating against her and snapping her senses to attention. Hoofbeats pulsated against her stomach and vibrated up her spine.

"If ye stay to my side and make nary a sound, no harm will befall ye. But if it's fight I must, run like the sidhe and stay hidden until I come, if I am able." His eyes narrowed in grave concern. "Pray all the gods ye know it be me who comes, lady. Ye ken?"

"Aye, I understand," she answered and inched closer to him.

"But I give fair warning, if ye scream, it's a knife to the throat from me or them, whichever comes quicker."

And his eyes commanded her to lie still as stone.

There were about twenty horsemen in all. As they crested the spine of the hill, their armor became a ghostly etching against the black canopy of night. Their horses were shod, for the ring of metal crashed against stone but turned to dull heavy thuds as the animals made their way along the wet, boggy road. Brigianna trembled, feeling the clank of heavy armor as well as hearing it. Massive beasts shook ground; power rumbled earth. Riding in single file, each man with helmet, halberd, and shield, they looked like specters from the dark world, coming to claim their due.

Suddenly a swelling scree of wind funneled around the horsemen in a hideous cry. The horses answered the wailing wind with terrified, shrill whinnies and bolted. Men shouted guttural curses in a dialect Brigianna didn't understand. Iron scraped against leather as they tried to force their animals back into line. Frenzied and wild, the horses ignored all commands. Instead, they reared and pawed the air, clawing wildly at some unknown, unseen enemy. Lunging forward and crashing into each other as they came down, metal scraped against metal with so much friction Brigianna saw flashing streaks of blue sparks.

Beside her, the man grew as stiff as iron rodding.

Dark-armored men tried to pull their animals under control, but to no avail. The horses pitched and roiled in the slick mud, trying to catch their balance, but the mud only made them spin and crash into each other with greater force. In the agony of crushing bone, muscle, and sinew of man and beast alike, shrill whinnies and angry, guttural cries rose to meet the high-pitched wail of the wind.

It is said that the faeries move their camps but twice a year: on May Day, the Feast of Beltaine, and then again on Samhain. Only moments ago, it seemed, Brigianna had been safe inside her lodge, ready to celebrate. She remembered hearing the admonition, "It's not good to be out in the dark of Beltaine. The faerie wind will whisk you away, and ye'll ne'er be seen again."

The scree of wailing wind funneled madly around the terrorized men and beasts. But around Brigianna and her captor the air was perfectly still.

"It's a fey," the man whispered, his voice tight with fear.

"Aye, 'tis," she said with absolute certainty.

As quickly as it had come, the wind died down, and the animals fell into line. And the moon shone with menacing clarity.

The warriors' helmets boasted large horns; their shields were knobbed with spikes, and their longspears bore wavy blades like shafts of lightning. As they rode by, Brigianna watched facemasks of hammered iron, each with long snout, form grotesque, ungainly shadows. They rode with grunting fury, like wild beasts routing the night.

"Black Dhurmod and his Pig Men," the man spat in curse as soon as the horsemen were out of sight.

"Who would that be?" she asked, retrieving her cloak. Without waiting for the answer, she crawled out from beneath brushy tangle.

"Bedams if I know," he said, "bedams if anyone knows. Striking terror into the heart of all, he is, raiding what's not his by preying on landmen who live outside a clanbind. He swells his ranks by promising freedom, yet reigns by terror, for he burns their fields if they do not obey. . . ." Moonglow caught his look of anger as his voice trailed off, hardening his firm features into cold granite.

"He's a terrible terror, not man enough to fight on the battlefield of honor. No one can catch him, by horse or by foot. Chase him to the wood, and he and his men become as trees, lost in dark shadow."

"Then I'd best be keeping clear of the roads," she said with a grave look and drew her knees up to rest her chin on them.

"Aye, which causes me to ponder. In a lifetime of wandering it's not been my good fortune to meet a maiden fair on the roads in the dead of night. May I be asking who ye are and where ye be going?"

"Brigianna—uh . . . just, Brigianna," she replied all too quickly.

"Just Brigianna?"

"Aye. Just Brigianna. On the way to the sea. I've business to tend." She drew a footpath across the grass with her left foot, the way she always did when not telling the truth.

"Mmmmmm, well, Just Brigianna, Kevin here. Kevin the McErin it is. And it happens I'm going that way myself." He announced his name with pride, as if she should know it, and smiled wide as he reached for her hand to help her up.

But his look gave her the nervous fritters.

The grating call of the corncrake, matched by a warbler's lilting descant, woke Brigianna up. She opened her eyes to see the sun sprinkle dew-laden grass with coppery rays, making it glitter like a jeweled carpet. Rubbing her eyes to chase away the sleep, she glanced back at the road, thinking that in the golden light of morning, last night's vision was only nightmare soon to be forgotten.

Trees hugged the riverbed like jealous children, marking its path. Kevin was down by the overhang, bending over something, she could not tell what. He had stripped down to his loincloth, and all his belongings were folded neatly into a pile beside him. Not a twig snapped beneath her footfall as she walked down to the water's edge to watch.

"Ho there, it's time ye were about. Long's the day ahead."

"Aye," she agreed, wondering how he knew she was there.

His skillful fingers worked quickly as he wove the river reeds into a large square mat with a hole in the center. Freshly cut strands of sedge lay beside him, and one snapped as he fitted it in. His fingers appeared to have eyes of their own as they rummaged about for replacement, since he never looked up.

Inching closer, brows knit into curious frown, she asked, "What are ye doing?"

"Weaving a bonnet."

"A bonnet? Why, that is women's work."

"It is at that." His blue eyes didn't betray his thoughts when he looked up. But his hearty laughter warmed her soul like a hot mug of tea come to chase away the last dregs of sleep.

"A warrior's work falls to that since we Fian seldom take women with us," he commented, standing now and towering above her.

"Fian? Warrior of the Fianna?"

As he worked, the rising sun played shadows upon his fine muscles. His bushy mane stiffened by limepaste gave him a gruff exterior belied only by dancing eyes alive with the lusty fervor of life. He looked like a bronzed god, crafted by a skilled artisan who took delight in molding sinew, bone, and muscle into a masterpiece of motion. With not a dram of fat to spare, his belly was lean and hard as his shield. His legs, strong as oaks, retained their supple spring from years of woodrunning. And in the sunlight his wide-set square shoulders looked hewn and hammered into raw power.

But it was the limepaste, sculpting his hair into flaxen folds and framing his face to show off his long curling mustache, that made him appear to her as a god.

She gasped in awe, for tales of the Fianna had ridden the wind and sparked many a winter's tale. In spite of the fact that Balfe often sang of mighty Fian, Brigianna had never met one. Few chieftains were wealthy enough to retain such warriors, and they were said to grow surly when there was no fighting to be done. A simple tradesman like her father, whose wealth was measured in cattle and who kept no horses, was of no interest to Fianna. Their outrageous exploits and ferocious acts of bravery rivaled those of the gods; their deeds often gave the gods fair competition when it came time for storytelling at the triannual clan gatherings of Uisnech.

"For true? Ye are Fian?"

"The same. And now, Just Brigianna, we've a river to cross and no time to waste. Take off your clothes."

"Begods, no!" She jumped back in horror. Her hands flew across her breasts, her eyes darted furtively back and forth, looking for escape.

"Come, come, m'lady. I mean ye no harm." His well-guarded smile vanished as he thumbed toward the river.

"It's my guess Black Dhurmod is headed for the sea, and I do not plan on leaving tracks he or his Pig Men can follow. So it looks like it's the river for us, lady. If ye swim it with your clothes on, ye'll catch your death. That is, if ye make it. 'Tis a fine cloak you be wearing, but one that heavy will drown ye in passing and, if ye survive, take as much as three days to dry. So do as ye're told."

His sense of command was so complete, Brigianna didn't

dare question him. With a shrug of her shoulders her heavy green cloak crumpled to the ground. She kept her eyes on him, afraid to look away as she undid the shoulder ties that laced the folds in her simple maidenshift. But she closed her eyes and swallowed hard when she felt it skim over her and fall at her feet.

"The boots."

Obediently she stepped out of the pile of clothing and leaned over to undo her laces. He squatted beside her and folded her garments, placing them next to his. Without looking up, he reached out and she gave him the boots, rolled together and neatly tied.

Kevin quickly undid them, grabbed the laces and tucked them into his loincloth. As the boots unrolled, his hand rested upon something sharp. Her dagger. Brigianna's eyes grew dark with alarm; her hand flew to her mouth. Hard looks passed between them; his questioning and hers a challenge.

But his eyes flashed with sudden pleasure as he drank in the gentle outline of her nubile body. Then his eyes steeled quickly in hammered reserve as he laid her boots aside.

"Come," he commanded, holding blue eyes steady.

Her flesh blossomed out in goosebumps; her face flushed to a rosy glow, and discovering that she couldn't look him in the eye, she turned away.

She had seen her brothers naked many times. Her clansmen often went around with little or nothing on, especially after the baths when they grabbed their cloaks and were soon enveloped in a comfortable layer of steam. When steam and sweat got too stifling, they tossed cloak or clancloth aside, preferring the close contact and easy camaraderie of warm skin. Even traders who came to the clanhold joined in after the trading was over and the boar finally done.

There Brigianna seemed not to notice. But now, standing naked in front of Kevin McErin, warrior and Fian, she was flustered. The McErin was a different sort of man. His eyes danced with godbolts and could see right through her.

When he put a hand out to brush away a strand of hair, fingering the blackness of it, she trembled at his touch. "Why, 'tis a virgin I've got me," he mused and quickly drew his hand away.

Her palms flew to her breasts and she cried in astonishment: "Ye can tell just for the looking at me? A man can know that of a woman?"

"For the looking at ye? Well, now, let me see."

Kevin stepped back and propped elbow upon hand in shandy stance and with a rakish grin let his eyes meander, slow as a summer day in a lazy meadow, down the full length of her body and back up again.

She was thin and well built, with the short, sturdy thighs of inlanders. Her breasts budded to high rounded mounds pulled taut from the cold. Her waist had narrowed and her hips had rounded, but they weren't the hips of a woman roughened from childbirth. Her nervous heartbeat pulsated her navel, gently, making him yearn for the touch of silken-smooth white skin.

Aye, he thought to himself, she is virgin all right, and like a wee deer, come to the forest's edge, cautiously savoring the sweet smell of spring.

"Virgin ye are," he announced aloud. "Though it be not for the looking of ye I can tell, but by your trembling at my touch. For that a man has questions. There is no belt or girdle to announce your station. Are ye spoken for, m'lady?"

"No!" Brigianna shouted, too quickly. "I'm freeborn, my own woman."

"Aye?" he mused as he reached for a hand and carefully examined her pinked nails. "A freewoman with hands that show no sign of work, boots of the softest leather, cloak of finely teasled wool, and dyed by laurel perhaps?"

Brigianna jerked her hand away and set her jaw. As she did, her fingers brushed the welt of a long scar that marked his forearm from elbow to wrist. The thin dark line that shadowed her lids deepened, quick blue eyes demanded an answer. Now it was his turn to look away.

"The scar of my blooding, when I was proclaimed warrior. A small wound . . . considering." Sensing her woman's ability to disarm a man at his weakest point, he stooped down, fumbled for the mat, then coughed to cover his wariness and reestablish his prow. "We've a river to cross and no time to waste. Come," he said harshly, standing back up.

The hole in the center of the mat formed a perfect headband.

Securing it, he placed her bundle of clothing on top. "Here," he ordered, flopping her hand on top of the bundle to hold it.

Whipping leather taws from his loincloth, he put them between his teeth. Next he divided Brigianna's long hair into four even sections. These he used as ropes, bringing them out from beneath the woven sedge and crisscrossing them over the mat, thus forcing the mat to wrap around her bundle as if it were a basket. Finally, he tied the sections of her hair together with a lace. "Shake your head," he ordered, and grunted with satisfaction when the bundle didn't topple.

His bundle was wrapped in his furs, turned skin side out with enameled longsword, javelin, armbands, and greaves jutting through the center of the roll. This he tied with the other lace and lifted the roll above his head to announce, "In we go."

Normally the Boyne would be easily fordable, but it had been a wet spring. High-watered and treacherous from angry storms, it cursed its course like a woman in the throes of childbirth. Like the goddess for whom the river was named.

Brigianna stared at tannic waters. "It's cold!" she wailed.

"'Tis," Kevin agreed. "And Dhurmod's blade swift and warm."

"How do ye know I can swim?" she hedged, hugging herself to keep warm and slowly inching back up the bank.

"If ye cannot swim, ye are no freewoman. If ye stay behind, ye will not be free for long." One bushy brow shot up in stern command, but Brigianna only inched farther backward.

"It's grateful ye should be I saw fit to keep your hands free for swimming! Now, jump!" he bellowed in quick temper.

He waited and when she didn't budge, his temper roared full. His blue eyes frothed like the North Sea; his neck muscles reddened and twisted like heavy knotted ropes. He gritted his teeth, then forced his smile to a firm, formidable line.

With strident and certain step he marched behind her and shoved.

Chapter 3

Her scream ended when she hit water. She gulped as she went under, came up coughing, and screamed again.

The bundle atop her head bobbed around like a cork and weighted her down, anchoring her to it like a hopelessly tangled fishing line. Water, sky, and land whirred before her eyes in one continuous stream. Gasping for air, she thrashed wildly about, trying to stay afloat, and searched frantically for Kevin.

Certain the bundle would force her under, she screamed an angry curse. And in one sucking swill, the hollow sedge filled with water, swelling the reeds to capacity. Now her bundle was twice as heavy and her ears rang. "Oh, help me!" she cried as she was spun around again.

A large rock jutted up from the middle of the river like a tower. With trembling hands Brigianna reached for it, but was whipped backward. Barrel-rolling right into the whirlpool, she catapulted toward the rock with frightening speed. Certain she was going to be gnashed to pieces, she held her breath and was shot into the center of the river with the force of an arrow. There the current was even more deadly.

"Kevin!" she cried in a rage that turned to anguish as she went under.

White-hot pain cramped her leg, doubling her over and forcing her down again. She fought for air, gulping huge mouthfuls of it every time she surfaced. Desperately she tried to force herself up. But her leg would not obey. Pain had turned it into a raging fire. Muscles balled up and hardened; tendons stretched and snapped.

The tannic river slowly laced icy tentacles around her leg, ready to pull her down, ready to devour her. She could feel its tiny streams searching her with icy claws, fingering her tighter in its grip. Her leg lay in its hold, and she, paralyzed in pain and fear like anesthetized prey, waited to become the victim.

Waters lapped around her, dark as the color of strong tea, and she knew if she went under again, Kevin would never find her. Fear prickled the tiny hairs on her body, and even in the midst of that raging river, she could feel each one of them. They made her aware of herself and aware of life, and in that moment she refused to die.

In a last determined burst of strength, she beat the water, frothing it into foam around her. But her leg, deadweight at her side, dragged her down.

Dread chilled her blood. Quick energy spent, her arms weakened first. With a garbled cry she gave up.

In that instant, that tiny brief second when she relaxed, her bundle toppled so that the weight of it fell to the back of her head, where it should have been in the beginning. Where it would have been if Brigianna had not fought the waters as she fought everything.

Now she bobbed around like balsam with her face up and the bundle a pillow. Breathing deeply, she savored each delicious breath, babbling in jubilant cry as she filled her soul with this elixir of life.

"Almost there, m'lady. Just a little farther. Ye can make it."

Kevin shot the words out between short breaths as he swam to her side, and even in the icy waters she was warmed by his presence.

Soon the rocks grew rounder and more numerous, and the force of the river beached them into a pebbled inlet. She groped in the shoals, aching with pain and too weak to move any farther. Finally Kevin dragged her ashore and dumped her in a tuft of clumpgrass, then went back to the water for his bundle.

With concentrated effort Brigianna reached for a handful of grass. Staring at her fingers through blurred vision, she willed them to curl the succulent stalks in her palm. With a choking sob she buried her face in the sweet-smelling grasses, reassuring herself she was still alive. Her sob was followed by another, and another. They came with racking speed, and she shook violently with the force of them.

Down by the river Kevin looked up warily. His face froze in alarm. He ran to her side and, cradling the back of her neck, hurriedly tugged at the mat. He tossed it aside and pulled her to her feet, grabbing her shift as he did. Much too wobbly to stand, she fell hard against him, her expression still and waxy, and her breaths alarmingly far apart.

His blue eyes darkened with worry. "Oh, lady, lady."

He slapped her face with a resounding whack that left its welt. When there was no response, he slapped her again. "Come, Just Brigianna. Ye'll make it, I know ye will." When there was no response, he braced his feet wide apart and propped her up. As he struggled to get her shift down over her head, her arms flailed against him, pliable and rubbery as hens' wings, as he tried to poke them through the sleeves.

When he reached down for the cloak, her head rolled back on her neck as if severed at the cord. She was spineless as a doll stuffed with bog cottons and stared straight ahead, white-faced and unseeing.

"Of a truth, m'lady, sorry I am, but there was no other way."

Hugging her to him and rocking her back and forth against his warmth, he worked his strong hands up and down her back and around her shoulders, fast as he could make them go. Feverishly creating as much friction as possible, he worked so fast the wool crackled and made tiny blue sparks. Tawny brows guarded his narrowed eyes like the cliff guards the river. Grimly he studied her face with breath held in check, waiting for her color to return. When it didn't, he shook his head in dismay. "By the gods, have mercy," he whispered hoarsely, and carefully laid her down.

As he worked, the air trapped beneath the naturally oily cloak warmed to form a soothing cocoon. With the skill of the well-trained warrior who had learned to be father, mother, brother, and friend to himself, the Fian massaged her body. He gave himself up to her with the patience of mam to sick child or warrior assigned to a long night watch.

Beginning at her fingertips, he moved up her arms; spreading his palms wide, he worked down her sides. Trained fingers gently woke traumatized organs back to life. He worked her legs, down sturdy thighs and dainty calves. When he picked up the cramped leg and felt it resist, he took stock of the knotted muscle with grim-set chin, worked his fingers back and forth over it, patient as a woodcarver determined to bring burl in line with fine grain.

At last he picked up the foot, braced it against his chest, and worked it back and forth between his palms so vigorously her entire body shook. Slowly her color returned. With a wan little smile she opened her eyes briefly, then fell fast asleep.

Brigianna woke to see the evening star courting the silvery slice of moon in the western sky. Eager for his nightly romp, the star pursued his lady moon through the twilight, as together they chased the golden ball of sun hiding behind the purple hills in the land of nether. She was seated beneath a stately willow that wagged tender trails of fresh spring green. Her cloak was tucked around her like a blanket, and she was fully dressed. Searching through the last fuzz of sleep, she tried to remember where she was and what had happened. Her first thought was her brooch. Alarmed, she reached for her boots and felt along their side. Relief graced her face when she discovered her boots carefully laced, knife and brooch safe inside.

Kevin bent over a fire and, seeing her awake, called out, "No fat there was for perch frying, so I spit the fish on alder to keep the fat in. But methinks the alder too wet to be worth the trouble. Ah, me, did ye sleep well?"

Laughter tumbled from her lips. "Aye, and it looks like all day, too," she said, walking over to the fire and sitting down beside him like they had been friends forever.

"I've had time to me thoughts," he mused, moving aside a polite space but still keeping his attention on the fish. "How fares your leg? It got badly battered during our tumbleroll, not to mention the river."

She stretched her toes and turned her ankle around. "Except for the bruises, good as a greening sapling. What magic powers do ye possess?"

"Patience, m'lady. Just patience."

In the time between the two lights the slipping sun made his hair look like spun gold. The river had washed most of the limepaste away; now his hair fell to his shoulders in soft curls. Still, the lime had bleached streaks into it that were lightning white, and when Brigianna looked closer she saw wisps of gray.

The shadows caught in her hair, making it richly blue-black, as dark as ravenfeathers. And in the flash of a second she saw two ravens flying in a golden sun and wondered again of their meaning.

Kevin pulled the spit from the ground and turned the trout to see if it was done. "Not fit for a maiden fair," he said as he offered it to her. "Sore, but it will have to do."

At the smell of food invading her consciousness, the vision vanished. "Beholden," she said and grabbed the skewer, moving away from him to guard it like a hungry animal.

Absolutely ravenous from exhaustion, she attacked the fish, devouring it in huge unladylike mouthfuls. When she was through, she held up her hands and the fish grease dripped down her forearms.

"Well . . . I amn't about to try the river again," she

informed him, so he reached into the tuck of his belt and tossed her his square of rabbit skin. She winced when she caught it, for she could tell by the stains that it had been used many times. Nevertheless, she wiped her hands and face on it and tossed it back. "Beholden again."

He tucked the skin into his belt, then reached into a leather pouch and pulled out a comb and tossed it to her. "Your hair."

When she caught the comb and gently fingered it, her eyes widened in delight. The horn had been cut and polished so that its many layers rivaled the inlaid mother-of-pearl beading across its bridge. The rakes were widely set, some of them long, some of them short, and all of them sharp. The naturally curved handle settled easily into her hand.

"How beautiful," she murmured with the hush-toned admiration only those bred to the patience of art crafting could understand. She leaned back against a large rock to begin working at her hair, starting up from the bottom. "It really is. Beautiful."

"Keep it," he said casually, as if it were every day he gave away something that had taken a month of firelight and thinking time to make.

They stared at each other across the fire and into the long silence.

The fire hissed and crackled from the wet wood that had to be used, and Brigianna marveled at it. Rarely had she seen a wood fire. It smelled much different from the mushroomy turfs she was used to.

With its crude noises it was hardly a fire to sleep by, so she continued to work at her hair, holding it with one hand and combing it with the other, so as not to stretch or snap its fiber. Firelight bathed Kevin's features in a golden glow. She caught herself wondering whether or not a bronzesmith could carve their mold, and if he did, what they would look like on a drinking cup.

He followed the gentle curves of her body with his eyes, imprinting the whole of her being upon the farthest recesses of his mind. A warrior's life was given to long hours of solitary duty where silence grew deep and memory was the only company. Rare were the moments he enjoyed the pleasures of a woman. Even more rare was time to enjoy watching a woman do womanly things. For an unguarded moment he set aside the rugged discipline of the Fian and eyed her with the lusty longing of a man.

Catching himself, he turned his head away. A warrior's life held no promise of tomorrow, and sore's the making of promises, come morning. He had spent a lifetime learning that bitter lesson.

Brigianna was not used to long silences. Her people prattled endlessly, whether they had anything to say or not. Even when they were not talking, they exchanged thoughts, by nod or gesture, so that no one was ever really alone. Only Lochobar locked himself away in the privacy of his head, and that was because he had other places to go. Communication with the spirit world demanded this.

"It's true, ye are Fian?" she said, breaking the silence.

"I have said."

"Ye can recite books of poetry and other stories as well?"

"Aye."

"If that be true, Kevin McErin, then tell me a tale."

With eyes shining bright in expectation, Brigianna set the comb aside, plucked a strand of oat straw, and began to chew on it.

With only fire glow to illuminate the unblinking night, Kevin the McErin turned to pace the dirt in front of her as if she were the Ard Ri himself, and he, master storyteller of all Ireland. For to refuse her would blacken the bronze of his hard-earned reputation.

" 'Maeve and the Brown Bull of Cooley'?"

If she had heard this story once, she had heard it five score and thrice. Still, it was her favorite. "Say on!" she cried.

Kevin pawed the dirt with his bare foot, flared his nostrils as the brown bull himself, and began to tell of the famous Queen of Connaught, who, thinking to outdo her husband, King Ailill, staged the war between Connaught, and Ulster and, in so doing, won back the prized brown bull, thus making her herdwealth greater than her husband's, the king.

Brigianna inched forward, ready to race by Kevin's side in her mind's eye as she was trained to do, quick to pounce before the next sound was uttered if he got so much as one little word out of order.

Rugged, angular features turned soft and beguiling as he became the conniving, unrepentant queen. Tawny brows canopied the creeping suspicion of a wary king, then vanished in petulant pout.

And the oat straw fell from Brigianna's hand, unnoticed.

He beat his chest rapidly to simulate running cattle, then with shoulders hunching into the run and splayed fingers forward, he began the rampage. When he lunged, she clung to the rock at her side with breath in check. Her brilliant blue eyes darkened, like sapphires in the heat of making.

Suddenly he tossed his golden hair back over his shoulders in queenly arrogance—scowled, stoop-shouldered as the defeated king—it was over.

A stricken look crossed her face. Her spirit winged above her like a blackbird, hovering over the last, lingering word until it faded away into darkness. A soundless "ah" escaped her parted lips, and she sat back, certain she had heard this story for the very first time.

Kevin looked down at Brigianna, who was too full of childhood and too new at womanhood to be tainted by its sharpness, and held himself in check. He did not go on to say that Ailill soon tired of a woman who would not be his subject, either in bed or out. That he cast her aside and took her sister instead: Ethne, sweet and willing as a butternut.

No, he decided, that was a tale best reserved for the warrior's camp; a tale designed to make dutybound men grateful for a cold bed.

Instead, he cleared his throat, patiently waiting his due.

Brigianna's expression wilted like forget-me-nots in the rain.

"Oh, Kevin, it's terrible, just terrible."

"It is? What do ye mean?"

Caught off guard by this unprecedented insult, he crossed his arms over his chest in ready defense. Never before had Kevin McErin failed to charm a lady. "I said every word, exact," he declared with pride.

"Of course, of course," she said kindly, unwilling to pay the penalty for insult and brushing his feelings aside as if they didn't exist.

"Kevin?" she demurred. "Is it not true such a tale could not be told if Queen Maeve were not a true Celt? A freewoman?"

"Aye," he said, slightly baffled.

"The queen owned cattle and lands of her own?"

He welded his bluff to the fore by reddening his face, though his eyes narrowed in suspicion. "Aye," he agreed. But cautiously.

"Cattle and land were hers—she was free to do as she pleased?"

"Aye." He nodded, getting the distinct feeling he was losing a battle he didn't know he was fighting.

"Then what is happening to Mother Ireland if her women are bought and sold like cattle? Are they then free?"

The dam of her reserve broke, the river overflowed its banks, and tears fell in torrent. She sniffled and wiped the tears away with the back of her hand, and smudge marked their path.

"Mmmmm, I see," Kevin mused with newfound understanding. His temper left as fast as it had come and he went to her side and fell to his haunches. "Methinks, Just Brigianna, 'tis more to your tale than ye are willing to tell. More than . . . Just Brigianna."

"McColym. Daughter to the chieftain, Tormaigh."

"The McColyms? No whit! I've heard of them. Fine hammered gold, well-set jewels, most delicate fretwork, smoothest of torcs, of which tradesmen speak with great fondness. Am I right?" he said, stopping to let the question hang.

"The same," she hedged, then paused. "Kevin? When a woman's seasons are set by blood and she feels that aching for pleasure, is she not free to take pleasure with any man of her own choosing?"

"Aye," he agreed calmly. "It is law."

"Well, I'll have ye know, mighty Fian, I would marry whom I will. But no!" she lashed out. "Brigianna ni Colym is slated to marry the Finucane and secure the northern border. Father's not a fighter, like ye, Kevin. He would easily become sept to the Finucanes and let them fight for him. He would even sell his own daughter, just to keep peace."

"That decision is his as chieftain, and as father, too," Kevin said in singsong voice that rang with respect for law above all things.

"Well, I'll not marry me an old man with a dinger in a slinger and a dong gone wrong. Balfe even sang of it."

"Ye believed him?" Kevin exclaimed with jolting peal of laughter.

"Oh, ye do not understand, do ye? Balfe shamed me. My father's own bard shamed me. The women laughed. How can I save face?"

He placed firm hands on her shoulders. "For shame on yeself, Brigianna McColym," he said, laughter gone and voice grim. "Ye are the daughter of a chieftain. Thicken that skin till it's sturdy as the cloak ye be wearing. Where's your spine, lady? Everyone's been spurned by his bard at one time or another. They think it their job, to keep us all in line. Sure now, it is no reason to run."

Brigianna trembled beneath his touch, alarmed by this strange man who could be so tender one moment and so fierce the next. "I did not run. I was banished," she blurted out, and then put her hands to her mouth, wrestling with the import of her words for the first time.

Kevin's tawny brows evened into fine line and his hands

fell to his sides. "Banished?" he said with a dry throat and grave look. "If ye are banned or fugitive, I've right to know since it befalls me to keep peace. I've more to do than fight McColyms, so I warn ye, speak truth. What did ye do? What trouble falls me on your behalf?"

At his sharp command she quickly set her jaw. But his eyes churned dark and foreboding, and her muster quickly vanished.

"I defied my druid," was her slump-shouldered admission. "He was to use me for prophesy so the clan would approve of my marriage to secure the northern border. And I fought him, long as I could."

"Ye did?" Kevin said in utter disbelief. "Ye challenged prophesy? Ye defied your priest? Ye stood firm in the face of your chieftain?"

"I'll not marry me an old man," she snapped with enough force to make the air around them crackle. "I'll marry the man I want!"

Her cheeks reddened from anger, and her eyes glowed like the gemstones her clan was famous for. Her jaw set in determination, and Kevin drew back daunted. Never before had he seen such resolve in a woman, certainly not in one just beginning her woman's journey.

"What would happen if ye went back but did not marry this old man?"

Stunned by the question, she thought a moment. "I do not know. I am priestess trained, so I suppose I would be given to Lochobar."

"This Lochobar. He is old as the Finucane?"

"Aye, by several lifetimes, I fear."

"Ah," Kevin said, tossing back his head so the firelight caught the glimmer in his eye. Tugging at his mustache, he ployed the question.

"Sure now, there must some handsome young buck who catches your eye?"

"None, I fear, and isn't that a sadness?" she said innocently.

"Pride is not such a hard thing to swallow if it brings bread and broth in the morning, and sure now, not a bad thing for a chieftain's daughter," he said simply, but unwilling to let the matter rest, he pressed on. "Ye would not bed an old man to secure your father's lands? Ye would not endure sour breath to become priestess to your people?"

"I am Celt, and for that I am free," she lashed out.

"Ready to stand by your own spit and spittle?"

"Whatever do ye mean?"

"Ye forget I am Fian?" he said, pulling her to her feet. "By liege and loyalty it is my duty to protect the innocent with naught the wit to protect themselves, and those caught in disaster, be it of their own choosing or otherwise." Stepping back a pace, he challenged her. "Hold up your hands, Brigianna McColym, and prepare to spit."

"Why, it's not given for women to spit. Spits, oaths, and loyalties belong to a man's world. Surely ye know that."

"That I do," he agreed. "But a clanswoman stands before me claiming to be kinbroke, a fact that must be sworn and sealed by spit, surely ye know that. From now on ye stand behind your own spit, lady."

In spite of his towering presence and stern command, a playful smile brightened her face as she thought the matter over. To be free, no longer under her father's thumb, that was a winsome thought. But to be free of her own clanpower was to fall prey to everyone's clanpower. And to declare an oath was an awesome thought. No man, or woman for that matter, ever goes back on spit. It simply isn't done, for how else could there be law?

"As one of the people, I am freeborn. No man is ever going to tell me what to do," she declared, and her statement only confirmed Kevin's deepest suspicions.

They both stepped back the measured pace, coughed and discharged a wad of spittle into their palms, rubbed them together, and with hands outstretched, pressed their palms to each other's.

Against the backdrop of the ancient forest where all things

began, the firelight enclosed them in a sacred circle. They sealed their pledge while the unblinking sky, discreetly veiled in darkness, watched in silence. Only the thin slice of a silvery moon and a single star witnessed this resolve.

Kevin spoke first. Brigianna did not know that this voice, one filled with measured respect, was one he normally reserved for men.

"I, Kevin McErin, declare myself to be the protector of Brigianna McColym. I pledge her my fealty and provision, and by all that lies within me as a warrior, blooded and seasoned, I aim that no harm come her way when I am near. I choose by my own free will to defend her honor, and"—he coughed and forced himself to add—"I will, above all things, respect her freedom."

Seeing in him the warrior's protection, Brigianna's face radiated her pleasure, and like a true lady, she smiled her acceptance. At the very least he would grant her safe passage, a place to sleep, and if the gods smiled, warm food in her belly. He was a ringfort of safety, the scar that showed as a fine, white seam down his forearm a banner of courage. Whispering, shimmering happiness fell over Brigianna, as if she had been kissed by the gods themselves.

"By the Great Raven above, the twelve standing stones of Crom, god of this land, and Macmannon, god of the sea—by Bel, goddess of fire and protector of women, and by Ban, god of might and men . . . and, oh, me . . . all the hosts of heaven too many to remember, I place my life into the hands of Kevin McErin and happily accept his protection. I declare myself a freewoman and promise to live such that my honor can be defended, never using my freedom to harm another."

They lowered their hands and Brigianna absentmindedly wiped the excess spittle on her cloak. She glanced up to see the crescent moon and its consort star and smiled in the face of such a good omen, remembering that an upturned moon meant a cradle full of happiness.

"It is true now," she pressed, "I have declared myself a

freewoman, but ye have only offered me your protection?"

"Aye," he said with a sly smile tucked safely away beneath his mustache. "After a manner of speaking, that is."

Chapter 4

Lochobar lay on his furs, suspended somewhere between this world and his other. Never in all his years had he been so disturbed.

Decisions came quickly for him. They came of their own accord, with a sense of urgency and inner calling. It had always been that way.

Even as a child he had possessed the fierce energy that marked him as special. That, and the ability to see through people as if they were fetches: mere ghosts of themselves. Confident and independent, he passed through his first rebirth with ease and claimed his druidic calling, smugly gratified by the power he now held over his peers.

But now came this thing with Brigianna.

Her name hung like leadweight upon him; like the last vestiges of flesh clinging to bones too weary to care; like the last store of his many years now buried in dimmed memory. It seemed an eternity since his heart was free to run like the wild deer he once stalked. "That is the trouble with eternities," he muttered and turned over, scratching his behind but not feeling the sickly, oozing bedsore. "One never knows for certain which eternities have been lived and which are yet to be faced."

His years stretched out behind him in a vast wasteland of yesterdays. At first he attributed their great number to his own stubbornness and then to his longset, sturdy bones.

He recognized the Sight even as a young sapling. Singled out by druids more powerful than he, he sat at their feet memorizing every word, like sandy loam filling with water during the spring runoff.

According to tradition, when he came of age, he spent his cycle of nights in the forest alone, and there was reborn. True to the druid's word, ravens came to pick his bones and gorge upon his soul. He cried out in anguish, mourning his own death, seeing it from his detached other body floating above his true self, looking at it and feeling it at the same time. After that, he rolled up into a little ball, shaking with fear and from the rain-drenched cold, and whimpered like a baby. He faced his embryonic beginnings, only to be plunged once more, headlong and at dizzying speed, back into the land of the living.

Alone in the forest, he defied the gods by demanding life. He stared at death, screamed in its face, and stood as a man.

But when he returned to his clan, he seemed a hundred years old: born of an eternity that dipped its treacherous, sticky fingers into deep, unknown crevices of knowledge hitherto hidden from the heart and mind of man. Tormaigh, his friend of friends, appeared adolescent by comparison. His confidant was gone; now all he had was an innocent, inquisitive lapdog yipping at his heels.

Tormaigh's father died suddenly, and the two men assumed the roles they were born to, ready to stand by each other's side for the good of the clan, ready to fight each other to the death if necessary.

"Sure, it is unnatural for one to live so long or know so much," he cursed, still not feeling the pus between his fingers.

Smoke from the central fire penetrated the shadows of his domed hut in searching, tender tendrils before spiraling upward and outward through the single opening. Unresponsive to its warmth, he tossed and turned, coming in and out of feverish delirium. In his most lucid moments his breath hung in the air, suspended, a white vapor above him. Now even the wind seemed to whisper "Brigianna."

He could see her, with his inner eye, never far from him. He breathed easier, knowing she was safe in the company of that tall, blond warrior. He would care for her as a true Celt and, by Celtic law, not violate her virginity. In due time she would accept her marriage to the Finucane and, he hoped, forgive him for banishing her. What was called forth out of darkness would run its course and come to fruition. Of this he was certain.

His breath rattled inside him like the strum of a harper uncertain which tune to play. Annoyed, its rasping sound made him challenge faith, questioning the games gods played.

But had he done right in banishing Brigianna from the clan? he asked, and the harper's song within sweetened on his breath to calm his soul.

No, it was not Brigianna that disturbed him, he realized. He never reneged on a decision nor tolerated those who opposed him. Brigianna must learn to set her feelings aside, just as he had done. She must understand this: it is the clan's way. Yet something was awry.

He still saw her as tiny and trusting, full of bubbling mirth and questioning not. He remembered the first tremor of excitement coursing through him when he recognized she was gifted, and took refuge in her curious, agile mind. That scintillating moment came when they were both fully aware of their inner selves; when their minds were fully exchanged. He wondered even then if they would ever share pleasure and make a child. And when menarche came and the seasons of her blood became certain, she walked by his side in hip-swaying grace, and he found himself asking that question more often than he cared to admit.

A sudden chill overtook him, and as he shivered, it grew worse. A racking spasm tore at him as if he were caught in the grip of some evil outside force . . . and he grew more certain his real worry wasn't Brigianna.

Something on the night wind froze his blood. Something loomed in the eternal darkness, something against which marrow, sinew, and sweat could not prevail. It was as if Mother Ireland were caught in the talons of a giant bird, like those raucous, nagging ravens he so adored. The gory, enigmatic creature laughed at her screams for mercy and greedily tore into her flesh.

Lochobar filled his lungs with acrid air and tried to chase away the dark. But he could not, nor could he quiet the haunting in his bones.

Shivering, Tormaigh squatted outside the priest's hut. Mother Ireland woke slowly from her winter's sleep this spring. He drew his banty legs under him so his furs would shield him from the bitter wind; his wiry muscles, taut from cold, hugged his lean frame. In an open, deliberate manner he rubbed his beardless face with the palm of his hand, to mask the uncertainty he felt inside. Although he appeared to stare straight ahead, his eyes scanned the doorflaps of the surrounding huts, taking note who was watching.

Ground fog came and went at will, bringing him first a clarity of reason, and then, just as quickly, a shadow of doubt. Courage came, then vanished, as the mists lay heavy in the dips. The central fire spiraling a feathered trail above told him that Lochobar's spirit had not departed this world forever, for no one, not even priest in trance, would let a fire die out.

He grew impatient; Lochobar had lingered in his spirit world long enough. Lifting the stiff leather doorflap, Tormaigh stepped inside.

Cautiously he walked to the wicker platform where Lochobar lay and searched among the furs, barely able to make out the dark, lipid form lost among them, as still as a piece of furniture, and winced. Even the comforting smell of peat was soured by the old man's fever.

Too old and uncaring to hunt new furs, Lochobar had no woman to complain or goad him into providing better ones.

Sweat poured from his feverish frame, and grimy streams ran into the already matted skins.

A certain resolve marked Tormaigh's movements. As warrior and chieftain, he had smelled death often, understanding its meaning all too well when he buried his own father in the caves of Dunbar. Death may hold no fear, but it certainly had a way of changing things: Today he was chieftain and father of seven sons and two daughters; yesterday he lay by the river, lulled by the sounds of salmon in roe fighting their way upstream, and lost in the wonder of his lovely Fiona.

Shaking the thought away, he put his ear to his priest's mouth, carefully awaiting a struggling breath. The old man's flesh matched the waxy drippings from his single candle; he smelled like soured milk. Only rapid movements behind closed lids told him he was alive.

Death for one so necessary to the clan as Lochobar was not something Tormaigh was willing to face. He hovered closer, blowing great blasts of ale-filled breath into Lochobar's mouth, determined to call him back.

Lochobar's eyes flew open, staring ahead, like a dead spirit in a dying body, and Tormaigh jumped back in fear.

"Well?" Lochobar grumped, scooting backward on his pallet until he was braced against the wall and pulling his furs around him like an angry child who had not finished his dream.

"The women brought ye broth and herbs and ale daily. Me own mother fed ye barley water and sponged ye down between the shadow time of day and night. Three days now it's been." Tormaigh stepped back in reverence as he spoke, then squatted on the dirt floor.

"Amabel's been in here, with me? Like this?" Lochobar cawed, jumping to his feet and stomping his pallet, like an angry jackdaw.

"Aaaaaaye," Tormaigh stammered.

"Well," Lochobar sniffed in a haughty jeer, "she is nothing but an old woman, I am nothing but an old man. So what are my goods to her?" With a magnanimous wave of his hand, he brushed his indignities aside.

Relief spread across Tormaigh's face. He scrambled to his feet, meticulously rearranged his cloak, sat back down on his haunches, and assumed the relaxed air of the chieftain he was. Lochobar only grunted and drew in a long breath to chase away the dregs of sleep.

Naked, and in the light of the pitifully tended fire, Lochobar looked thinner than ever. He barely had head room in the small hut, and as he stretched, he looked like a mass of confused bones. The fine muscles he boasted of in his youth clung to him like string.

Worry crept back into Tormaigh's face. "I must be telling my women ye are up so meats can be set." But as he rose to go, Lochobar fixed him with bloodshot yellowed eyes, and Tormaigh sat back down.

Lochobar splashed icy water over his face and down his body without shivering. Noting the ice forming on the edge of the wooden bowl, his face turned grim. "These bones are so cold I cannot tell when the water's been warmed or the fire's been lit," he muttered as he reached for his loincloth. He tied the square around his middle, then reached through his legs and pulled the flap over the tie at his waist so it fell forward like a skirt. After snapping his leather gird and adjusting his tunic, he grabbed his scratchy woolen robe, a simple two-toned maud, but thought better of it.

"Your colors?" Tormaigh exclaimed as Lochobar reached for his ceremonial robe.

"More than you are entitled to," Lochobar grumped with a pompous turn of his head and threw the length of his clancloth over his shoulder, piercing it with a fibula. He clasped Tormaigh's shoulder in a sharp-nailed grip. "Come," he said lightly, *seeing* Brigianna safe in the arms of the Fian, yet *knowing* that something dreadful, deep, and dark rumbled dangerous and deadly in the pithy parts of his gut.

Tormaigh hurried ahead to lift the doorflap. "My Brigianna? She be well?" he asked as the priest bent down to go through the door and they met, momentarily, eye to eye.

As Lochobar stepped into the morning air, he drew in a deep breath of morning air to reassure himself. "Well, indeed," he announced.

"Himself's about!" Amabel cried. "Hurry, now. Shoo! Shoo!"

Late morning cooking fires were at a full roar, and rich smells of savory herbs and hot fat ladled over spitted meats filled the air. Wooden bowls of grain had been set by the fire to swell for morning, along with honey and herbs for tea, ready for those childish enough to break their fast. And Amabel was well pleased.

Fiona looked up; wingtips of graying hair softly hid the sadness behind her eyes. "Brigianna?" she whispered. But priest and chieftain walked by without noticing.

The overly tall Lochobar walked with a permanent list so he could hear everything Tormaigh was saying. The chieftain paused and scooted around to his other side, and the old man's bones creaked as he stood up straight. Patiently he bent his head the other way.

Gray faded Tormaigh's hair, making it look like a wool rag that didn't take the dye, but his body was as wiry and ready as any of his seven sons'. Lochobar, walking beside him, looked like the ravages of death had already played its game. Sensing this, Tormaigh became more solicitous of his priest than ever.

The *clickity-clack* of bone shuttles from lap looms lost their timbre as the men walked by. Women sat with their legs out in front of them, weaving boards on their laps, backs straight and toes curled up, their faces quiet with haunting questions. By the fire Fiona raised her arm, pretending to ladle fat. "Brigianna?" she whispered.

Amabel, who mothered everyone, even the chieftain's wife, whispered, "Hush, dear, it's not to worry. Himself knows what he's about. Why not sit with your yarns while

I tend the meats." Obediently Fiona put the ladle down and joined her weaving women.

Just as the men veered onto the path that led away from the clanhold, Doughall, the youngest of Tormaigh's seven sons, rounded the corner. It had been Doughall's lot to stir the dredges of offal and dung into the ever-foul, ever-decaying glue pit, and he, being most obliging of Tormaigh's spirited seven, agreed.

"Ho there!" he cried, swinging tar-covered leather buckets from the pole across his shoulders. "'Tis a fine day, and glad I am y'are about."

Tormaigh merely nodded and went right on talking. "The cows. Where are my cows? Brigianna is gone, and if it's to the Finucanes she has gone, then where are my cows? Ten of the finest, I was promised."

"Yes, yes," Lochobar said, irritated. Tormaigh scarcely noticed. He went right on lamenting the fact that a contract had been made between the McColyms and the Finucanes. In exchange for his daughter he was to receive ten milk cows, and he had not received his merchandise.

Ignoring Tormaigh's demands, Lochobar stood straight, turned toward Doughall, and fixed him with a penetrating gaze. Tar-covered buckets still slimed with glue dropped to the ground as confusion and finally acceptance played tug-of-war with Doughall's simple features. Caught in the wake of those yellow eyes, Doughall had no choice but to obey. He knew their mesmerizing, commanding power well.

"Go to her," they said. "Be my eyes, my spirit, my mind, my heart. Watch over her carefully, see no harm befalls her. Let her know that she is loved, even though I am not there. Report back to me. By runner if you must, or run the wood yourself. I shall see no harm befalls you."

Doughall's dark brows settled down into a fine even line, and his thin lips drew tight in measured pride. He had never been given such an honor in his life. It far outdid carting dung and offal. He braced his feet wide apart; his left arm crooked at the elbow so his hand rested on the hilt of his knife. He balled his right fist and crossed his chest, hitting it with a resounding *whack*. Next he tipped two fingers to his forehead to seal his sacred vow.

"Father," he said simply, and took off to disappear in the copse.

Tormaigh, lost in his raincloud of dark thoughts, scarcely noticed. "If she be not with the Finucanes, where is she?" he stormed. Throwing his clancloth back over his shoulder, he faced Lochobar, demanding audience.

But before Lochobar could answer, Dierdre ran up to them and took Tormaigh by the hand. "Good morning, Daddy," she yipped.

"The colors! Sure now, ye see the colors?" he growled, knitting brows in worried frown while looking nervously at Lochobar. Dierdre paid no attention. Instead, she leaned against her father's arm like a pup that, if scratched behind the ears, would follow him anywhere.

The trail narrowed, and Dierdre scooted in between them. Tormaigh, knowing his moment lost, marched on ahead, bemoaning his fate.

Unlike Lochobar, who must be respected when wearing clancloth, Tormaigh seldom had the privilege of such privacy. As his people's chieftain, he must be the best among them yet still approachable. His seed found home between Fiona's legs nine times now; his bow remained the strongest, his quiver always ready. It was he who saw that amethyst, beryl, and topaz were set with the intricate, circumlinear patterns his clan was famous for. The McColyms had tradable goods and had eaten well because of Tormaigh. Now Brigianna's marriage would strengthen those trade routes and bring him even greater wealth.

Muttering, Tormaigh marched on. Lochobar had been lost in his spirit world for three whole days. That was enough!

"Look!" Dierdre cried, stopping suddenly to point to a spider's web shimmering on a nearby brush. Lochobar bumped into her, catching her by the shoulder as they both stumbled forward. Tormaigh turned around. He saw Lochobar smile, then reach for the tip of Dierdre's single braid and tickle her chin with it. Tormaigh gave them a surprised stare and then huddled back under his storm of angry thoughts.

Dierdre laughed and fell in step with Lochobar. Slipping her hand in between his gaudy robe and tunic, she rested it over the back of his leather girdle. Fog lifted, and sunshine warmed the morning. And Dierdre's laughter filled the pathway like field flowers.

Lochobar smiled but, instead, saw Brigianna. His mind's eye traced brows that fell in gentle arc across a wide forehead, hooding heavily fringed lashes dark as ebony that shadowed forget-me-not-blue eyes. He remembered her short nose and the way she always jutted her jaw forward. Saucy, that one. Briefly they walked the fields again, foraging herbs that cured, those that brought sweet dreams and strange visions, and he was young once more.

But when his eyes refocused on Dierdre, he saw no beckoning fire. No mysterious ravens flying the golden sea. No uncommon mystery.

With the fickle heart of an old man he pushed the child away.

"Tormaigh!" he grumphed.

Tormaigh turned around. "Have ye heard a word I say? Have ye been listening to me at all?"

"Of course, of course. We march at moonrise. Will you be ready?"

Chapter 5

Brigianna ran by Kevin's side in the predawn darkness, comforted by his presence and patterned breathing. They traveled in concert, matching stride for stride, needing little in the way of conversation.

The rolling cloud bank above looked like the master craftsman's darkened rag burnishing the golden bowl of morning. When the furze shook its yellow head, or the ruffled branches of the hawthorne swayed in the breeze, then the earth would laugh in glory and goodness. But this early in May the earth held its breath, like a promise waiting to be born. And Brigianna greeted the dawn with this same breathless wonder, eager to experience what lay ahead.

"Do ye not believe in eating? Or does that march against what little faith ye've got?" she goaded, remembering the warm horn of cherry-bark tea Kevin offered her just before breaking camp. He had boiled water in a square of pigskin, then carefully peeled the cherry bark from his supply. She marveled at how he was always able to produce what he needed, yet seemed no more burdened down by belongings than she.

And gods knew she had nothing.

"Oh, I believe in eating when there's food to be had," he said, crooking his left arm over his head to block the sun's glare. Brigianna caught the smile resting in the shadow of his invisible shield and matched him one. "But ye are right in that, for often as not, faith is determined by how full the belly." His last words were lost to the wind as he suddenly gained speed on the downside slope of the hill.

"Faith, it is," she muttered, rubbing her stomach and scurrying to keep up with him.

Since he used his upturned spear as a walking stick, the momentum of his steady thrusts forced him on ahead. His fox-fur cloak billowed like a sail behind him, keeping his back warm and body cool.

By midday the sun reached its zenith and bathed the earth in bountiful goodness. Brigianna itched furiously beneath all this goodness. It was said that summer could be told by whether a woman was carrying her cloak or wearing it; Brigianna's was too heavy to carry and now too hot to wear. Earlier she had plaited her thick hair into a single braid, but even that didn't help.

She tossed the braid over her shoulder, determined to chin up, but just then her foot came down on a jagged rock. She cried in pain as her calf muscles knotted up, but Kevin was too far ahead to hear.

Through soft leather boots she felt everything earth had to say and recoiled at the reprimand. The once beneficent sun beat down without mercy, and the resilient earth turned withholding beneath her touch.

Kevin's sandals were hard-soled; studded bosses on wide leather straps wound around his legs served to clear his path. Living in the wilds from May to November made his muscles solid as hammered iron. Even the soles of his feet were tough as shield leather. As they ran, Brigianna's only grew more tender and more painful with each demanding step.

Years of woodrunning had hardened him to this task. He pounded his javelin to the ground like a drummer beating time. Even his hot, heavy breaths marched in tune. She squinted her eyes against the sun, resolved to meet his demands, but when he showed no signs of stopping at high sun, she began to falter.

Nothing but tired and hungry since she left home, she

cried out, "I cannot, not without food," and fell down by a clump of maidenfern.

"I've a stag's leap to run, m'lady, and only a hare's breath for time. I cannot stay."

"Ye offered me your protection!" she charged, and sensing he had neither time nor pity for weakness, fought back her tears.

"That I did. 'Tis my duty, for I am Fian. But I did not offer to turn my life about on your behalf. I am no fool, lady." The shortsword at his belt dangled in the dirt as, panting, he dropped to his haunches.

She stared back at him coldly. Without dancing firelight and courting moon to cloud her thinking, she saw only the hard lines of a warrior's face. A man committed to peace but trained to kill. And a face to fear when sternness set the jaw. It was framed by lightning streaks at the temples, bleached there from the limepaste. Instinctively she knew even sorcery would be useless against this man. Nothing could keep him from being what he was. He was like an arrow set to its course, even if that course meant death.

"I see," she said in a voice as flat as a day without breeze.

"I've no choice, for I am foresworn. I must return to my liege by Midsummer, Lughnasa at the latest, and there's no time to spare." Sweat funneled down his cheek into his long curling mustache as he spoke. Radiating the heat of running, he smelled like his furs.

"The warrior's life is not given to choices. This is a new thing. Choices." He gulped a huge mouthful of air, wolfing it down like a hunk of meat. "Life gives me none. 'Tis mine to obey. But ye be free, to go or to stay. That I cannot decide. I can only ask—are ye coming with me? Or am I absolved from my pledge before its time of testing?" His eyes bore the steel edge of flint, shielding his feelings as he waited her answer.

"Go," she ordered, angry that promises made by moonlight meant so little to the mighty Fian, angry that she had been so foolish. "I can fend for myself, I can."

He reached into his pouch and tossed her a small dark object. She caught it, then stared at the square of hide in disgust.

"Chew on it," he ordered and took off at a steady pace without backward glance. But the spark in his eyes grew dim, like a flame dying, and the quick spring that lightened his step turned leaden in his path.

Brigianna tossed the chunk of leather into her mouth and laboriously chewed on it as she watched him go. His hair flew out behind him, highlighting the gold and red of his fox-fur cloak. The distance between them widened; he bounded on, with leaping strides, jabbing the earth with his upturned spear. Obediently she chewed the foul square of hide, dismally watching him get smaller and smaller.

She spat and kept on chewing.

Kevin's javelin pierced the sky; a barbed insult against its gentle skin. How different the Pig Men's spears were, she thought, and blanched. Angry spears like carved godbolts filled her vision. Lochobar's gleaming yellow eyes came into view. She saw him wave his cloak like the wings of that dreadful bird, and two ravens appeared. Two ravens, flying in a golden sun. Two ravens, certain of their course and bidding her follow. Always beckoning, and always beyond reach.

Stomach juices started pumping, her mouth warmed with saliva, and she jumped up to spit out the slimy chunk of leather.

By the time she caught up with him, her breath felt like tongues of fire. But wind cooled her brow and lifted her spirits.

And the leather had cleared her head . . . as Kevin knew it would.

He said nothing as she fell into pace, but he slowed down ever so slightly, a subtle, unobtrusive drop in speed. A true Fian, he kept his eyes straight ahead and his smiles to himself.

By late afternoon they managed to steal a forgotten cache of hazelnuts from two angry squirrels. He smashed the store open in the crotch of the tree with the hard hilt of his shortsword. Still, they both attacked the food like voracious animals, grunting and wolfing it down with little regard for manners or each other.

When they left the wood this time, grasses turned thick and reedy. Blossoms had come and gone like brief snowfall, newly pollinated trees leafed out in gladness, and the wheatear's call heralded the arrival of spring. A flock of whinchats nesting on a wild plum tree filled the branches like succulent, overripe fruit. They took off in a chattering black cloud as Kevin and Brigianna walked by.

And a lone raven stared at them from behind the foliage.

Startled, her breath caught in her throat. She whirled around and cried, "Oh, Kevin! 'Tis the sea! I can taste the salt on my lips and smell it in the air even before I see it!" and ran on ahead of him.

The windswept land turned sharp and foreboding. Angry hordes filled the road, determined to give little.

"So many people," Brigianna whispered. "Can a clan be so big?"

"'Tis no clan, 'tis the gatherings. Already they are coming to buy and sell before heading inland to Uisnech and the feasts of Lughnasa."

"Pogosh! For all your faults, mac Erin, 'tis a poor liar ye are."

"Aye, 'tis a poor liar I am, but something's amiss. I cannot tell what, but these people move with quick step, and it's not in families they travel." With foxlike wariness he drew his features back. "Cling to my side like second skin, and I swear by death or by honor I'll see ye safely through."

"Fair said," she murmured and slipped her hand beneath his cloak. He tensed at the unexpected tease of her touch, and she looked up at him, puzzled, then took refuge in his rock-hard strength, fitting into his steps like a soft-soled slipper.

Men tall as Kevin pushed against them, bearing the sea-burned look that turns human hide into leather, their features pulled taut by sun and wind, their expressions stolid and unyielding. Women with spirit and hair like fire made Brigianna suddenly conscious of her black hair, white skin, and delicate, short stature.

Tripping unexpectedly on the hem of her cloak, she fell against the woman ahead of her and knocked her aside. "Careful, colleen," the woman snarled through browned and rotting teeth. Then suddenly her eyes widened, and her scream pierced Brigianna like a godbolt.

"Jump!" Kevin shouted just as the horsemen appeared. Bringing his arm hard around Brigianna's shoulder, he knocked her onto the soft dirt flanking the roadbed. She tore at tufts of salt grass as she hit the bank; Kevin fell over her, catching her in his roll. "Who are they?" she cried, grabbing onto him.

"Bedams if I know, though I've got me suspicions."

Behind them a cheer went up from the crowd deep as a tidal roar, and as the horsemen came around the bend, the cheer turned into a chant in time.

Beside the horses a core of heavily muscled men ran pace, beating back the admiring throng with iron-studded gaffing sticks.

The lead horseman was as hard-hewn as his cudgel and rode standing up: oilskin covered straight legs, and crotch pressed firmly against his straw-stuffed saddlehorn. He was hooded, and his cape of skins furled behind him shiny and black as the deathbird.

He whirled his whip around overhead three times, then suddenly lashed it out. With snapping surety it parted the crowd.

A piglet squealed and bolted straight for the horsemen, screeched in pain, then screamed in confusion as huge hooves came down flat upon it. The swineherd tore through the crowd, swearing his wrath. The second horseman clubbed him aside, and he fell to the dirt, eyes glazed and blood streaming down the side of his head.

With angry guttural shouts the horsemen brought their animals in line and headed out.

Badly shaken, Brigianna grabbed Kevin's furs with both fists and buried her head in his chest. Men nearby laughed: harsh laughter spattered with obscenities Kevin understood only too well.

"Quick, Brigianna. Run!" By sharp and ready instinct he shoved her ahead of him, just as a burly man gave Kevin a knowing sneer.

"Begods, woman, do ye want to get us killed? A freewoman does not cower at the sound of a whip, nor does she think a swineherd worth a moment's thought. Dagda! Do ye want them to mistake ye for my whore and lop off my head for sport?"

Reddened neck muscles twisted like knotted ropes as quick-tempered words tumbled over themselves. "A Fian never travels with his wife, so I'd be sparing ye the honor of that."

Blood rose to his cheeks as his skin grew tight. Drawn into slits, his eyes were more frightening than Lochobar's.

He drew in a deep breath to gain control and said with measured calm, "Now, march by my side like a woman of station. Hold your head high, and by gods, woman! Don't gawk. Ye do be virgin?"

"Aye, I have said."

"If ye prize it, then mark my words. Flesh be cheap, and yours would bring fair price."

Thrusting his lance against the dirt, he turned heel and marched on. She followed, staring straight ahead and, trying her best not to step on dung or offal, clutched her stomach to keep from retching.

Rathdun was a walled fortress with the staves fencing it whittled at the top like a garrison of arrows pointing to the sky. Set at the mouth of the Boyne, it commanded both river and sea. Outside the fort merchants hawked their wares. Beneath a thatched, unwalled building stood the blacksmith's shop. Grassy slope gave way to the sea there, and beneath it black waters slapped against the cliff.

"With a wee bit of cunning I may be able to steal us a ride," Kevin said, in better humor now. "Linger by the stalls and look like ye've important business to tend." Brigianna nodded, posted herself by the heavy wooden gate, and Kevin disappeared.

Annoyed by her presence, the animals snorted and rammed into each other as they moved away from the fence, and she shuddered, not certain she wished Kevin success. Since her father kept few horses, she had never ridden before; their size and unruly temper frightened her. Just then a wagon creaked by, boasting a comfortable bed of hay and solid iron-rimmed tires. Dark brows shot up like ravenwings in flight. That, she thought, would be more to her liking.

Inside, the smith, a swarthy man with powerful knotted muscles, lifted his square hammer and brought it down to forge a blade. The sword kicked back in the process, and the hard ring of metal hitting metal was echoed by the hollow answer of metal crashing against stone. Raising his hammer for another blow, he eyed Kevin carefully. Though tall as the DeDanaan, Kevin's lean frame seemed slight by comparison.

Apprentices looked up, silently acknowledged Kevin's presence, then went back to work: stretching taws, coaxing flame, sorting charcoal, or hammering bosses. The smith snorted, and a burly apprentice moved to where a sixteen-hand bay, with his rump to the fire, waited shoeing.

The stench of burning charcoal and molten metal overpowered the sweet sea breeze, and Kevin loosened the neck of his tunic as the heat got to him. "Yo!" he shouted in greeting, praying he knew the correct dialect and method of bargaining. The smith merely grunted and kept on working, so Kevin made his way through the tables assessing the workmanship.

The hissing sear of hot metal plunging into the stone trough of icy water startled him; he spun around quickly and, as he turned, caught the smoky glint of hammered iron. Weapons and armor lay poorly concealed in ungainly piles beneath oiled tarps. As he eyed the weapons, storm clouds rumbled through the recesses of his mind. Even though he couldn't see the crests, the shape of the armor seemed vaguely familiar. Pieces jutting out from beneath the tarps appeared to be the misshapen, dented discards of battle, now ready to be rehammered and reused. The horns were common enough, certainly, but the way the browshield had been elongated to form a nose cone worried him.

At Kevin's questioning look, there came a slight but noiseless shift in movement. With steady eye the smith pulled the sword he was working on out of the water and set it on the firebowl. Patting the bay on the rump, he stepped forward.

As the veil of steam caused by the plunging iron cleared to leave the air blue and crisp as sea breeze, Kevin saw that the men had risen from their benches. Glancing at the cache of hidden weapons, he realized he'd fallen into a trap. If that was the Pig Man's armor, kingsman or no, the smith was not going to let him live to tell about it.

Silent consent crossed matted brows; raised tools became weapons. Nearby a dark, bent-shouldered man eyed him with a salacious grin.

Kevin's lips drew over his teeth in feral snarl; neck cords drew tight as bowstrings; eyes darted furtively back and forth. Gripping the satin-smooth wood of his longspear, ready to toss it and reach across his belly for his shortsword, he tested the spring in his knees.

Sweat beaded his forehead as he cursed his folly. By law he could run from no fewer than ten men. Now he was outnumbered by a score.

* * *

At the pens Brigianna grew impatient. She was tired, thirsty, and, more than anything else, irritated. *How dare he make me wait outside like some lowly water girl. Hold my head up high and walk proud, he says. Well, I'll give the likes of him a thing or two to think about!* Resolute, she turned heel and marched toward the shop.

"Kindly be stepping aside," she snapped as she elbowed her way through the closed circle of men. "Aside, I said."

Startled, a man nearly as large as the smith himself let her through. But the man next to him raised his square hammer, holding it with both hands and closing one eye. Kevin's lips furrowed narrow as he sensed men in shadow, circling behind him and closing in. A low growl formed in the back of his throat.

Like the loosened rock that tore moss and packed mud as it tumbled down the hillside, Brigianna marched through the row of tables, making havoc and scattering small pins and scraps of uncut metal in her wake.

Kevin guarded his ray of hope from turning to a smile, for through the workbenches in Brigianna's wake ran a single, unwatched aisle.

"There ye be, ye ungrateful wench!" he shouted and, like the flashing blur of a hawk's dive, rushed her.

"Brazen little tart! I'll be thanking ye not to come marching in like this, just when I was about to offer these good men honest trade." With a snap of his wrist, he twisted her long braid around his fist and yanked her to him. "'Tis a sound lesson ye be needing."

Releasing its grip, his hairy arm crooked out to pitch her forward and throw her across his hip like a sack of meal.

"Put me down! Put me down I say!" she screeched and sank her teeth into the fleshy part of his hand.

"Bedams it, woman!" he shouted and, in reflex, shot his left foot out and caught the man crouching behind him in the bow of his knee; the outstretched javelin in Kevin's other hand cut a path through the air as he swung it around and the man went sprawling forward.

At that the smith whooped in pleasure. Smiles broke out and weapons lowered. Laughter, mild at first, quickly turned deep-throated and earthy; Kevin's hackles rose as he feared the outcome, made even more horrible by his buffoonery.

"Yah!" he yelled and flung his foot high. The metal bosses of his boot tore at a man's throat; his eyes bulged as he yelled in surprise and gargled blood. Kevin threw his head back and bared his teeth in challenge. Determined to keep her tight against him, he crouched, ready to leap the tables, shouting loud enough to drown out Brigianna's terrified screams.

By using his longspear as cudgel, he ran the gauntlet of shouting men. Swift as the young buck, he sprang over the first table to cut a ragged path in the dirt. Laughter hardened and forgemen sprang into action.

With the scream of the sidhe, Brigianna was butted through the wall of angry men, and in the wake of that bloodcurdling scream, those men drew back. Kevin's cudgel beat through the air. Gripping her tighter, he whirled around, ready to aim another well-placed kick.

As Kevin sprang, the bay, tethered and hooded, jerked its massive head backward, and the butt end of the javelin swacked it in the rear. With a frightened shriek the animal bolted forward. Its head crashed through the poles of its tether, but the stakes halted its run and jerked it backward with such force it went crashing to its knees. As bones hit the forgestone, they gave way in brutal snap, sending the hapless animal sprawling to the dirt.

The sword, hot and raw in the making, spun around and fell over the side of the firebowl to do a head-over turn. As it scored the horse's tender underbelly, the air filled with the stench of searing flesh. The animal thrashed in jolting pain; its brain burst in a gush of blood that came spurting through its nostrils, and, still kicking in its last dying breath, it sent up a shower of hot coals.

"Eeeeeeeyah!" Kevin yelled and gripped the length of

his javelin, cudgeling it ahead of him as he forced their way into the open air. Brigianna, gagging involuntarily at the stench of blood and coals, desperately gulped fresh air to keep from passing out.

In horror the smith watched the horse go down. Tools and armor were tossed aside and workbenches overturned in the scramble that followed.

"Good Crom, my forge!" he yelled, grabbing red-hot tongs with gloved hands. "The life of the Fian against one good horse—after him!"

Curious hawkers and skullies from nearby stalls had come running at the sound of the maddened horse and, in the onslaught, crashed into one another like the waves of the sea below.

"There he goes!" someone shouted, and the swelling tide turned.

Kevin saw them coming and whirled around, dropping Brigianna to the dirt. "Dog my steps and run, lady, for if ye fall, I'll not be able to come for ye." He held his arms up to brace the lance in front of him, and Brigianna quickly darted behind him.

Fearing for each breath, she saw every action with such intensity it slowed down so she could weigh its import. Lochobar had painstakingly stitched this knowledge into her soul, and now she fought for life with disciplined obedience and iron will.

She ducked when Kevin ducked, she leaned left when he leaned left. She whirled about to land behind him, following his movements like a shadow. Unarmed, except for a useless table knife hidden in her boot, she had no choice but to become one with the wind or die. Her eyes darted back and forth with feral quickness and her nostrils flared with bloodlust as the angry horde closed in. The smith led the pack, shouting, "Twenty cows for my horse!"

With both hands free now, Kevin brandished his lance in front of him and reached across his belly for his shortsword. Years of woodrunning had hammered his legs into hardened iron, his lungs into the firebreath of the winged steed. By clout and cunning he gained ground. Behind whipping hair and billowing cloak, Brigianna flew by his side as fetch.

She could not keep up with him for long, he knew, and he did not even want to think of what would happen then. For that his breaths were numbered; his hope of making merry in the land beyond slipped from his grasp if he were to discredit the Fianna and die a coward.

Then he spied the pens.

"The gates!" he shouted above the din of angry clansmen closing in on them. "When I open them, roll in behind. 'Tis our only hope."

Fear steeled her nerves and she squinted to take aim. She rolled back against the fence just in time to see him leap for the gate and pull the heavy iron bar. With a wild shout he snapped his cape and waved his arms, then rolled away.

Unaware of what lay ahead, the smith and his cohorts rounded the path. The animals poured from the pens with the force of a raging river. Men rolled for cover as thundering hooves scissored by.

The gate hit Brigianna full force, pinning her between two walls of wood. Sucking in her breath, she huddled between fence and gate. Outside her narrow coffin frenzied animals battered against her like raining boulders. Cursing men dodged the torrent and ran the other way.

"Brigianna?" Kevin hissed as he fell between the two walls of wood. She reached out, but could not see him crouching in the shadows. "Come, lady, give me your hand. There, there, that's it now. When I say run, run like the sidhe and not a moment before. Ken?"

"Aye," she whispered, her voice drowned by thundering hooves and obscene, angry shouts.

As the last horse ran by, he grabbed her hand and shouted, "Now!" as he pushed the gate forward.

They ran the sloping path to the sea, backtracking the cow trail until they hit shore. With lung-burning speed they ran its edge. Water lapped their heels, and they didn't stop until they came to a deserted inlet well north of the firth. Panting, Kevin threw himself down on the sand, and she crumbled beside him.

"Beholden it is," he said quietly. "Ye saved my life, so it's beholden, I am."

"Well, if it's grateful ye are, Kevin McErin, ye have a strange way of showing it," she said in a breathless huff.

Chapter 6

"M'lady! The smith would have killed me. Me!" He thumped his chest with a closed fist. "Kevin, warrior of the Fianna."

Brigianna looked at Kevin soberly, a thousand questions crowding her tongue. "Ye did not start the fight? But then, why . . . I mean who would dare kill a kingsman?"

"Of a truth, I do not know. My life is forfeit to Mother Ireland. Had they killed me, my kin would be none the wiser, for by law I cannot be avenged. By might or by kindness, whichever is needed, I must defend the people. I am the sword, I am the law. So to kill Fianna"—he paused to ponder this—"that is serious business. No one challenges Fianna, except on the battlefield of honor." His eyes glinted like hardened flint as he twirled the end of his mustache. "Unless there be more concerning that rubbish of discarded armor than I first surmised."

In deep thought he grabbed a stick and began drawing in the sand. "Look, m'lady, here is Rathdun, and here are we." He drew an X in the sand and boxed it in with wavy lines. "Lucky it is we crossed the river when we did, for the fort commands both river and sea, and blest be the gods, we headed north. My clansmen are farther up the coast, along about here." Again he drew an X, then laid the crooked stick down at an angle. "McColyms would be about here, winter sunset from Rathdun."

Brigianna's brows shot up like two ravens in flight.

"Kevin, what did ye see in the smith's shop? Do ye think—"

"Black Dhurmod bribed the smith of Rathdun? It's even possible he's burrowed nearby? Aye, I suspect that and more."

"I must warn Father!" she cried, jumping to her feet. "He must be told of this Pig Man."

"Ye cannot go."

"What do ye mean, I cannot? Ye forget I am free?"

He uttered a troubled sigh and reached for her hand. "Come, walk the beach with me, we've things to say."

At his simple command she did his bidding. They walked the dimming light of evening, where shadows cannot be told from stones, hugging the cliff for safekeeping. She unbraided her hair, loosening it with her fingertips to let it breathe, till at last it cascaded over her shoulders like a shawl. All the while she waited for him to speak.

Padding footfalls on spongy sand became night song between them.

She watched in fascination as audacious sea pinks dared eke out a living in the treacherous crevices of the cliff above, splashing the seawall with dollops of color. Terns fortunate enough to find level tuft nested there. One swooped down now, darting through the last shafts of light and over the breakers to bomb the waters and disappear below the surface. It emerged again with surprising speed, the trophy clamped tightly in its black beak, and soared above to its waiting hatchlings.

"Brigianna?" he said, finally breaking the long silence. "When ye ran from your father's lodge, did ye stop to think how he would feel when he discovered ye gone?"

"Faith save me, of course not. Madder than a stuck pig I was. Him thinking to marry me off to that old man Finucane. Me, a bonny virgin, forced to bed a dry old stick. Never! And Lochobar—to betray me like that!"

Sunlight cut through the gray-green stillness, a sword-thin blade of light, and in her mind's eye she saw two ravens flying across the shimmering sky. Lochobar's eyes narrowed, and the ravens were no more. She felt the sting of being cast from his inner presence. Like a haunting, he followed her everywhere.

"I told ye I was banished. I defied my priest and he bid me go. I told ye that from the beginning."

"Aye, and for that ye cannot go back. Were ye to return and your priest still bid ye go, ye would become betagh in your father's eyes—a person without a soul. Grant him grace and stay, m'lady. Ye must not shame him so. And ye must not cause him to defy his priest by recognizing ye, else the whole clan be in danger. For to come out from beneath priestbind is to face the gods alone."

"But my people are in danger!"

"Aye, m'lady, but ye cannot leave me, else ye shame me, also."

Looking up, she saw in his eyes a worry she had not noticed before. "I do not understand," she said. "Ye offered me protection only, and in your own words, 'I'm not about to turn me life around for such as ye.'"

"Fair said," he harumphed to shield his embarrassment, "but well ye know, ye cannot be protected by the gods unless clanbound. Ye stood before me, kinbroke. Clanless and, therefore, godless. I pledged ye honor, m'lady. If ye were to leave me now, and if ye were to, shall we say, come to uncertain end? It would be"—he hung his head and dropped his voice low—"an embarrassing thing for me to explain."

"Me, soil the face of the mighty Fianna? Ye are impeccable. Invincible. Kevin, that's impossible! I don't believe a word."

"No, no, listen up, now. If ye were to go, it would be counted against me as pledge unkept. Ye knew we Fian are fated to roam the country six moons of the year, from Beltaine to Samhain, and for that to keep peace and uphold honor."

He spoke in sobriety reserved for only the most serious judgments, then, when her mocking scorn settled into serious concern, guilelessly suggested, "To add to the demise of damsels, most especially if there is known danger about, would certainly discredit Fianna, and therefore our respective clans, would it not?"

She considered this predicament with utmost care.

"Are ye asking me to stay? I mean, are ye asking me? Not telling?"

He fidgeted. "Aye."

"But it's for honor ye bid me come. Your honor, most certainly, and not mine?" Her brows winged tight but smiles tugged her mouth.

"'Tis for your protection!" he blurted out in exasperation.

In pawing urgency he pulled her to him and beggared the question, "Come with me, m'lady, come to my father's clanhold. Be under his protection. Promise me that there ye'll stay. It's life and limb I'm speaking of, long as Dhurmod is about, and not just pot's fair share. If another clan took ye in and ye did not go to the chieftain, why, ye'd be forced to do betagh work. A cow, ye would become, mite that ye are. Shoveling shit, shipping slops, grinding grain till your back is broke. Stationed women would walk all over ye and leave ye hurting—beat ye with no cause to tell or ears to hear. Without kin to stand by your side, ye'd be broodmare, workhorse, common cow."

"Stop it!" she cried, jerking away and pressing her hands to her ears. "Gods bite your tongue!"

Angered, he caught her by the shoulders. "Nay, it matters I say on. Ye must come to my father's clanhold. Ye must promise me that much."

She drew her body tight in stiff reserve. To fall on the wrong side of one called Kevin McErin is a fearful thing, she concluded, and nodded in agreement. As for now, there was no other pot from which to beg.

"Ye'll promise?" he beggared shamelessly. Again she nodded and brushed the sacred temple of her brow with her forefingers, making the promise as certain as if it had been sealed in spit.

In exuberant relief he buried his face in her hair, and the flint reserve of his eyes changed to fiery blue. "Brigianna, Brigianna," he murmured, trailing a handlock through his fingers. In an expression of wonder his stern features eased out and washed the years away.

"Have ye noticed how very different ye are?"

"I'm not different where I come from. 'Tis quite ordinary I am there," she murmured, conscious of raventresses against golden hair, like ravens flying in golden sun. And how small she was next to him.

The dipping sun sent a prism of light against the eastern horizon just then, and its rays skipped the waves to fall at her feet in a ring of golden baubles. She shrieked and jumped back, chased into his arms by the skittering tide.

Her smile played laughing games across her face, brushing her worries away, and his laughter joined hers in full-bodied timbre. His fox-fur cape fell back over his shoulders, and the scar of his blooding showed above his wristband as a fine white seam down the length of his forearm. Without the limepaste his hair fell to his shoulders in silken strands, and the sun fingered the golden curl of his long mustache.

Pungent smells of fox fur and woolens, strongly laden with musk and made more heavy by the sea air, penetrated her being. Aroused by the feel, the smell, the touch of him, she breathed deeply, glad to be alive. Not at all unschooled in the ways of men, but certainly untried, feelings wakened within her; feelings she had not known before. Deep yearnings and tremulous, unspoken fears that seemed to have been there from time immemorial, stood on the threshold, awaiting their calling.

"Ye are one of a kind," he insisted, swooping her up off her feet.

Beside them a bevy of gulls, gannets, and 'trosses took off in raucous flurry. "Ordinary, indeed. Why, ye are no more than a pansy shaking its head after a spring rain. A good man would have to lump the furs well, just to find ye again come morning, so tiny ye are."

The last of the sunlight danced across the stretch of water like a bolt of silk unraveling. Sand, sea, and sky turned to a purplish blur. Round and round they went, she giggling all the way, especially when his mustache tickled the nape of her neck.

"Put me down," she said, laughing. "Oh, I beg, put me down."

"Never," he whispered as his arm fell 'round to cradle her thigh.

Caught in the magic of the moment, he whirled her around faster and faster. "Never it is will I let you go!" he shouted for sea, and sand, the wind, and sky; for all the hosts of heaven to hear.

Whirling around with dizzying speed, Brigianna gasped for breath and kicked against him like a young filly quickened by the breath of spring. Her hair cascaded over his face and shoulders to become part of the gossamer blur of sand and sea.

But drinking in her woodsy smell of winter's sage only reminded him of personal pain and dreaded vigil of battling long and lonely nights.

"Kevin!" she cried, her voice whirled with panic, and he snapped from his reverie. For a brief moment time stood suspended. Their eyes met and his expression sobered. Slowly he loosened his grip.

The whisper of promise skimmed past his reach as she slid to the ground. Her slender body, lingering against his, resilient and yearning as the rose of promise, sent tremors rippling through him. Such a slip she was, girlhood past, but womanhood not yet come.

A warrior's mettle is tested by patience, his training spoke within. But a man's body is tested by hunger, his soul cried back in outrage.

For a brief moment he fought himself for himself, then for Fian's honor, stiffened and dropped his arms to his side.

She felt firm, hard flesh pressing against her, causing her to tremble with wonder as she slid to the ground. Beneath her fingertips scratchy tunic gave way to shammy-tanned forearms stretched over iron muscle. She traced the scar of his blooding, that tiny slice of vulnerability, and felt his pain.

As he stepped away from her, rising wind whipped his fox-fur cape around his shoulders and blew his hair across his face. "Begging your pardon, m'lady," he stammered, looking suddenly awkward and foolish.

"That was clumsy and untoward of me."

"Aye," she said soberly. "'Twas."

"And foolish, too, considering the smith is not apt to let me off so easily and Black Dhurmod's men be roaming about."

"Agreed," she said, standing her ground.

Above them a lone raven flew by as a dark shadow in a blackening sky, taunting them with its haunting cry.

They spent the night cosseted in the crevice of a cliff only to waken the next morning with stiff, unyielding bones. Even before sunup they were scuttling along the shore like sand crabs, making their way north and counting on the tide to dampen their trail. Not willing to take time or leave evidence, they ignored the clam spouts, even though their stomachs grumbled in protest. But in the rocky reaches of a protected inlet Kevin plunged his arm into the icy waters and smiled triumphantly. Soon he had a neat pile of crusty oysters.

Brigianna watched as he held one up on the tip of his knife and downed it raw. Involuntarily her stomach quivered. With a rueful look she turned and headed inland.

He saw her go, hungrily wolfed down the last of his catch, then put his hand to his brow and scanned the horizon to see if they were being followed before he tossed the shuckings back into the bay and hurried to catch up with her.

Stubbornly Brigianna marched on, her back bowed against

the howling wind. Without warning her shift caught the snapping tentacles of a low-lying bramble. It whipped her backward, and she cried out in protest, then miserably picked the brambles loose. "Are ye sure ye know the way?" she called in a voice that fell on Kevin's ears like the shrill, mocking cry of the gull.

"Like the wrinkles of my palm," he snapped, grousing out his chest.

"But I cannot see where I'm going," she complained.

"Then hold on to my lance," he ordered. "It's naught but a day's run in fair weather. Ye cannot fail me now." Obediently she reached out to grab the pole and, by holding it, was able to anticipate his next step as they left the beach and climbed the ridge.

Soon they found a large rock, sea-bleached and slick, cleft by insistent roots and covered with curly gray-green lichen. Wind-whipped myrtles bent over it, their backs braced to the sea like a conclave of women surrounding a well. The travelers crawled inside to rest and would have broken fast here had they any food. Instead, Kevin squatted down on his haunches, leaned his head back against the cool stone, and instantly fell asleep. Knowing he could rise to an attack position even before he was awake, she took comfort and curled up beside him.

For her, sleep came and went in the flash of an instant. Kevin lay beside her, breathing deeply, and she mused for the moment at how her dark hair and cloak were lost in the gray-green shadows of the rock. But his bleached tunic, golden hair, and fox-fur cape only mirrored the perfidious beams of low-lying, scudding clouds. Not wanting to disturb him, she crept silently from his side to stand in the open air. She happily wriggled her toes in boots that had taken a long time to bend to her bidding, and stretched her arms, glad to see the wind had died down.

As she started back toward the overhanging cliff, she heard voices. Instinctively she dropped to the ground, scuttling again like the sand crab. Tiny hairs at the nape of her neck prickled up as slowly she inched to the edge of the cliff.

Below her a brigade of horsemen ribboned their way up the rocky beach. Round-rumped war horses shied at the incoming tide, knocking their riders against the rocks.

Spittle stuck in her throat as she watched, for they were armed but not with weapons and shields like she was used to seeing. These men were armored. Their shields weren't common boards covered with leather but round metal disks that hung by their sides and clattered like gongs as they rode. They wore padded tunics that were banded with iron, helmets bearing angry horns, and—Brigianna's blood ran pale—facemasks. The brow and nose shield common among warriors had been elongated and hammered into ugly, twisted snouts to make them look like killer beasts.

Scrambling to her feet, she flew back to the rock while visions of Beltaine stormed overhead: a faerie wind rising, a renegade army, a roiling boil of angry horseflesh, wavy bladed spears thrust into the sky by hideous pig-masked men.

"Up there on the cliff. Something's a-running!" a man shouted from the beach, and his voice was drowned in the thunder of pounding hooves.

This was no fey, she realized. These men were real.

Brigianna threw herself between the trees and into the cloven cleft.

She hit Kevin with a hard swack, rudely knocking him to his senses.

He woke ready to spring to his feet, but the look of horror on her face staid his hand. He reached for his javelin and drew it to his side just as Brigianna loosened her cloak and spread her arms so that it fell over them, tenting them beneath its voluminous folds.

Battle-ready, his flint-sharp eyes narrowed. Quickly she pressed her brow against his and, with pathos born of Sight cried out to him in her spirit-voice. Ravens flew overhead, and Lochobar's golden amulet swayed before her eyes. Years of intrinsic training had honed her into a tool of beckoning, and she gave herself up to the danger before her like the reed yields to the power of the wind . . . and lives.

Ye must not fight. Ye must live. Do ye hear? Close your eyes. Breathe deeply. Ye are destined to live, and for that ye must retreat. Retreat, ye hear? 'Tis no dishonor I ask. Oh, Kevin, I beg my soul that ye should live, and if honor be questioned, then for aye! let the spear fall on me. But to live, ye must do as I say. Become the rock that stands sentry-still. Become the tree, gnarled by the wind. Become sand and sea, each in its own place, each in its own time. Oh, Kevin, Kevin, can ye hear me? Draw into yourself. Become one with earth. Become as rock that lies beneath your head, quiet and still. The roaring sea grinds powerful, jagged boulders like this into fine, smooth pebbles. Yet each still lives, the rock, the sand, the sea, because each knows its place. Oh, hear me, I beg ye. Draw not a breath. Be as stone.

She closed her eyes and pressed her forehead against his, catching his breath and pulling it into hers, matching breath for breath, slowing it down, until it barely was. Molding into his being, she became part of him, until she was no more. Feeling flint-gray eyes relax to become warm blue fire, she concentrated on the heat of this soulfire, blotting out all else. His soulfire burned within her womb of being, so that his every breath became, for her, life itself.

"Nothing here, I say. Nothing."

The man who spoke was less than a spear's length from them.

"Probably just some animal," said another as he reined his horse in. It snorted in displeasure and began kicking time. Massive hooves sliced air less than a hair's breadth from Brigianna's head.

"Probably scared it off," he added, "but just for certain I'll match ye one run with spoils going to the victor." He raised his spear and nodded toward the trees. "Yah!" the first man shouted and took off.

Brigianna felt him coming, felt the tremors running through the earth as the warhorse turned and, with fetlocks flying, ran directly toward her. Rocks sent shockwaves that reverberated right through her.

The horseman let out a bloodcurdling yell. His lance zinged its course above them and fell to the ground at the other side.

Beneath tented cloak, eyes grew wild as whites gleamed with fright. Brigianna and Kevin faced each other as death masks.

"Ho!" the second man shouted and thundered his course. When the Pig Man got to the rock, he pulled his steed in tight, making the animal kick and prance, but did not throw his spear. Instead he thrust it forward, withdrew it, waltzed his horse to the other side, and raised his arm.

"Yah!" he yelled in hungering bloodlust, and the spear came down.

It tore through Brigianna's cloak. She looked up to see a silver blade pierce the darkness and stop only a hair's thickness from Kevin's throat, and a scream exploded inside her.

She forced it to rumble the hollows of her gut by gouging her nails into Kevin's arm. Steadying herself, she willed the scream to stay inside of her. By might and power of all that was, she would force that scream to stay inside her!

Through the tear in the cloak Brigianna could see a hairy leg bound by thick leather bands that were studded with crude-cut bosses. Quickly she turned her eyes away, lest their flashing curiosity, lest the intensity of her unbridled anger, give her away. Her spirit-self leapt up to claw him in raven madness, yet her body remained suppliant as the curly lichen covering the rock.

"No one here—they could na come this far. I say we turn back."

"We march on! I have orders."

"Ah, but there is something here. Look!" cried one of the men in the remainder of the company as they rode up. "Rabbit holes. Scores of them. 'Tis a harebin."

"Then get these horses out of here before one of them breaks a leg!" the Pig Man shouted. "And ye, there! Return to Rathdun. Tell that smith we've lost the Fian, and I still expect the work I commissioned finished by my return."

The horsemen were well out of sight before Brigianna dared throw back the cloak. Overcome by the sweetness of life, she looked at Kevin, face awash with tears she didn't know she'd shed.

He gently traced the tears with his fingertips, brushing them away and caressing her cheeks as he pulled her face to his. With reverence he kissed her forehead, both cheeks above his fingertips, and the nub of her nose, then drew away.

"We are alive, Kevin, alive!" she cried. Never had the sunlight been more beautiful, never had the earth seemed so solid beneath her feet.

"Aye, that we are." His easy mirth broke the floodgates, and she joined him, laughing and crying at the same time. "Alive, alive," she sang over and over.

"Praise the gods!" he shouted as he dragged her into the field. "Praise the gods, all of them, for now I love them all."

"Such daring! What would your clan god say to that?"

"Summer's my own time, lady, and look, there's rabbits to be had, more than we could cook and clean in a year."

Brigianna looked around her. The earth was runneled well with rabbit holes, and now that danger was over, several were braving a scamper.

"No, Kevin, there'll be no killing here. For a life spared a life must be granted, 'tis the balance of things. Sure now, your priests taught ye that much?"

"Aye," he admitted, "that they have."

She looked at the rabbits with second thoughts and with regret, rubbed her aching stomach before walking on.

That night, instead of bedding where they fell, Kevin took great care to clear an area near some trees and lay a bed of green boughs.

"What are ye doing?" she asked.

"'Tis Fian's bough I'm making, lady. Seems only proper."

He turned back to his task of laying moss upon the greens and then covered them with rushes. When finished, he motioned to her. She eyed the smooth, green pallet with appreciation.

"Beholden," she murmured.

"'Tis I who am beholden. What spells ye bind, I dare not ask, for when I rallied, my legs were gluey as calves' hooves set for pudding. . . ."

His voice trailed off. Graciously he held out his hand, and she stepped onto the pallet like a queen to her bower.

"A Fian is always armed, he sleeps with his sword, so for tonight I keep my belt buckled. A Fian also stands by his promise. It is his life; it is his death."

With a firm finger he lifted her chin so that she had to look at him. "How goes it with you, lady? Do ye stand by your promise?"

"By spit," she declared.

"Then ye understand why ye cannot shame your father by going back, and why ye cannot risk the journey alone if Black Dhurmod is about? Now can I trust your word? Ye will stay at my father's clanbind?"

"I have said," she insisted once more.

"Fair said, for to break promise will cause your death . . . and mine, too, I fear," he said and turned toward the fire.

The forest wove its black blanket of silence around them.

As a man who had tasted many battles, he had taught himself to trace the quiet moments of life indelibly upon the sacred corners of his mind, corners that remained privy only to him.

And in spite of how tired she was, sleep didn't come, which surprised her. In times past she slept as the dead after portents or visions.

She lay on her back, knowing he was watching her. At first this upset her. McColyms lowered their eyes while speaking, in deference to one another's privacy. To stare openly invariably meant a fight.

He stood to stir the fire. Night shrouded them in darkness, bathing him in fire glow like a golden statue emerging from the smithy's forge.

Her heart flew to his side, to gently trace the thin white scar of his blooding, or softly stroke tawny brows and call forth sparkling blue soulfire to light cold gray eyes. She longed for the brush of his lips at the nape of her neck and that kindling warmth he called forth from deep within her warm and waiting womb.

But, instead, she lay perfectly still.

Fianna walk this land as gods.

And this one, she decided, was frightfully human.

Chapter 7

As Brigianna and Kevin neared the Cafferty stronghold, an old woman looked up from the cooking fires and squinted into the sun. "Kevin? Kevin, it is!" she cried. A young girl standing beside her mused, "Kevin's a come?" and quickly tossed her cooking tines aside. They ran down the road, followed by a chattering trail of women and children.

"Grannie, Grannie!" Kevin called and held out his arms. The old woman ran into them, and he planted a warmhearted kiss on her cheek. As he whirled her about, she demurred a titter behind a fanned hand.

"Ye left before Beltaine, and sure now he's been carried off by the fay, some said, but not I," she wheezed. "It's not to worry, Kevin knows what he's about, says I."

"That I do and look what I've brought." He chuckled. "I warn ye, fay or no, this one will bewitch ye all with her charms." He reached out and pulled Brigianna to his side. "Our beloved Grania, the fairest woman in all Ireland," he said with a sweeping bow, then turned to the other women standing nearby. "M'ladies: Brigianna, a freewoman who has consented to dwell with us Caffertys."

She noticed he did not say "Brigianna of the McColyms" and forced herself to smile at the line of curious, staring eyes.

"This be Yvonia," Kevin announced as a tall redhead stepped forward, "and Catriona, and Maire, and Darcy and—" he stopped short and looked down, "and Rollie, dear little Rollie."

Kevin swooped the toddler off the ground and into his arms, ruffing a mass of coppery curls. Surprised, Brigianna turned to him.

"Are ye married, McErin? I never did ask."

"Me? Married? No, lady, I like women too well. Isn't that so, Rollie?" Pinching a ruddy cheek, he set Rollie down, and Rollie went scampering to the woman named Maire.

She smiled and asked, "A freewoman? What trade do ye offer?"

"Brigianna comes not for work but for protection, Maire. Mind the women understand."

"Aye, m'lord."

"Yvonia! Tend to the lady's needs," Grania ordered, then turned to Brigianna. "Yvonia is a biddable wench and faithful to her duties. Ye'll do well to mind what she says. I'll be doing the honor of bathing, and for that the Caffertys bid ye a thousand welcomes."

Duty aside, she turned her attentions to Kevin as arm in arm they walked the winding road toward the lodge. At their coming, men lined up in formal greeting.

A large wolfhound bounded out of the crowd to lather Kevin with affection. "Max!" he shouted as the dog planted both paws on his shoulders, and they both danced to keep balance.

Yvonia sidled to Brigianna's side. "Such a rich green, and the wool, how soft it is! It must have taken forever to comb it," she murmured, fingering her cloak. "But what's this? A tear in it?"

"'Tis nothing, just the pitfalls of travel."

"Aye. Well, we'll have it mended in no time."

Like Kevin and his people, Yvonia was tall. Her flaming hair blazoned like the sun at its set, but her green eyes smoldered like a carefully banked fire. Brigianna found herself warming up to her, yet taking careful note to mind her cloak.

"'Tis doubtful she did her own combing with nails pinked like that," Catriona teased. Flaxen-haired, blue-eyed, and diminutive compared to Yvonia, she smiled graciously to reveal fine even teeth.

"No woman sits idle in the Cafferty clan when there's work to be done," Maire grumped, taking Rollie in tow.

"Well said. Lord Gawain is not one to be kept waiting, so be off," Yvonia announced, taking command by steering the chattering women to the main hall, where they filed in through the several unguarded doorways.

At best these doorways were windbreaks, set aside from the actual entrance a few feet, to form narrow hallways or porches. Since only dirks and drinking horns were allowed inside, the walls were lined with arms, cast aside in a treacherous jumble. Brigianna stepped gingerly but still tripped over a discarded weapon belt. "Take care, m'lady," Yvonia said and held out her hand to guide her.

Once inside she brightened to the warmth from the central fire and savory smells of the huge boar roasting there. No daylight ever entered this hall; instead, firelight cast ghostly shadows on the heavily carved oak and hollywood furniture. Men gathered around Kevin in a boisterous rabble of seemingly well-ordered confusion and, after exchanging greeting, went back to their own furs. Most of them had discarded their baggy checkered breeches and other field clothes, choosing to wear finer tunics or short kirtles of clancloth or leather instead. But for his scratchy traveling tunic and hard-soled shoes, Kevin blended in with his flaxen hair, build, and brawn. Even in passing, Brigianna couldn't help eyeing the heavy wristbands, fanciful twisted armbands, thick torcs, and long golden earrings worn by both men and women. One burly man with ruddy hair wore a gaudy necklace of abalone bound by copper tubing, and even the young men wore their hair braided and secured with baubles.

"This way," Yvonia whispered, leading Brigianna through a narrow passageway. She tried to catch Kevin's attention as she passed by, but he was deep in conversation.

* * *

"Drop your clothes here, m'lady," Grania announced as they stepped inside the women's quarters. "Yvonia, tend her. Catriona, see that the water is hot." Grania punctuated her words with a sharp handclap, and both girls moved quickly.

As Yvonia reached out to undo the taws that fastened Brigianna's maidenshift together, she informed her that Grania was first wife to Gawain, lord of the Caffertys. In a land where marriages existed by the exchange of a vow, and were often forgotten by less, Grania had accepted her role of castaway with dignity, but still demanded rule over the women's quarters. Her girdle was loosened and tied to the left, signifying that her moonsets had come and gone, and that she was free to take her pleasures at will. Provided her affections remained steadfast, of course. And to prove that his seed was fertile, Gawain was free to take younger women. If a woman proved well through childbearing, and if she continued to bring the king pleasure, she might be considered for a wife.

Brigianna listened to Yvonia's prattle curiously at first, but then with a dark tremor of apprehension. And with an embarrassed flush as she realized all the women and children were staring at her. In her clanhold families slept together; she had never faced the curious eyes of little boys who weren't her brothers.

Grania stepped forward. Brigianna often watched her mother bathe strangers but had never been so honored herself.

"M'lady," Grania said graciously and held out her hand.

In Grania Brigianna saw a woman very much like her grandmother, Amabel: a comfortably fat woman, sure of herself, oblivious to the sorrows life had to give, and smiling from eyes as sweet as the solitude of a hidden meadow on a soft summer's day. Brigianna, warmed by her charms, stepped forward, then suddenly froze.

Yvonia, bending over her clothes and fingering her soft leather boots, was definitely curious about the hard lump within. Aye? And what is this? her green eyes flashed in silent question.

Brigianna's eyes smoldered dark as sapphires: 'Tis mine to know, so leave it be.

"M'lady," Grania snapped impatiently. "Clabber could curdle with ye standing there."

"Begging your pardon," Brigianna said as she watched Yvonia gathered up her clothes and disappear.

The water was slightly too hot as she slipped into the heavy stone trough. As it swirled over her, she wriggled, fishlike, trying to adjust. Soon she was ringed by onlookers of all ages who began to pinch and prod her like curious, savage children. Grania elbowed them aside, stood over her, and took a handful of Brigianna's long, wet hair.

"Winter's sage, it is," she concluded after holding it up to her nose, then turned to rummage the ledge filled with tiny vials: petals fused in oil to be placed on the pulse points; and simples, herbs mixed with rainwater for splashing over the body. At home Brigianna was given no such variety to choose from. There she had been given winter's sage by her mother and told to guard it carefully. She had come to accept the fact that she smelled like winter's sage just as she accepted the rising and setting of the sun.

"Perchance tonight I would like to smell like wood roses," she proffered suddenly, surprising herself.

Grania drew back.

"Did I say something wrong?" Brigianna asked, puzzled.

The old woman hesitated, knowing it was the mother's prerogative to choose the scent for a daughter. Then, with a twinkling smile that unwittingly brushed the past aside, she announced, "A fine choice, m'lady."

Brigianna was dizzied with delight as the spicy drops of oil hit the water, and she would have gladly simmered in this sweet sea of nothingness forever. But when the women finished scrubbing her, they tossed their sponges aside and rudely yanked her out of the stone tub and onto the hard-packed earthen floor.

"Her hair is as thick as a horse's tail," Catriona complained with a pout. "The sun will rise and set with me still standing here, and ye will be dancing the night away without me, and when Kevin's a come, too."

"We'll be plaiting it, then, that's what," Yvonia purred. Her startling green eyes were like closed doors as she began parting the strands of hair with her long, sharp nails.

"So many braids, Yvonia?" Catriona wondered, watching. "Won't she look . . . strange?"

"A single braid will take forever to dry, and for that ye would still be standing here till morning, silly goose. Now, come help me. And keep your eyes off Kevin. I have first claim!"

"That was long ago," Catriona sulked, and Brigianna's ears perked up.

"Ye leave Kevin be, ye brazen little wenches. I have words for that man meself," Grania scolded as she handed Catriona a bowl full of crushed petals and beeswax. Like a cat who obeys only when its master is about, Catriona took it and began rubbing Brigianna's feet.

Soon Brigianna stood in front of the heavy bronze mirror clad in a shift so fine, it was like the silken strands of a spider's web. With candlelight behind her, her tiny figure appeared as a beckoning shadow behind a gossamer veil. Her hair was now braided into a score of tiny braids, each twined through with scarlet threads and knotted at the ends with beads of shell and bone. Reflected in the bronze shield, women moved behind her in mottled shadow like towering giants, as she, only a darting sprite, danced in delight, dazzled by her finery.

"Ye be so clever, Yvonia," Catriona cooed in spite of herself.

"Of course!" Yvonia eyed her handiwork carefully.

"But it still needs something. Ah! I know just the thing."

She dashed off and quickly reappeared, trophy in hand. Brigianna started when she saw her precious brooch but determined to say nothing. Yvonia skillfully fastened the fibula at her shoulder, where it glimmered in all its glory. That it was placed there for beauty's sake, and not for practical purposes of securing clancloth, made the women stand back in awe.

"Such a bonny thing!" Grania exclaimed, examining the filigree.

"Aye, and from one of your lovers, no doubt?" Catriona purred.

"That and more." Yvonia's green eyes crackled as she held up a golden torc and placed it around Brigianna's neck. The metal was cold and stiff to her touch, but Brigianna, knowing the ways of metal well, fingered the softly hammered gold with respect, certain it would shape itself to her throat as easily as the one she had left behind.

"Beholden," she said politely, knowing that by accepting the torc she was in debt to this woman.

Yvonia's eyes crackled with pride. "Aye, it's a pleasing sight ye are. But ye are so small I fear a man could sneeze and find ye gone come morning."

"Us, too. In the wake of Lord Gawain's wrath, if we be late!" Maire cried and dropped her clothes. The women, absorbed in themselves, splashed in the dregs of the tub as they hurriedly primped for evening, and Brigianna was left to be.

"Yvonia, ye are simply shameful." Catriona fluttered her dark lashes as they entered the main hall.

"All I said was that after his days on the road, Kevin might prefer a woman with experience. Now, where's the harm in that? Ye think to announce your wares by the tightening or loosening of a sash? Ye think ye can tell a maid virgin or no by the looking at her? Come now, where's the truth in that? Ah, Catriona, ye weary me, holding on to childish games with pretended innocence, when ye certainly know how to bring a man his pleasure. Ye were taught as well as I, ye know."

Adjusting her own sash, she glowered at Catriona through smoldering eyes. "If ye really wanted Kevin, ye would have had him by now."

"Yvonia!" Catriona gasped.

Yvonia fluttered her lashes and clasped her hands to her ample bosom. "Yvonia!" she mimicked, then her ire rose full timbre. "Sometimes I tire of feigned illnesses that leave ye unavailable for the evening and me to pleasure the men at their will. What will it be tonight, Catriona? A headache? The moonset? Or one of Grania's special teas?" She lifted the curtain as Catriona lashed back. "As kingdaughter, 'tis not expected of me, and well ye know that fact, so leave me be. But ye have chosen your bed, now lie in it."

"There ye be wrong, Catriona Cafferty," Yvonia said in dead earnest. "Only once did I choose my bed, and that, as ye say, be long ago."

Brigianna, listening to their tiff, tried to avoid Yvonia's eyes as she followed Catriona inside but found herself eye to eye at the doorflap.

"Ye be virgin?" Yvonia hissed.

"Aye," Brigianna reluctantly admitted.

Yvonia let the curtain drop and let out a low chuckle. "Well, we'll soon be taking care of that!"

Chapter 8

Brigianna lingered by a support pole, trying to ignore Yvonia's remark and to clear her head. As she tried to see through the smoky haze, the pungent smells of charring meats overwhelmed her. Nothing edible had come her way for an entire day, and savory smells made her mouth water in anticipation.

The spitted boar was braced by the central fire. Maire stood by, ladling the drippings over its charred and crackling skin. Other meats were already set on hot rocks to keep warm, their juices oozing onto heavy wooden platters already swimming with blood and rendered fat. Maire tossed another meat, squirrel or hare perhaps, onto the platter, and the swill dripped down into the fire with a hiss and sputter.

At first the central fire held Brigianna's attention, but as her eyes adjusted, she noticed the men ringing the fire pit. They sprawled about on their furs and were freshly washed, well oiled, clad in loose furs, brilliant checks, or plaids, and laden with gaudy jewelry. Radiating the sweet scent of musk, they aroused her senses, making her tingle with excitement, and more, too, for she had never before smelled the heady aroma of common lust preceding a feast.

"Yah!" a large man yelled from the shadows. Beside him Max, the wolfhound, jerked to attention and bounded over him to land in the dirt beside the fire. His enormous head fell to the ground in bewilderment when he discovered there was no bone to fetch. At this the Caffertys laughed uproariously at the dog's expense, and with much backslapping and rib-punching, shared an overflowing drinking horn.

"Hah! What have we here?"

The voice stampeded through the hall like a hundred head of cattle. Laughter sliced to silence; hush swelled like the rise of the wave.

Brigianna jerked back in alarm, came face to face with a wall of calculating eyes, and quickly turned away. Wringing her hands to quiet her trembling, she looked for some clue as to what to do next.

Finally she realized whose voice this was: Kevin's liege lord.

Gawain of the Deformed Eye, Lord of the Caffertys, and High Lord from sea to central valley.

She knew she should drop to her knees, but curiosity overrode her fear, and instead, she raised her chin and met him in the eye.

The Cafferty stood taller than Kevin and bore the fighting weight of a much older man. His cloak, cleverly designed to be worn furside out when hunting or in close company, or clothside out, to herald his seven colors as a panoply of power, hung loosely about his shoulders. His nearly hairless chest, glistening with sweet oils, was laden with gold. His left eye drooped badly as the result of a sword's cut that fell short of its mark and left him disfigured but not blinded. His curling, golden mustache ringed teeth that were cleft in the middle, and with a smile he held out his hands, beckoning her to come.

Trembling, for she had heard of this man, Brigianna was determined to keep her chin up. It was rumored that he intended to make himself next high king at Lughnasa. He was not content with the sea strip to central valley, but would, if he could, claim the whole valley and then Ireland.

The clansmen watched her. Grania came to her side and

whispered, "The king finds favor in ye, lady. Go to him." Catriona, Yvonia, and Darcy looked at her, trying to prod her on.

When Brigianna didn't budge, Grania swatted her rump. "By the mercies of heaven, Lady Brigianna. Have ye no manners at all?"

Propelled forward by Grania's swat, Brigianna stumbled toward the low benchlike table that separated her from the king. Just as she pitched forward, he let out a lusty growl and swooped her up and over the table. He dropped her to his furs and then fell down beside her. Gawain's meaty hand caressed her many braids and ran its course down the length of her delicate body, well outlined through her sheer gown.

The piper's wail broke the spell, and again the lodge came to life with raucous laughter. Women took their stations; Yvonia and Darcy to fill amphorae, and Grania and Catriona to join Maire at the meats.

Brigianna slowly realized Kevin was sitting beside her, staring straight ahead. She felt the sting of his silent reprimand and thought to put her hand to his arm, but there was a sudden ruckus at the main entry, and she turned away instead.

"'Tis the Cafferty lot to give sanctuary to all homeless tonight, Father, for look what I've brought." The man speaking was the one wearing the abalone shells she had noticed earlier. Though his hair had lost its rudd and was tinged with streaks of black, he looked remarkably like Gawain and even bore the same split-toothed grin.

"Aye, Cagney?" Lord Gawain said as he set his drinking horn aside and wiped his thick lips and mustache.

"Dregs of the rainbarrel. Found him hiding in the copse." Cagney grinned and spun around to draw a dark form from the shadows and hurtle it forward. "A Shameface, no less!"

Cold, noncommittal eyes watched the Shameface fall to the dirt and roll forward, then try to right himself beneath his heavy wooden mask. Brigianna drew back in horror. She had heard of Shamefaces, certainly, but in her father's clanhold there were none. Tormaigh McColym was a lenient man, too lenient, some said, in not putting the blade to the face in discipline.

But here, groveling like a pig in its mire, was a Shameface. A man who, for some crime, had had his face shaved away by the slice of a king's sword. One who had lost a nose, a cheek, perhaps even a jaw, but still lived. One who was forced, because of his ugliness, to beg for daily rations and to live like an animal; forced by a people who worshipped beauty and considered physical deformity a curse of the gods.

Gawain stood, with hands on his hips, eyeing the outcast carefully.

"How say ye?" he demanded.

The Shameface, a short runt of a man with a stocky frame, rolled over and came to one knee. With both hands he steadied the heavy wooden helmet that formed his prison. As he rose, his right leg turned inward, refusing to bend. As he stood, his left hip bulged in ungainly compensation. Both legs were wrapped with rags, then laced with leather bands. When he raised his hands in silent plea, a stretch of bare leg showed between the rags and his tunic.

"Dumb, ye are, then?" Gawain growled with his hands still on his hips and his good eye narrowed in suspicion. "If it's 'defend me or spend me' ye cry, I have to have some way of knowing."

"My lord, is it wise to bring such dregs as the gods despise to the mighty Cafferty camp? Do not the gods demand beauty of both body and spirit among our people?"

Gawain turned to face Conor, his nearly chinless, ferret-like priest. "Is it wise for the mighty Cafferty to turn the hungry away?" he challenged.

"For aye!" the king's brother, Lord Eric by name, shouted with a slam of his drinking horn upon his hollywood table. Thwarted, Conor retreated beneath the shadows of his cowled robe.

"I repeat," Lord Gawain bellowed, enraged by Conor's

interference, "if ye pledge your liege and for that demand my protection, I must have way of knowing it."

The Shameface nodded and his heavy head nearly toppled him forward. He balled his right hand to a fist and thumped his chest. A shout of acclamation went up from the clan as horns were raised in drink. But Gawain put his hands out, palms down, and again silence reigned.

"Fair sworn and fair witnessed!" Gawain thundered. "Work an honest day, and the pot's fair share be yours, as is the warmth of my fire, my sword, and my shield of protection. But be it known, if it's fugitive ye be and ye be avenged, then my sword shall fall to my side, for I'll not pay your price. And if need arise and ye do not raise your sword in my defense, then mine will lie buried in your belly without a moment's worry.

"Again I ask. How say ye?"

Once more the Shameface beat his chest with a balled fist, and shouts of acclamation were followed by drinks and laughter.

"Make him feel at home. Make him fight for his food, make him understand what it means to be a Cafferty," Lord Gawain said and sat down.

Amid the peal of rousing laughter and slamming drinking horns, a boy ran from the shadows, slammed into the Shameface, and forced him to his knees. The Shameface grappled with his mask as he lost his balance and fell forward. The youth quickly straddled him. Lean, with a thatch of fiery-red curls and eyes flashing bloodlust, the youth saw his vantage point and went for his knife.

Brigianna's scream was cut short as Kevin's hairy arm lashed out to brace her hard against his chest and twist her face to meet his. Her eyes widened in fear as she met his gaze. The short-lived scream was lost in the din and unnoticed by all but Gawain. He gave them both a split-toothed grin, then went back to laying wager.

"Rory! Rory!" Caffertys shouted.

Kevin pressed his drinking horn to Brigianna's trembling

lips. "Drink, m'lady, and enjoy the honor bestowed upon ye of sitting kingside to watch the evening's entertainment."

She blanched, knowing it was an order, and fluttered her lashes in assent. With cold reserve Kevin acknowledged it.

As Rory's knife plunged forward to splinter what would have been a cheek if the Shameface were not masked, she forced her screams to silence. The Shameface rolled away from the deadly knife and lay on his back, panting, his anguish and newfound shame betrayed only by a pulsating belly. As he rolled, the wooden helmet shifted, and Brigianna gasped in spite of herself. His locks were black as midnight.

Rory drew his knife back slowly and got to his feet. With eyes blazing bright in triumph, he gingerly ran a fingertip along the blade, as if he were wiping away blood.

The Caffertys roared with laughter, and Gawain, amused by Rory's ribald humor, raised a thumbs-up. The youth nodded, coughed up a large wad of spittle, and aimed it so that it fell to the side of the Shameface's head. He strode confidently toward the boar and plunged his knife into the juicy meat to claim a choice morsel, accepting the loud cheers and foot-stomping as his rightful due.

Back in the smoke-filled shadows a youth, slightly older than Rory, cuffed his brother. Soon they were in a scuffle, rolling and tumbling on the ground even before they left their dais. Growling like animals, they tore into each other and shouted gainsay—each barbed insult intended to be worse than the last. Catriona and Yvonia giggled at this, and even pinch-faced Maire smiled in amusement.

After them came the next pair and the next. Except for Brigianna, no one noticed when the Shameface rolled away from the fray, got to all fours, and leaned forward, trying to find the strength to get up. A cold wind rippled through her soul as she watched him leave with his ungainly, clubbed foot leaving a snail's trail behind him.

Gawain soon tired of the evening's sport and turned to Kevin. "Teach your brothers a lesson," he demanded, eyeing the hacked-up boar. He rubbed his hungry belly, determined to stave off his hunger.

Kevin rose. He met Gawain's eyes and held them as warrior to warrior. Gawain lowered his first, well aware that in his younger days he would have challenged his sons one by one and fought them himself for daily rations. "Go," he cursed with a wave of his hand.

Twirling the end of his mustache, Kevin walked the length and breadth of the cleared area. Suddenly he stopped, braced his legs apart, and folded his arms across his chest. He eyed the remaining haunch, the victor's cut, and by his stance issued silent claim. Unless challenged in hand-to-hand combat, it would be his.

A guttural roar came from across the hall. Kevin whirled around to face Cagney, the oldest of Gawain's natural sons, who stood with legs braced wide apart and shoulders hunched forward. Bared to the waist, he had shed the heavy abalone disks and now growled his challenge.

"Cagney! Cagney!" some shouted as they pounded their fists on the tables. "Kevin! Kevin!" retorted the others, banging horns and platters for added clamor. Gawain's upper lip curled in a cleft-toothed sneer.

"Ho!" Kevin yelled and tested spring. "Ya hay!" Cagney roared. They dug heel and rammed into each other like two stags in rut.

Kevin laid into Cagney with his face twisted against Cagney's chest and smothered by his scraggly hair. Cagney's muscles knotted up as he hulked his way over the top of Kevin's shoulders, intent eyes bulging with strain. But Kevin grunted as he butted his strength upward against Cagney's brute power and turned his face to the side, gauging the right moment to topple the giant with a quick, unexpected movement. Gritting his teeth beneath his mustache, he gave way, just enough to let Cagney think he was gaining ground.

"Yah, Cagney!" Caffertys stomped their feet in clamor, and in spite of Kevin's earlier warning, Brigianna cried out.

Gawain was too interested in the outcome to look away, but at her outcry he reached out and pulled her to his side. She gripped his furs, trembling as she crouched beside him.

"Why, the lady shrinks like the morning glory in moonshine. Here. Drink," he ordered, adding a hearty peal of laughter as he plunked a leather tankard in front of her. She gulped down the warm liquid, startled by its strong bite.

Kevin's thighs buckled under. His neck muscles drew into tight cords, and his whole body quivered beneath the force of Cagney's brace.

Brigianna gripped the tankard tighter and gulped the last of the swill. It burned its way down her throat and settled in her stomach like molten metal. Though a flaming river, the brew left an aftertaste as sweet as honey. She slammed the tankard down on her hollywood table, and it was immediately filled by a waiting maid. This she downed just as fast, all the while keeping her eyes on Kevin and Cagney, who were, for some reason, getting farther and farther away.

Gawain watched her unsteady arm slosh swill, and he chuckled. With the sureness of one used to getting his way, he grabbed her by her many braids and pulled her face to his. His kiss was wet and heavy, and she felt herself helplessly drowning in its swirling current, like the day she was pulled downstream by the angry river.

Succulent, supple, and squirming beneath him, she awakened his appetite, and he suddenly lost all interest in fight or food. With an experienced hand, he downed her on the furs and sidled her rump into place. Enlivened and hungry now, his kiss demanded that his appetite be not only satisfied, but satiated.

Grunting in the force of Cagney's vicious grip, Kevin's features stretched tight as he twisted against its power.

Then he saw Brigianna, and his anger kindled.

His cry of anguish sliced the air like lightning arcing to fissure granite. Gawain jerked back, eyes riveted on Kevin. Caffertys hushed. Cagney the Brave loosened his grip and stepped back in alarm.

At that moment Kevin lunged. He dropped Cagney to the dirt. On top of him now, he battered his brother's jaw with a closed fist. Cagney cursed and made an attempt to roll away from Kevin, but failed. Again Kevin's fist came down in solid swack, and Cagney bellowed in rage. Grunting in pain, Cagney drew up his powerful legs, bent his knees, and braced his feet firmly on the ground. Then he bucked.

Kevin was pitched forward. He rolled over even before he hit dirt, but Cagney landed to his side and grabbed a fistful of golden hair to use like a rope and force Kevin's head down. Cagney raised his balled fist, ready to lam.

With great effort Kevin slowly drew one leg forward so that it crossed his own stomach. With practiced cunning, he thrashed his head to the side, just missing Cagney's blows, and waited for the right moment. Cagney raised his arm again, and Kevin's foot shot up and caught Cagney at the throat.

Cagney bellowed and rolled backward, and Yvonia came running up to them. Eyes blazing and red hair shaking, she looked down in disgust.

"Enough of this, I say!" she shouted and ran to the boar. Drawing her knife from her sash, she sliced a thick slab of meat from the ham portion and threw it to the dirt. "Eat—like the pigs ye be!" she cried and ran from the hall.

Gawain guffawed, and with meaty hand shoved Brigianna away from his side. "The woman is right, pigs we are. Now eat. And enough of this. We fight in earnest soon enough."

Cagney and Kevin faced each other in stubborn stance. Neither would bend first to eat of the truce shank. Impudent and arrogant both, they strode to the platters of meat, cursing and elbowing each other for the choice cuts. Quickly Catriona hurried up to the main table with the king's platter and thrust it down in front of Gawain. Gawain eyed the grandly overfilled platter with caution and crouched down to make a pretense of eating as he tore little bits and pieces from the bone and tossed the rest aside. Max bounded forward, skidding into a nearly untouched shank, and happily sank his teeth into it. Soon the hall was filled with the clatter of burping and satisfied diners.

Kevin returned to sit at another table, down from Brigianna and, with eyes straight ahead, defiantly wolfed down large hunks of meat, followed by generous swills of fiery brew. Glowering at Cagney, he glanced at Brigianna to see her smile brightly at Gawain and turned away to stare stonily into the fire.

Gawain belched marvelously and reached for a bone to pick his teeth. His hand strayed to Brigianna's arm, where it stayed only momentarily before finding its way to her shoulder, to knead and prod a bit before sliding down to a waiting breast.

"Kevin, my son, give humor to an old man and quiet this rabble with a song," he said.

Still sweating from battle furor, Kevin hesitated. His eyes met Gawain's with measured respect alloyed with fear. He sighed and set his meat down. "Aye, m'lord."

Firelight burned low as Kevin McErin was once again transformed into bard. The harper strummed softly as his voice rose to full timbre to haunt heartstrings with visions of maidens fair and warriors strong.

Slowly Yvonia stole back into the hall to sit at Brigianna's feet, her green eyes sparkling with inner fire and her face unabashed with admiration. Kevin's eyes were soft blue, and he smiled her way but refused to look at Brigianna. He went on to sing of Ireland's fertile land and of warriors' glory from battles long forgotten.

Catriona went to sit by Cagney's side. She jabbed his ribs so that he moved over, and with pussycat smile she took the better seat. Maire held little Rollie, who eventually fell asleep in her lap. And Grania smiled proudly, but refused to leave her seat by the fire.

Brigianna listened, lulled by the flickering fire and fiery brew, wondering how a man could sing like this and fight, too. How can a man be tender as the turning of a rose, yet hard and forbidding like the sword of blooding?

As the fires in the great hall burned low, the slow breathing of sotted Caffertys hummed steady as the fire. Gawain, drunk from several tankards of potent brew and considerably mellow, finally broke the trance of Kevin's song.

"The night grows old, my son, and so do I. Ask of me anything, and it shall be given ye."

Before the McErin spoke, soft blue eyes scanned the hall carefully, giving due attention to adversary and admirer, alike.

Chapter 9

Kevin drew in his breath and marked each word well.

"Were a crown and a kingdom to lie at my feet this very night, I would ask only for the smile of Lady Brigianna, that and that alone."

He dared not look her way but kept his eyes on Gawain instead. Not a tremor in his voice nor a flicker of his eyelids betrayed his feelings. There was nothing imploring or pleading in his voice, nothing that spoke of love's desire, as he said, "I would that I could have the honor of taking this fair woman first. Even in my father's house."

At those words Brigianna bolted upright, and warmth spread throughout her body.

The few Caffertys sober enough to weigh the import of this grave offense fidgeted nervously and turned round-eyed from the shadows, their faces now luminescent and alive with curiosity. Yvonia's gaze quickly turned to green ice, and Grania clamped her eyes shut and hung her head low.

Lord Gawain eyed Kevin from behind a glazed and drooping lid. His hand shook slightly as he grasped his drinking horn tighter at its base. Very, very slowly his neck reddened. Cautiously he surveyed the faces staring back at him like a ring of glowing lanterns. Inwardly he weighed his prow with his waiting women and to his surprise was unable to look at Grania.

The few eyes remaining at attention were well schooled at hiding behind hooded lids, and Gawain recognized this semblance of alertness for what it was. Secretly envying them their freedom, he made a great show of drawing in a long breath and giving the matter the same concern he would have given a border raid, a cattle exchange, or a well gone sour.

Kevin did not lower his eyes in the presence of his king. Instead, he stood guard as he had throughout countless battles, body alert, challenging fate's cold, hard game. Meanwhile, Cafferty hands moved noiselessly within the shadows, laying wager, and Brigianna watched with trepidation shivering cold chill up her spine.

Reluctantly Gawain let his hand trail the curve of her shoulder, trying to ignore the stirring in his groin. Even though his seed was warming within him, he realized that the woman was a pawn. A succulent sweeting to be sure, but a pawn, nevertheless.

Concluding there was no saving grace in forcing the issue, he eyed her with deep regret, then raised a drooping lid to search Kevin's expression, longing for words that did not come. The split lid fell back over a disconsolate eye. "Bed her well," he said.

Had Brigianna entered this chamber directly from the main hall and not by the outer path, she would have stumbled along in drunken obedience. As it was, the night air brought her sharply to her senses, making her think of the time she and Lochobar had gathered cobwebs to use for bandages. They had tugged the matting loose, wrapped it around their hands like a spinner gathers wool, and magically the darkened cave was swept clean. She followed Grania's surefooted steps, thinking of that day as happening a lifetime ago and belonging to someone else.

Above them a thin slice of silver moon graced the star-studded sky: the virgin, crescent womb cradling the unseen with her consort star watching in contemplation. She smiled at the omen. Were they fated perhaps? And would there be a baby?

Grania's soft leather boots were noiseless as shadows as she traveled what was for her a well-worn path, out the back and into one of the side chambers by way of a narrow corridor. When she drew back the curtain, light reflected calm, complacent eyes. She smiled shyly and was gone.

The room was terribly small, most of it taken up by a pallet stuffed with new straw. The air break between the walls and roof displayed a thin strip of starlit sky as if it were fine tapestry, framed by golden thatch that overhung it by a double handspan and shielded it from the cold. A single beeswax candle lit the room, its sculpted folds laid waste by the heat of burning. Even though this chamber had no fire, it was well warmed, for its inner wall shared common bond with the main hall, where fire was always going. Inside the hall songs of merriment quieted upon the lips, and well-sotted diners slept where they fell.

Brigianna fingered the soft ermine- and rabbit-skin coverlets, knowing that furs of such whiteness could only be caught in winter, when the animals had fully changed color; and knowing, also, the painstaking hours it took to sew such skins together. A length of wool in rich woaden blue, finely teasled and soft as shammy, was carelessly tossed over them. Lost in thought, she did not hear Kevin and jumped when he entered.

"Did I startle ye, lady? Ye knew I would come."

"Begging your pardon, but I was taken by such fine furs and woolens, and aye, ye startled me."

"Ye find them pleasing, then?"

Bare, except for the loincloth kirtled in the front as a short skirt, and unarmed, except for the small dirk tucked in the waist, he suddenly seemed very different. He wore no jewelry or symbol of rank. Candle glow, enhanced by a moonbeam's silvery touch coming through the transom, bathed him in soft light and made his body, well rubbed with sweet oils, glisten.

His legs were like the oak, well turned by the craftsman's touch, young and pliable at first bidding, but now seasoned by the bitter winds of winter and able to withstand almost any force. Thin runner's legs they were, strong, sinewy, and hardened by the many standing battles he had fought, for he was footman, not horseman. With them he was able to kick as high as he was tall but not miss a step, pick a thorn from an enemy's chest, and yet not crush the grass beneath his feet. They were the mark of his trade, his legs.

"Aye, it pleases me," she said, looking at his legs. Anxious eyes, flashing dark as obsidian, finally dared look up, expecting to see the waiting hunger a man holds at bay when he is in want. She saw, instead, a bladed slice of a smile and firm-set features framing steeled eyes blunted cold with anguish. He towered above her, feet braced well apart and arms folded across his chest.

Shattered by this walled rebuff, she quickly turned away.

Quiet veiled them. And she thought of the baths and talk of maidenheads broken, and womanhood come, of milkteats and panting men. As a child, she surmised that when the men were alone, they, too, spoke of such important matters as fecundity and bellies made fat by ripening seed.

Listening, she would wonder what it was like, that first moment between two lovers. Was there fear or pain? Was there mourning at the virgin's loss of innocence? Or tears shed beforehand for sorrows that lie ahead?

Like a child peering through the flaps to view sacred ceremonies, she waited, burning with curiosity and tormented by her own eagerness and wanton desire to be loved.

But now her moment of reckoning had come, and the woman waiting within, ripened from time immemorial and eager to experience the tender art of love, stepped forth from the darkness of eternity to face a man, blooded and bound. A man, withholding in stoic reserve all that she saw explosive and fascinating.

Fervently she wished for some enchantment to put on him. But of men and women Lochobar had said little; and no woman, certainly, ever spoke of a man not willing.

Fingering the coverlet, she mustered courage to speak.

"What makes ye look upon me with such reproach? By king's honor, ye played with me no song of the roads, and yet ye begged me come. 'Come to my father's clanhold, be under his protection,' ye say. But for what? Why did I come if ye take no pleasure in me?"

Daring to look up, she stifled back her tears, and in meeting his walled silence, her ire began to lick its flaming tongue.

"What do ye fear in loving, mighty Fian? Why not take? Why not have? Would not the warmth of loving be kindling against the cold of a thousand winter's nights? Or is a warrior's life so uncertain of its morrows that it cannot venture love? Are pathways of duty so narrow they be holding no compassion for moments like this? Or is it that ye could love me? And that ye truly do fear?"

She tilted her chin upward and forced a smile. The single beeswax candle sputtered in the circling breeze. The shadows of night loomed dark around them, making Kevin appear taller and more godlike than ever.

Whispering awe traced its indelible finger upon the recesses of her being, for in demanding her due as a woman and reveling in this stirring wakening and relishing more to come, she knew she was a child no longer.

She longed to run her fingers over the curve of his shoulders, longed to feel his strong and sinewy thighs wrapped around her. The forced tug of a smile had its wanton way, and in warm, chuckling mirth she acknowledged what had happened to her in those long days upon the road.

Hungering eyes played the planes and shadows of her gossamer gown. Nervously she put a hand up to brush back her hair and was startled by the unaccustomed feel of braids and beads.

"Come now," she braved, "the king has given me to ye. For tonight, at least." Rising, she took a step forward.

"Ha!" Kevin roared as he slapped an angry fist into his palm. He spun around to lean his head against a lodgepole, his brow soothed by its smooth coolness. His thunder made her draw back.

"Gawain Cafferty allowed me grace of saving honor, m'lady, so ye would not know the agony of an old man's dreams." Gripping the lodgepole, his knuckles turned white, and glistening muscles turned into angry knots. "Oh, for aye," he wailed and swooped his hand, "he gave ye to me to sport with for the night, ye who are still bound by your father's oath to wed an old man."

"I am not!" The seductress vanished and cheeks rudded in quick ire. "I declared myself a freed woman, and we spit of it. So I'll not be having the matter thrown at me feet. Ye knew of this at our first meeting, and by your own doing I am no longer bound by such honor."

"Ah-ha!" Kevin badgered, spinning around. "The lady has no honor? The lady is free to lie with Fian or king, whatever suits her fancy?"

"Lie with the king?" Brigianna snapped. "Has the McErin gone mad? How dare ye speak to me like that!"

"How dare."

He gritted his teeth in calculated control. "How dare," he repeated. "Me, who has the common sense to rescue ye from the Pig Man's rampage. Me, who warms ye, finds ye shelter, and feeds ye at your whim. Me, who sees ye are bathed by Grania herself. Me who sees ye clothed in finery, properly presented, and given a seat at king's table! Me!"

He thumped his chest in angry tambour. "For the trouble ye've cost me, Lady, that's how I dare call honor."

"I said I was beholden," she said, scurrying back to ermine safety.

"Beholden enough to make sport with the king? To

smother him with the kisses of a camp woman? In the presence of my clan, before claims are made? To shame me?"

"What are ye talking about?"

"Think, Brigianna, think."

She put her hands to her temples and gave him a puzzled frown.

"The wine?" she cried.

"Aye, the wine," he said as he moved forward and took her by the shoulders. "Only 'tis no wine, and far more potent than ye are used to. Here we call it 'water of life,' and it's not to be guzzled."

"Was I too unseemly?" she asked, shaking aside the raven madness clawing her dignity.

"Unseemly enough. If it's Lady ye are."

The moon had risen to its crest, and soon its turning would bring the light of morning. Brigianna winced as sobriety hit her, and fleeing skirts of drunken fancy took off like raucous ravens, leaving a throbbing head in their wake. She shivered in the coming chill and felt suddenly shamed; a discomforting feeling and one she was not used to.

With a sniffle she felt the warm, waiting furs. "I did not come to this chamber to be reminded of duty or honor," she pleaded. "I came thinking to learn something of love, grateful in my secret heart that it is not by the king I must learn it."

"To learn something of love?" he attacked, ignoring her plaintive cry. "For all I've done, it now befalls my lot to school ye in love?"

Then, almost of its own accord, a low chuckle bubbled up. "Well, Lady, the night grows cold, and this chamber is not ours forever. Since I brought ye here, we'd best be on with it," he said, seizing her.

His mouth came down hard upon hers, fierce and demanding, and he forced her down upon the pallet. His breath was as sweet fire, hotter and more burning than that stuff they call the water of life. She shivered, tingling with delicious excitement, lost in a whirr and blur of feeling that made her murmur nonsensical little noises.

She felt him grow hard and full against her as he fell over her and pressed her deep into the straw. His hand skimmed the silken flesh of her thigh, easily slipping beneath the sheer gossamer gown to cradle her butt in the crook of his elbow and pull her down farther beneath him.

Deep fire rose up within, wakening something previously forbidden.

Hungrily, fiercely, she kissed him, with a strength she didn't know she possessed. Her lips parted and his tongue found hers, in searching, questioning demand. She clawed his shoulders, pulling him tighter and tighter against her. Everything was dark, and getting darker, as she sank into murky oblivion, where time no longer existed and space became an endless tunnel of careening, swirling, thrilling, tumbling trills.

Their breathing deepened, it became as one, taking long strides and short, panting halts, as hungrily, and for the want of each other, they matched pace, like the days they had run for hours by each other's side, saying little, thinking little, only letting their blood pound out the rhythm as their bodies melded into one.

With a deep cry and full longing, his hand slipped between her thighs and, with knowing firmness, parted her legs.

But something dark and primordial cried out within.

She gave a spasmodic shudder and turned her head to one side.

Kevin's expression turned waxen. Without word he rolled over.

She scooted backward, shaking as she pulled the coverlet over her.

"What is it, Brigianna?" he asked in an even voice.

"I do not know. 'Tis like the sea, different from what I imagined."

"And how did ye imagine love to be?"

"I thought . . . " she began, trying to choke back tears

that eddied into hot splash anyway. "Well, I supposed that if babies are so wee and gentle . . . that love . . . I mean, the making of such creatures could be wee and gentle, too."

"Ah, I see," he said in deep and bitter sigh, and turned away to perch on the edge of the pallet and lean forward to rest his chin on his hands. In the dimmed light of the waning moon, with shoulders rounded and head buried in his hands, he did not seem so powerful and godlike. He looked to her at that moment, lonely, forlorn, and terribly human.

Instinctively she slid over to him and rested her cheek against his bare shoulder. Hot salty tears bathed her face and warmed his back.

"Surely all men are not like my father's brown bull. Surely ye have loved a woman before, and with kindness?" she whispered.

Taking her in his arms and cradling her tightly against him, he slowly brushed the teardrops away.

"Have ye not, Kevin?" she pressed, tracing with pulsating fingertips the curve of his lips, soft and certain beneath the golden mustache. His brows were silken beneath her touch, firm in wide arc, and his forehead no longer set with deep worry lines.

When he kissed her this time, there was a mellow sweetness to it. Her entire body flooded with shimmering warmth and soft tingling sensations. And from the palms of her hands, she felt power leave her; the life-force held within her flowed freely into him. She felt it leave, and felt it return, each delicious, ebbing, pulsating tide.

"I had thought ye a willful lass bent upon her own way," he said as he drew back for air. "Careless of duty, wanton and headstrong. . . . I—ah, it's not to matter what I be thinking." He stopped and shook his head, his smile turning tight and grim again. "A man's thoughts be best kept to himself.

"Ye do not belong here among my people, Brigianna. Your gentle heart, your kindly ways, ye are different than women here. It's rash I was to bring ye here."

"Shhhhh," she whispered, putting a finger to his lips to silence them. "When choice was made upon the road, I did not come because I had no place to go, I came simply for the liken of ye. But still I have to ask, for why did I come?"

"Is it for love, then, Lady Brigianna?"

Her smile told him all he needed to know, and with her kiss, eager and unafraid, he felt his body stir once again. Not wanting to hurry the moment, he took a tiny braid, slowly undid it, then another and another. When she giggled in mirth, so did he.

"Ye are not a man much given to laughter."

"It's not for much I've had to laugh."

"And I make ye laugh? I make ye happy?" she said, slipping her arms around his neck and kissing the smile tucked safe beneath his mustache.

With teasing eyes she reached to undo the knots at her shoulder. He cupped her breasts in the palms of his hands as the gown slipped, and kissed them each. His warm breath stirred yearnings deep within, yearnings no longer bewildering or mysterious, but still yearnings too wonderful to speak of.

With womanly confidence she lay back down on the pallet.

Slowly, with longing eyes, he caressed her body, exploring each tiny crevice, savoring the full sensual delight of each gentle curve, marking upon his heart all that was to be remembered for a day or a lifetime: the wonderment of Brigianna.

His hands ached to touch her, but he stopped just short of completing that act of loving.

"Tonight I just want to fill my being with looking and longing." His eyes, livened by hunger, shone like sapphires, hardened to brilliant perfection. Yet behind that brilliance, and even at this moment, he trembled with deep, unquenchable despair.

She quivered beneath his gaze, unaware that his hands had stopped touching her.

Her soul seemed to burn and cry out in its loneliness. Loneliness she did not know existed until this night. A virgin still, she lay before him, a child no longer, threshold crossed and womanhood come. From this point on her life would be a dull aching nothingness unless he was near.

And in that moment she vowed: No man would ever touch her, save Kevin the McErin.

"Do ye not want me?" she cried when she could bear it no longer.

"Aye. I ache with want. And I will be in torment until that want be filled."

Tenderly he kissed her. A hand fell to her waiting breast. Then with a look of unbearable sadness he pulled it away.

"Brigianna, I am Fian and bound by oath. If ever a time comes when your loyalties are tested by priests, remember well this night and its price paid."

Leaning now upon the doorpost, he turned his face away and whispered:

"I give ye permission to say what ye will. I ask only that ye remember promises made by spit, and that ye do not leave."

Turning, he gave her one last, longing look and was gone.

Chapter 10

Stubborn pride forced Brigianna to suffer the indiginity of spending the night in the sleeping chamber alone. Tears cascaded down smudged cheeks. Finally she realized that crying was just a vexation of the spirit and had not, after all, brought Kevin back. When sleep did come, it came with the heaviness of a boulder sealing a darkened tomb.

By the time she wakened, the Caffertys were well into their daily tasks. Brigianna, thinking to steal quietly back to the women's quarters, stopped by the rain barrels to splash chilly water over swollen eyes, and sensing she was being watched, stiffened. Patting her eyes dry with the hem of her shift, she turned to see the Shameface leaning against the outbuilding, watching her.

"Good be the day," she said politely and walked on. Knowing dark eyes watched her through the fearsome carved slits of his mask, she quickened her steps, hurrying to lift the flaps to the women's quarters and duck inside.

"There ye be," Yvonia said as she entered. "Tea is warm, come."

Yvonia shoved a leather mug of steaming brew into her waiting hands, reached down to grab Brigianna's cloak, and all but pushed her back outside. She led her to a sitting stone, away from prying eyes and listening ears, and with palm to shoulder, firmly sat her down. Brigianna gratefully cupped both hands around the mug and lifted it to her lips, but comforting as the tea was, it didn't warm her bones. Setting it down, she reached for her cloak, for the dampness this close to the sea chilled her. When she looked up, the Shameface was gone.

"Well?"

"Well, what?"

"Well," Yvonia said again with a knowingly wicked smile.

Brigianna fussed with the collar of her cloak. With lowered lids, she sipped her tea.

"Mmmmmm, 'tis a sad cricket that does not chirp by the hearth," Yvonia mused and reached over to finger Brigianna's cloak. "Such a finely teasled cloak, soft as baby's swaddle. But the tear here, it causes me to ponder. Who are ye, Brigianna? And why the tear?"

Brigianna ran her finger along the ripped edge of her cloak and forced a lighthearted laugh. "'Tis a wonder it's not torn to shreds, for the time we had in getting here."

"Aye, though not a burr's been caught in it, and no brambles stuck in the threadlines." Yvonia quizzed her brow, eyeing Brigianna as carefully as she did the tear. "Perhaps Grania will loan me her best bone needle, and I can tweeze the threads back to order."

"That would be a kindness."

"But it's not to everyone Grania gives her best bone needle."

Brigianna waited out the moment. "'Aye, 'tis beholden I am."

Yvonia's smile acknowledged the debt. "Good. Now come. Morning is upon us and there are eggs to gather."

"How fun. Let me fetch bread to last until we return."

Yvonia gave Brigianna a puzzled stare. "Ye'll hardly die of hunger when the hens are right here."

"Ye know where to find them?"

"Of course, right behind the brush. Did ye not keep hens at home?

"Keep them! Lucky it was to find them. Of a truth, when mother set a coddled egg before me, and I had to face that terrible green stuff before the light of day, well, I made it game not to find them."

Given to laughter like some people are given to sadness, Yvonia filled the morning with mirth, then reached down to gather the waiting basket filled with corns and bread crusts. "I do not like plover, nor grouse, either, for that matter. But ye'll like these—big, yellow, and fine-tasting, they are. Raiders brought the hens from across the sea. And that's the only good thing I can think to say of raiders!"

They made their way down the narrow trail in back of the meadhall. Brigianna followed, intent on the hens and trying not to think of Kevin, or of Rathdun's seething horde or plundering marauders. Still, fierce lances flashed before her eyes, making her remember her promise to stay.

As if knowing her thoughts, Yvonia said: "Forget him. He's a fickle-hearted lover. Gone six moons of the year, sour and surly when he's back." As she turned to face Brigianna, her dazzling emerald eyes clouded over. "Forget him."

Never, never would she forget McErin, she declared inwardly. Out loud she asked, "Ye have prior claim?" not wanting to know.

"A fickle-hearted lover, that man," Yvonia said, forcing a smile.

"Ye are not Cafferty, then?"

Yvonia turned to hold a threatening spear of bilberry bramble so she could pass by, and Brigianna could not help but note that Yvonia seemed ageless; a beautiful woman, with fine high cheekbones, stately grace, and a swanlike neck with skin so clear her veins were as lace webbing.

"Not by bloodset, but I might well be—so many times I—" She caught herself. "I'm just a straggler, come to stay." She let go and the bramble snapped behind them.

"Is that why ye vex Catriona so? Because she is a Cafferty?"

"The king's own."

"Catriona is Gawain's daughter?"

"Aye, and looks forward to marriage for life. She's been making mew eyes at Kevin since she was a kit."

"Kevin stands to wear the crown?"

"Aye, and Cagney, and Rory, and Brian, and even little Rollie."

"Rollie is Gawain's also? He's just a baby."

Yvonia laughed again. "Aye. Got by Maire, and the woman's complained of nothing but backaches since."

Making clucking noises, they stepped into the downy clearing to scatter the corns: both barley and wheat. Russet-plumed biddies scratched at their feet, then parted way for the cock, let him pass through, and closed in quickly behind him. The morning breeze quickened, making Brigianna's frizzed hair whip across her face. She shivered in the chill as she struggled to balance her basket, and forgetting about the eggs, thought of a nice warm fire and a hen roasting.

"There!" Yvonia pointed to the brush. "Follow that broody and she'll lead you to her nest."

Brigianna darted after the broody and into the brush, soon to find an egg, soft, nut brown, and still warm. Gentling it into the basket, she parted bramble to search for more. A biddy ran across her path, and laughing in tune to the hen's noisy clucking, she ducked into the brush as it closed in behind her. Suddenly a shadow crossed her path.

"Begods, what fortune awaits? Do ye come running to my arms the moment Kevin turns his back?"

Cagney Cafferty, on his way back from the squatting pits and taking the back way, stepped from the shadows to bar her path. With his thumbs resting in his wide leather belt and his feet braced well apart, his overpowering presence filled the darkened clearing. He smelled as rank and dank as bramble itself, and in fleeting recognition, Brigianna detected another odor, one that harkened back to childhood memory, one that rang of fire and molten metal.

"I . . . I . . . ." she started and her hands flew to her breast. The basket fell to the dirt. Eggs rolled and splattered, but she scarcely noticed.

Eyeing her with amusement, Cagney let out a peal of laughter like a preyer enjoying the hunt but in no hurry to end it. Bushy brows canopied slitted eyes, so that his expression was lost, but his fat-lipped smile made her shudder.

She turned to run, but bramble barred her path, making all the breaks in the brush look alike. Darkness closed in. But a narrow shaft of light lay to her right and she dived for it. And he was on her in seconds.

His smile widened to reveal yellow teeth that rimmed his gums like a rockpile fence. His battle-roughened paw grabbed her by the shoulders; she spun around, stumbled slightly, and was swooped up off her feet. Holding her up in the air and crushing the breath out of her, he gripped a handhold of hair as he force her lips down to his. She pounded closed fists upon his chest muscles, which were hard as iron, and screamed, pushing him away.

"Come, come, kitten, it's only a morning's sport I ask," he cajoled as he pursed fat lips together and pulled her closer. "If Kevin's warmed the pan, then faster comes the dinner for me," he chuckled, gusting garlicky breath. "And if the Fian has left the lady wanting, it's Cagney at your service."

"Ye let Kevin's good name be!"

"Oh?" Eyes widened and lips furled in amusement. He plunked her down to the ground as rudely as he would a sack of meal. Earth was spongy beneath her, and she stumbled, only to fall against him again.

"If it's your heart he's stolen, lady, I care less. 'Tis only your body I'm wanting. And that, be assured, I will have soon enough." Arrogance turned his words into stinging arrows. "For if Kevin's left ye wanting, my sweet, I'll soon have ye begging for more. But if ye thought to stay and bring him pleasure, it's not to worry, ye will soon learn to close your eyes and think only of me."

Grabbing her hair again, he forced her against him while his other hand reached inside her cloak, and she screamed in terror.

Suddenly branches parted and the light inside the bramble brightened.

"Let her be," Yvonia demanded.

She stood bathed in sunshaft, her stance resolute as any warrior's. Fires flashed within, making green eyes crackle. Her hips began moving back and forth, her feet dug their toehold into the dirt, and her arms shot up as she readied her first move.

It had been a long time since she had fought the Cafferty.

But Cagney was too quick for her. He lunged forward, spinning Brigianna around as he did. Yvonia's forearm shot out, and Cagney ducked the blow. He grabbed Yvonia around the waist and pulled her to him, and just as Brigianna was about to slip between the brambles, he yanked her backward and forced the two women face to face in crushing embrace.

"Methinks, considering the circumstances, it fair sport to be having ye both, for after all, I've not yet broken me fast." Laughing uproariously at the joke of this, he showered them with sour breath.

"No! No!" Brigianna cried, struggling to free herself. Cagney crushed her to him, nearly snapping her ribs. Slowly he released his hold at her waist and gripped a handhold of dark hair and pulled it taut. Paralyzed like a kitten in tow, she yelped in pain.

"What think ye of that?" he chortled, turning to Yvonia.

"Unhand the maid," Yvonia answered calmly. Understanding crossed Cagney's face. Their eyes met in silent agreement.

"Fair said: appetite could find no better reward, my sweeting."

With lips curled in hunger, he cast Brigianna aside. She would have been lacerated by the bramble's thorny spines if it weren't for the broom growing there that cushioned her fall.

"Go," Yvonia commanded.

"Ye cannot mean that, sure now . . ."

Brigianna dared to look into the Cafferty's eyes: they were calm and territorial; beside him, Yvonia stood firm in command.

"By your leave," she mumbled and left.

Yvonia watched her go, then turned to Cagney and said, "Begods, ye smell of a man fresh from a hard night's ride."

He let a handful of richly red hair trail through his fingers. "When it's a crown ye are wearing, ye'll not be complaining."

Her eyes narrowed with cat's-eye greed. Ignoring his fetid breath, she kissed him soundly.

The Shameface barred Brigianna's way back to the lodge. The moment she saw him, her hand flew to her mouth to stifle a cry. Still shaken, and in no mood to speak to anyone, she looked around to see if there was some way to avoid him without offending him.

He made no attempt to let her pass, and she was instantly angered and puzzled by his impudence in not letting her pass and by his brazen behavior. Certainly he knew that he had no more stature here than the animals!

The morning sun played games with the clouds and won the first round by brightening the day, but not her mood. With memory of darkened brambles and Cagney still fresh on her mind, the Shameface appeared as an ill omen: a specter pleading to her from another world.

Before she could turn away, he shot a hand to his throat and made guttural sounds while shaking his other hand wildly in the air. Both hands were mitted with crude leather wraps, and as he grunted, he shouldered from side to side, looking to see if anyone was watching.

Humiliation washed over her. Of course the man couldn't speak. But what did he want of her? Favors? Provisions?

Rolling mists had been chased into oblivion by a determined sun. Now sunstreams beamed down to ring the misfit in noble light.

When he stumbled forward and closed the gap between them, she was surprised to discover he was not much taller than she. His bound leg turned clumsily inward, twisting the clubbed foot at a painful angle.

Surely he must be used to such pain by now, she thought, but wondered if anyone ever got used to such pain.

Through that horrible mask, she imagined she saw the agony of a young man who was as ordinary as any lusty young man, tormented by fate to wear his crime as a banner, his story told and retold in the ribald carving of the heavy oak mask.

"Aye?" she ventured.

He reached out to touch her cheek with grimy mitted hands still stinking from the task of groveling for his daily fare. Yet his touch was tender as a lover's as he brushed her brow, cheeks, and forearms; everywhere the brambles had scratched her.

Then wordlessly he turned and limped away, his ungainly walk painfully stretching out the day.

Later that afternoon, after the breads had been set to cool, she saw Kevin again. Ashes of the fire pits had grown cold. The washing was pounded and set over bushes to dry. Women cozied by their lap looms, nimble fingers stiffened in slumber. And babes, well suckled with teats forgotten, slept, while milk trails drizzled down their chins.

The clamor of battle sports declaring Cafferty foment and prow lay dead in the field. Tethered horses swatted flies stuck in their foaming sweat as it cooled. And cattle bawled lazily from too much comfort.

She paused when she saw Kevin coming in from the sparring fields; sword, still warm from parry, now hanging in his wide leather belt; sweat dripping down his chest; cheeks red from the foray and eyes shining from the love of it. Like Brian his younger brother beside him, he was bare to the waist and dressed in checkered trousers. He guided the boy along with an arm o'shoulder, and the boy kept putting in an extra step or two, just to keep up.

"How goes it, m'lady?" Kevin called in greeting as they met by the large oak that stood on the path to the fire pits.

"Fair's the day, I would suppose," she replied politely.

"But not so fair as ye, m'lady," Brian gushed, unabashed in his delight of the beauty before him. The fervor of sport still shone in his eyes, and, grinning, he wiped a shock of tousled red hair from his forehead. "Kevin says I did well on the fields today, Lady Brigianna. I did, didn't I, Kev?"

Kevin kneaded the boy's shoulder in affectionate camaraderie. "Killed me twice, ye did."

"By the gods?"

"Would I tell a falsehood?"

"No. Or not be Fian," Brian teased.

"Well said. Now put some clothes on, or better yet, get to the baths. Grania tells me there's salmon for dinner."

"Aye, Kevin. Lady Brigianna." He bowed politely and turned to go, calling, "On the morrow I will kill you thrice!"

Brigianna watched him, secretly envying his easy place in Kevin's heart. Kevin leaned against the tree and took great care in fingering the twirl of his long mustache. And silence fell between them.

By now mistletoe was safely nestled in the mighty oak, and the oak, richly leafed in the breath of summer, gave the holy parasite sanctuary. Come the winter solstice, it would be cut down and its ripened white berries become part of the sacred ceremonies. But even before then, druids would steal to the oaks in the dead of night. And, from the concoctions they brewed of mistletoe, would stave away the rheumatoid aches that beset common people of wet clime. For it was well known that druids lived for an ageless span.

The druid's bough rustled above their heads, and a large

raven flew out, and as he flew away, he dropped a greening berry at Kevin's feet. Kevin watched its wingtip against golden sun, then turned to Brigianna. "Ye are certain it goes well? 'Tis from the day's work ye came by the scratches on your brow?" he pressed, embarrassed by his own question. She started to speak but held her tongue, wanting instead to trace the tiny seam of his blooding that ran down his forearm and reassure herself that all hurts can be healed. She wanted to tell him the scratches he saw from the brambles were on the outside, that they mattered little compared to the jagged nicks inside. No women's gossip had warned her it would be like this, and she wanted to go back to last night and begin again.

Before she could speak, a voice boomed from behind: "Ho! Brother!"

Cagney approached the oak in confident air, his abalone necklace a seascape mural across his chest, his leather jerkin darkened with sweat, and his lance butting the heavens to make way for his presence.

"Lady Brigianna," he acknowledged, then turned to Kevin. "'Tis a fair sweeting ye've brought to father's camp." With a split-toothed smile he braced the ground with his spear end, then let his eyes fall to Brigianna's feet and travel very slowly upward. "And a warm summer we'll be having, unless ye care to stake claim."

Kevin's features drew back in canny quickness. "The lady is spit clean of clanhold or promise. She is free to make her own choices."

"Kevin!" Brigianna whirled around, quickly angered at him for not claiming her and declaring her bound. Cagney chortled and put a hand out to her shoulder.

And Kevin's arm shot out to intercept Cagney's grip. "I pledged Brigianna provision and protection. She'll not be treated as common woman in this camp," he growled.

"Brother! Ye said the woman is free to make her own choices." Cagney cried in feigned surprise and laid a possessive hand upon Brigianna's shoulder.

"Unhand her," Kevin demanded with fingers turning vise around Cagney's bulging biceps. When Cagney only chuckled, Kevin's free arm shot forward to clip his brother across the jaw, and Brigianna was flung hard into the oak.

Kevin's blow knocked Cagney off balance. He flew at him and they went skidding down the slope, Kevin on top. They slid onto a flat space. Cagney's spear fell aside in the tumble, but Kevin was still armed. Cagney immediately sprang to his feet, standing with clawed palms forward, his only defense in rendering Kevin helpless.

By Fian's honor, if Kevin drew sword now, the death knoll would be counted against him. With deliberate gait he waltzed around Cagney to goad him into attack.

Cagney hunched his shoulders forward and lunged. Kevin, bending backward as a greening sapling, carefully gauged Cagney's run. With uncanny timing, he avoided the collision by a backward roll. Cagney, propelled by his own force but not meeting the intended impact, fell forward, just as Kevin's foot shot up to kick him in the groin.

Cagney cursed all the powers that be as he went down.

Brigianna ran down the hill shouting for help. Men dropped their weapons and hurried in from the fields, shouting and taking sides as they ran. Women left fire pits and looms and came running to see what the fracas was all about. Yvonia rushed up and grabbed Brigianna and pulled her aside. Taller and much sturdier, she was able to clamp Brigianna against her in ironlike embrace.

Kevin readied for the charge as Cagney reached inside his belt and pulled out his table knife: a small bronze dirk of pearled inlay with cylindrical blade designed for spearing, not for slicing. Muscles bulged in heavy wrestler's thighs as Cagney thrust a leg forward.

When Caffertys saw the upturned blade, the women hushed their babble. Brigianna drew back, leaning tight against Yvonia and, as the children standing beside her, watched with wide, fearful eyes.

"Yah!" Cagney yelled and charged.

Kevin saw him coming and spun around to kick the dirk out of Cagney's hand, but missed. Enlivened by battle fury, Cagney's eyes shone with vacant madness; his leather jerkin turned slick and dark with sweat. He snapped back and ran at Kevin with his knife raised, ready to plunge it into Kevin's chest.

Kevin saw the knife coming and whirled around so that his baggy checkered trousers danced behind him in a swishing flurry of mottled color. By the time he landed, his shortsword was aimed at Cagney. His arm shot up as he feigned his roll, but even as he swung, his arm was halted midair by some unseen force preventing him from driving the blade home.

Seeing his moment, Cagney jumped him, knocking the blade awry. They both went down on the grass. Kevin was ready to roll over and spring to his feet from all fours when he saw scarred leather boots standing in front of him. He paled and, like a dog, kept his eyes to the ground.

"What is this?" Lord Gawain raged.

Kevin looked up slowly, eyes beginning at the soles of scuffed boots and traveling upward, to see his foster father towering above him. Gawain's head parted the heavens; his split lid gorged with anger, and his neck muscles knotted thick as heavy ropes.

"What fighting is done will be at my command," Gawain bellowed. "There will be no fighting in my clanhold unless done for sport and done by honor, and there will be no fighting over women."

Lord Cafferty of the Deformed Eye grabbed his two oldest sons by their hair at their crowns. With the butt of his boot he sent them sprawling to the dirt as beaten, whimpering dogs.

Next he turned to face Brigianna, standing in the center of cowering onlookers. She lifted her eyes and quaked beneath his gaze.

"Ye will be brought to me later," he announced.

Chapter 11

Brigianna sat by her pallet, only halfheartedly listening to the gossip, trying to make herself as unobtrusive as possible. She fingered her possessions, each in turn: the small silver dirk tucked in her boot; the brooch that carefully secured her cloak; and Kevin's hand-carved comb resting delicately in the palm of her hand. Realizing this was all she had, darkness stirred her bones.

Inwardly she fretted over Gawain's frightful words—"Ye will be brought to me later"—but outwardly she made great pretense of having worrisome hair. But now that she had been formally welcomed and properly presented, Cafferty women were much too busy with their own affairs to be bothered, and her facade went unnoticed.

"Ye look no different than when ye came," Catriona mused at dinner call. Her merry blue eyes were unusually lackluster, as if an ill wind had blown through the camp.

"True," Brigianna agreed, forcing herself to rise.

She had donned her everyday maidenshift and braided her hair into its customary queue. Her head still ached from the pull of those tiny braids Yvonia thought so splendid, and she was thankful not to be so scantily clad. She reached for her cloak, surprised to see that Yvonia had already mended it, and quietly followed behind.

By the time the women entered the hall, the salmon was well roasted. Even when spitted on alder, there was no guarantee its oils would stay in the fish. Grania worried over it diligently, making certain the meat didn't flake and fall to the fire. The fish's head would be reserved as victor's cut if there was fighting to be done. Wild strawberries were just running the vines, and she had gotten honey. Shamrocks, sorrels, lovage, lamb's lettuce, and other potblacks filled out the meal. With gruel to the side, bellies would be full.

"Tend to the fire and stay by Grania's side," Yvonia whispered as they entered, then disappeared among the men with her large jug of mead. Dutifully Brigianna walked the ring of packed dirt circling the hearth to where Grania was standing.

Brian gave her a mischievous grin as she walked by.

Scarcely older than she, he was but half a handspan taller; a tender stripling with greening muscles, eager to be tested both in bed and in battle. She flashed a smile set with teeth even as strung pearls, met Kevin's steeled gaze, and scuttled toward Grania for comfort.

As she hurried by, she saw Yvonia bend over to fill Kevin's drinking horn with that fiery water of life. Flaming tendrils cascaded over his cheek, and he made no attempt to move aside.

Lord Gawain raised his hands to signal the evening formally begun. But before he could speak, there was a commotion by the main entrance.

"Make way!" Cagney shouted, and barged into the hall. Gripping his lance and butting its blunt end to the ground, he marched forward with strident steps and stopped one pacelength from his father, the king.

"What is the meaning of this?" Gawain shouted, then sucked in his breath and held it long enough for his split eyelid to engorge.

Cagney brushed his father's quick temper aside, and ignored the sudden gasps of the women and coiled wariness of the men. When he was certain he had their attention, he stepped forward, commanding audience.

"This!" he cried as he thrust his spear into the ground. The shaft was thick as his wrist, the blade long as two hand spans, the dirt beneath packed solid as firestone. The spear only went in a third of the way, then stood there, quivering.

Seeing fragile balance lost by the intrusion of weaponry inside the sacred hearth, Caffertys gasped in horror and Conor leaped to his feet in protest. "This does not happen unless war is to be called," he cried.

Cagney ignored him, and with an angry scowl raised a clenched fist to the ceiling. As he did so, two thick-bodied men in baggy trousers entered, towing a large object wrapped in a dark tarp. When they got to the fire, they let go of the tarp. It fell open to reveal the grisly severed head of a bull.

Grania gagged and immediately reached for Brigianna. Catriona whirled around to butt into Yvonia, who gave her a quick look of disdain, but put her arms around her to shield her, nevertheless. Instinctively, Kevin reached across his belly for a sword that wasn't there.

Once Gawain's finest, the bull's sorrel skull was now covered with gore. Its horns, symbol of pride and prow, lay cracked and impotent and dangled over its ears. Terror froze its face.

Gawain's lid lowered to shield his thoughts as he studied the spitted head. The staff on which it was posted stuck out as warning: hardly the work of wolves. And the two men who carried the head kept their eyes to the ground, furtively glancing back and forth.

Cagney's chest swelled to where it looked like he would burst the seams of his buff jerkin. He gripped his lance firmly with his right hand and rested his booted foot on the curve of the blade, which was still stuck in the earth. With eyes smoldering like well-banked embers, he turned to his father.

"To council."

Gawain's gruff voice reverberated through the lodge like a rumbling war drum. He marched through the hall and out through one of the narrow side doors with his long blue cape stirring wind as it whirled behind him. His retinue quickly followed. Not included in this company were the elderly, the untried, and the disfigured, such as the Shameface. But it did include Conor.

Grania looked at her beautiful fish with remorse. Knowing she tired so easily of pork, Brian had brought it as a gift. The summer's run with the first of the wild strawberries was to be an occasion. Grania watched them go, then turned to her waiting women. "My salmon. Who will eat my beautiful salmon?" she lamented.

A split-log table stood in the center of Gawain's quarters. On it sat a bronze pitcher for wine, a vial of distilled woad used for ink, a smaller vial of the squid's darker fluid, quills with shaved points, one square of badly soiled linen, and several maps scrawled on rolls of hide. There were no chairs or benches, and it was the only waist-high table in the Cafferty clanhold.

Gawain tossed his cape aside, rummaged the map heap, found the roll he needed, and laid it out flat. Both curious and apprehensive, his men leaned over the table. He moved the pitcher over to secure one edge, the vial of woad to the other. One of his men reached down and picked a rock up from the dirt floor to secure the bottom edge.

Leaning forward with his palms framing the sides of the map, he squinted and his eyeball disappeared beneath its lid. "Of the bull, what say ye?"

Rushlights caught the glimmer of Cagney's sweating forehead as he elbowed his way to the map. He smelled of leather, sweating animals, and fresh blood, and in such close quarters the men stepped back. That he would even come into the main hall without bathing was unthinkable. Fresh from the baths Kevin leaned against the opposite side of the table. There shadows gleamed a golden fire dance across his flaxen hair and oiled skin. Flared nostrils and stern features revealed nothing of his feelings. But blue eyes scanned father and brother carefully.

"There," Cagney announced, pressing thumb to the center. "My men say they picked up the head there. Posted. Stuck to the sod on our western border, just before Finucane territory."

Excitement mingled with dread ran crosscurrent among Cafferty men.

Gawain studied the woaded center of the map representing the large lowland valley. It separated the two clans and provided pasturage for both. Blood had been spilt there in times past, but of late, spit-sealed hostages had been exchanged in fosterage. Generations passed in truce; Cafferty and Finucane had both grown fat on the bread of peace.

The valley formed the hinterland of Leinster before it bucked Ulster. Caffertys were protected by the sea. Finucanes backed the western rim where great oak derries served as barrier wall. The valley represented sustenance and security: there a man's wealth could graze fat and his reputation grow sleek.

That wealth, and that reputation, now threatened, Gawain turned grim.

"Ye think it Finucane and not Pig Man?" Kevin asked.

The remark hit Cagney like lancemark, and Kevin's brow quizzed in question. Gawain raised his chin slowly, his unruly mustache dangled down his chest, and flickering flame danced his eye in ghoulish shadow.

"Ye know of Dhurmod, Kevin?"

Gawain eyed the men around his table with careful scrutiny. Except for Brian, only recently counted in this privileged company, these men were seasoned veterans with families of their own. All had able-bodied sons aching to be blooded and hungry for the taste of war.

"What did ye learn of him?" he pressed.

"Nothing that gives me clue to his whereabouts or the name of the coward behind the mask. My sortie was cut short to give the Lady Brigianna safe passage." He humbled himself by lowering his eyes, and there was an aye of assent, showing that his actions were deemed honorable, for by Fian's honor, he could not abandon a maid in distress nor lead her into further jeopardy.

Nodding acceptance, he raised his eyes to see Gawain staring at him impassively. Beside him, Cagney itched with impatience.

All eyes were on him as he pointed to Colym's cuirnen, a lay of land that protected Brigianna's clan like a large drinking horn and cut them off from valley trade. His trailing finger continued through the river valley and on to Rathdun. "We first spied a raiding party here, and again farther north when we were backed to the sea."

He paused to contemplate the wisdom of relating the skirmish at Rathdun, thinking it better mentioned later in confidence, and started when Gawain's fist came down hard on the table.

"Here. And here. The same raiding party, or different?"

"Dhurmod, we saw here," Kevin said, pointing to the cuirnen. "At Rathdun we saw troops of horsemen riding roughshod, with little regard for man or beast. I remember thinking the dun restless at the time, overcrowded with mercenaries out for bounty perhaps, or taxed by too many families headed inland for the games."

He sighed, deep in inward thought. "Begods, Father, I know not what to say of those men. What do ye know?"

"I know hollow-eyed men flee the Pig Man's wrath to fill our ranks, that is what I know!" Gawain erupted in unbridled anger. "The swelling cry of 'defend me or spend me' lies like a death knell upon my ears, now my quiver grows too full of arrows and hungry for the hunt."

"If Dhurmod is so fearsome," Brian challenged, eyes ablazing, "let him taste a Cafferty blade, and we'll be seeing how fearsome he be!"

With a shout of "Ya ha!" Caffertys tightened the circle.

"Ho there!" Gawain's older brother, Eric, cautioned. Like the king, he had commanding presence and massive bearing. Rushlight caught red highlights in his golden hair as he entered the circle, and his eyes were sharp as a blade fresh from the whetstone.

"Hold it, young Brian. Ye are too like me own Donny, itching for blood. It takes no priest magic to be knowing ye'll taste it soon enough," he warned. "Then your belly will ache for warm grains, and all ye'll have to eat are your own words."

The old king sighed. "Aye, lad. Dhurmod cannot be fought. He is like the faerie wind. Here and there at will. No warrior can flush him out. And those that flee his wrath know not where he strikes next. Say ye aye to that, Cagney?"

"Aye, and then some," was Cagney's stonefaced answer. "My men return from the night's ride weary, and with no trophy to tell of it. Their women grow sullen and cold with fear."

"That booley where the head was found lies as a sweet memory of our childhood, brother, and there be no sign of Dhurmod there," Eric pressed. "But I fear if we venture too far west, we will push Finucane temper too far and have to face it come morning."

"But we are forced to enlarge our borders to feed our hungry!" Gawain shouted. Silence rolled in like ground fog, and in quiet voice he continued. "Ye say there be no sign of Dhurmod near the Finucane border, yet that's where my bull spilled his blood?"

"That is what my men say," Cagney affirmed.

At those words foreboding reverberated through Kevin's bones like the aftertone of bell clapper hitting metal. "Ye would fight Finucane, not turn and fight Dhurmod?" he cried, unable to mask his surprise.

"No, son, of my own accord I would not fight. But I would not be robbed, either."

With a sidelong glance at his brother, Eric stepped in. "Cagney?"

Cagney cowered slightly in his uncle's presence, then turned to his father. "'Cafferty! Cafferty!' people shout wherever I go. Your name rides banner over them, and they swell your ranks from river to sea. So it would do ye no honor to ride forth to king's crowning next summer with a border skirmish not brought to call. If this Pig Man be a threat, how do we show our might with a weakened flank? How do we ride with honor, if these puny Finucanes nip and chew without reprisal?"

Gawain peered into his son's face, but bushy brows fielded his gaze. "Are ye certain my bull met his death by Finucane hands?"

"I have no evidence but the obvious, Father."

Gawain studied his men carefully—his brother, his sons, his clansmen—thinking of their women, and their babes; those born, those still waiting like arrows in the quiver. And the keening cry of widowhood haunted him.

Conor, who had seated himself comfortably on a pile of furs to watch, now stood.

"M'lord," he began, his chinless grin revealing a ring of stubbed brown teeth, "it is I who must face the gods to know if their portents bring blessings or cursings. With your permission. An augury. A nightly vigil and tertiary answer by morning."

"Without heart, lungs, and liver the gods desert ye," Gawain snorted.

Conor looked up, but his lids were hooded and his eyes rolled back so that only the whites showed. "Need I remind my king that the seat of the soul is behind the brows?" he said with feigned indulgence. "And now. The bull's head?"

Gawain bade them leave, but held Kevin back.

When the doorflaps fell, leaving the two of them alone, Gawain reached out to clasp Kevin on the shoulder. His mouth started to form words, but his lip quivered, and with head low, he fell silent.

It had been a long time since they stood alone as father and son, unarmed, barefoot, in simple tunics, and not as liege to lord.

The rushlight sputtered. A dollop of wax fell to the table, and the sound of it was magnified tenfold in the ensuing silence. Gawain's hand still rested on Kevin's shoulder. When Kevin's voice finally nudged the stillness aside, it bore that little-boy quality so long ago forgotten.

"Was it not ye who stood by my side, patient as the oak and me a greening sapling, while I fitted my arrows to the bow, and played pickup sticks forever, it seemed, until I learned to do it right?"

With a slight nod the worried crease in Gawain's brow eased out.

"And ye who gave me the knife and weighed its balance in me hand?" Kevin continued. "The first of me swords, a wooden plaything it was, then later, the sword of my blooding? Does not that same enameled hilt stand proudly in its sheath and warm to my bidding even to this day?"

Gawain's eyes mellowed as he painted his mind with memories of young Kevin, the would-be warrior, and he, the mentor. They seemed forever away now.

Kevin's voice turned thick. "And who butted my strength and rivved me clean through, twice score in a day's time, until it was that I killed him fair in the sport of day? Oh, what a day that was, Father, the shouting and the clamor of it! Do ye remember?"

Remember the day Kevin turned man by challenging him—mighty Cafferty—and claimed victory on the gaming fields? Gawain beamed, just thinking of it.

"Endless hours I spent learning the legends, reciting the poetry, while ye munched bread and curds at my tortured expense. 'Not to leave the copse until ye get every word right,' ye said. 'But that is druid's work,' I said, but nay, ye insisted. ''Tis a man I'm making and that is a father's right.'"

"Aye, who fitted ye with a man's shield but me? Your chin rubbed raw against the rim for two moons straight until ye proved strong enough to handle it." Warmed in heart, Gawain chortled in spite of himself.

"I was there at your blooding, wasn't I, lifting ye up out of the trench, binding your forearm with my own robe, that is, before Yvonia took ye aside." Sallow cheeks rudded up, recalling the grandness of that day, and his hand fell from Kevin's shoulder to trace the fine, white line with reverence. "That same scar ye wear now as badge of honor."

"Aye, father," Kevin said with calm conviction, "that same badge of honor I wear as Cafferty, in service to my king."

Gawain's smile widened. Even his eyes smiled, and the slitted lid did not seem so fearsome.

"When I reached my majority, ye bid me go. And I said nay and pledged my oath anew. So it's not to worry, Father. For 'tis bound by law, upheld by honor, and sealed in spit. My duty must follow your glory to old age, to your grave, and even beyond, if need be. It is law."

"Aye, that, too, is a day I remember well," Gawain said solemnly, then suddenly he torqued in anguish:

"It's a crown ye should have begged, and not a maiden's favor! I laid my kingdom at your feet—yours for the asking! All eyes were turned in witness. Ye should have forced me to declare ye tanist, Kevin, ye should have forced your future sealed in spit." He drew back to ball his fist and slam it into his palm. "It was your right! That woman would have waited. It was a crown ye should have asked."

Welling tears made Kevin's clear blue eyes sparkle. "I covet no crown at the expense of the face I see before me," he declared.

Gawain fell on him in one gruff, backslapping embrace before he pulled away, then turned and placed his arms against the edge of the table, determined to face the darkening void of his aching loneliness.

Kevin paused at the doorflap, his head against the post. "The woman, Brigianna?" he dared to ask.

"I will take her in. I will see she is well cared for."

Kevin turned, Gawain looked up. For the first time they

faced each other, man to man. It was a long, steady look.

Gawain was first to turn away.

"Do what ye must," he whispered hoarsely, "and gods go with ye."

Chapter 12

Safely secured at Tighmohr, Lord Erin Finucane stood at the door of his great wooden meadhall. Summer winds beat upon the wooden shutters of his balcony, and the banging of wood against stone made him conscious of the fact that he had been sleeping in unguarded luxury for most of his years. Leaning his hand against the window frame, he surveyed the valley that stretched endlessly before him. It was as fertile as a ripened womb, and it dimmed on the eastern horizon, where it became Cafferty territory.

Even his most reliable bards could not recall the tale or sing the song of when the alliance began. In time Caffertys claimed right to clanpower and were no longer considered sept under Finucane protection. Though never regarded as law, cattle from both clans meandered a similar path. Even booley boys were instructed never to graze a hill so that it couldn't be fed upon by another and never to muddy a watering hole. "The land is our mother, and we her common sons," they were told.

Daughters intermarried, sons were exchanged in fosterage, cattle grew sleek, and with no tales of valor to sing, old men grew quiet. Erin Finucane's reign had been an idyllic existence until now.

Three days ago his men had come across a young bullock with its belly slit and its neck broken. Erin was certain it was not the work of dogs. Nor was it the work of renegades like the Pig Man. Having no territory of their own, men like that stole and killed in order to eat. Having seen marauders come and go in his lifetime, he was not concerned: they were a different worry. But in order to keep them out the clan must defend its borders. His main concern was the central valley and his portended quarrel with the landed gentry, namely the Caffertys.

The Finucane was a slender man. Even in the best of his battle years, he had not put on the burly weight his kinsmen so admired. His hair, gold as turning flax, had only just begun to gray. His bearing belied his age; the gray at his temples and curve of his beard only added to his dignity. At threescore and two, his eyes still spotted the hawk hidden in the branches before its sudden dive.

He stood naked to the waist, and the sudden shift in wind made him shiver and reach for his plaids. His colors—soft blues, bright oranges, even brighter yellows, colors gotten only by the ancient knowledge and patience of his women—were like him, only slightly faded with age.

"The festivities of Midsummer are upon us," he announced with a grandiose wave of his hand.

Corm, his faithful thrall sleeping in the corner, grumped himself awake. "What say ye, m'lord?" he mumbled as he scrambled to his feet.

Erin gave him an indulgent look. Corm was magnificent. Not a day passed that Erin did not thank the gods for him. Sufficiently dull-witted to have no cunning ambitions, Corm patiently waited upon his king, filling the lull between duties with well-paced snores, thus leaving the Finucane to his coveted solitude.

"I said, bring me my mirror, Midsummer is upon us. Let us feast. Let us dance. Let us spill seed by the bonfires of life!"

"Aye, m'lord," Corm muttered. Hunchbacked, with scuffling feet, he hurried to the outer wall, where he wrestled with the heavy bronze disk. Gripping it with both hands, he leaned it against him, even though he could not see where he was going. As he dragged it back across the room, the well-polished bronze caught the glowing embers of a lazy fire and ricocheted the reflection back like a stream of miniature godbolts.

"Begods, man! Ye blind me with my own mirror?" As Erin's forearm shot out to protect his eyes, he accidentally cuffed Corm on the shoulder. The mirror toppled and Erin jumped to steady it. Bracing it against his faithful thrall and thus mentally dismissing him, he combed the ruff of his golden beard with an admiring glance.

When the Finucane nodded, Corm hastily set the mirror aside. He struggled as he leaned it against a support post and shambled to the door behind Erin like an obliging shadow. Erin stepped outside and thrummed his chest with deep breath and watched the laying of the bonfires in preparation for Midsummer's feast. Let the matter of the bullock be, his council wisely advised: "If a lone incident, it will soon be forgotten. If a warning, the enemy will soon show his face. If the breaking of a time-honored truce, there's blood to be spilt. If the work of renegades too surly to be contained, there's land to be held. So if it's a war to call, let men drink and dance and sleep with their women. For men who drink and sleep together will fight together; and the babes that warm the womb will live to fight another day."

"Kevin's gone?" Brigianna cried out with such surprise Grania instantly pricked up her ears.

"Why, child, himself's never about come summer. He's out and about by king's commission, so it's not to worry."

They were sitting on the edge of Grania's pallet, and except for Darcy, quiet as a titmouse in the corner, their quarters were deserted.

"The morrow has sorrows of its own, but for now be glad the Fian left ye well fed and in good care." Grania's wrinkles turned into laugh lines as she leaned forward to take Brigianna's hand in hers and stroke it lovingly. "If it's a seedling to warm the belly he's left behind, then your heart will be happy. Ye'll see. It's time he had himself a son and wed the woman who bears it, says I."

Ravenwings flurried the edges of Brigianna's composure. She jerked her hand back, and Grania's woolly blue eyes took on the contemplative look women wear when their hearts are set to ponder.

"Speak, m'lady. What is it?"

"'Tis nothing, really, nothing, I—"

Grania's browset made Brigianna fidget even more, making her voice her innermost fears. "Oh, Grania, Grania, is it that I am so ugly? Kevin did not touch me, and, gods forbid, I am virgin still."

"Ugly ye are not! Have ye not set by the pond on a clear day? Or shined up a plate of bronze and taken a look? Sweet pea of springtime, never should a thought like that build its nest in your head."

With grandmotherly calm the old woman brushed an unruly strand of hair back from Brigianna's forehead. "Tell me true, for I must know. For all your travels he has not had his way with ye?"

Brigianna's face reddened and she shook her head.

Over in the corner, Darcy looked up from her mending.

"Then himself, the king, must be knowing of it," Grania said.

"Ye would tell him? Ye would say: naked, Lady Brigianna could not arouse the Fian? Ye would shame me so? Oh, Lady Cafferty, have pity."

"It is not for your shame I be telling Lord Gawain, Brigianna, dear. But if it's the Cafferty's protection ye beg, then 'tis the Cafferty himself who must make provisions. Sure now, ye understand that?"

Her father's face flashed before her eyes. "I know, 'tis king's rights," she muttered, then mustered courage to speak. "Kevin insisted I come, but without promise, mind. And I thought, after our travels together, that he, well—" Out of words, she shrugged in despair.

"Ye thought rosewater and a shadowslip gown a bit of magic, did ye?" Grania chuckled and her belly fat quivered. "For all we women think, men are not playthings, my dear. They've much on their minds, especially my Kevin. Loyalties. Commitments. Things not of their own choosing.

"But sometimes a man's prowess is cut short by a bad day in the fields. Or perchance, too much garlic in the broth. One never knows. It is a very great mystery, even to me," Grania whispered in earnest as her blue shawl fell down to her arm and she fretted it back into place.

"With some men the rutting season lasts all year. But others quake at the thought of celebrating Midsummer. Why that is so is the greatest mystery of all." Her merry blue eyes turned crescent as she mused, "Of all a woman's charms, patience is the most needed, methinks."

"And is that how it is with ye now, Lady Cafferty?"

Startled by Brigianna's impertinence, Grania's eyes flew open. But quickly realizing it was simple curiosity, she turned candid.

"I fear even patience has lost its magic for me. Brian is my youngest living, but not the youngest born. Sure now, I thought me women would have told ye such things."

Seeing puzzlement on Brigianna's face, she went on to explain. "I am Gawain's first wife, and for that I keep charge of the women's quarters and my life is spared. Twins they were. Boys, and pretty little mites, too. Knitted together in life as in the womb. They had to be killed, of course. It so happened the gods called them to life when they called the old priest to death. Conor took over immediately. It was fair balance, he said." She looked up, her expression fogged with mists of yesteryear.

"Ye would've liked the old priest, Brigianna, a kindly man he was and not like our Conor here. Well, anyway, Conor said I should leave Gawain's bed, for I bore him bad seed. Himself should be free to make good seed. And little Rollie, got by Maire, proved his good stead.

"Now Gawain warms his bed at will, and the Grania sleeps alone. Ah, me, such a cold bed it is, too."

This time it was Brigianna who stroked Grania's hand as the old woman bid yesteryear's sorrows away.

Suddenly Grania jerked forward, stern planes reshaping her doughy features. "The Fian has turned your heart, I see. Thirty and two years I've waited to see my Kevin wed a good woman. But not Kevin. Off and running he is, ever about his liege lord's business. Oh, women he's had, sure, but no bonny yet has stolen his heart, so more's the pity."

She paused momentarily: "Now ye see why I must tell Lord Gawain?"

Worry winged Brigianna's brow. "I beg ye not," she pleaded.

But Grania was firm. "The Fian brought ye here, and it's Lord Gawain who must decide your fate."

Leaving Grania with her memories, Brigianna huddled with her own worries outside. As she did, she saw Conor quickly dart behind the lodge. Ever since they'd discovered the bull's head, the camp had turned quiet. And Conor had been seen going here, going there, always on urgent business and begging for more time. Most of the women were busy laying bonfires for Midsummer. Watching them, Brigianna was struck by how somber everything seemed, and quivering of darkness crept over her. To her Midsummer was a time for laughing and dancing. And this year, she hoped, for making love. But Kevin was gone. As Grania said, his mission took him away the summer months. She had known that in her head, yes, but not in her heart.

Feeling suddenly abandoned and inexorably lonely, she plunked herself down on a sitting stone.

Did her mother feel this way when Tormaigh didn't return from the hunt for several days running? Did Amabel feel this way when Grandfather left for the land of the eternally young?

If they did, they didn't tell her.

* * *

Brigianna stepped into the porthall that led to the main lodge and, faltering in the dimmed light, stumbled into Cagney the Brave, who greeted her with a smug grin.

"Kevin is gone and once more ye stumble into my waiting arms?" he chided. "Begods, how easy goes my path."

He barred her way, as menacing as the double-bladed ax leaning against the wall behind them. Her blue eyes flashed in quick anger as she looked to the doorway beyond. "By your leave!" she demanded.

"Come, come, prettykins," he snickered. "Might as well get used to me, for I mean no harm, so if it's to sup we go, we might as well share a common table." Making a great show of reaching across his belt to undo his buckle, he dropped his shortsword and heavy girdle.

As he stepped out of his belt, his shammy tunic loosened and fell to his knees. Brigianna smiled, thinking at least there would be no serious fighting tonight. A man like Cagney, with thighs thick as lodgepoles and stomach muscles bulging like the staves of a well-filled liquor barrel, cannot fight full strength when his loins are not girded.

Cagney, catching her gentle sigh, misinterpreted it.

With a split-toothed smile, he reached forward to run his hand over the single braid that nested in the cowl of her cloak. "Come, sweetkins, share the hero's portion with me tonight."

Brigianna spun herself away. "Unhand me, knave!"

"Knave?" He fairly choked on the word. "Ye would call the king's son knave? Why, that is rich, lady. Rich indeed. I thought only to protect your gentle reputation, lest someone else seeing ye with the Shameface, as I did this day, be thinking your honor sullied by that lowly earthworm. It was the Shameface I saw ye speaking with?" he ended with bald-faced innocence, bringing her up halt.

"Oh, ye needn't worry, dear Brigianna. I have no scruples on such, though I do not know how ye be standing the smell of pig dung that clings about him. Ah, me. Now to dinner, lady?"

Gallantly he lifted the doorskins for her to pass by, then leaned down to whisper, "There will be a day when I bid ye come . . . and ye will come. But until then, ye are as ye came to us. A freewoman."

As Brigianna stepped into the firelit warmth of the main hall, an icy fingertip slithered up her spine, and she shivered in the sudden chill.

Chapter 13

Brigianna and Cagney disappeared into the shadows, reappeared inside the rim of golden firelight, and hastily sat down next to Gawain Cafferty. Slamming his drinking horn down on the low table in glaring reprimand, he lowered his other hand as signal for the evening to begin.

Wrestling a large flagon of wine, Yvonia hurried the serving women inside. Maire followed with a platter of bread that was crusty on the outside and still steaming on the inside. She set it in front of Lord Gawain, and he held a round up, split it, and split it again, so it fell onto the wooden plank in fourths. He took a farl for himself, motioned her on, and then bit into the chewy fiber, jerking his head back like a hungry wolf to snap a section loose.

At this, pipers struck up a high-spirited tune.

Within seconds a kniver appeared, juggling three long-handled knives as he danced barefoot around the fire ring. Baggy breeches skirted his ankles, and with toes trained like fingers, he searched out his path. Keeping his eyes upon the swirling knives, he threw one high above the others, then leapt into the air. In hushed wonder Caffertys watched the gleaming blade circle overhead, swishing in its cut and rumbling as the hilt caught up with it. Wide-eyed and intent, Rollie gouged little fingers into Grania's sturdy thigh.

The kniver landed on the balls of his feet, dug his heels

back, and with thrashing cuts, slashed air with the other two knives. As the circling knife came down, he caught it in his left hand. Quickly, even before Brigianna could realize what was happening, he tossed the knife into his right hand, then threw it in a skilled, underhanded pitch.

The bronze stiletto spun through the air. Whirring like a small comet, it pierced the ham shank of Midsummer's festive spitted boar. Juices trickled down the quivering blade and sputtered as they fell.

"Yah!" Caffertys shouted, pounding horns and tankards on low tables. Conor, seated near Brigianna, smiled. Gawain shoved his platter out for filling, and his engorged lid drooped lazily over the bulging eye.

"M'lady," Cagney said with a grand sweep of his hand.

Marching to the boar, he gripped the slippery knife and withdrew the blade. With his meat knife in the other hand, he cut off a sizable chunk. Piercing it with the kniver's stiletto, he wiped his dining dirk on his knee before sheathing it, then held the trophy up. And the crackling skin acted as dish to keep savory juices from being lost.

Bushy brows lowered to guard his eyes; thick lips parted in semblance of a smile. "The king's portion," he announced, walking toward Gawain, who reached forward to take the honored piece.

But Cagney snatched it away. A breathy gasp echoed in chorus, and a puzzled frown flitted across Brigianna's face as she noticed Cagney was not wearing his abalone disks or other gaudy jewelry. With his eyes still on his father and all eyes on him, he signed victory. Lowering the meat, he calmly tore off a mouthful and methodically chewed it.

In quick rage Eric sprang to his feet, his meat knife ready. In the course of cursing him back to his seat, Gawain sent his wine spilling.

"Ye would eat the king's portion? Ye would eat our father's meat?"

Startled, Gawain and Eric turned to see young Brian scream from the shadows, leap over tables, and knock good tankards and drinking horns aside in his wake. Women quickly bent down to shield their children as he clambered by.

With the bendable spring of a sapling he leaped into the arena and tackled Cagney. Surprise flew to Cagney's face as Brian hit him full bore and flattened him to the ground before he had a chance.

The meat got knocked off its spear and thrown in the dirt. Max bounded—a streak of gray—across the clearing and tackled the meat as it tumbled by. With narrowed eyes the animal dragged his trophy into the shadows, snarling and snapping at everyone in his way.

Cagney cursed as air was knocked out of him. He rolled over Brian, they scuffled dirt, and Cagney's gut ballooned out. He heaved and panted, trying to gain air. Thin and lithe, Brian easily slipped out from beneath the roll and came down on top. A thatch of red curls whizzed by before Cagney caught him and was on top again.

Brian feinted: fingers spread out and headed straight for Cagney's eyes. Brian bared his teeth and shoved his hand forward. Cagney ducked his head aside, and Brian's nails ripped his cheek instead. Blood spilled down Cagney's cheek. In quick-tempered bloodlust Brian reached up to grab a hunk of Cagney's ropy hair and yanked hard.

Seasoned as burled oak, Cagney rolled aside with a deliberate, almost clumsy movement, and his features darkened in menacing scowl.

There was a quick flash of bronze. Brian Cafferty fell back. And the screams that followed cut to the quick the bones and marrow of man. Smiling, Brian lay good as dead.

"Brian! My baby!" Grania cried as she rushed forward and skidded to her knees beside him. Pillowing him upon ample breasts, she looked down to see her son staring, sightless, straight ahead.

Her blue eyes blazoned bonfires of fear. "Cagney Cafferty, ye are no son of mine," she lashed out, her face now set with hard lines of grief. Choking, she threw her head back to begin her keening.

But Brian stirred. "Mother?" he moaned. "Mother?"

At that Brigianna started to rush forward, but Yvonia was upon her instantly. Gripping her forearm, she forced her to the ground.

"Let them be," she snapped with stern command. "This be no concern of yours. It's brothers they are, and it's their quarrel, not yours."

Brigianna tried to wrestle free. Sweat beaded her brow. Yvonia's nails gouged her tender skin and brought her down.

"Hush, lady. Listen! Even Lord Eric was forbid this quarrel."

Obediently Brigianna turned to see Gawain standing. He shook from inner rage, more terrible than battle fury, and fear quaked within her.

Again Eric bolted forward, features handsome as his brother's were frightening. Again Gawain waved him back, and Eric halted mid-motion. Gawain cursed generously, and slowly Eric lowered his knife.

"M'lord," he muttered stiffly, and Conor rose and walked over to where Grania huddled Brian.

Unlike the rest of the men, who were dressed in short tunics or kirtles, the young druid wore his flowing robes and longcloth of station colors. His shadow fell over Brian and Grania. With trembling lips Grania looked up. "No," she pleaded. There was no audible sound; her mouth merely formed the word.

With a backward cuff of his hand Conor knocked her aside. And with a hawk's quick dive he reached down and pulled the knife free.

Brian screamed as the knife was torn from his shoulder. Jerked forward by the force of Conor's grip, he convulsed in quick, short spasms, then fell back, unconscious.

The force of the pull sent the frail priest spinning, and the long blade dripped and splattered blood in its wake.

His eyes widened. Horrified by blood, he flung the blade into the fire to discipline it.

Catriona rushed up with a leather bucket of water and tore Brian's tunic open. Just as she lifted the bucket to throw, Cagney spotted the weapons the kniver had dropped in haste and dived for them. Snarling, he gripped one knife in each hand and pointed them at Catriona.

She stared at Cagney in amazement, then with stony defiance tossed the bucket of icy water over her wounded brother. Cagney blanched slightly and sliced air with both blades.

Covering her face in shame, Grania fled into the shadows.

Meanwhile, Conor stood by the fire, his hands clasped in front of him, his narrow eyes flitting from one person to the other, assessing every detail, observing every innuendo.

Cagney spun around, knives still in hand. "I say we fight. This be no time for celebrations, not with Finucanes overrunning our borders and slaughtering our wealth. I say we do not wait for evidence or priestly portending. I say we lay blood at their door. Now! While they are too sotted from feasting to lift their swords."

Caffertys stiffened in apprehension, but Gawain made no attempt to step out from behind the protection of his low table and call challenge.

Cagney looked down at his father, who had fallen back to the solace of his furs, and his angry brow smoothed babyskin-soft in disbelief.

"What have we here?" he shouted "Clansmen! I ask—what? A king afraid to sport with his sons? A king deformed? Sure now, we know it was in the battlefield of honor . . . but a king deformed, nevertheless. And now a king too cautious to call war and save honor?"

The knives fell to the dirt as he lowered his arms and turned around slowly to mark each Fian with his eyes. His clenched jaw pulled his features taut over his skull like a battle helmet. Slowly he let his eyes wander full circle, knowing that like the rockfill that shores the fortress, the clan would become his source of power once he became their leader.

Around him tension riveted bones erect and stirred nervous groins.

When his eyes fell on Brigianna, she blanched and scooted backward. His upper lip lifted in the merest hint of a smile as magnanimously he waved a hand her way. "Or do we have a king too old to sire children? A king so past his prime, his desire has waned?"

Inevitably, there was a snigger of laughter, and Cagney stepped back a pace. With a smug look on his face, he glanced at his priest.

"Enough!" Gawain crashed his fist upon the table. "I say enough."

"Ah, forgive me, dear Father and Lord." Cagney begged quarter. "'Tis the future I'm concerned about. Oh, not yours, m'lord, nor mine. Gods have decreed what lies ahead, and ye'll choose tanist wisely. After all, ye must name your successor from among the contenders so there be no fighting over your crown when ye've gone. It is not law?

"And is it not song, also, Father? And of the Cafferty future I speak? When we are gone, will the bards sing of Caffertys too fond of feast and too soft of belly to fight? Will they say Caffertys laughed and made merry while Finucanes danced upon their graves?"

"That is enough!" Blood at Gawain's temples throbbed noticeably as he barked his gainsay in quick, short barbs. "Will bards sing of Caffertys that broke peace? No, I say. Finucanes have been our allies for decades. If honor is to be called, we must first go in peace."

"Aye? When that Pig Man, Black Dhurmod, is about?" Cagney roared as if the absurdity was some kind of joke. "If we do not solidify our borders, what are we but waiting hens to a hungry fox?" With a clenched fist he shouted, "I say we fight!"

"No!" Eric yelled as he bolted forward with food dirk raised.

"Aye!" dissident Caffertys shouted as they jumped to their feet.

"No!" came the hue and cry on the backswing. The din grew louder as furor grew, then suddenly silenced.

Conor stood at the center of the ring. Using the meat tongs that lay by the boar, he had reached into the coals and gotten the knife. With both hands he held it up in front of him. The blade was so hot it was white. Even through thick wrappings the hilt burned his hands.

Beyond feeling, his eyes crossed, then uncrossed. Now they stared straight ahead, unfocused and mesmerized by the blade. In reverence Caffertys hushed and fell to their furs and leathers.

In slow and deliberate gait Conor walked over to where Brian lay. He raised the knife high. Absoluteness of conviction shone through his eyes in golden gleam. He faltered only a moment. Then, like the invincible arm of the gods, he quickly brought the blade down.

Hissing steam rose in white column as the knife lay flat against the wound and the stench of seared flesh filled the air.

Brian's eyes flew open as the blade hit home. His mouth echoed wordless surprise when the wound was cauterized. He looked down in wonder, amazed to see his own flesh burning. It was as if the bonfires of Midsummer had exploded inside of him.

His scream wrenched itself free. His wailing filled the dome of the great hall like the howling of hounds.

Once more his body convulsed, and he fell back as dead—forever marked by this fine red seam, his only claim to glory.

Conor held the blade high to command complete attention. Transfixed, Caffertys watched its blue-white stem slowly turn crimson. Brian's terror ended like the last groanings of a dying wind, followed by the blade's siren song as Conor threw it back to the fire, where it crashed against the stones and fell to earth in dull thud.

With outstretched arms Conor stepped forward till his shadow fell over Cagney. Sweat beaded up across Cagney's brow; his buff jerkin oozed sweat. Silence reigned, and to Brigianna it seemed eternal.

"It is I who decrees when war shall be fought. It is I you have defied, not your father," he said in a voice like the wailing wind.

Visibly Cagney paled.

Turning, Conor ignored Cagney the Brave as if he were a dog. With feigning smile, he lifted his hands high. "Comes now the feast of blessing. Comes now the sacred cup."

His words had not even cooled on his lips before the sacred cup, flasks of water and wine, and more bread were set before him.

"Auguries have proved our suspicions correct. This bull and those in the fields before it met death by Finucane hands." With raised brow he paused to let the weight of his words sink like a grappling hook into sponging minds. Sure his words had taken hold, he brightened up.

"Come, 'tis Midsummer, time for dancing, feasting, and making love. Let us drink the blood that binds. Whether you drink wine of war or blood of peace will be revealed to each of you, for we are clan, and you will know in sacred communion what choice you have made. Midsummer's Feast is at hand! Let us knit our hearts together in drink."

Brigianna watched as Conor whirled around so fast that his long robes twirled the other way behind him. His shadow carried to the roof of the long hall to fall over them, looming large and ominous, threatening to find them wherever they might hide.

But when he mentioned Finucane, she jerked her head upward.

"Hush," Yvonia hissed and yanked Brigianna's braid to force her down. "Do ye wish the gods leave us in darkness? Keep your eyes closed and pray."

Brigianna, with no choice but to lower her head, determined to watch as Conor poured the blood-dark berry wine and clear spring water into the sacred chalice. Then he reached into his magic purse and sprinkled a handful of crumbled leaves over it. When he lifted the chalice high to intone the blessing, Brigianna gasped in horror.

The chalice was a human skull, overlaid in gold, with its base of bone wide enough for Conor to have a firm handgrip.

The skullcap was cut clean away to form an open drinking bowl large enough for two men to share. Gold, hammered skin-thin, sheathed the pearly skull. With wine casting shadow behind thin golden-glazed sockets, it shone magnificently in the firelight and became the dark, uncaring eyes of judgment.

With solemn face Gawain stood. "Drink as your priest bids ye drink, and in drinking, listen to his will, for who are we—chieftain or beggar—to defy the words of our priest." He acquiesced with circular motion to the sacred temple of his brow.

Smiling to reveal stubby teeth, Conor approached each woman and child. At the Shameface his eyes blazed as bright as the sacred skull. With a jerk of his head he hoarded what was sacred and hurried past him.

As the sacred cup came her way, Brigianna reached her hand forward but it stopped, staid by an invisible shield that pressed upon her fingertips. Trembling, her neck hunched back into her shoulders.

"What is this?" Conor shrieked, swooping the skull upward, his eyes riveted to the skull as if enameled upon the gold. "Need I remind Lady Brigianna that our forefathers drowned those who once walked among us, but not of us, in a wellpool of sacrificial blood?"

Rushlights dripped tallow, and turf whispered brooding secrets. Again Conor's free hand swooped over the skull, and within, the surface shimmered as more crushed leaves fell into it. "To purify the holy and force the unclean from among them, of course," he canted on.

Beside her, Yvonia shook with the spasmic force of the

bewitched. "Oh, begods, Brigianna, drink," she begged.

Behind sightless eyes Brigianna felt Conor's piercing gaze bolt through her like the shaft of a poison-tipped arrow. Refusing Conor like she had refused Lochobar, she opened her mouth to speak in the dark voice of prophecy.

"Masked men ride the night. Rivers run red with blood. In the rising tide children cry. And kings no longer wear crowns."

"Stop it! Stop it immediately, I say!" Conor shrieked.

The whites of Brigianna's eyes rolled forward, and she looked at him, unseeing.

"Drink!" Conor demanded, shoving the sacred skull in front of her face. Refusing to put her lips to that golden forehead, she instead thrust a chew of bread into the dark sop, then put it into her mouth.

The sop hit the side of her tongue, and immediately its metallic aftertaste swelled her tongue so that it lay thick in her mouth. Eyes widened in fright. She reached forward, but already her hands were numbed and unbearably heavy. Pupils dilated, but orbs remained fixed, seeing nothing as darkness set in.

"Kevin, I must find Kevin," she whispered before this darkness enshrouded her in numbed, cold coffin.

Chapter 14

Cafferty warriors rose. Excitement coursed through their veins; the sweet smell of blood filled their nostrils.

War! Already its bittersweet power whetted their appetite.

They woke with one single thought in mind: from the aged scarred body that knew glory did not come without pain, to the virgin young, lusty and eager for the thrill of the cutting blade.

Some mystical force, its presence called forth from the eternal darkness by Conor's bidding, had pervaded the entity of their dreams. Throughout the night silent whispers hovered above them, gathering assent, knitting them in heart and mind to common accord.

Ever since that first young heifer had been found in the wood two moons ago, unanswered questions had haunted their being, following them on their daily walks and making the close-knit clan go about their tasks with muted hushtones of winter at a time when fertile summerlands called them to joyance and laughter.

Then came a young bullock with a slitted belly; now the bull's head. Why had Gawain not raised his hand? they murmured. Why did Cagney the Brave ride out by night? Why did Lord Eric stalk the borders? Where did Kevin go alone? And why did he return without full report?

Why are our sons afeared, why do they creep to their

pallets at night, still-voiced and somber?

Throughout the night thoughts became the single dark line of the weaver's thread and knit brother to brother, warrior to warrior. Now they woke as a single fabric whose warp and woof stood firm.

"Whether you drink wine of war or blood of peace will be revealed," Conor had said as he raised the sacred cup.

Rich red wine, laced with magical herbs only Conor knew by name, coursed through them to become their blood, their bones; finally the lurking question was settled.

War: its sound was as sweet as honeycomb. Too long had blooded warriors rested like spinning women, forced to play the crone when wombs ached to be quickened.

Gawain concluded from the light coming through the transom that morning was well underway. He tossed his bedroll back and got to his feet, thinking of the sweet red wine with the aftertaste of gall.

"They will not let me grow old in peace. To war I go," he grumped as if it were common knowledge, little realizing it was not yet fact.

Without warning his face torqued in agony; sweat beaded up across his forehead and splattered down his cheeks. Both eyes bulged out as he grabbed his chest to quell that horrid pounding. Begods! A battering ram shattered him from the inside. He envisioned fragments of bone and sinew and marrow flying through the air as it thundered incessantly against his chest.

He felt torn asunder, ripped apart from within. He tried to swallow but could not. He was exploding inside.

Its force threw him across the chamber and slammed him against the doorpost. Just as he reached out to grab the jamb for support, another spasm hit. The larch post, hardened like granite and smooth as beach pebble, slipped from his grasp as he fell forward.

Now the power knocked him backward. Then forward. Like a giant tree toppling in the forest, he crashed down upon his pallet, sweating so profusely his loincloth clung to him like swaddles.

In his haze he saw the metal rod of his brooch pin. He swiped at it but missed. With fingers stretched out, he reached for it again, got it, and clamped the cold metal rod hard between his teeth. A cry of agony welled up inside him and became gargle in his throat.

The battering ram inside was too powerful. With bludgeoning force, it crushed aching bones, leaving no breathing space between. Propelled by a force that made him double up, he was knocked back to his pallet.

As snaffles gore the horse, the rod gouged blood from his gums. His deformed eye swelled into angry banner as blood pooled behind it.

Finally he cursed the bitterness of his being: he cursed Conor and vile liquids that bring night sweats; he cursed Finucanes and their bedamnable greed; he cursed vanguards of dishonor like that filthy Pig Man; he cursed his sons for chawing at his heels like hungry wolfhounds; and again, for good measure, he cursed Conor, for usurping his authority in such a way that he could not be challenged, thus making him play the fool.

With grit he bore down hard as he could until a tiny veinlet inside his bulging eye burst to fill his vision with blood. Seeing nothing but red spray, he cursed himself for cursing Conor.

Darkness swept over him, the dark, dark, murky end of human life, and there he wrestled firsthand with his will to live.

The pain was too much, but no, he would not succumb, not Gawain, not the mighty Cafferty. He must outwit death. He must.

He let himself be drawn into that darkness, just to the point where he felt his body relax. A tremor of excitement coursed through him as in his semiconscious state he thought he felt the battering ram weaken. Then, with the tough-minded, maleated ore and alloy of warrior's mettle, he slowly drew his knees to his chest and wrapped his arms around them.

Slowly—because the pain was so intense it blinded his every thought—he forced himself to believe he was at the squatting pits with a rumble in his gut the size of a boulder. Only he, Mighty Cafferty, well-honed warrior with muscles of solid iron, could force this boulder out.

Though his eyes were open he saw nothing but red veil. Gut straining, he pushed against that boulder. He listened to his breathing patterns, as he had listened to women in labor who, in surrendering to death, find strength to live. Gritting his teeth, he pushed harder.

Like magic that leaves nothing behind but unanswerable questions, pain vanished. Quickly as it came, it left.

"If this trickery is Conor's doing, then his head shall hang on my lodgepole, but if this is warning gods are calling me, then pray they grant me mercy to stay alive until Kevin returns.

"Life is for the living!" he declared with a thrum of his chest. "Today, I shall break my fast with the children, perhaps even tell them a story. They need to be seeing me laugh so's to remember me a kindly man. Especially if I must lead their fathers to their death."

Brigianna lay with her long hair spread over her like a shawl and her face buried in freshly laid straw where warm air currents filled her nostrils with the smells of sweet earth. Even though morning was bustling, the women ignored her as she tossed about in drugged sleep.

In her slumbering vision two ravens appeared. Down from the golden sky they swooped, wings flapping in the slow motion of dance; each rising and each lowering a song in flight. They skimmed the sun's golden pathway along the water's surface, then flew through rings of gold. Her spirit soared with them, feeling at peace in the dip and lull of undulating swell. Smiling in her sleep, she snuggled deeper under the coverlets. Farther into the golden sea she went, becoming a part of the ravens, or one of them, or watching them . . . she could not tell.

Yielding everything that would pull her back to darkness, where mortals live, her soul ached in euphoric hunger to become part of the mysterious ravens and float in endless serenity above the golden sea.

But they got smaller, darkness closed in, and she uttered a tiny cry of longing. In that darkness two golden orbs stared at her like two golden suns with ravens flying in them. Darkness swept around the golden rings like tar slick, making them float above her, and when she looked again, the golden light had become green at its turning.

Green stretched into slitted half-moons. Behind them, not clearly discernable in the shadows, was the figure of a man with a broad forehead glistening with opalescent sweat and skin hung upon his bones like peeling wax.

Lochobar!

She bolted upright, not fully awake and with no recollection or comprehension of how she got there. Yellow eyes bore through her, and she chilled as she always did when brought under their power.

Something would happen, some portent; she could feel it stirring.

Suddenly she screamed. Pain gripped her chest like a battering ram and knocked her backward onto her pallet. Thrashing back and forth, she screamed again. Pain invaded her with the force of twelve legions. Her vision filled with blood. Gasping hungrily for breath, she clawed air, desperately trying to get free of the madness within.

"M'lady! M'lady! What ails ye?" Grania hurried to her side and shook her by the shoulders. Yvonia shouted, "Brigianna!" as she fell on top of her and pinned her shoulders back.

Sapphire-blue eyes tried to focus. "What be the matter?"

"That is what I'm a-wondering," Grania chittered.

As Yvonia rolled off, Brigianna pointed. "There. Do ye see him?"

"All I see is a dying fire and a cold pudding," Maire complained, annoyed that the commotion disrupted her solitude.

"Then mind ye tend to it," Grania snapped. "Now, tell me, Brigianna, whether dream or real, what did ye see?"

Brigianna shook her head at the blur of curious women. Yvonia's russet locks nearly matched her fox-fur pelt; Grania's tunic, dyed in poplar, was a muted orange; but Maire hung back as a thin dark line, demanding explanation. Concentrating, Brigianna brought the women into focus.

"Oh, 'twas nothing, I suppose. I thought I saw a man, that is all."

Grania threw both hands up in laughter. "Now, that would be a merry bag of pudding. Imagine! A man in the women's chambers. Why, no man would dare set foot here, and even the young laddies are only too eager to leave when their time comes.

"Doesn't that be so, Rollie?" She gave the toddler a loving wink, intending to follow it with a hug, but her attention got diverted by rustling wings in the corner. She jumped to her feet waving her hands and shouted indignantly, "Scat, you wicked jackdaw! Scat, I say!"

The raven, too quick for her, winged its way through the transom and roosted on the beam just long enough to cock its head and stare through yellow eyes before crying its mocking taunt and winging off.

"Nightmares always haunt the lazy, so let that be a lesson," Grania chided. But Brigianna was already lost to her own thoughts, for upon her furs lay a tailfeather still warm as she reached out to pick it up.

"By your leave, Lady, I must be seeing Brian," Grania said, turning to go, but Yvonia leaned over and whispered something and her woolly blue eyes turned crescent. "Aye? Mmmmmmm.

"It appears Lord Gawain is resting for the day but has need of ye come evening. Yvonia, see that Lady Brigianna is properly arrayed for the king's pleasure. Now, ladies, I truly must tend my Brian." With that she nodded politely and walked off.

"Time's not now to fret of Kevin," Yvonia purred with green eyes warming. "The king has need of thee."

"Kevin's not a man easily forgot, I'd say," Catriona jibed as she danced by with bouncing curls and honeysuckle breeze.

"Oh, cats bite your tongue, Catriona!" Yvonia snapped with the aid of a sharp handclap. "Hurry, for Brigianna's hair will take the day to dry. Maire, Darcy, prepare the baths. Catriona, lay out her gown, and not that coarse maidenshift, for the gods' sake." Both Darcy and Maire wore dubious scowls, but obeyed.

"Please, Yvonia, surely ye can see I—"

"Hush, Brigianna. Whatever makes ye babble like that? 'Tis an honor to be called to the king, an honor no woman declines. Sure now, a lady knows that." Yvonia looked at Brigianna for a candid moment. "Sometimes your lack of manners astounds me."

"Manners or no, it's clear that strong drinks befuddle your senses," Catriona said, giggling. "Stars alive, m'lady, but we had to drag ye back to your cot last night, and it's more than a bit wonkey ye were."

"How much farther?" Tormaigh demanded of Lochobar as they squatted by the river fishing. The salmon run was good this year; Tormaigh's women would grow fertile from the rich roe and liver oils. The McColyms had taken along sufficient store of nuts and grains for their journey, but now that Midsummer was past, they could look forward to berries and other succulent taste treats.

"How much farther?" he asked again, more than a little worried about his mother. "Amabel whimpers in her sleep, too proud she is to complain of the aches that beset her."

Lochobar raised a sleepy eye. He had hiked his robe up over his knees so that the long vein that throbbed nastily when he walked too far could get some sun. He had also shed his sandals and now leaned against the tall blackthorn to get some much-needed rest. It had been a long night.

The blackthorn's white flowers had ripened into juicy sloes, and Lochobar's mouth watered, just looking at them. "Two moon's risings, perchance," he said. "Not much farther."

"This Finucane, he is a man of honor?"

Lochobar groaned. How many times had Tormaigh plagued him with this question? Twoscore? Threescore?

"He is."

"Brigianna is safe? I will get my ten cows? The Finucane will fight by our side if need be?"

"Yes, yes," Lochobar blustered with waving hands, then with a grunt he drew back to cant rhythmically. "When the bridegroom comes, the bride will be waiting. What better jewel could a man ask to hold in cache than our fair Brigianna? What better fortune could the Finucane seek than to have his lands joined to ours? When he knows the full length of the fertile river valley, stretching deep into his backland forests, aye, my friend, the Finucane would fight by our side if need be."

Tormaigh mumbled his satisfaction and turned his gaze back to the fish. Lochobar gave him the same indulgent look a father gives a child.

Tormaigh thought not of fish but of the oak, sacred tree of mankind. Already he coveted those vast forests, untouched by the blade, and the great wealth gods held in store. Thinking of chewy acorn bread, his mouth watered. His heart quickened, thinking of the hunt that would bring down the stag, or the excitement of facing the wild boar at his charge. He thought of thick hazel and birch copses skirting the derry's edge to house gamebirds and an endless supply of red meat.

He imagined his artisan's hands busily crafting solid drinking tables that would become heart and hearth of home. He thought of sturdy carved chairs, large enough to ease out a man's weary bones, made of wood that was supple when green but hard as an iron shield when ripened. And shelter strong enough to battle the winter's rain, strong enough to thwart the heart of any raider.

He had heard of such wonders, certainly, but never seen them. And he tired of living inside mud-daubed huts, tired of moving from place to place, tired of slashing willow to pen his cattle, only to have the withes sprout and take root, so the task must be done again.

A ripple under the water's surface snapped him out of his reverie. His fingers eeled their way to his quiver, and noiselessly he fitted his bow. Then he stood. There. A dark roiling shadow.

His arrow parted the waters. Dark shadow burst from the deep to become a flashing ray of silver. It splashed back into the clear waters to send up a spray of blood.

Tormaigh dashed into the stream, churning up a wall of water as he went down. He plunged under the surface with the fish, then came up, triumphant. He hooked his fingers through the gills and threw the fish on his back as he waded back to shore. The fish, nearly as tall as he, flapped hard against him and almost knocked him over.

"I fight my sons for the roe of this one!" he shouted, voice warm with pride, and whipped out his knife. With shining eyes he wrestled the salmon to the ground and finally clubbed it with a rock, grunting in satisfaction as it quivered and was still.

"Tell me once more, so I know it as a hunter knows his arrows. My Brigianna, she is safe?"

Lochobar stared at the fish, the broken arrow shaft sticking out its side, its belly glutted in red stream, its eyes glazed over in death, and its last panting breaths barely noticeable. His eyes slitted into green wedges and slowly began to turn yellow.

Tormaigh watched Lochobar retreat to his private world, where, as holy man, he lived untouched by the cries of man.

"Aye. I be thinking as much," Tormaigh said quietly.

Chapter 15

As Yvonia shook Brigianna's boot, Kevin's comb fell out.

"My, ye are full of surprises!" Yvonia's coppery brow crooked upward as she quickly retrieved it, then swept a handful of Brigianna's hair back from her face and secured it with the comb. "A work of art worthy of a king's ransom, I'd say," she marveled as she fingered dark strands forward to frame Brigianna's face. "Ah, there, how fine it looks."

Brigianna immediately pulled it back out.

"It be dear, this comb?" Yvonia asked, puzzled.

"Very dear," Brigianna whispered with eyes brimming. "Oh, Yvonia, ye must know. Surely ye must understand that I cannot—"

Yvonia stiffened. "'Tis the Cafferty himself that calls, and 'tis the finest of our jewels we offer. Yet ye refuse? Lady, ye are churlish!"

She quickly fumbled along the ledge for a large medallion set with carnelian and beryl and held it up as enticement, but Brigianna only protested louder.

"As ye wish," Yvonia sighed, putting it down. "I do suppose I could send word ye are indisposed, or worse, thought better of it. Ye are freewoman, so it is a matter of choice."

A catlike smile appeared. "The choice being if ye care to eat or not, of course."

"Aye," Brigianna said. "As ye say."

* * *

To deny the king, Yvonia informed Brigianna as she led the way to Gawain's chamber, brought a fate worse than death. Lord Gawain was not a cruel man, but to insult him openly by refusing him would certainly lessen his stature in the eyes of his clansmen, would it not? And does it not defy the senses to demand protection from the very one you have insulted?

Brigianna tried not to listen. Her head filled with grisly visions of Conor bearing a delicate gold-plated chalice that was once upon a lifetime the Lady Brigianna.

The chamber was so much like the one she and Kevin had shared, she caught her breath when she entered it. "No!" she cried and whirled around, but Yvonia had left her to face the thunder of her heart alone.

Had Yvonia gotten her way, Brigianna would be wearing only loinskirt and jewels beneath her cape. As it was, she had protested loudly enough to at least be decently clad.

"Oh, Kevin," she whispered in dismay. He had saved her from the king's taking before, and he would have saved her forever if he had laid claim. But no, he was foresworn. As Fian he was destined to protect the people in war or in peace; for six moons of the year he was to wander the world homeless; if killed, he could not be avenged.

He had told her that from the beginning.

Oh, why did I not believe him? she thought. She slumped down upon the pallet and fretfully toyed with the furs. Why did I foolishly hope? Why did I promise to stay with the Caffertys? Kevin would never forgive me if I fell back on my word; he would not even want me then. Tears welled up in her eyes, and she brushed them back just as Gawain stepped inside.

"Lord," she said and instantly got to her feet.

"Ye are comely as a rose, lady," he said in greeting.

Without preamble Lord Gawain tipped her chin upward and with well practiced hand, fingered her cheek, then caressed the delicate curve of her throat. Bravely she met his eyes, for to look away now could mean swift and sudden death if perchance the lord mistook shyness for insult.

His bulging eye stared down at her. Up to now, whenever she thought of him, all she could think of was that eye. But now, dwarfed by his giant embrace, she began to see beyond the eye and into the man. And for reasons she did not understand she felt like protecting him.

Misjudging tenderness for excitement, he stooped to bring his face down upon her neck and clumsily nuzzled it. But he exuded the smell of a man who had eaten and drunk too much in a lifetime. Involuntarily she turned her face away from sour breath.

He crushed her to him, and she thought, How strange it is to be a woman; we quake at the mighty, and yet we are born to learn of their weaknesses and in compassion love them still.

Up close, the Cafferty was not nearly as ferocious as she imagined, and in spite of his ugliness there was a certain largesse about him. Cosseted within the tangle of his embrace, she discovered that with her eyes closed she could well pretend he was Kevin.

She dared to trace across the split lid. Startled, Gawain drew his chin back into his neck, for her touch was as soothing as the pearl was smooth.

"No one but Grania has ever touched me so," he whispered.

"Does it hurt?"

"The hurt of my eye lies in here, lady," he said, balling his fist to his chest. "Handsome and fit as my brother, Eric, I was, when I was young. Ah, then Grania loved me well, for I was the best of Fian." In the sudden gust of memory he grabbed her again. "Such sporting good child's play we had!"

But it was not for child's play that he called her. And what Kevin had wakened demanded audience, making her body cry out in torment.

He rummaged along her back and her skin tingled at the friction against her silken gown. She leaned warmly against him, for it felt marvelously exciting. His breathing deepened. And her senses took their leave to counsel in secret chambers and deliberate what must be done.

To bed the king is an honor not given to all, and the sweetmeats of warm bed and choice food are its reward. Insult, however, would incur wrath and bring an empty belly. Had not Yvonia said so?

As a freewoman, she was prey to every man's courting game. And with Kevin gone, there was no one to protect her from Cagney. Yet to wait for Kevin was folly. She was still a virgin, and by his own hand, no less.

The thought of his name called him to her mind's eye as surely as if he were standing by her side: the even blue eyes and soft curve of tawny brow, the curling mustache he thought kept his smile safely tucked away.

No one will ever know I dream of one man while I bed another, she told herself as she chased the vision away. Why not spill my virgin blood and grow fat on honeycakes and rich cream? After all, if I find favor with the king, my honor will be established and I can be given to some fair warrior, someone handsome and wonderful as—

Kevin appeared in her mind's eye. There was no smile beneath his mustache, no sparkle in his eyes. And she knew without a doubt, she could never bed any man but him.

"No, my lord!" she cried, pulling away. "I beg ye, be merciful." Gawain gave her a pained look, and sat down on the pallet.

She fell to his feet, babbling nervously. "Let me be doing that," she said as she reached for the double rings of his bootstraps.

"Whether for sport or for pleasure, ye came of your own free will. Yet ye back away. Tell me, lady, what do ye think of me?"

"Why, I think ye a kind man, given fair chance."

"Kind," he mused. His features eased so that high cheekbones gave plane and pride to what, surely, was once a handsome face.

"Aye." Her fingers flew to the ties of her shift, whether to protect herself or undo them she would never know, for Gawain staid her hand.

"Let it be, lady, for I mean no harm. It was only a bit of comfort and closeness I was needing, that be all. But for all that's said of me, I need no priest magic to tell me all my men find ye a fancy tart and would na mind giving ye a tumble. So I pulled ye to me, for your protection and for mine. I cannot let one lone woman destroy my camp."

With regret he pulled his hand away from her shoulder. "What do my gossiping women say of me these days?"

"Only that ye be telling the wee ones strange tales to brighten their day. Little Rollie came running in while I was still at my bath, his face aglow. And that ye are down in your cups." She hesitated, then giggled slightly. "And that I am down in mine, also, for neither of us could rise after last night's festivities."

"Aye, our strong drink proves too much," he mused, then leaned forward in earnest. "Kind, ye say. My sons would mistake kindness for weakness, especially for an old fox like me. Do ye not see it so?"

"No," she said honestly, and a knowing smile passed between them.

"If I offer ye kindness, would ye not repay me likewise?"

"Aye, I could not do less, for 'twould be unseemly."

Sputtering rushlight danced the brawny planes of his skin as he stood. Though he burned with hunger, the memory of his heart attack was too fresh and too frightening. He must stay in control: not to eat too much, not to drink too much, not to love so fair a maid. Not to have his head leave his body and journey to that land beyond on the pithy barge of lust. He had heard of stronger men than he dying while plowing their heifers. He would not be one of them.

Like an unblooded warrior, he groped for the right words.

"What I must ask, dear Brigianna, is this. If I spare ye

my bed but give ye my chamber, will ye frequent it and more, will ye speak well of me come morning? Kindly, as in what befits a man's prow, I mean."

"A dinger in a slinger and a dong gone wrong," Brigianna blurted out before she could stop herself.

"What's that? What's that ye say?" He spun around, florid-faced.

"Nothing, oh, nothing, m'lord, just some bawdy song a bard did sing. I am begging your forgiveness, for truly I did not mean a thing by it."

She fretted so nervously that Gawain couldn't help but laugh. "Pray the bards do not sing that of me," he chortled and, disarmed by her innocence, plunged headlong into the candor of the moment. "Forgive my treachery, but 'tis clear my sons have designs, and I thought to remove them from temptation. I cannot afford their quarrel."

He eyed her suspiciously. "Lady Cafferty says it's virgin ye are."

"Aye," she admitted, reddening with shame.

"Hah!" he shouted with a rounding slap to his knee. "Then 'tis a perfect match we make, with such reputations at stake."

Caught off guard, she giggled shyly.

"Ah, that's better," he said as he slipped down to her side and put a comforting hand to her shoulder.

"M'lady, what Kevin has not claimed, Cagney will take, so I beg ye consider this little collusion. I cannot have the entire war camp fighting over one woman. Did ye not hear the assent of my men? It's the Finucanes we fight and we march on the morrow."

"Finucanes!" Brigianna cried and pulled away in sudden panic. "Then I cannot go, m'lord, I must stay behind. I must. Oh, Lord, Lord."

Her words tumbled out in ungainly gush, and he raised a baffled brow.

"Why, this is no simple cattle raid I speak of. If war is called, it will be grand. Surely ye would not miss a battle such as this? Besides, what concern is it of yours who we fight? It matters not who ye are against, little one. It only matters who ye are for."

"Ye do not understand!" she cried with pupils dilated fully black. "I am Brigianna of the McColyms. 'Tis the Finucane I am fated to marry, and himself an old man. I cannot marry that man. I cannot march."

The Cafferty looked at her with utter astonishment. His natty little string game had suddenly bagged him a bird in the bush.

"What a shame it is that I do not claim king's rights over ye," he said with honest regret. "But it's not to war I would go. 'Tis the will of my people that prods me on, and for them I must claim victory."

Ravenlocks slipped through his fingers, and the bulging eye widened in newfound appreciation. "And ye, precious plum, are going to help me."

Chapter 16

Grania poked the dying embers with an iron rod until she unearthed a glowing coal the size of her fist, then blew on it until the turf sprang to life. Quickly she tossed it into her smallest cooking pot and clamped the lid shut. Next she carefully wrapped the pot in a blanket and tucked it away among her belongings. The coal, reincarnated with each new fire, had been passed down to her by her mother before her, and her mother's mother before that. Through her careful keeping it would live forever. Grania could not remember being without it.

"Best hurry, Brigianna. Himself says we march when the sun is full above," she called and hurried off to her chores.

Watching her, Brigianna was ashamed to realize she had no hearthstone to offer; she had called her sacred right forfeit when she ran from her father's clanbind.

Her fingers pussyfooted their way up the taws of her right boot, securing the bulges of her meager belongings. Her father had given her the brooch at her first bleeding. Its fine hammered metalwork curved with laugh lines of its own, like her father's face when he had handed it to her and pronounced her a fertile breeding woman ready to be given.

The dirk came from Lochobar, to use when they went foraging. She had not needed it here, for Caffertys set out common knives for their women to share. The dirk rested against her calf, tucked into the leather flap sewn inside her boots, and it was well no one knew she had it.

Inside her left boot, leaning against the ravenfeather, was Kevin's comb. She had wrapped rabbit skin around the rakes so they wouldn't gouge her skin. Only when Yvonia had discovered it had she taken time to appreciate its pearly perfection. The bone was silken to the touch, yet well fitted to its purpose. Bred with an artisan's patience, she knew the long hours that went into its making. Beyond price, it was unsurpassed in beauty. Created as a labor of love, it was the only part of Kevin she could hold.

In spite of Yvonia's urgings, she could not bring herself to flash it about and say, "Oh, for aye, Kevin gave it to me." But she was never without it, not since that night he gave it to her.

Her hair now lay around her shoulders in all its untamed luxury. She ran her fingers through it, realizing there was no time to braid it into the accepted fashion. Tossing her cloak over her shoulders, she secured it with the simple bronze fibula recently given her, thinking she would just have to appear as the wanton woman they thought she was.

A little smile twitched her lips. Perhaps she was wanton, in her own way at least, for she was certainly not like Cafferty women. Turning, she met Maire's pinched face, and her smile stretched to a smirk.

"Must ye watch my every move?"

"I must, Lady. Lord Gawain ordered it so."

"Oh? I suppose ye must follow me to the squatting pits as well?"

"There are no squatting pits on the road, m'lady."

"Then by your leave," she snapped.

Brigianna stopped by the great oak long enough to address the god within it on near equal terms. "The women assume I have bedded two men, and for shame I have bedded neither. If I begin to bed their men, the women see me as a threat. If I have no tasks to do, the women see me as lazy. Already, they snatch my food. Already, they speak sharply to me. And what of Kevin? What will he think of me? That I am wanton? Or lazy? Or merely selfish—as he said before? Oh, Great Oak, ye are so full of wisdom. What's to do?"

Caffertys massed their bulk into a single queue, ready to head out. By the time she fell in line with them, the Cafferty longhouse looked forlorn and empty.

Little Rollie clung to Maire's side, and the looks she gave him were much the same as she gave Brigianna. Never far from those searching eyes, she thought to lose herself among the women and children. But the moment she tried to scurry back into the shadows, guards standing sentry herded her into line with planted javelins.

But as the swelling horde pulled out, Rollie tugged at his mother's skirt and diverted her attention. Brigianna found herself falling behind. Soon Maire turned around and, with a hand to shield her brow, squinted into the roiling caldron of faces behind her. She spotted Brigianna, who slyly waved her on. Maire nodded and, with satisfied smile, turned her eyes forward and her attentions to the road.

As far as Brigianna's eyes could see, Caffertys filled the horizon. Like the mountain spring that becomes the mighty river, they made their way across land. Engrossed in the activities of the women's quarters and main hall as she had been, she had no idea the clan was so large.

Nor had she seen so many horses. Her father kept some pack animals, and traders often rode through on magnificent mounts. But her people were more interested in crafting fine metals than amassing great fortunes, and her father more interested in outwitting the stag than matching brute strength in war games. Well, no wonder, she thought. Father would scarcely disturb the hair beneath the armpits of these mighty warriors.

A vanguard of dark riders led the march, followed by armed footmen. Next came Lord Gawain, then Eric and his council, all family men with fighting men of their own. Babbling women and children preceded the oxcarts: huge two-wheeled shandrydans piled high with supplies and rimmed with magnificent iron tires. Horses were strung together on girtlines. Surly with pent-up energy that comes from greening timothy and alfalfa at summer's high, they snorted and pawed dirt and rumped into each other as mounted riders gaffed them into line. Max led the pack of yipping war dogs eager to sport grouse or hare on the run. Behind them, grim-faced men in buff jerkins rode rear guard.

Brigianna was drawn to the horses, yet frightened at the same time. Even when they stopped to graze or make water, they possessed a latent energy that defied command.

A big bay near the head of the line snorted a deep rumble and tossed its head back to twitch its tail and swat flies. When its hoof came down on a rock, there was the unmistakable ring of metal. The horses were shod, then? Wagon wheels tired? Axles well greased?

She looked around: tarps bulged, overstuffed and ungainly, from sharp pointed objects constrained within. The cattle, in whose honor this march had begun, had been left behind. The few cowherds left to tend them were bereft as new widows.

"Brigianna!" The voice darted through the air like a songbird in flight, and she whirled around to catch it.

"Brigianna!" It came again, but no one near her paid any heed.

Baffled, she turned to see the Shameface peering at her through the line of horses. Despite his tender concern, she shuddered. Even in daylight he was grotesque. Kirtling her skirts, she hurried back to the wagons.

Panting, she leaned against a shandrydan for support and looked up, surprised to see Brian sprawled atop the supplies like extra baggage. Boots, gird, and arms lay at his side, and beside them, Grania's pot.

"Brian! Are ye faring any better? Grania reports ye doing well, but her face is without cheer at the mention of your name," she called, amicably enough. His once cheerful countenance had grown wan with pain, and when he snorted and turned away, her eyes blazed blue fire. "Well, it's not just for the passing of the day that I ask!"

"It's too old I am to march with the children, the women bid me off, and now it's too weak I am to march with the men. Ye dare ask a king's son how he fares? Be off, Lady, I have no need of foolish prattle."

"This is not like ye at all." Moving closer, she put a hand out to calm him. The tunic was wet; his chest oozed slimy liquids, which gelled to bandage his clothes to the wound. And his vitals were swollen.

"Sure now, a cauterized wound should be on its way to healing," she ventured. Unless struck again by a blow from the outside, or forced open from pressure on the inside, she thought, answering her own question. A worried frown crossed her brow as she reached up to touch the wound. Discovering the stuff sticky, she instinctively put her fingers to her nose, then drew them away quickly in disgust.

"A plenty's been done to be sure." His sharp bark made her brows knit in curiosity. "Conor has given me this draft. 'Take it three times a day,' says he. Well, me bowels have turned to pudding, me legs are soft as a greening willow, and sure now, the hole in me chest gets greener by the day, almost as green as the awful stuff Conor gave me to drink."

"Aye? Let me see that stuff."

Reluctantly he handed her his horn. She uncorked it and smelled the sickly brew. "Borage, and fennel, and oh, me, senna, too? And with a piney smell, mmmmmm. It's no wonder ye've the runs." She handed the vial back to him and forced a smile. "Perhaps I can find some knotweed, or perchance a daffodil bulb. Though it's late in the year for such. But sure, the women have dried clover? That thickens the blood."

"Perhaps the lady would consider nightshade. That thickens the blood, too. Though in a most curious way."

Conor had crept up behind them. Smiling, he rocked back on his heels with his hands folded inside his sleeves. His clean-shaven nearly chinless face shone with savage delight, and his eyes glinted like well-hammered iron as they made their way slowly over her. Realizing the remark was meant for her, she froze, thinking of the draft of nightshade, the dilated pupils, the drugged trance it produced, and the slow death that followed.

"I-I mean I—"

"What have we here?" a big voice boomed out from behind them.

Cagney reigned the big bay against its will and, with its ears laid back in rebellious submission, brought it into line. He leaned forward, thick tongue pressed against parted teeth, awaiting answer.

"Nothing more than a curious wench, m'lord, asking about poor Brian here, and how he fares." Though his tone was light, Conor's deadly smile quelled any protest Brigianna might have made.

"Brigianna, fair," Cagney said indulgently as he leaned against the back of his straw-stuffed saddle, "'tis unseemly for ye to be worrying your pretty little head with such concerns when others certainly more skilled than ye are giving the matter their utmost attention. Come, I am certain the king has need of thee."

Before she even realized what was happening, Cagney hoisted her over the saddle stock with one broad sweep of his meaty hand.

She screamed in surprise, then in earnest, and pounded her fist into the horse's withers. The bay's eyes blazed bright and it shook its head, trying to rid itself of the aggravation. But all it could see were flailings whirring the air in the gray spots behind its line of vision where it could not see color or distinguish objects.

It jerked back and heaved upward with a shrill scream, and its forelegs pawed the air. Its head rolled backward from the sudden upswing, and Brigianna was butted into

Cagney's belly as its head came down. Men standing nearby leapt back in horror, as it looked like the animal was going to tumble backward and crush both riders.

Conor's arms shot out; he jumped clean away as the horse's rump butted into the wagon. Sharp rods beneath the tarp goaded the horse's rear. Nostrils flared, and with shrill whinny it lunged forward.

Cagney got knocked off-balance when Brigianna hit him. He shot both feet forward and hunched over to match the incline of the horse. And Brigianna got wedged beneath him as the horse bolted into the field.

Earth rushed beneath her like a raging river. Greens and browns and yellows all muddied together. Silvery horseshoes flashed in front of her eyes, and she screamed as she was pitched into them.

Cagney grunted and pushed against wind to grab her. With a snapping wrist, he pulled back with so much grit that red welts appeared across his face. Barely catching her in time, he yanked back so hard she choked in pain.

Mayhem exploded behind them as tethered horses roiled and churned, trying to get free of the gantline. Cafferty men, shouting obscenities, grabbed whatever was nearest and beat the horses back into line. Gantline slipped from their grip; horses bucked and thrashed. And there was the unmistakable snap of broken bone as the first Cafferty fell.

The remaining caravan burst its seams as the bay bolted and went running after it, thinking to close it off and ring it back. But the bay, trained to plow through war lines as unrelenting as the waves of the sea, ran through this horseshoe of waving hands and into the fields.

Brigianna's face was thrashed against Cagney's knee. In panic she groped the ridge of the horse's spine to handlock its mane and hoist herself back up. But she couldn't do it. Wind beat her down. She was certain she would slip over the side and be flayed alive.

Welts on Cagney's face reddened as he lifted a thick-muscled thigh and pulled her legs beneath it to press it in a vise against the horse. Blinding pain nearly rendered her unconscious, but through it came a glimmer of hope as she realized she was secured beneath him.

Straining muscle against muscle, iron will against iron will, the horse ran on, maddened by Brigianna's sudden kick in that dark, shadowy space behind it, where eyes do not see and instincts only react. Blood coursed through the animal's temples, drowning out everything but the sound of thunder. Blood and thunder. Thunder and blood. They worked in perfect harmony, each becoming the other, until the horse was beyond recall, until the horse was beyond the reach of human mastery.

Shouting, Caffertys ran to catch them but could not. Eric and Gawain ran back. Cutting the gantline with flashing knives, they each mounted a steed and charged after them. Too late, they realized they had no saddles, and thus, no anchor to act as ballast.

Cagney grabbed the reins, twisting them around his forearm to shorten the horse's pull, and yanked. But he could not bring the animal down.

It coursed on in mindless oblivion. White froth whipped the sides of its mouth. Snaffles gored in. Streams of blood joined white froth.

Blood pounded Cagney's temples, hammering his senses. He plowed forward, as mindless as the animal beneath him, yielding to death.

In the darkness that spun around her Brigianna felt this same rhythmic plodding. It coursed through her with relentless force. She was powerless to fight its undulating lurch and pull. Its heaving roll held her in hypnotic power.

The horse was losing strength. Time began to lag between strides. Simultaneously it dawned on them, and they tensed in apprehension.

Behind them came the thunder of charging steeds and angry cries.

Beneath them the massive head lunged forward. Withers heaved in a half twisted roll as the right foreleg stretched out. A hoof lifted. It came down with labored effort. Bloody froth filled the air, sinuous as red ribbon. Hairy fetlocks floated in silken strand.

The head lolled to one side. Withers rose again. Now the chest lurched left, and Brigianna rolled with it. Now the left front hoof came up. Slowly the right-rear flank rolled forward to meet it.

And the horse pitched over.

Brigianna rolled away as Cagney fell to the dirt.

Gawain and Eric braced into an abrupt halt. Behind them Caffertys filled the line, their clamor lost to the wind.

Cagney rolled over and fell against the horse's heaving belly. The last blood-filled, foaming rush of breath from the dying horse surged through him as if it were his own. He looked down in disbelief. The horse was dead.

Ignoring his father, his uncle, and his clan, he looked at Brigianna.

With burning breath, he heaved one arm forward. Then slowly, the other, and crawled away from the crowd and over to her side. Angry fingers knotted around a handhold of hair. He yanked, and brought his face down upon hers.

"That was a good horse," he spat. "Not only is a good horse dead, but it seems ye have disrupted the order of things and have need of knowing a few simple facts of life."

He leaned closer to fill her face with a garlicky spate of breath. "If a woman comes to our midst and our men have sport with her and she does not protest, then fair's the fair. Do ye not see? She is entitled to her pot's fair share, and the men are comforted by her presence.

"But if a maid comes to our midst and she keeps her legs well crossed except for her intended—whether she be with child or before—and he crowns her with clanbadge and takes her to wife, then he claims her children, and she, in turn, claims his hearth. Again there is balance.

"And if a maid is fair and to the king's liking, he may take her, for that is his right. If he tires of her and a clansman takes her after that, that is his choice. Once more there is balance."

Her brows became charcoal slashes in the pull of Cagney's grip. Gurgling laughter rumbled his gut, and when she started shaking, his laughter settled out to even enjoyment.

"Ye, Lady, have upset the balance of things. First ye bed my one true rival. And the moment his back is turned, ye bed his king." He rolled his eyes around in his head. "I wonder what he will say to that, I surely do. For 'tis fair manner to bed the king before ye take your warrior . . . but begods! Not after."

"Ye leave Kevin's name be. Ye leave me be. Stay away! My life is no concern of yours," Brigianna dandered in tear-stinging rage.

But he caught her and rolled her backward. "Ah, there ye be wrong. Now, I personally have no concerns about your skirts at present. But it's to war we go," he leveled, and once more his narrowed eyes took on a glazed look. "And war or not, the old king cannot live forever.

"So mark my words, time will come when I will call, and ye will pay."

He thumbed toward the horse: "That was a good horse. Ye owe me."

A meaty hand shot out and gripped Cagney's shoulder. As he looked up, the smirk was wiped clean from his face. Gawain towered above him, the blue furl of his cape bannering rank and his javelin piercing the sky in judgment. Their eyes met and locked gaze.

Rollie came toddling up to hold out a chubby hand. Before Brigianna could take hold, Maire swiped it away and twirled the toddler around to bury his face in her skirts.

"Lady Brigianna," Lord Gawain said stiffly and walked away.

Chapter 17

With the death of the horse a pall fell over camp. Uniformly they blamed it on Brigianna. Giving her wide berth, they marched on.

Now they spread out to quilt a marching path of their own making, only loosely following cow trails threading the central valley. Fetlocked hooves dug up huge clods of turf, wagon ruts scarred the boggy sod, and the Shameface scraped a zigzag path pockmarked by regular plantings of one sure foot. Not even in the lark of summer's wanderlust, or in search of greener pasture to booley cattle, had they wandered this far. Grohens chuckered at their passing, warblers and wheatears heralded their coming, but the Caffertys remained oblivious to the wonders of summer. For this far away from clanhold and clangod, they felt unprotected.

Ahead lay the great hall of Tighmohr, where Finucanes now slept and where Caffertys were servitors in the dark ago. When Caffertys rallied power to break clanbind and be recognized, the valley became a pillow of peace between them. Now that pillow lay threadbare with a tattered edge.

Only the thought of Kevin's return kept Brigianna going.

"Come to my father's clanhold. Be under his protection, and promise me that there ye'll stay. For 'tis life and limb I'm speaking of as long as Dhurmod is about, Lady, and not just the pot's fair share," he had said in voice as resonant as the timbre of a fine bowstring.

"Aye? For why do I come?" she had asked then, and asked now as well. Brushing a hair back from her brow, she wished she hadn't been so quick to spit herself clean of honor, or so quick to accept Cafferty clanbind.

Fields, ribboned with golden furze, purple heather, and pink and white clover, danced around her. Caffertys, not wont to be sober for long, bubbled bits of conversation here and there that soon became noisy hubbub. But Brigianna sensed within that conversant caldron the stirring of raven-wings gathered for war.

She must speak with Gawain. But Maire mortared herself to her side. Rollie clung to Maire's skirts and, in the smack of her dour disposition, subdued his tousle-topped curiosity.

"Step lively, Lady, and mind ye give me no trouble," Maire snapped.

Brigianna's temper was thin. "Must ye lay shadow to my every step?"

"I must, m'lady. Lord Gawain bid it so."

Brigianna adjusted the folds of her cloak, wrinkling her nose involuntarily at the smell of horse sweat and Cagney, which was still upon her.

It brought to mind the many hours she had spent, quiet as a cricket, watching the McColyms' smith. Fires burnished his skin like the golden statues he made, and he had a robust scent about him that was mixture of sweat and leather, and more animal than human.

Brigianna knew that molten metal had an unmistakable odor about it. As gases escaped, metals were freed to their purity, and the air filled with rich life.

For it was the working of air, earth, fire, and water—the four elements—that allowed Ban to birth his wondrous art. Mingling human sweat with molten metal, the god bound creator and created thing as one.

Filling her thoughts with memories of home, Brigianna trudged in line with the noisy hubbub of Cafferty horses, wagons, and stock. Suddenly her drooping eyelids opened wide. Why was Rathdun different—did they not honor Ban? And why did that fire smell linger so in her memory?

Inscribed in her bones and marrow was the smell of the forge. She knew that smell as an animal knows its master.

Even after the baths the smith still smelled like fire, for it lingered in his hair, dry as death. By contrast, Brigianna's hair was luxuriantly rich and earthy smelling.

She took a deep breath, thinking to brush the cobwebs of worry away, and a shiver of precognition coursed through her. Dancing furze, heather, and clover suddenly erupted into rivers of blood that smeared her vision with waves of red that blotted out the soft summer day.

Surrounded by his council, Gawain trudged on, unaware of what lay ahead or behind. By now the red pool in his eye was clearing, the white beginning to show. His labored breathing stirred the battering ram within, and to free himself of its impending doom, he let his mind go easy on him. Like cattle pulling ungainly shandrydans, he plodded on, uncomplaining. Eric put an arm across his shoulder in easy camaraderie, but when there was no response, he marched by his side in silence.

Cagney rode up and down the lines, absent of any jewelry, his simple buff jerkin a tan blur astride the dark black.

"Would m'lady care to ride?" he asked, reining up, as if yesterday had not happened.

Brigianna clutched her aching ribs and gave him a defiant chin-up look. "M'lady would care to walk!"

Bushy brows knit to form dark streaks above the slashed red welts that were still drawn on his cheeks from wrestling with the horse. He leaned forward and, with an arm resting on the saddlebuck, started to say something, but thought better of it. Instead, he reined the horse's muzzle into its neck so that it bucked time.

With a cavalier "good day" he goaded it on.

"Ye've a pretty morrow acoming," Maire chided. "When the king tires of ye, his son will be waiting. Though methinks patience is not Cagney's lot." An old woman beside her parted cracked lips to show brown stubbed teeth and made a cackling comment.

"Ooooo, m'lady's in a snit, I'd say." The crone's wrinkled features pulled taut in mock surprise, and her hands flew to sagging breasts in feigned distress.

"Mind ye keep your thoughts to yourself. The both of ye!" Brigianna commanded.

"Tend to me own affairs, ye say? Lady, the making of babies be everyone's business. Now, a wee taddie to round that flat little belly of yours would name your place at table. Mark my words, young'n. Ye'll ken soon enough how a woman earns her keep."

"Oh, leave me be," Brigianna pleaded and pulled back in line. Others quickly filled the space in between, and soon she was several steps behind. Nervously Maire glanced her way, then leaned over to whisper into Rollie's ear. Grinning, he scampered back to tag Brigianna's skirts and coyly offered a chubby hand. But Rory came to his side just then and, scooping him up, perched him on his shoulders.

"Wheeeee, Gianna, look't me," he squealed in freckle-faced glee as his brother pranced him off, bucking him like the stallion in spring. Rollie left a trail of giggles behind, and up ahead Maire, with eyes dutifully road bound, was none the wiser.

With Cagney on patrol, Brigianna kept her smiles to herself as Kevin did, and fell farther behind. Her supple hide boots made no trail at all, for she was bred to the art of footing her way through grasses so they could spring back at her passing. But everyone could tell where the Shameface had been. She sobered quickly when she discovered him to her side, walking with spastic difficulty, his left buttock bulging larger than his right to accommodate his thin, useless leg.

For the first time Brigianna was close enough to see through the slits of his mask. With the sunlight just right she could see his eyes.

Impossible, she thought, and quickly turned away to focus her attention on Cagney. Riding to the head of the line, he reined his steed around, then circled back.

A strange feeling swept over her, the fleeting perception that something had radically changed. With a slight shift in movement, Caffertys fell into line when he was near. But when he passed by, they fell out of step to once again become common rabble.

"Come," Cagney commanded as he neared her way and leaned forward on the saddlebuck, the hair upon his arms sweaty and matted from riding.

"No, m'lord," she parried as the Shameface quickly stepped forward.

"Ye fend the lady's honor?" Cagney mocked. His fist shot down before the Shameface could duck and clubbed the butt of the mask.

Quickly putting his hands to his chin as if to steady its thudding ring, the Shameface was thrown further off balance by his crippled foot. He fell to the ground, rolling over and over like a runaway barrel. Caffertys burst into nervous laughter and fell out of line to ring around him, taking sport in his downfall, but pretending to urge him back up.

He hit a rock and pitched to a sudden stop. Thrusting his leg out front, he awkwardly tried to gain balance, then with a steady movement brought the stiffened leg back, tested his weight against it, and grunting at the effort, slowly stood up.

Sober eyes watched him as he made his way back to the lines. With shoulders bent he stood in front of Cagney the Brave, who jerked his head back, signaling him to follow. Dutifully the Shameface hobbled behind, leaving his zigzagged trail.

Brigianna's hand shot to her mouth to muffle her cry. The padding at the curvature of his spine had shifted, and a lock of hair, dark and thick as hers, had fallen from beneath the mask.

* * *

Leaning forward to catch his breath, Lord Gawain thrust the butt of his lance to the ground. As he swung his arm out wide, his nephew, Donny, hurried to take his shield from him, then backed off to leave the lord alone. Sweat beads fell to Gawain's side like raindrops. Wiping the drenched hand on his cloak, he drew away from the crowd.

"They follow us?" he asked as Eric stepped forward with bent brow to survey dark shadows skirting the edge of copse. "Dhurmod's men?"

In that thoughtless, plodding march where reason vacates the soul and senses become honed to every change of light and shadow, Gawain had become aware of them through the eyes of his mind rather than through the eyes of his head.

"There are no parries? They do not attack?"

"We are too many for them, m'lord. The Pig Man is not known for his bravery," Eric replied calmly.

Air whistled through Gawain's parted teeth. "Is it wise to call the Finucanes into battle and let this cur live?"

"Methinks wars are fought for honor and wealth, Brother, seldom for wisdom. We are of the people, and it be by the people's will that Finucanes suffer, for if they have wronged our cattle, they have wronged us. I say, let the rabble be, we will have them for dessert after the main battle is finished. It would be a waste of men to scour the woods for one cur when there is battle to be fought and glory won."

Gawain turned to his brother and saw a reflection of himself but without flaws. His handsome face bore no sword slash that in splitting lid, removed his shield of privacy and forced him to stand sentry even when he would rather be asleep. Gods had even given him fine teeth. "Father would have done well to choose ye king and not me," he mused.

"Gods' truth, Gawain, 'tis not like ye to speak that way." Eric drew his chin back into his neck, furling his lips into concerned scowl. "Well ye've served our people and well ye'll serve them after this little skirmish is over. A fine wife and sons I have, I'll thank ye to know. So I've no need of the crown."

"The crown will not stay long on this old head; its hairs be numbered," Gawain lamented.

Eric's features turned grim, his clancloth furled behind to catch in the folds of his baggy trousers, and he rubbed his chin in deep thought.

"Let me call the battle cries. Let me cry challenge. We be of common height and bearing. Not even my Ainne would know."

Tempting as the proposition was, Gawain brushed it aside. "For that I might well let Cagney call the gainsays of war. Nothing would please my son more."

"Ho! That son of yours loves to fight so much he would die just for the thrill of it," Eric jested, then grew serious. "Ye should have chosen tanist and given this battle to your successor. Ye have earned rest, Brother. It would not be counted dishonor."

"Kevin has not returned," Gawain mumbled. The statement hung like leadweight.

"Now, there be a true Celt. Brave and fearless in the face of death. 'Tis no wonder womenfolk like him." Eric put a firm hand on Gawain's shoulder and gripped it warmly. "But the fearless are often fools, for methinks he should not have brought that woman to camp. She is upsetting the balance of things, and gods be fickle, Gawain, when balance is upset."

Gawain's eye strayed to the copse, where shadows haunted their passing, and for a moment he wrestled with the temptation to confide in his brother. Instead, he drew deep breath and thrust the butt end of his cudgel into the earth.

"Mark the women do not wander from the lines; when they take to the wood to relieve themselves, they must go in parties of three or more, and men must stand sentry. Children are to tag their mother's skirts. No longer can they run in packs like untamed hounds. Make them eat by their own campfire so as to be accounted for. And starve old

Max. I want those dogs tough and hungry. Brace night camp in full circle, with armed guard at its ring. Unless they swear clanbind before me, anyone coming into camp or murmuring gainsay from within will be killed on sight. Alert your men and prepare to ride. Send your men scout, forward west. I want full report of the Pig Man's strength. Command Cagney's men to retrace our steps; see that Cafferty clanhold remains safe. Station armed guard there and deploy men to guard our march from behind and on both sides. I do not want my enemies to think we have a weakened flank or that they could ambush us from behind. My Kevin should return with full report on Finucane strength—then we shall test the full measure of our mettle."

"Aye, Lord." Eric's face shone with unabashed pride as he addressed his king, but as he turned to go, it softened in concern.

"Ye should ride, ye should save your strength."

With flaring nostrils and blazing eye Lord Gawain thumped his chest. "Like ye, I am woodrunner. Father was Fian. I am Fian. Kevin is Fian."

"Aye," Eric agreed. "And methinks honor a poor bedmate come nightfall."

Chapter 18

When they broke march, Caffertys took to the wood to relieve themselves, with women trailing off in groups of three or more, nervous as deer who must drink, knowing the wolf lurked nearby. They had entered enemy territory, but they were still uncertain who was the greater enemy. Men stood sentry, sensing Black Dhurmod was watching, yet a surging hunger rose within that called for Finucane blood.

To prepare men for battle, horses raced at regular intervals and war games were set up in the fields at night. Back at the Cafferty stronghold, Brigianna had been kept too busy to enjoy such sport. Now she watched, and with great fascination, as prow pitted prow in staged matches and men twisted in the ungainly positions of mock battle. There was no doubt Cagney was the best of them. With his long ruddy hair flying like a cape over rippling muscles, he could beat anyone.

Suddenly a man fell, his shoulder sheared away by a double-bladed ax because his ankle had twisted against a rock. He was hauled away, screaming his torment mid shouts of joy and victory, and Brigianna had serious misgivings about the glory of war. It did not pump McColym blood or cull McColym young as it did Cafferty, and in spite of pulsating bloodlust that flared nostrils and quickened step, its lure escaped her.

Lord Gawain's comrades marched with him by day and ate with him by night. Tall, blond, with trailing mustaches and beardless chins, bound by blood and by fealty, they slept, drank, and fought together. Their young cut their teeth on tales of glory and ached to become a part of this inner circle even before they left their mam's skirts.

But now, at Lord Gawain's orders, families grouped around small campfires. Children no longer ran at large but reported to their parents, and slowly Brigianna began matching them up.

Men joining the march from farms and fields were large, well muscled, and swarthy. But the scragglers and vagabonds joining them along the way seemed to be an entirely different lot. Their women had grit-lined faces and skin that was tanned like leather by the harshness of outdoor life. When she met them at the cooking fires, she found in them no humor at all. And she wondered about Cafferty ranks growing day by day, and of bulky supplywagons carefully kept behind guard, and of Brian back there among them with a wound still sore and festering.

Defend me or spend me, was the hue and cry. Lord Gawain deliberated each freeman's case with sincerity. To accept allegiance increased his clanhold, but to feed them mandated that he stake claim against Finucane territory and put end of this border dispute.

As Brigianna walked by, Lord Gawain raised a disconsolate eye. Thinking it was beckon to come, she stepped forward, but javelins immediately barred her way. Behind them Lord Eric and Donny stared at her with forbidding eyes.

"M'lady!" Maire cried, aghast. " 'Tis for men to determine law. Ye must never tamper with a man's world, 'tis unseemly."

Yvonia joined them then, with a deliberately goodnatured, "Scat, Maire, shoo, I say." Maire gave her an indignant frown and insisted, "M'lord Gawain says I'm to shadow Lady Brigianna."

"Pogosh, Maire. Where would herself be going in the dark of night, and sure now, Rollie has need of thee?" Maire's pinched features masked relief, and she quietly left.

"Come, Brigianna, ye must eat."

"Truly, I am not hungry."

Yvonia gave her an inquisitive look. "On the march all day and not hungry? 'Tis no wonder the women be wagging. After the raven and the horse, they say ye have a fey, and consort with the spirits."

"And ye agree with them?"

"Aye," Yvonia said with poke-faced wink and pointed finger. "Kevin has bewitched ye, but ye have bewitched Cagney!"

Her quick rain of mirthsome laughter caught Brigianna off guard. "Ah, that's better," Yvonia purred, seeing Brigianna brighten up. "'Tis only gruel and greens tonight, Lady, but ye must eat."

Summer sun cracked the nether that lay between earth and sky. Turning and tossing in worry over Brian, Brigianna woke to a dew-drenched mat, to see in that dancing sunstream the laughing, slender daffodil. A wry smile crossed her sleep-filled face as she thought, Ah, now, why didn't I think of that sooner? The bruised bulb, mashed in poultice, will surely draw the poison out. But again worry set its frown: this late in summer the daffodil had long lost its golden head, and to perchance a lily could be fatal.

Mists lay heavy in the dips, veiling her disappearance through ghostly walls as she slid between the golden beams and away from Maire, who slept soundly at her side. Shivering, she slipped her long hair inside her cloak as she pulled the hooded cowl up and crept into the forest. Intent on her quest she was unaware how easy her escape.

Brian was not getting any better. His continual retchings made him stink, and no one would go near him. Death had called him, they said. But she, bred to the curing arts, set stubborn store in the daffodil.

Thinking of the many remedies Lochobar had taught her, her eye fell on some shepherd's purse, which grew rampant. With no way to brew a decoction without being noticed, she thought she might get away with steeping the leaves in cold water. She knelt down to pull the dirk from inside of her boot, thinking it safer to dig shepherd's purse than chance a bulb that might well be poisonous, and wandered on. Her trail led her to an open clearing, where mallows and sorrels bedded aside shepherd's purse in plentiful supply.

As she knelt to dig, it dawned on her how easily she had escaped. She could hear the noises from camp, the general stirring of Caffertys as they wakened, the wail of a child, the neighing of the horses as they were herded into line. Trees formed a natural barrier that riveted sounds back and forth in capricious reverie. Yet she was shielded, easily to slip behind the fern and scrub and wait their passing. The thought dumbfounded her, for with Brian so heavily on her mind, she had not thought how easy it would be.

Staring at the silver dirk in her hand, she realized she had with her all she owned. Its blade was no longer than her finger and could lie in the palm of her hand unnoticed.

She quailed. Dhurmod's knife would be longer, certainly.

She turned the blade over and over in her hand: to return meant Cagney's lust, Gawain's schemes, and Maire's vise-like grip. No! She chinned up. Sure now, Kevin would know she was in more danger if she stayed? Sure now, he would overlook spit and promise and say that it was for life that she ran?

Rising mists ringed golden sun shafts to make trees appear as ethereal visages of a haunted realm. Dampened moss and lingering ivies became murky shadows, trillium trailed darkened tunnels, and sunlight made dappled patterns on the forest floor. With dirk in hand she gingerly followed their beckoning call.

A breeze flitted through the forest floor, stirring rustlings that all too quickly quieted like the closed door of a darkened tomb. Her hands grew clammy, making her hackles rise and her skin grow prickly. The wood had turned ominous, honing her senses and making her wary.

At a dark movement within the shadows she froze. Unable to tell if it was man or animal, she called timidly, "Who goes there?"

Likely the wood would be full of stragglers by now, Caffertys relieving themselves before the morning march, she told herself.

But no answer came. Silence tightened around her like a slipknot. She raised her dagger. "Who goes there?" she called again, unnerved by the raspy edge in her voice, for if Cafferty it was, why the silence?

Backing up against a sturdy oak to use as shield, she stood still as the tree. At a movement within the brush her hand began to sweat so badly that the knife handle slipped.

She looked at it, frightfully aware of its limitations and realizing, also, that there were no low-lying branches to catch her swing. She was too far from camp to outrun whatever was hiding there, and if animal, and if startled into charging, her scream might bring sudden death.

Now footfalls trampled brush, and something unseen rutted ground. Cocking her ear, she could hear grunting noises coming closer. They stopped, with pig eyes intent on quest. Slowly large, curling tusks parted brush. And a huge boar stood no more than a rod away.

Brigianna paled and willed herself to become a part of the tree, urgently paying homage to the oak, sacred mentor and protector of mankind. Forcing her breathing still, she prayed: "Gods will it does not pick up my scent."

Large, gray, and ugly, its tusks curved wide, dipped into half arcs, and rose again as deadly pointed spears. Its ears lay flat against its head, and as it came into the clearing, its snout twitched wind.

With an angry grunt it spun around on all fours. Pig eyes narrowed, surveying territory, and its squealing cry ruptured the stillness. With head down and rump swaying back and forth, the boar dug sharpened hooves into boggy sod and rutted in for the kill. Hairs on its spiny back bristled in fury, and once again it screamed shrill.

Flattening herself to the tree and frantic with fear, she drank in every detail, determining each minute chance of escape. Slowly she slid her back down the trunk so that she had just the right amount of spring in her legs and readied to dart behind the tree as the boar charged. If he came too close, she would have to leap, roll, hunker backward, and be on her feet again before he could turn to trample her.

The silken strand of the spider's web survives the storm; the willow weaves backward and is not uprooted, she canted inwardly, only half mindful of the charms Lochobar had engraved into her being. Still, the taste of copper coated her tongue, and she smelled her own blood.

With all that lay within her, she blotted out the day and crawled into her dark center of being to will the sun and moon and stars to her bidding. She knew well the timelessness of the elements, for at Lochobar's consent she had been singled out from birth to learn druidic ways. By bending her will to the will of the heavens, time would become cyclic and eternal and, in that way, pass more slowly.

Now what could happen in the slice of a knife could be seen in the detail of suspended time. By opening her senses to powers beyond her reach, time would be called forth from eternal darkness, time given to carefully calculate each movement and weigh its import.

Yet to call darkness to her own defense by the power of incantation and ward off attack would be to break truce with the gods that called her from darkness into human life, and in that, unleash their fury.

Death is but the simple passing of one life to another, she reminded herself. Through shaded lids she saw the boar lower its head to rut earth and snort territorial outrage. And white blotches welted across her forehead, down her throat, and onto her breasts.

Like the boar's, Brigianna's lips furled back to bare her

teeth in snarling defense. Unconsciously her breathing deepened and her hips swayed back and forth as she became the enemy she would destroy. She swallowed hard. Death, if it must come, would come quickly.

The boar lifted its head, filling the air with chilling cry, and charged. Brigianna shook with the earth beneath her and whirled around, for, from the other side of the clearing came an ear-splitting growl that was scarcely human.

In a whir of movement so fast it was no more than a shadow passing, the Shameface hurtled himself across the clearing, landed on top of the boar, knocked it off balance, and clubbed it on its skull with the heavy wooden mask. The boar whirled around, its former quarry forgotten, and dug earth, routing up clods of mud and turf and snorting vindictive fury in vile siren, frantically trying to shake the Shameface off.

Wide tusks slashed the air like swords as it jerked its head upward, then veered to reverse course. The Shameface was tumbled full somersault over the boar but landed on his feet, surefooted as any young stag. Legs apart, he hunkered backward, and his gurgling roar was as guttural and animal as that of the boar.

The boar turned, lowered its head, and charged, its high-pitched scree the chill of death.

In continuous motion the Shameface pulled the heavy mask from his face, held it above his head, and dropped to his haunches. The boar ran head on, certain of its kill, and came within a breathshot of impaling the Shameface before the hard wooden mask slammed down on its skull.

Deadly tusks cracked the oak, but the oak, hardened by time, did not splinter. Brigianna's scream joined the boar's as it went down.

The Shameface braced a handhold inside the mask, threw himself on top, and bore down with all his might. Both man and beast screamed in anguish as the boar bludgeoned the Shameface's gut in fierce, frightful skirmish. Finally the Shameface riveted the pig into the earth by battering his own weight against the mask and using it as shield.

Stunned by a blow to the brain, and with tusks plowing ground, it was rendered helpless. Before the pig could bend a knee or raise its head, the Shameface was on his feet. Long black hair spilled down over his shoulders as he whipped out his longknife and rolled beneath.

The blade plunged into the belly, and its death cry cut wake through wood so that not even a bird moved. Mayhem had attacked Cafferty campsite at the frenzied squeals of the boar, but at its death cry men froze with alarm. Now they dived for arms and went running to the wood.

Blood gushed in fountain from the boar's heart, and the Shameface rolled clear, bathed in such a smear of gore that Brigianna didn't recognize him at first. He cleaned his blade on his leg wrappings, then wiped the smear of blood from his face with the back of his hand.

"Doughall?" Brigianna cried in astonishment and ran to him. "My own brother with me all the time in this dreadful disguise? Oh, pray the gods, Dough, but I do not understand this a'tall."

"Be hushed, little one, we've only moments to spare before Caffertys find us. If they were to discover me legs fit, and me face good as any of theirs, it's me hide that would swing in the wind just for sport."

Gulping air, Doughall McColym gathered her to him, and she, happily, buried her face in his neck, scarcely noticing the pig's blood.

"Tell me, quickly, how ye fare. The king is gentle?"

"So much so I be virgin still," she lamented. "But mind, I'm not about to marry that Finucane and play broody to an old man's chicks, so I won't be going back." The corner of her mouth twitched up into a half smile. "Truth is, Brother mine, it's for the McErin me heart is set."

Doughall smiled back, fine-featured and handsome as any man. "Aye, I thought as much, when first I saw ye together."

Brigianna blushed slightly and pressed on. "But, Doughall, it's woe is me. Kevin bid me pledge upon my honor to stay with the Cafferty camp. But I cannot stay. Kevin's a gone and regardless of king's rights, Cagney would make me his woman whether I be willing or no. But now Lord Gawain knows who I am and has me under watch, for it's against the Finucanes we march. I'd fare better taking my chance in the wood, but with Dhurmod about, what chance is that? Oh, Dough, what's to do?"

"Of a truth, I do na know," he said, staring at the still, gory form of the dead pig and thinking well it could have been him.

"Did ye know that Father is marching on Tighmohr, thinking ye there, and his insides a beehive because he didn't get his cows?" he said.

"Well, curse those cows! If it's banished I am for the price of the cows, then it's banished I'll stay till it's certain I am that Lochobar has had a change of heart!"

"Banished!" Doughal replied, dumbfounded. "Ye were banished?"

"As certain as if Lochobar proclaimed it aloud. It was his eyes."

"Ah," he said, truth dawning. "And I be here because Lochobar sent me, for it is as ye say. When those yellow eyes bid ye do something. Well, ye do it, and later ye ask why."

Her cheeks were streaked with blood, and now new fervor edged her voice. "But with Black Dhurmod and his men around, it's a double trap. We must warn Father! But how?"

"I do not know. And I suspect there's more to your tale than even Lochobar knows." Pressing firm lips to her forehead, he held her quiet.

"Tonight after ye have eaten and the men are tired, listen for the warbler—the male, then the female in echo—and come to me. I will gather me aching bones and me wits and know by then what's to do."

"I cannot go with you."

"And ye cannot stay."

The noisy thrashing and shouting of men approaching made Doughall scramble to his feet. He dropped his long-knife as he ran and, with no time to retrieve it, called, "Remember—the warbler," and disappeared.

Just as a score of men entered the clearing with arms raised and Cagney at their lead, Brigianna lunged for it. Turning, she held the blade, dripping with dark pig blood, up in front of her and smiled.

Chapter 19

Cagney squinted to get a better look. "Gods grant mercy. M'lady Brigianna with knife in hand and the fierce and mighty boar dead at her feet? Come now, ye daren't tell me ye killed this boar yourself?"

"Gods' truth!" a large, raw-boned man next to him cried. He bent over the pig and grabbed both ends of the mask. His biceps knotted into round balls as he twisted it. With a resounding crack, the carved oak piece split in two and he wrenched it free.

He held the ugly mask up for all to see. Brigianna's vixen smile faded as she saw the splintered features and thought of Doughall.

"'Tis the work of the Shameface, Lord," the man said, then added with a puzzled frown. "But if so, where be the body?"

Lord, Brigianna thought as she lowered the knife. Did he say Lord and not the commonplace m'lord? Quickly she averted her eyes.

From that vantage point she saw a hairy forest of leather-wrapped legs. Once again she salivated copper salt, for the bosses on their shinguards were sharply familiar. Her mind's eye flew to that granite cleft and myrtled canopy by the sea, where she had cowered next to Kevin. Her dark green cape, their only protection, had been torn then, by a javelin strikingly similar to these. And now these men standing before her, swarthy and hard-muscled, clearly claimed Cagney lord.

"It was the Shameface himself that saved me. I had come to the clearing when I heard the boar rooting. Like a flash, he was in the clearing, ready to charge," she blurted out, not daring to look up.

"Enough! Where be the Shameface now?"

"I do na know, m'lord." Her hands flew to her face and she peered at the men through the cracks in her fingers. "Terrible, just terrible it was. Shocked, I was. When I set eyes on that dreadful face. Oooooh."

"Bedams it, woman, quit wailing," Cagney demanded as he reached down to pull her hands away. "Once more, where is he?"

Brigianna kept her eyes to the ground. "With a face like that, how could he bear common company?"

"Bah!" Cagney spat on the ground just inches from her feet. "What's to worry over a cull like that when we have a pig to roast. Right, men?"

"Ho!" the men shouted approval with clenched fists. One of them lifted his ax and began hacking away at a spindly hazel. Another man, much younger, tried to fill his helmet with blood, but cursed violently when he realized the heart had stopped pumping and the earth had drunk most of the warm, salty brew. Soon longpoles were rigged. They bound the pig's feet to them with wide leather thongs and, grunting as they heaved to shoulder the load, staggered, then weaved back and forth beneath its great weight before they steadied.

"Fetch Conor," Cagney ordered the blond-haired youth standing nearby. "These guts must get to him before the blood cools." Turning, he said:

"Come, Lady. Let us see what our priest has to say about this pile of pig shit." With pealing laughter, he held out his hand. She took it, expecting to be lifted to her feet, but Cagney brushed it aside.

"The knife," he demanded.

* * *

Catriona was first to spy the men coming back to camp. Waving her hands and shouting, she roused the Caffertys. Soon they clamored around the pig, wanting to know every detail, demanding to hear it again and again. Women ran to get knives, scrapers, and wooden bowls. And Conor stepped into the arena to shout in full timbre, "Crom be praised!"

Men gathered around to watch their women whipping knives with flashing precision as they cut the hide free. Gutted in its fight for life, it had lost blood, and seeing that, Conor raised a dubious eye. When the entrails lay heaped in his wooden laver, his eyes turned to dark slits. Clumsily lifting it out of the reach of hungry dogs and eager children, he hurried away, hoarding his precious information.

"That liver is mine!" Cagney bellowed, and Conor, with enough map work to do in unraveling trailing intestines, didn't challenge him. Cagney grabbed the quivering mass, still dripping blood, and sliced off a chunk. In boisterous laughter he downed it raw.

The quiet of gods' breath fell over them as the heart was pulled out. The blond youth respectfully placed it into Conor's smaller laver, then went running after him.

Cagney claimed the tusks in trophy. "Not so hollow or well rounded as good cattlehorn, I say, but impressive, nay?" He looped them through his belt, complete with grisly shaft of hide and gore.

"Ah, my wizened buttercup. Be not quick to make judgments, or ye will find others willing where ye are not," he said at Yvonia's reprimanding smile. Pinching her cheek, he left it rouged with fingerprints of blood as he looked back over his shoulder to Brigianna, who turned away in disgust.

When he met Conor with his laver swilling pig gut in hand, Gawain realized the march had come to a halt and decreed a feast. Needing the rest, he retired to his quarters, there to do private battle with the battering ram within and the ever-waiting dark ravens of war.

Soon the pig was set to boil in its own hide. Below the hide caldron, the fire roared mellow. It was banked well to keep a slow boil, but not so well as to singe the hide and crack the precious crust.

Under the careful eye of men at guard, women combed the fields for garlics, leeks, irises, field carrots, borage, shamrocks, and sorrels. From the wagons emerged a precious ration of salt. In spite of her own worries Grania bossed them in good humor. Summer was up and berries were pungently juicy. At sun's crest Rory boasted his find of honeycomb, holding it up in triumphant trophy. At last handfuls of barley were tossed into the boil. The grains swelled, binding the fat and setting the top with a skim of gluten paste, thick as jelly.

As the boar simmered on, the day wore away to its frazzled edge. Stock was watered and fed and babies tended. But Caffertys were away from the comforts of home, on forced march and keeping cautious eye to the wood. Max and his fellow hounds had to be tethered far afield, and within the clan, tensile strength tempered thin.

After Brigianna refreshed herself, she happened to corner Catriona. "Brian, does he fare well?" she asked. Catriona answered with a worried frown and scurried away.

Conor bent over the entrails, diligently arranging and rearranging them. Grinding stubby teeth in consternation, he cast aside the first augury as an ill betoken and began again. The second was more favorable. But to be sure he cast them again. When he was certain his prognostications spelled victory, he hurried back to the fires.

He happened to arrive just as Grania pronounced the boar done. Caffertys looked at Conor's exultant face and Grania's raised meat fork, as with dirks in hand and stomachs growling with hunger, they elbowed each other aside like starving hounds. But soon good-natured laughter followed rounds of foot-stomping and they fell to feasting in earnest.

"Make way," Cagney demanded, and Caffertys parted at his coming. "More's the better." He strode up to the makeshift slab table and with careful eye looked the meats over. Prodding the jumbled pile, he pierced the ham shank. Juices spurted in savory goodness.

He held the ham shank up, puffed out his chest, and sweeping low, he offered Brigianna the victor's cut.

Blue eyes danced in jest as she reached forward and took the prized cut. Smile threatened to sneak into smirk as she raised it high and with steady gait walked the path to where Gawain sat.

Careful not to let caprice run away with her, she watched Caffertys watching her. The closer she got to Gawain, the more she could sense Cagney's bafflement gaming up on him.

"To Gawain Cafferty, acknowledged and beloved king of the Caffertys; lord of this valley; protector of us all," she proclaimed, surprised at the lyrical clarity of her own voice.

Lord Cafferty stood. Radiating pleasure at the honor bestowed upon him, his rising arms furled his king's cape in magnanimous gesture.

"To Brigianna Mc—" he began but caught himself and quickly harumphed a cough. "To Lady Brigianna, mistress of beauty and kind heart, who graces our hearth with gentleness."

As he took the meat, she demurred with a smile and, with lids properly lowered, slid down beside him. "I must have word with ye, m'lord."

"Be quick," he mumbled as he lifted his palms up to show his approval, and in turn the Caffertys shouted theirs.

In molten anger Cagney turned heel and barged through the crowd.

And pipers quickly struck up a dancing tune.

Hungrily Gawain sliced a thick slab from the bone and speared it with his knife. His sudden appetite surprised him, making him hold back with caution. Too much meat in his stomach hung like lead and caused the battering ram within to waken. It became harder to keep this matter to himself on the march as he no longer had his privacy. His split lid lowered over the bulging eye as he watched his camp turn to merriment and dance, and sullenly he pretended to eat.

"We must talk," Brigianna persisted. "I forebode within, Lord, and I have reason now to understand why. But first I must know of Kevin."

Gawain gave a wry laugh and raised his hand to signal for more wine. "So? We both await Kevin's return, but for different reasons. Aye, m'lady. He should have returned before now."

"Ye do not understand, m'lord. There is more ye should know. I have reason to suspect—" Her words came to a halt as she realized they fell on deaf ears, for Gawain's attentions had turned back to his men.

The sun left a bloody trail as it dipped over the western horizon, and fires burned brighter. The pig had rounded their bellies, and for that there was little fighting. Well sated, they began to snore.

Nervously Brigianna slipped from Gawain's side and edged toward the outskirts of camp to listen for the warbler's call. Maire followed her with her eyes, but with Rollie nested in her lap, did not get up.

Like a silver blade, a high-pitched scream cut across the piper's wail. Catriona threw herself at her father's feet and, grabbing ash from the sleeping fire, smeared her face with the mask of death.

"Brian's died," she howled. "Oh, Father, Brian's died."

Her soft blond hair hid her features as she ripped her shift to bare her breasts. Then she threw her head backward and began her keening.

"Brian's died? My baby?" Grania cried.

Brian Cafferty, youngest living son of Lord Gawain by Lady Grania, was dead. He had the senseless grace to die on the eve of a great feast when there was merrymaking to be had and loving to be done. In that he aborted the natural flow of things by upsetting the balance.

When they laid him on the funeral pyre that next morning, he took with him his knife and good drinking horn. Torchmen hesitated as they set the flame, for the pyre was rich with sap in the run of summer and would be slow to catch flame.

"To the spirits we bid Brian farewell," Conor intoned. "For what is life but a passing from one world to the next? What has been created by fire is now purified by fire, and brief here was the journey."

Gawain, Grania, Cagney, Catriona, Rory, and Rollie stood at the head of the pyre. Had Brian not died when the Caffertys were on march, he would have been buried in the family cave, there to rest beside his ancestors, ready for the glories of war that lay beyond the grave. As it was, his tunic was well fouled, his body acrid from Conor's drafts, his unwashed hair oily and full of lice. Brian Cafferty, just at the brink of manhood, was borne across the seventh wave with little to offer the gods in the name of glory.

A strange grief filled Brigianna's soul, welling within as an ominous dark. It was quite clear the clansmen did not know of Conor's draft, and it was also quite clear that she was in dreadful danger. For seven days and seven nights time would stand still as she patiently, then frantically, listened for the warbler's call.

Meanwhile, Lord Cafferty held court. And by consent of his council he turned no man, woman, or child away. Setting his weight of grief aside, he resolved to march on Finucane territory to save honor and to secure stock for his hungry horde.

"Ye are not feeling well, m'lord, and 'tis not grief that ails ye. Your gait is heavy, and the shine be gone from your eyes."

"Trust a woman to see what a man cannot," Gawain commented as he pulled Grania to his side. Impulsively he braced himself against the thick tree and her against him. "Oh, Grannie, Grannie. How foolish I was to cast ye aside at Conor's command."

"Because I left your bed, I did not leave your heart, m'lord," Grania whispered softly, fearful of a rebuff for nestling up to him in public.

He turned to take both weathered hands in his. "Mighty oak, sacred tree of mankind. Sacred oak, strength and power of us all. We pledged our love beneath such a tree. Do ye remember?"

"What a time we had then," she tittered, surprised to discover she could still blush. Warm eyes bathed the years away from the other's face. Come again was the youngbuck, chafing and eager to show his prow. Come again was the trusting virgin, willing as the young doe. Then she could but look at him, and his groin would stir and lovemaking begin. To him, she was still that young doe, not the bent old woman whose body had taken on the shape of a well-simmered dumpling.

Obediently, at his priest's orders, he had taken other women, the last of them that pinch-faced Maire. But no matter whose bones creaked beneath his weight, his heart bedded Grania. Finally he had given up.

Then came that delicious plum, Brigianna, and he found he could not. He cursed the dry stick that scratched between his legs, for at last his heart pounded lusty as the stallion who smells blood. But at the delight of its twisting, turning, growing pleasure, the battering ram within wakened that night in warning. And he dared not.

"My lands are too small, my sons are too many, and I grow old."

"For aye, ye do grow old and ye are not alone." Grania pulled away and in sharp-toned practicality asked: "Have ye thought now of Kevin?"

"He was free to choose when he came of age, ye know that. He chose to remain Cafferty; his allegiance to me is bound by spit. What could be more simple? He fights by our side."

"That much I know. I was only thinking how different he is from the others, that be all. Remember how it was when he first came to us?"

Hearth fires, well banked but not quenched, put sudden sparkle to Gawain's eyes. "Like yesterday. Even as a wee taddie he was one to curl a father's heart, but a baffle to his elders, I fear, for his love of the arts seemed soft as a woman's touch. Now his skill in war games goes unmatched, and his prowess is told over a score of lodge fires."

"True," Grania agreed. "But harken, Lord, he has no spirit to fight if there be another way. Not like Rory or Cagney, who fight for the sport of it, and I fear, even little Rollie, too. Of a truth, sometimes it wearies me. And heavy-hearted I am that me Brian is gone . . . " Her voice faltered as her features pulled against themselves. "Gone without honor! For it's not on a battlefield he died, but by his brother's hand."

"Hush, Grania. We all know it was an accident, for it was done in fair sport. The wound should have healed, and it didn't. That be all."

Sadly she reached up to trace a lip line whose warm touch she barely remembered. "Pray for Kevin's quick return," she whispered softly.

Later that day Gawain called his men to him. "Once more ride out, scour the brush, and give me full report."

"When we are in mourning?" Rory's features knotted in confusion as he tried to comprehend his father's order.

"Aye. Ye are to head south, and take Cai, here, with you."

Rory, who was not yet blooded, looked at Cai. His cheeks reddened at the challenge and his curls danced in restless energy. His first mission: Brian's honor was quickly forgotten.

"Cagney, take a handful of men. Head south, but veer east and circle back. Ye brought me no certain news last sortie, yet blood tells me Black Dhurmod's men comb these woods. Assess their strength and report their numbers. And do not fail me this time."

Cagney's thick lips furled back. "Aye, Father," he said, fingering his abalone amulet. "My sortie will be sure, my blade quick."

"No, Son, it will not. Ye are to test this Pig Man, not kill him. If clan must rise against clan, I'll not have a weak flank or men lost in skirmish. Strength must be saved for the Finucane. Understand?"

"Aye, Father," Cagney said with narrowed eyes.

"Eric, ye are to scout the Finucane border, but not to trespass their territory. I want to know how many cattle are lost, how the borders are posted. Once more I must assess the Finucane's strength. And Donny? Be going with your father. It's man ye'll be soon enough."

Donny and Rory exchanged grins, and arrows panged Gawain's heart. So young they were, so hungry for blood, so like Brian. Ah, Brian.

"Be back by three moonsets."

As the men turned to go, Gawain waved Eric back. "Do ye know what day this is, Brother?"

Eric rubbed his chin, thinking, then a look of shock smeared his frown away. "Why, 'tis Lughnasa, the day of feasts and games and—"

"Aye. Lughnasa it is, and we Caffertys march north to settle a paltry border dispute that has grown into clanwar. We are plagued by a marauder we must lure onto the field of battle. And we are delayed by the ill-timed death of my darling son. The gods turn against us."

"No, Brother, it is the gods who give us life and choose our path."

"Hold your tongue! Ye sound as bad as Conor."

Eric snapped his head around, ready with quick retort. But in seeing the weariness in Gawain's face, he rested his hands on his lord's shoulders instead. Scratchy war tunics chafed their skin, leather strappings dug at their calves, the tensions of war rose tumescent within them.

"I say it again: well ye've led the Caffertys, and well ye deserve your rest. Ye know I be no man to beg, but I would give ye my life, Brother." Flush rudded his cheeks as he gouged his fingertips into Gawain's shoulders. "Let me fight this battle. Once more I beg."

Steel-blue eyes braced in deadlock. Gawain's golden torc shielded the light rays and bounced them back into the shadows. The deadlock grew more tense, and Gawain's eyelid began to pool thick with blood. And without their knowing it, their breathing matched breath for breath.

Finally Eric backed down. With a clenched fist he butted the edge of Gawain's chin. It was a gesture he hadn't done since they were boys, a gesture he hadn't dared try since Gawain was made king.

"Death, they tell me, is but the beginning of a new life," said Gawain. "Ye would deny me that honor?"

"No, but that life only comes after death's pain is fully tasted."

"Would ye have it come quickly? Or would ye have it knock on my door, slowly, day by day. Already I eat little, my pallet is drenched by night, and even now the battering ram inside me is waiting."

Eric rested his head on Gawain's shoulder and gently stroked his graying hair. "Brother," he whispered as he let his arms fall around him and pulled them tight. "Brother," he whispered hoarsely once more.

Gawain drew away. "We understand each other?" he said.

"Aye, Brother. Too well we understand each other."

Chapter 20

Clan McColym gathered at the clearing that marked the border of Finucane territory. Tormaigh pulled his coarse mantle around him, thinking it better to save his otter cape for later when they were feasting and a show of wealth appropriate. But to declare station and show king's coming, he wore his coronet of hammered gold inlaid with delicate fretwork and inset with amethyst.

His cheeks sported high color and his heart quickened with anticipation. "Ye are sure," he said to Lochobar, "Brigianna is safe? It's ten cows I want for her hand, and so far I've not seen them."

"Ten cows. An honorable price for one as fair as our Brigianna." Lochobar's indulgent tone comforted Tormaigh, who grunted in agreement and turned back to his own thoughts. Ten cows would greatly increase his honor among the tribes. His sons stood beside him, seething in the fitfulness of youth and ready to storm Tighmohr if the Finucane proved stubborn; Clan McColym had honor and would bring it to call if need be.

Adjusting his coronet so it was markedly noticeable in his tumble of graying curls, Tormaigh waved his men behind and his women to the side.

Lochobar stepped into the clearing with him, unbearably weary from lack of sleep and dark hauntings that plagued his dreams. He adjusted the folds of his longplaid around his neck. Even the reflection of brilliant reds, oranges, blues, and yellows against his sallow skin didn't bring his color up. A deep frown creased his ancient brow. He put a hand on Tormaigh's shoulder as if to steady himself and, instead, felt reassured by his chieftain's simple faith. Quietly they waited.

Soon a white horse, streaming jets of hot breath, appeared. Blue mantle, bordered with metallic needlework, spread out behind the proud rider, tenting the rump of his mount. Ermine tails, caught in winter's trap, when they were their whitest, bordered the cloak and bounced as the man rode. Lance rested against black boot, and the butt of it sliced the sky, ripping the heavens apart to herald his coming.

Adjusting his quiver, Tormaigh watched the approach with a nervous eye. He lifted a hand to his mouth and trilled the warbler's call. His men spread out to line the edge of the copse at strategic intervals. Now brush swelled their ranks and made them appear more numerous.

Finucanes spread out in phalanx behind their king and filled Tormaigh's vision as far as he could see, but to his relief, only the king rode. He came within fifty paces and stopped. Now both McColym and Finucane advanced to hold the line between them at ten paces; their priests remained a respectable distance behind.

"I come in peace, mighty Erin of the Finucanes. I come also to save my honor. Ten cows it was we agreed upon in exchange for my Brigianna. Beltaine is gone, Lughnasa is past, still I am without my cows."

"By what right do ye speak of honor, O Tormaigh of the Colyms?" Erin railed. "By what treachery do ye betroth your daughter to my clanhold, then be so bold as to claim your bride-price without sending her? Bah!"

Erin reined his steed in tight and with his right hand lifted the lance from its mounting. He drew it back, and the blade spun through the air with a deep-throated rumble to dig turf at Tormaigh's feet.

Tormaigh jumped back in alarm. "Brigianna is not here?" he cried, whirling around to face his druid. "Brigianna is not here?"

Lochobar stood stiff as death from shock and began to babble. Inside his head, thoughts crashed into each other with wretched force.

Wasn't Brigianna with that blond warrior? Didn't he take her with him to his clanbind? Hadn't . . . ? no . . . no, he admitted, that was when the dark cloud hovered and the vision became distorted. Bah! That is the trouble with visions: you cannot always tell what they are or what they mean, and when you wake from the trance . . . the memory is gone.

"I demand answer!" Tormaigh shouted and bolted forward to grab his druid by the cowl. "I am in no mood to await your ecstasies or listen to your babblings. Give me my daughter. Give me my cows."

Lochobar was about to speak, but Erin's hand shot up to stop him. "I'm not one to trifle kindly with treachery. Priest? How say ye?"

Before Lochobar could defend himself, the Finucane druid stepped forward. An ascetic, who lived the life of the hermit, his dirty, ragged skins stood out in stark contrast to his king's finery.

"Speak, Angus," the Finucane demanded, but the priest only stood by the horse's side, waiting. After a moment of strained silence the Finucane cocked his ear and leaned to the side. Silver-tinged brows shot up. "The Wise One tells me we have important matters to discuss."

Erin took his lance from a runner and fitted it to its holding, then announced in resonant tenor, "I bid ye a thousand welcomes, Tormaigh of the McColyms. Follow me. My men will see to your needs and my women your baths. We meet again at dinner."

With his feet thrust forward and his right arm braced against the lance for ballast, the Finucane turned his mount around. Lines that parted at his coming closed again behind his billowing cape.

"To Tormaigh the McColym," Lord Finucane said as he raised his horn high. "May our clans dwell in safety and may our lands lie in peace. May your daughter's womb be fertile as the valley that lies between us and bring us many warriors."

Warriors resounded agreement and Tormaigh nodded, graciously lifting his horn. Warming to the strong drink, mellow and pungent from the oak in which it aged, he set his horn down and signaled for more. His women were huddled off to the side with Erin's own. Fiona looked especially lovely, so frail and delicate, compared to these statuesque women with ample breasts, wide hips, and gaudy finery, he mused as a maid filled his horn. Perhaps I have been too withholding; with more jewelry my lovely Fiona could stand among those women as their queen.

As Tormaigh walked the line behind the Finucane, he was awestruck at how vast the land was. The dun was well fortified. Inside the longhall he was warm and comfortable, for there were no fickle drafts coming through fallen chinks as in his wattle and daub. This hall of fine-hewn wood, hardened by its years, was strong enough to withstand the raging winds that blew in from the North Sea. Rock work, shaped by adz and patience, secured huge lodgepoles to the earth. The vaulted ceiling was spectacularly timbered, not covered with simple thatch as most of his dwellings were, and the triangle bracings supporting the roof formed air holes to divert the smoke. His own lodge had one central air hole, and sometimes the smoke chose not to leave. He had thought himself a wealthy man, but compared to this Finucane, his wealth was shoulder high.

He stood and raised his drinking horn overhead. "To Erin, Lord of the Finucanes, and to me own fair Brigianna. May the pledge that lies between us seal our blood. May blood and land and goods and bounty course their way between us like a mighty river and bind us in current to one accord."

He rumpled graying curls, eyeing clan to see if his toast was well received, then fell back to his seat and leaned over. "And now, m'lord, where is Brigianna? What sport is this ye play with me?"

"It's more important matters we have to discuss than the bedding of your daughter," Lord Finucane said sharply as he tore a string of meat from the bone and swilled it in his sop. Juice trailed down his newly combed beard, and a page leaned forward to fastidiously wipe it away.

Tormaigh gripped both sides of his coronet and his nostrils flared. But Erin staved him off. "No insult intended, m'lord. Now, harken."

"Our lord speaks well," Angus cut in, seated at the other side of the king's table on his pegstool of judgment.

Tormaigh leaned forward, offering the wizened man his horn. "Say on."

But the priest brushed the brew away and cleared his throat with spring water instead. Setting his gourd back down with deliberate movement so to capture everyone's attention, he leaned forward on his blackthorn staff, exposing forearms twisted as his walking stick.

"You there! Priest. Lochobar, is it? Tell me what you see."

Fear yellowed Lochobar's green eyes as he fidgeted in his seat.

"Come, brother. I ask in peace. Is it not priest's duty to lay down his life for his people if need be? Is it not the people who must ultimately interpret the dream? Do not be withholding, for if we are brothers in blood, we have nothing to fear. If the gods have made dwelling place within us, are we not then committed to each other?"

"Of a truth," Lochobar warily admitted. Unused to being backed into a corner, he forced his weary bones to stand. Facing the Finucanes, who numbered so many, brought a nervous edge to his voice. "I see my beloved Brigianna safe in the arms of a tall warrior. I see her again with his women, well attended. But . . . I see a black cloud that overhangs them all, and of times in that black cloud I have seen banners of red like rivers of blood," he admitted in raspy voice.

Murmurs of surprise rippled through the lodge. Babes were quieted at the teat, and chunks of half-eaten meat were set aside as the clans shouldered forward and strained to hear. Amabel and Fiona huddled together in the darkness, and around them glowing coals of curiosity burned like dark fire.

"Rivers of blood swell in number, and banked on each side like a huge forest, dark men, cloaked with iron, move like shadows. At times I see them coming in great waves like the sea, for they are horsemen, fierce and terrible, unlike any we have ever seen."

"Ye did na tell me this!" Tormaigh shouted. His coronet slipped and he caught it midair. Bandying it in front of him as a weapon, he challenged his priest. "None of this I know!"

Lochobar's bony shoulders sagged. "Perchance it is not given me to tell you all," he muttered, rubbing his arms to stave off his chill. Speculation among the clan burst out like the chatter of blackbirds, and Angus pounded his cudgel on hard-packed flooring to bring back order.

"Your portent of death is not amiss, for I, too, have seen visions. Gods be fickle, for it is not given each man to see everything. Only that wee bit which concerns him most."

Lochobar sat back down, and reverently awaited Angus's words.

"Black clouds cast the spell of death, and the banners are the blood of the innocent. A man they call the Pig Man rapes Mother Ireland even as I speak. His powers grow stronger, his slaughters more merciless. Chieftains fall in his wake, clanholds lie masterless. These he offers protection. But this fealty is based upon fear, and as his numbers swell, his bloodpath grows wider. No man can track him, for he is more cunning than the fox. No man can face him for he wears the face of many. No man can single him out for he walks among us."

"Who is this man?" Tormaigh ventured in a quavering voice as he lifted his horn. A maid behind him obediently filled it. The Finucanes make a good brew, he thought in passing. He must remember to ask them about it later. "Does he not fight upon the field of honor?"

Erin decided to level with them. "Hardly!" he said. "He rides a mighty war horse and girds himself with iron, yet he attacks in a whirlwind, like faeries riding the night. He's not an honest man, nor does he offer fair fight. My women keep close to the valley floor, and my scouts ride our borders daily. My priest has come out of hermitage to give counsel. And even as I speak, no man knows he where will strike next. But, surely, ye have heard of Black Dhurmod, the one they call the Pig Man?"

"Not so. We traveled far to the west, where rocks and windswept reaches groan like a barren woman," Lochobar admitted. "It is not a land for which men fight. Seldom do raiders go there."

"Well said. But rich valley and great forests are worth the taking, especially if they harness access to ports of trade with raiders from across the sea." Erin paused to stroke his well-combed beard. "But fearsome as Black Dhurmod is, he's not the greatest of my troubles."

"How so?" Tormaigh eyed both priest and king with suspicion.

"The valley bed ye bargained your daughter for is in jeopardy. A young bullock was found, belly slit and hung on a stake, at the eastern border. This is not the work of the Pig Man. Wicked as the Pig Man is, he kills to eat," Erin said evenly. "No, this is the work of—"

"Caffertys!"

The husky voice rang out from the back of the lodge, startling Erin so much so he stopped midsentence, shocked by this absolutely unheard of offense. Heads turned, women exchanged wary glances. And Lochobar's slitted green eyes strained through the haze to find its owner.

The Fian emerged from the shadows, naked to the waist.

Firelight danced flame in his flaxen hair and his blue eyes were lively with passion.

Stunned, Lochobar slumped forward onto the table. Standing before him was the man of his visions.

"Son? My son?"

Erin Finucane's voice was weak with emotion as he stretched a welcoming hand forward. Firelight, dancing planes, and shadows in capricious mirth left no doubt to all watching that he and this Fian were one. What was graven on one was graven upon the other. Worries of time had carved deeper passages on Erin's features, but the even brow, narrow bridged nose, and slate-gray eyes were as mirror image.

"Aye, Father. It is I."

Erin rushed out from behind king's table. With an effusive, backslapping embrace, he welcomed his son back home. Timbers rattled as the clan burst out in joyous shout and hurried up to them.

Tormaigh, seeing the blur of faces before him, moaned, and fell forward. "My cows! My cows!" he wailed as his forehead butted hard wood. Shamed, Fiona hung back in the shadows and clung to Amabel for comfort.

"When I get my fair Brigianna, ye will get your cows," the Fian whispered with a smile beneath his mustache, just before he was pulled away by bear-hugging men, embracing women, and trews-tugging children.

"If what ye say be truth, we are caught in double net," Lord Erin said in the narrow confines of his private quarters as the Fianna pressed against him. His champions held their fighting weight well, keeping fit for war with games. Hugh stood at his side, always ready. And Niall was even considered for the crown, though nothing yet had been said.

The McColym, surly from being wakened out of drunken slumber, was so short by comparison that a Finucane champion could issue a challenge, swirl a blade at shoulder height, and miss him completely. But he was wiry. All his men were quick, darting bowmen. Their priest looked strangely out of place. Tall, ungainly, extremely thin, and those eyes: translucent as topaz. Erin's own priest, Angus, sat in a corner with eyes turned inward, as if the mundane matters of men did not pertain to him. Already thinking of the deer in the fields, no doubt. Erin mentally dismissed both priests and turned to his men.

"Ye are certain? After all this time the Caffertys march against us?" he asked the Fian. "Ye were given in fosterage as a peace token, yet they dare turn to fight?"

"Aye."

Erin waved his hand in irritation, and the sudden air current made rushlight play ghoulish shadows on grim faces. "No man can call this Pig Man to honest fight; he gnaws the warrior's pride like the wolf who weakens the herd before attack.

"Now ye tell me this rapine marauder is but a simple worry. Instead, Caffertys move west like scythe on the threshing field, intending to mow us down like grain if we do not pay them liege? Bah!" Lord Erin spat. "Caffertys were once our hounds. They think Finucanes will lick their heels? They think they can laugh at Pig Men as if they were fleas to be scratched? I am appalled. Is this the message Lord Gawain sends?"

"No, Lord. This is the message my runners have returned to me since I left Lord Gawain's side. I was sent to spy on your camp and assess your strength. On the way I discovered gutted cattle set as bloodbait at both borders. Lord Eric's men report that the call for blood rides high in the Cafferty camp."

Around him was the unmistakable creak of leather and of metal slapping iron-hard thighs as Finucanes turned to their arms.

Erin nudged the silver streak in his tawny beard. "They gut our cattle, spy our camp, raid our border, and call for blood."

"And your men, I see, are not unwilling to fight," Kevin said evenly.

Erin's bare feet made dull thuds against hard flooring as he brushed his long cape back over his shoulder. His loose breeches ballooned behind; he braced his fists at the wide leather gird hung loosely at his thinning belly. Breath came in anxious spurts.

"Kevin, my son. I must ask ye before witnesses, and I must know the answer ye give in the heart of my mind, whether it cries victory or death. Ye chose Cafferty allegiance at your majority and, thus far I have honored that request. Why did ye come back?"

Taller, and in mirror image, Kevin, son of Erin, stood before his natural father, the king, and gave word before witness. Word that, if failed, would be held against him and demand his death.

"Ye are my father. By your love and your loins I was given life. For that, m'lord, I cannot lift sword against ye."

Erin Finucane stroked his beard, all the while keeping his eyes steady with Kevin's. "Yet ye fight for Cafferty honor? There must be more to this than ye are telling."

Silence grew loud as the din of wardrums. Finally Kevin spoke.

"I suspect this be no small border raid."

Lord Finucane whirled around so that his blue cape billowed behind him. "Dismissed," he barked. "Hugh. Niall. Stand guard."

When the chamber was empty, Erin Finucane sat back on a bed of fine furs and expensive woolens. "Now, tell me all ye know," he said evenly.

Outside the door Kevin heard the unmistakable clank of iron.

Chapter 21

Three times the moon rose and set. Cagney, Eric, Rory, and Donny returned to camp. Gawain called council behind dark tarps, but Conor refused to attend. Instead, he scuttled about on secretive missions, weighing omens. Watching Conor and muttering complaints about makeshift accommodations in the rainy days that followed, the clan drew into itself.

Anxiously Brigianna waited for the warbler's call.

And when Lord Gawain summoned her, she came eagerly, hoping to relay her suspicions to him in private. But her pleading words fell on deaf ears, his disbelief turned to snoring, and she spent the night at his feet.

In the morning, on the way back from his quarters, she spied an egg that had been left in the ashes. Seized by sudden hunger, she pried it loose with a stick, then frowned as it went tumbling down the slope. She went running after it, but when she caught it, it was still too hot. Forming her skirts into a makeshift basket, she danced the egg around.

"Behold, the maid dances when the clan is still in mourning?" Hearing the voice, Brigianna spun around. "Dance on," Cagney said with an ingratiating smile. "I, too, have no taste for mourning."

"But for ye, Brian would live!" she accused and, immediately realizing the import of her words, came to an abrupt halt. The egg lolled in the sway of her skirts and fell to the ground with a thud.

"So, ye are brave enough to voice what others dare not?"

"Stand aside and let me pass," she bluffed, with a stomp of her foot.

"Knave. Do not forget to call me knave, remember. I am but the king's son and ye the lady who graces his bed. Still, ye call me knave."

"Knave!" she conceded sarcastically.

Suddenly he grabbed her wrist and yanked her to him. "Would ye scream, Brigianna? Look about ye, what do ye see? Your watchdog, Maire, tending little Rollie. Yvonia, there, pulling the last of the breads. Men sporting for battle. Grania, waiting her days and singing of Brian.

"Scream? Think better of it, Lady." His free hand found the nubbin of her breast, and his fingers gouged into her as he hungrily kneaded it.

She recoiled in revulsion, and with lusting laughter he pulled away.

"Would I really force ye in broad daylight with clan as witness? Come now, Lady. Should ye scream and men come running, what could I be saying in my defense? 'Ah, but the maid tempted me sorely, and imagine that, m'lords, the very maid who warms me own father's bed.'"

Brigianna sucked in her breath and waited.

"Ah, that's better. Now, do sit down, for 'tis such a fine day." With gloved hand he played the gallant gentleman. Having no choice, she sat on the grass and he sat beside her, reeking smells of fire and metal.

"For now ye may warm my father's bed," he said with husky voice as he fondled the tip of her single braid and then brushed it against her cheek, "but the old king cannot live forever, and when my time comes, I will treat ye as a woman should be treated. Do ye not fancy that?"

The braid fell from his hand; his flashing eyes met hers. "But for now, tell Father this. His people cry for a king to drive Black Dhurmod from this land; one who will solidify the forces of the central valley by taking a stand against

Finucane raiders. The people demand a king who will bring honor to the Cafferty name."

His face came down against hers, eyes wild as a winter's storm. "When ye warm old cold bones, tell the king he will not live to see his grandsons unless he does what he must. Force him to choose his successor while he is still living; force him to do it with his people as witness. And tell him more, Brigianna—tell him I stand waiting."

Quaking beneath his breathy passion, she pulled back, fighting her anger and shame. Her hand strayed to her boot and, in the pretense of adjusting it, rested upon the ravenfeather hidden there.

"I stand waiting," Cagney repeated, with eyes as sharp as an angry blade, then walked away. She watched him go, her hand still on the ravenfeather.

Overhead the sky turned dark, as if a violent storm were brewing. Soon stormclouds parted, slashed wide by a silver sword. Out of them came hordes of angry, black-clad riders.

Her hand fell from her boot, and once again the sky turned bright and sunny. Puzzled, she put her hand back to the ravenfeather.

But the vision had cleared. Riders had passed by before she could see their faces, leaving only an unsettling foreboding behind.

Maire's dark silhouette stood over her. "People talk, Lady, and I'll not be having Lord Gawain's name sullied while it's under my care ye be."

Brigianna stood to follow Maire back to the fires, but as she got up, her hand brushed the edge of Kevin's comb, and loneliness rained anguishing torment upon the window of her heart. "Kevin," she whispered within.

Catriona greeted them, blue eyes round with terror. "They say it be Black Dhurmod's men." Little Rollie went running to his mother's skirts as an old crone with sour breath and wizened eye stepped up to Catriona's side and whispered,

"The lad's belly slit. Dhurmod haunts us as fey, for he cannot be found and we are under a terrible evil—but Finucanes are men that can be found, and to fight them will bring back balance." Her eyes blazoned black, and her splayed hands shot up over her eyes. "Fight the Finucanes and curse this fey. Drive away this Pig Man."

The murmur of assent among the women was broken by Yvonia's cry. "There ye are, Lady Brigianna! Ye must not wander to the fields," she cajoled, and Brigianna fell into her embrace like a wagging cur.

"What has happened?" she asked, leaning against the heaving bosom.

Features of fire turned to ice. Baffled, Brigianna drew back. "'Tis the Pig Man's doing!" Yvonia pointed her finger. "Look! Over there!"

The babble of women huddled around the thick oak parted as Brigianna and Yvonia approached.

"Doughall!" Brigianna screamed. Her hands shot upward in helpless plea. "Oh, Doughall, oh, begods, oh, dear brother mine. No, no, no."

"What says she?" the old crone asked sharply.

"Is it the lad's name she calls?" said another.

"I do not know," came a third.

Too late she realized her grief should have been borne in silence.

Doughall McColym lay propped up against the tree, clutching his belly, outstretched hand lost in his own gore. Cut clean through the length of his abdomen, his blood gushed with arterial force and splashed down his legs. Even as Brigianna fell down beside him, the pulsatory fountain came slower and with labored effort.

Through his haze he saw her. His mouth tried to form her name. Quivering lips painfully tried to force it. "B . . . B . . ."

Wretchedly Brigianna watched the last sparkle of innocent passion burst into sweet flame, and for brief moment savored the sweeting fleetness of memories shared but so easily forgotten. Then the doors behind those passionate eyes closed . . . forever.

"Doughall," she sobbed, feeling her life-force pulled from the palms of her hands to seep into the ground with his.

Cagney forced his way through the crowd to stare with disdain at the mutilated body now replenishing the ancient oak with blood.

"'Tis the work of Black Dhurmod, methinks," his young knave said.

"Aye," another chimed in, and soon the chant picked up pace. "Black Dhurmod!" they cried. "Pig Man! Pig Man!"

Cagney held up his hands. "Enough!" he demanded. "Who is this man?"

"No one knows, m'lord," the old crone called. "Doughall, herself there calls him."

Cagney turned to Brigianna. "How do ye know this fellow? Say on."

Just then a young boy came running up with a leather sack in hand. "We found this on 'im," he announced and thrust it at Cagney's feet.

The leather wrap fell open to reveal a chunk of wood, carved something like a nose piece. Leather wadding, bound with thongs, lay beside it. Protective padding for a shoulder or a hip perhaps?

"The Shameface?" Cagney exclaimed. "What be the meaning of this?"

The large abalone disk at Cagney's chest caught light in mesmerizing glare as Brigianna looked up, and in the boar's tusks dangling from his wide leather belt, shortsword and dirk, sharp-studded wristbands and thick shinguards, she saw an entire army. Turning white with fright, she remained silent.

Cagney yanked her to her feet, his blade to her throat.

"Lady, ye came to Cafferty clanbind by Fian's honor; Lord Kevin named your place," he said, nicking at her with the point of his blade.

"It's honor I had, but honor now forfeit for Cafferty clanbind."

Cagney's brows shot up as he drew her closer. "Ye are fugitive? For ye, Caffertys are to be avenged? Speak, Lady, who, then, is this man?"

The blade pricked blood. And she shook involuntarily, from the base of her skull to her toes. "My brother!" she cried.

"And ye?" he demanded, pressing his blade harder against her throat.

"Brigianna McColym, daughter to Tormaigh, slated to wed the Finucane."

Cagney burst air like the wind had just been knocked out of him.

"Curse Crom!" he snarled and with the butt of his knee kicked her.

The old crone rushed forward with splayed-out hands. "A fey! Ye have cast a fey upon us. We must be avenged!" Other women followed, jeering insults. But men hung back, fearful.

"Father," Cagney announced as he marched through the tent flaps, past Gawain's guard, and threw Brigianna to the floor, "may I present Lady Brigianna McColym, soon to be a Finucane, I understand."

The look on Gawain's face made Cagney quake. "And ye knew it all along?" he shouted.

"Aye" was Gawain's slump-shouldered confession. "I thought to offer the maid as truce. I thought that if I offered her in clanbind, I could, well, spare bloodshed."

Incredulous, Cagney stared at his father. "Ye what? Ye offer a woman that war may be avoided? A noblewoman, no less, and the very one slated to marry their king?"

Lord Gawain stood his ground. "If they value their honor and the contract they have made for her life, then aye, we have bargaining power."

"Have the ravens racked your brains, Father? Ye've now

given the Finucanes good reason to slaughter all of us before sunrise."

Murmurs rippled through the crowd. Eric and Donny spilled inside the tent and stopped short. Grania, who had been sharing Gawain's couch only moments before, scuttled to the shadows, eyes wide. Harkers relayed the message, and soon it carried through the camp: they had been betrayed.

Cagney the Brave turned to face the council of lords gathered soon there. "What king is this who thinks to decrease our borders by turning his cheek!" he shouted in the full voice of battle challenge, and his gainsay was carried from earshot to earshot throughout the camp.

"Cagney Cafferty, ye are bone of my bone and flesh of my flesh," Gawain cursed through clenched teeth as the wellpool above his eye thickened. Instinctively he reached an arm out to steady himself. In the shadows Grania's brows knotted tight in confusion as she stared at husband and son.

Trapped, Gawain hurtled a wad of spittle that landed in front of Cagney's feet. "Ye are no son of mine. Ye rally my men to stand against me, and ye are out for blood, and that blood set against me, your king."

"By what treachery do ye speak? I stand here before your council in open gainsay. How dare ye accuse me of treachery! Why, your scruples put even that Pig Man to shame!" Cagney shouted.

Welts appeared on his cheeks as his dander rose. He cleared his throat and matched spit for spit in slimy mass that whipped Gawain's calf.

Lord Cafferty drew back as if mortally wounded. Cagney tossed his head back in silent jeer, and his voice grew low.

"Did ye know, Father, the Shameface is the Lady McColym's brother? Fit-looking as any of us—and the mask a disguise used to spy on us? But ye needn't worry, for 'tis bitter end he met. My men found him belly slit like our cattle. Some say 'tis by Pig Man's hand he fell, and even now your wailing women are babbling that we are bewitched and doomed by his hand. But look, Father. What say ye to this?"

Cagney snapped leather glove against his thigh, and his knave rushed forward, skidding to his knees in front of his king, and with head trembling and eyes lowered, held up his arms. There was a collective intake of breath as all eyes stared at him in disbelief. The longknife found on the Shameface still dripped blood. Stuck to it, in matted strands, was the torn fragment of a Finucane longplaid.

"Now do ye doubt that the Finucane is your enemy?"

Calls for blood rang out. Hearing his men and facing their anger, Gawain breathed deep to steady himself as the battering ram within wakened.

"Must I remind ye, dear Father mine, that the crown of a clanhold belongs to its people and that the lord only rules by will of his people and ye have withheld vital information from your council?" Cagney's low voice struck like a blade that hit home.

Shouting, Eric bolted forward from the shadows with itching fingers easing to the hilt of his longsword. And Donny jumped to his side.

"I speak not the truth?" Cagney whirled around, filling his barrel chest with deep breath. "Ye dare say I speak not the truth, Uncle?"

"Ye speak truth, the lord must rule by the will of the people. The ways of war are made by council and even the lord is subject to that council," Eric avowed with a steel-edged voice and backed off.

In the stillness that followed, Conor elbowed his way through the flaps and marched up to where Gawain stood. "My lord, I beg you," he began with beady eyes darting back and forth, "toss the Shameface in the field. Let the ravens pick his bones, let his blood warm the earth. Oh, Lord, listen to common sense!" he cried and threw himself at Gawain's feet. "Gods of my fathers be avenged. Through the boar and now the Shameface, they have spoken. We must replenish the earth. We must call for balance. The gods must be appeased. I beg you listen."

Gawain stood with his arms folded across his chest. "Beg me? Since when, priest, do ye beg?"

"Only for the Caffertys would I beg," Conor intoned piously.

"No!" Brigianna cried as she scuttled forward. "Lord Gawain, it cannot be so. Do not condemn my brother to the wanderer's grave. Do not let his soul suffer so. Purge him by fire, so he may live! Hear me, Lord. Conor speaks with double tongue. O Gawain, he is thinking not of Cafferty welfare when he speaks. I am bred to herbs and simples, I know by taste and by smell—I know what he has done!"

Hearing this, Conor's hand flew up and swacked Brigianna across the face so hard it knocked her to the ground. He fell over her, pinning her to the dirt as he rolled to her side. With his forehead to the earth, he slowly turned his head.

"You accuse me of poisoning Brian?" came his whisper beneath the mass of flowing robes. "Need I remind you of what it means to accuse a druid? Or the telling draft that follows? A simple, really, no more than cedar bark. But it does dissolve the bowels and death does follow shortly. So what matters the accusation if the victim dies?"

The look he gave her divided bone from marrow.

"I'd sooner ye eat pig shit than dirt," Gawain said, facing Conor. "Get up."

"Crom be praised, oh, Crom be praised," Conor babbled.

"Oh, begone," Gawain cursed, waving Conor away.

"Shameface aside, Lord, the Lady Brigianna is of grave concern to all," Cagney said evenly.

Gawain eyed him warily. "Say on."

"Your woman, Maire, is lax with her charge. And if the lady were to slip from our hands now . . . well." Certain his message had struck bone, Cagney continued: "The Lady Brigianna must be well guarded, for her flesh matters greatly. For to the victor her flesh matters even more. Yvonia is well schooled in such matters, trained well by Grania's own hand. With your permission I call her forth. Do ye oppose me in this?"

Gawain stared forward, eyes looking like chipped flint. "No."

"Fair said and sealed by witness, then," Cagney said as Yvonia was shoved into the tent.

Fingering a lock of copper hair, Cagney whispered, "Ye are to guard Brigianna well, my sweeting, and for that your reward will be great."

Yvonia's eyes flashed green fire as her talon-tipped fingers gripped Brigianna's shoulder.

Chapter 22

As they came upon increasing evidence of slaughtered wealth, battle furor grew hot. Shameface forgotten, Caffertys marched westward, invigorated by the call of blood. Some saw Gawain Cafferty as their true leader and clever king; others looked to Cagney as the Cafferty who would save them. But they marched united, determined to seize command of the central valley and to beat the lowly Finucanes like cur whelps beneath their feet. This grand show of Cafferty prow and power would make the Pig Man quail. And Caffertys would grow sleek on back fat.

Clouds revealed heavens ribboned in blue on this, the morning of battle. A grasshopper warbler swayed upon sedge, and behind him came the whinchat's call. Shamrocks pinked the fields, and the woodland apple was heavy upon the stem. Caffertys greeted this as an omen of victory.

Eager for blood, they spread out on the ridge. Families gathered around longpoles tied with bright banners that heralded station colors. Out in the field, where the men made sport in preparation for battle, these same colored banners hung from belt loops or lance rings.

Eric wore bright red, as did his son, Donny. Like Gawain, Rory wore deep blue. Cagney preferred yellow, gotten only when the broom, tansy, and chamomile were at their prime. Their mantles were embroidered with metallic yarns, and their shields shone as mirrors. But for safety's sake, when the actual battle took place, all fighting men would wear the Cafferty weave of red, deep blue, black, and yellow.

Brigianna's feet were hobbled together by a cord the length of a pace so she could still march. But her hands were crossed and tied at the wrist.

Now Cafferty women dragged her onto the field and threw her on the ground. Forcing her knees apart, they buried the lance blade in the earth between her legs so that the shaft held her prisoner. Already, she ached from her ungainly position. The only way to rest her head was to lean forward against the lance, and then there was no way to curl her legs. But as Caffertys pressed closer to the battle line, she became lost among them and part of the panoply of color bordering the field.

Dismally she watched men bid their families farewell. If they returned, they would celebrate life as if called back from the dead.

"Ye would think this a clan gathering or fine summer fair for all the bright banners," Yvonia commented as she dropped to the ground beside Brigianna and offered her a round of oat bread still warm and steaming.

"Beholden," Brigianna said. Hunching up to the stake and working around it, she tore into the bread, savoring its chewy sweetness.

Cagney rode up to them then, calling, "Good day, m'ladies. Bid me well." Brigianna clung to her shaft, fearful of deadly, prancing hooves. Boar's tusks dangled over Cagney's saddlebuck, and he wore his large abalone medallion. With a spate of breathy laughter he leaned over. "See ye tend the Lady Brigianna well."

Jumping up, Yvonia stood beside him, her long-nailed hand resting upon his hide-bound calf. She murmured in his ear, and his laughter turned deep-throated. A wry smile crossed his face as he bent forward to brush Yvonia's lips in a brief kiss.

He reined his mount forward a pace and, with a movement

quick as a hawk's dive, sliced off a clump of Brigianna's hair with his sharp palmknife. Yelping in surprise, she scuttled backward and discovered, in cunning wonder, that she could rest her hands on her ankles.

Cagney held her tresses to the breeze. "A charm to bring victory."

Yvonia watched him ride off. "More's the blood I've seen shed in sport as in war. Have ye ever watched a real battle, Lady?"

"No! . . . Yvonia? What happens if the Finucanes win? What then? And where is Kevin? Why is he not here?"

"By king's command, Kevin's always gone come summer, though it's not like him to miss something as grand as this." Yvonia tore off a heel of bread and examined it thoughtfully. Like Brigianna, she was seated with her legs out in front and her toes up. "Pogosh! Finucanes are no match for Caffertys. Why, look at how our numbers have grown. With that Pig Man about, settlers have been flocking to the clanhold like geese. Finucanes? Bah! Fat pigeons compared to a mighty hawk!

"Cagney the Brave be a fine warrior. And Lord Gawain the best of gainsayers. Have ye not heard him? There be none better, except for Kevin, perhaps. Besides, Conor portends victory, so what's to worry?"

Brigianna's own portents loomed dark above her: "Listen, Yvonia. What if? What happens then?" she pressed, trying to shove blackbirds from her mind. The Finucane king lay waiting; Kevin had not returned, Gawain had not spoken to her since Doughall's death. That left Cagney. She shuddered, pulling her cloak close even though it was a soft day.

"Perchance we lose?" Yvonia waved a bread crust in Brigianna's face. "Well, then, ye'll be warming a Finucane king and not a Cafferty warrior. And I'll be right there beside ye." She threw her head back in honest mirth, and copper curls ringed her summer-bared shoulder. "In times of war it's those that be old like the Grania who have cause to worry. Spark up, Lady, ye be of strong bone and round flesh. Ye'll not go a-begging no matter who calls victory. If this king be old as ye say, ye've nothing to fear. But even if he does win, he'll not last for long, and then, Lady, ye'll squat a hard and handsome cock in full measure! So hush, they are lining up, and I don't want to miss a word."

Finucanes and McColyms spread out on opposite ridges. The valley between was wide enough for the battle to take place without bloodshed if skirmish between champions or gainsays forced a forfeit. But it was too wide to hear the parlay, the very best part of battle, some thought. As champions came into view, both sides slowly inched forward.

Beneath green and white wolfhead banners, Erin Finucane rode his front lines, then circled back to dismount and stand in front of Kevin.

Tormaigh McColym stood beside them, bare-legged and in his leather kilt, quiver full and bow to his side. Niall and Hugh, both blond and even-browed, stood full head and shoulders taller. A heavy mace hung from Niall's muscular forearm; Hugh braced his double-bladed ax at his shoulder. Both men wore shortswords and carried knives in their leather girdles. Priests, unarmed except for tall walking sticks, knew well how to place the cudgel's brutal blow. Behind the ranks of fighting men, women and children dotted the hillside. An undertow of excitement bound them as with a silver thread.

Murmurings hushed as Lord Finucane stretched forth his hand. He met Niall's trusting eyes. Once again he wrestled with his fateful decision. Keeping Kevin under armed guard only afforded him more time, but in that brief time he had gotten to know his son, and now his heart was certain.

"Ye are prepared? Ye know what to do?"

"I stand ready to defend your honor, m'lord," was Kevin's reply.

Erin nodded, fingers straying to the large disk he wore

about his neck. Inlaid with beryl and carnelian, it hung from a chain made of interlocked squares, and he was never without it. There was a breathless gasp as he took it off.

"Would that your mother had lived to see this day. But fever took her, and shortly after that I pledged ye to the Caffertys. Ye be the only child of that union, and I had thought both my son and my wife be gone from me forever. But ye returned, and that of your own free will. Now time grows heavy; battle calls and a kingdom lies at stake. So now, with the passing of this medallion, a kingdom passes hand."

Erin's voice carried through the ranks to be rallied by heralds from earshot to earshot. Kevin, son of Erin, stood before his father, every muscle tensed in apprehension. Slowly, and with great ceremony, the Finucane slipped the chain over his neck and passed title.

Erin's eyes brimmed with tears long unshed. "Hear, Finucanes, hear me all. My son lives! Let it be known, I name him tanist, I claim him king. Pledge fealty to your king. I command ye."

Finucanes laid back in rank like grasses mowed by the wind. From across the field Caffertys stared in astonishment as the noise of the Finucanes' acclamation filled the valley like a drumroll.

Kevin fell to his knees. "Before I fight, before I die, I must know if my heart's wish has been granted."

Lord Finucane eyed Hugh and Niall, then balled his fist to his chest. Hugh and Niall balled their fists, placing them across their hearts, and Lord Erin said, "We three bear witness, it is as we agreed."

Kevin grabbed Erin's hand and began kissing it. But Erin jerked the hand away and placed it on Kevin's padded shoulder. "There be time for that later. Stand, my son. Fight valiantly and to win. Ye are invincible. Ye are Fian. Ye run with the gods."

Before Kevin could rise, Lochobar was at his side. "I beg you, take this also." And in a jerk of his hand he tore the sacred stone McColym loose and placed the amulet around Kevin's neck.

Tormaigh lunged forward. "Pray tell the meaning of this?"

Lochobar put out a waxy hand, and Tormaigh drew back to glower at the sacred stone suspended by a single golden chain.

"My dear friend," Lochobar beguiled. "Are we not on Finucane land?"

The McColym scratched his head and nodded.

"Are we not under Lord Erin's protection? While on this soil, does not his god watch over all? Including us?"

Tormaigh's wide eyes gave silent agreement.

"Does not Kevin the Kind march into battle on our behalf?"

Once more Tormaigh was forced into agreement.

"If the champion marches to war protected by more than one god, does he not double his chances?"

"Enough!" Tormaigh put both hands over his ears. He braved a smile, but worry spread over him like the pox.

Erin raised his hands, and Finucanes stomped their approval.

"Look well upon this crown," Erin said to his son and future lord. "Come evening, when we are back at Tighmohr feasting and Caffertys have become but smoldering ashes, it will be yours."

Gawain Cafferty took a deep breath and drew himself up to full height. He put one sandaled foot forward, planted his longspear upended in the earth as a walking stick, and held his leather shield close to his chest. Above him the colors of his gold and red banner fused together like a crimson sunset. Wind whipped the folds of his red, blue, black, and yellow clancloth, and the scratchy wool chaffed the nape of his neck.

Like an animal, he sniffed the wind and spat.

His heart felt like an unused cistern overgrown with

moss. To Grania he had said fare-thee-well. To Lady Brigianna he said nothing. For the aching emptiness in his loins he had no answer. For his sons he had donned full battle dress, standing firm as the mighty oak. For one last show this Cafferty would rise in towering strength.

Behind him Caffertys bandied their battle cry. As he marched across the field to enter the arena and call challenge, the war cry began. Its undulating pull matched cadence with Gawain's silent footfalls.

Now came the ululating cry of women. Heads thrown backward and palms covering mouths, tongues darted in and out fast as hummingbird wings.

Even above that rose the din of drums, tympans, ironware, shields thrumming, feet stamping, and children crying. Then, with a short tantara from Eric's horn, the noise clipped to an abrupt halt.

From the Finucane lines three men stepped forward.

Lord Erin rode his white mare, now masked with red eyes edged in fanciful blue lines. His blue cape unfurled like tapestry to reveal its border of Finucane colors: orange, blue, and yellow. His lance was upended, its staff end butting the fitting in which it lay. His wrist was turned and ready to throw. A very small man walked to his side, lost in the shadows of the horse. Behind them Angus the Wise placed his pegstool of judgment upon the battlefield of honor and sat down.

The two warriors spread out, and their champion stepped forward. He was well armed: pike and broadsword, dirk, and palmknife hidden. His tunic fell to his knees, his loose breeches billowed about his ankles. He wore no plaids. Instead, he wore a scarlet hood.

He raised his pike, and Gawain beat his chest. At that signal men behind him beat upon their shields and stomped their feet upon the earth to show they were not intimidated by the hooded one.

Din came to a crashing halt and all was still. Then, overhead, came the lone cry of the raven. Soon the whirring of wings filled the air in pregnant crescendo as ravens of war began to gather.

Gawain prepared to claim the first gainsay. He had spent the night rehearsing his lines. Lying upon his pallet and drenched in despair, he had ransacked his brain to think of the perfect line. He had done it before, many, many times, in his youth. Then words slid off his tongue like slippery elm warmed in honeycomb, trickling their way into the hidden crevices of a challenger's mind to slowly turn the disposition.

Ah, yes, he was the best there was, but could he do it again?

"We Caffertys grow like the sands of the sea, our numbers increase like stars in the sky, our fame spreads to the four corners of earth to be winged in glorious height by the voice of the wind. Daily our ranks swell. Who will protect us? they cry. Who will defend our honor? I will, says I. Mighty Gawain of the Caffertys. For ye scudding Finucanes are but a little island. A sneeze in the sea, a whiff of gods' breath, hardly to be noticed except when the tide is out." He stopped to draw himself up to full stature. "This valley be ours!"

There, fair gainsay for openers, Gawain thought and awaited repartee.

"Pith!" the hooded warrior raged, ramming the butt of his pike into the ground. "We Finucanes are a mighty river. We swell our banks, seas cower at our coming, for they can hold us no more. Ye Caffertys are no more than fish in roe. Your bellies grow soft and ripe for the taking. Stand aside, I say. This valley is ours."

Behind them din rose and fell with each chanting. But the caprice of the wind played haunting tricks, funneling frenzy in whirlwind, only to misplace it farther afield. Dismayed, both lines inched forward.

"We are mighty bulls in your presence, our horns are like great spears ripping the belly of the sky, thunder and lightning are our toys. Flame snorts from our nostrils, the boar quakes at our coming. The girth of our chest is like the spreading of the chestnut, our feet trample all who would cross our path!" Gawain shouted. "Stand aside, Finucanes. Ye are but spitbugs swaying on sedge. We trample ye when we feed and not even notice."

"Hargh!" the hooded warrior yelled, and the din from Gawain's gainsay quieted. "Your horns lie between your legs, shriveled and useless, like peasecod in fall. Your mighty pike, with its once proud, rounded head, turns away. A cowardly, squiggling worm it is. Your women grow fat with disuse. Their breasts hang like empty udders, wombs swing like discarded hammocks, your old men whine like women before the fire. But we Finucanes birth our babes with sword in hand. They tumble from our wombs running to battle. Our women do not sough like the wind. No! Finucane men are quick with the sword and just as quick with prow stick in bed. What have we to do with ye? Stand aside, I say. Forfeit honor that mercy may be granted and life spared."

Gawain stepped back a pace and circled around; his eye began to throb from pressure. The warrior was closing in. Shouts between each insult were getting louder; the high-pitched wail by which they were sustained was getting longer. Now his chest hurt and his breath came short.

"I can't even hear!" Brigianna complained. "What is happening?"

"I cannot tell," Yvonia answered. "One minute the gainsays go one way, and the next the other. Perhaps if I slither down on me belly like so, I can hear the challenges better. No one will notice."

Yvonia, engrossed in the stageplay before her, slowly inched the green on her belly. Brigianna saw her go, and a tremor of excitement swept through her. Judiciously she kept her eyes lowered, feigning interest in the champion's call. At the next clamor she hunched forward to undo the brooch that held her cloak secure. And with a shake of her head to camouflage her action, she let the cape slide off her shoulders to spread over her knees. Scuttling forward and bending her knees so that she could get her hands and feet together, she pushed its edges down over her boots, all the while keeping a careful eye on Yvonia.

Slipping beneath the folds, she leaned against the pole and fished for her knife. It was dull from disuse, but with consistent slicing she was able to cut the cord and break the bonds.

"Yah!" she shouted in praise at each scathing challenge, while beneath her cloak busy fingers worked away.

"Surrender before we crush ye beneath our feet. Ye are mealworms, unfit for human consumption. Maggots breeding in the rot of refuse . . . "

Gawain faltered; he strained forward, trying to see what his ears suspicioned. His mind blackened, and the words he so carefully rehearsed suddenly escaped him. The battering ram within reared its ugly head, and sweat drenched his palms. Behind him he could feel his warriors shouldering forward. He opened his mouth but no words came.

"Finucane soar above this land like peregrine falcons, watching ye weaken," the hooded warrior hissed between clenched teeth. "Your sons quarrel among themselves, nipping your heels like wolf pups, feasting upon your carrion while it still walks. Your men lie ready to kill ye, should ye fail to bring them glory on this day. Mighty Gawain, your foolery scares me not."

"What's this?" Gawain bellowed as he staggered backward. Temper swelled his split eye and pounded his temples, drowning out reason and calling forth bloodlust.

"Ye would dare call this Cafferty a braggart and a coward?" he raged. "Enough of word games. Prepare for battle; I call blood."

"Nay, Lord, I will not. 'Tis a brave fight ye would call,

for ye are my mentor." Slowly the Finucane champion reached for his scarlet hood. "I know ye too well: ye would not be here but for sons who force your hand and men who nip your heels. May my blood father forgive me, but I cannot slice the hand that fed me. I cannot harm the chest where once I rested safe and secure, because ye were a mighty warrior and I loved ye as father. I cannot harm a hair upon that hoary head so dear. Father, Father, can ye not hear my heart crying? Can ye not hear it bleeding? I beg ye, oh, begods! Do not make me do this."

As he jerked off his hood, Gawain's breath sucked in to lock him in gripping spasm, and he fell forward in astonishment.

"My son and my lord!" he cried as he slumped to his knees. "Gods grant us mercy. What treachery possessed us that we meet in battle? Ye are the son of my heart, Lord Kevin. I cannot lay sword against ye."

Like the beaten dog of war groveling before his master, Gawain fell to all fours. Slowly he lifted his head, ready to face the sword if it must come. For by rights Kevin could lift it, and better it was to die in dishonor than to live in disgrace.

But before death came, he would look once more upon the face he loved. Once more his eyes would behold the son of his heart.

"Kevin? Kevin!"

Tossing her cape aside, Brigianna scrambled to her feet and ran out into the open field. Her heart ran with the swiftness of the deer, eager to fall into his arms. "Oh, Kevin!" she cried. "Kevin!"

Soft leather boots, molded to her feet like a second skin, gave wing to her flight. Yet even as she ran, the distance between them seemed to pull them apart, like a thousand yesterdays stretching out forever.

The gap grew wider with each footfall. Suddenly she stopped. Her brows pulled back as her face knotted up in horror. And her scream cut across the fields like the wake of the wind.

Chapter 23

The lone horseman waiting in the shadows of the copse saw the Cafferty fall to his feet in surrender, and beneath his iron mask his face blackened with rage.

Black horse and rider rode forward.

Wild eyes painted dark with gore, and nostrils streaming black fire, his charging stallion tore through clods of turf. Gloved hand flayed the air, crackling leather whip. With menacing speed he came, evil as death, even in the bright of day. His helmet bore large horns that ripped the sky's belly; his eye shield and nose brow were elongated to form a huge snout. Calling challenge, he ministered death.

Pig Man.

Air above him churned in whirlwind as he brandished his double-bladed ax. "AIEEEEEEYAH!" he yelled, stretching his arm forward for the kill.

Spittle clotted Kevin's throat when he saw him.

"The Pig Man! Father, run. Begods! Run!"

Kevin drew back his arm, throttling his pike, and prepared to throw. Biceps balled into round knots; torso twisted backward. Honing all senses on the charging horse, he awaited the exact moment to raise his arm and thrust his spear. Even as he saw him coming, he realized his pike was no match for Dhurmod's heavy armor. Death fingered cold chill across his shoulders, knotting shaking muscles and tying tight neck cords in a constricting grip. Gulping air, his left hand fell to his side to flip the snap of the scabbard. When the pike was thrown, he would toss the shortsword to his right hand and go for the dirk tucked inside his leather gird.

Brigianna saw Black Dhurmod crash through from the trees, and her feet took root beneath her. "Kevin!" she screamed, cast like a wax mold in stilled motion. And in the split of a moment the Fian was distracted.

But Gawain saw it all.

As he knelt in front of Kevin, knees spread wide and palms knuckling ground, he felt thundering hooves riveting through him like current.

He looked up and his face torqued in agonized surprise. Fear congealed the blood in his heart even as it beat. Even before it happened: he knew. Death had opened wide its vacant door.

Breathing fire, the mighty war horse closed in. Hooves, large as bronze disks, lifted with agonizing slowness to reach out and churn the earth's surface. Earth absorbed the impact with undulating swell, to cushion each brutal blow with boggy resilience and propel the razor-sharp hooves upward again. The Pig Man's enormous shoulders, encased in black leather stretched over thick straw padding and metal quilting, heaved and lunged as he rolled forward. Ax blade flashed through the air like a silver comet. The horse's nostrils widened, and from them Gawain could feel the sting of death.

He looked up and in his mind's eye saw a river of blood and a lone, dark rider. The vision flowed before him, even as it was happening. Ebony-shadowed riders ridged death's rim, and the valley once held in truce turned into a sea of blood. At their master's call armed men leaped into the froth. Trampling one another, dead men twined like withy to become rafts, jettisoned against one another by their own greed.

Dhurmod's arm shot forward, and a gloved hand ran the shaft as it slipped along the smoothly worn handle. The Pig

Man's battle-ax sliced the air with a sickening sound and whirled above Gawain's head.

Dhurmod's dark arm followed it to its end; his hand jolted in spasm as it heaved forward in the bolt of the throw.

Gawain looked up to answer the gleaming call of death. Hardened by fire and pain, like the blade that called him, he lifted his head to face death squarely as man to man. As a Fian, he would die with honor.

The horse's flaring nostrils showered stinging breath over his shoulders. The ebon belly swelled before him, dark as an iron wall that divided the living from the dead. Kneeling, but leaning backward now, he felt death press against him. The battle-warmed belly flashed over him as dark hooves caged his involuntary and sudden crouch.

All the vile ugliness this world possessed bore down upon him encased in black armor. His turgid eye filled with blood.

And Gawain Cafferty saw no more.

"Father!" Kevin cried and raised his arm.

But Black Dhurmod closed in and rushed by with such alarming speed that Kevin had no time to throw. Instead, in the briefest of moments he stared, awestruck in grisly horror.

Gawain's head was cut clean from his body. The ax sliced through the neck and, with the momentum of the throw, did a full three-circle turn before landing in the field.

Gawain's head flew upward, splattering blue sky in crimson comet before it fell to the ground and rolled away.

Landing upright, it stared at Kevin.

Headless, Gawain Cafferty knelt in the calm repose of the prayerful before he finally toppled over to fall in humble submission in front of Kevin, son of Erin, Finucane tanist, and now High Lord.

"Lord Gawain!" Brigianna cried as she snapped to life.

Propelled onward, she ran the slippery field, with her hands outstretched and her black hair streaming a ribbony whip behind her. She tumbled at a hare hole and scrambled to her feet, clawing rock and long grasses that blighted her way, screaming, "Kevin! Oh, Kevin!"

The Pig Man circled back to recover his ax. He drew the horse's head into its chest, making it snort and pull against itself, so that when he loosened the rein, it would lunge forward.

"YYYYYAAAAH!" he yelled in bloodcurdling revenge.

Spinning around, Kevin gripped his spearshaft, braced his feet, and twisted his torso. Eyes turned cold and sweat beaded his brow.

But instead of coming for Kevin, the Pig Man ran the field in a wide arc. He thrust his feet forward and spurred his steed to a full gallop.

Finucane and Cafferty warriors on each side of the swell held back as if snared by a fey. They watched, dumbfounded, as the Pig Man caught Brigianna on the run and tossed her into the air.

He reached down, but not far enough, and she was thrown against his leg at the side of the horse. Her feet dangled dangerously close to the horse's churning hooves. The Pig Man grunted and tightened his burly arm around her as he tried to pull her up. But the weight of his armor jilted him sideways, and once more she screamed in terror. The animal whinnied a raged response, and its shrill cry drowned out Brigianna's cry. Finally the Pig Man pulled her back across the saddlebuck and braced her firmly against him. She drew her knee inward to force the leg to the other side and straddled the horse. As she leaned against him, sharp spikes in his armor dug into her delicate skin.

The Pig Man shattered her senses with his bloodcurdling cry. As he drove his stallion across the field, she could hear his breath blasting against his metal helmet. The horse bore down, running directly for Kevin. But when the dark rider closed in, he slowed down and swiftly released a broadsword from its scabbard. Clumsily he heaved to the side and, with sword arm outstretched, impaled Gawain's head.

It gushed blood and its eyes sank into their sockets as he held it up.

Brigianna saw it and passed out.

The Pig Man pulled his horse around to face his stunned audience. He let out a robust peal of laughter and, very slowly, pulled off his mask.

"Cagney!" Kevin cried.

"Aye, Brother, it is I."

When the Pig Man raised the grisly head and his war whoop shattered the silence, his horsemen came from cover. With an echoing whoop they rushed the field, trampling both Cafferty and Finucane alike. Warriors ran against each other in confusion. Eric barked his commands and let his dogs loose. Whirling around, he became caught in the trammel of action. Tormaigh's men became the arrows they shot, and the battle that followed was swift and brutal.

Stench rose like dragon's breath that next morning as Kevin walked among the dead. Kinsmen by blood and kinsmen by fealty surrounded him: mutilated, crushed, and ravaged human beings, with their life-force gone.

The whirring of wings came from above as ravens of war gathered to feast. Tucking their wings, they edged the battlefield in strutting arrogance, making it look like a simmering caldron containing the sumptuous feast. Glowering, but determined, they were kept at bay by Max and his fellow guard dogs.

Kevin eyed the dark ravens with honest hatred and shook as he bent down over the form of one man. Even in the posture of death and with the boldly bordered blue mantle soaked in blood knotted around him, this man possessed a graceful air and regal bearing.

"Father," Kevin whispered as he knelt to gently stroke the matted golden hair. "So young I was when ye sent me out. I barely knew ye. Now I meet ye in death, and ye burden me down by this awful mantle ye've spread over me. I would I could be free of it. In my secret heart I would that ye had let me be just a common man to woo my lady love. But now, brother rises up against me, my lady lies in peril, my fathers are dead. And without a king to free them, my people are lost."

With deep anguish he raised shoulders high to shake away his baggage of sorrow, knowing it could not be part of the warrior's armor, and also, thinking in passing, how cold life was without it. Lifting clear blue eyes to the heavens, he threw back his head. Deep despair rose to keen the wind as he beat his chest and cried his torment.

"Ye will pay for this, Cagney Cafferty! Ye will pay!"

Chapter 24

Cast aside like dunnage, Brigianna sat in the corner of the war camp's makeshift quarters with knees to chin and eyes seething. Cagney stood over her with feet braced well apart and thumbs tucked into his belt. His cleft-toothed smile was cavernous; oily strands of hair spread over his shoulders like licking tongues of fire. And Conor stood by him.

Brigianna hunched back against the earthen embankment that formed one wall of the makeshift shelter. Leather taws, placed on her wrists and ankles when wet, were now dry and dug into her skin. Seeing her discomfort, Conor gave her a salacious grin. And Cagney's men gathered round.

Brigianna bared her teeth and spat.

Spittle landed within a fingerlength of Cagney's right foot. He blanched as it hit dirt, his expression as grotesque as when he wore his pig mask. Beside him flickering torchlight formed hideous shadows on the high cheekbones and narrowed eyes of his Pig Men.

A hedgerow of angry eyes stared down at her. "I warned ye, sweeting. I said there would be time when I bid ye come, and ye would come," Cagney began.

He dropped to his knees and traced his fingertip up her calf, resting at the recess of her knee. With outspread palm he kneaded her thigh and hot, hungry fingers worked upward. Her cape had been taken in the capture, and now her ripped shift exposed a length of leg. Dark lashes fluttered over closed lids as he slipped beneath its edge.

"I would die first!" She lashed out with hands like talons.

He ducked those claws by grabbing bound wrists. Sour breath fell warm upon her face as he took her by the shoulders.

"Come, sweeting, it cannot be bad as all that," he cajoled. "Do ye hear me women complaining? Aye, they complain not." His breath grew heavy with anticipation, and in his eagerness he gouged her shoulders.

"When ye have been ravished, and I have had my fill . . . ye won't be complaining. Aye, men?"

Guttural laughter bolstered Cagney's spirits, and in quick glimmer, before he turned to bring his mouth down upon hers, the edges of his lips turned upward and his eyes signaled victory. His mouth parted, lust already warming his groin. But the abalone necklace bit her skin as he coiled a yank of ravenblack hair and brutally jerked her to him.

And she cried in pain: "Let me go!" and tried to kick him.

Enlivened by her struggle and anticipating victory, he panted: "Give me men a little show of what's in store for them. Whet their appetites, sweeting. 'Tis sure they'll be having ye when I am through. Let them ache. Let them drool like dogs while I have my sport. I am a hungry man, Lady, reknown for my appetite. Women leave my bed well trained. Ye should be grateful for this honor." Hunger begged its quarter, and his eyes grew dark in concentration.

"Aye, well trained they are in the art of pleasing a man," he mused, thinking how they got that way. He brought his mouth down, and a fat, curling tongue snaked its way across her teeth. Forcing them to open, it slithered down her throat.

She thrashed backward. A scream welled up inside her like vomit. Cagney forced himself upon her. This time his lips were gripping as a snail's slipshoe. She swooned as the vomit curdled inside her. He, taking this as response to his touch, quickened his desire.

Around them men pressed closer, radiating the heat of lust.

Her bound fists were forced into a round ball, caught between her belly and his. His penis swelled to hard force, rising like a great wand of power. Pulsating, insistent, growing large and tumescent, it thrust against her. Ramming and rhythmic, cod pounded smooth cupped palms, and shuddering in sweet ecstasy, he moaned with pleasure.

She whimpered in childlike terror and jerked her head away. Tears streamed the corners of her eyes, and her face contorted in pain. But his viselike fingers gripped her jaw and forced her backward.

There was a notable shift in breathing among the men. Pressing closer, they slyly, but eagerly, reached for their crotches and rubbed their shafts in eager anticipation. And Conor was among them, scratching furiously.

Gasping for air, Brigianna finally got her face to one side. Cagney halted momentarily, and in that moment Brigianna's expression changed.

The vixen's smile tugged the corners of her mouth; her brows shot up like ravenwings, and beneath them sapphire eyes turned almond-shaped.

A wicked smile spread warm and winsome across her face. "Why should ye take by force what can be given in pleasure?" she purred.

Sweat beads rained her face as Cagney pulled back; his forehead shone like a warrior's shield to mirror his hungry question. Brows lifted their hairy curtain to reveal open eyes. Twitching lips tried to smile. Brows lowered again to shield naked want, and the warrior in pursuit of prey settled in to claim victory.

Torchlight veiled her flirtation as she raised her mouth. Her tongue darted a beckoning trail across parted lips.

They paused to stare at each other with searching eyes.

Drawing in a deep breath to savor the moment, he slowly leaned forward. With inviting smile she tenderly waited.

His eager lips met sweet virginity and softened to its kiss, delicate as the brush of a butterfly's wing.

Lust rose within him to escape his lips in deep sigh. His body relaxed and stretched out upon hers. Already hard and hot, he hiked a knee over her while fumbling his trews in search for the opening. His fingers found smooth, warm head, and quivering, he caressed himself, pulling silky liquid upward, thinking only of the soft, moist cavern awaiting him. His eyes opened, but they remained unseeing, for his mind had clouded in dark pools of sensuous delight. Pulling his penis forward, pushing foreskin back, other fingers reached out to caress her face. Mindless now, he lifted his lips to hers.

She welcomed him gladly, drawing searching lips into hers, waiting until he was lost in swilling darkness like a tight cocoon.

Then she bit him.

He bolted backward, wiping blood with the back of his hand. Spurting blood splashed her cheeks as his balled fist knocked her aside.

"Slut! Cur! Little bitch whelp!"

In raging fit he slapped her, welting her cheeks. His blow knocked her against the earth wall, and she cried out as she hit.

"Milk puppy! King's whore!" he roared as he heaved forward.

"I'll never bed the likes of ye, Cagney Cafferty!" she shrieked.

Cagney's men drew back in horror. Slowly, with straight faces and hooded eyes, they began inching toward the door.

"Keep your stinking hands off me, or I swear I'll kill ye, Pig Man. Lay me, Pig Man, and I'll lay a knife to your throat. Dare to sleep afterward, and ye'll sleep forever. Call me before clan, and I'll tell them what pig swill ye really are. I swear it!"

She clawed him then, and her scream ripped the wind.

Quick energy spent, she fell back with shoulders slumped and hung her head in shame. Sniffling back the tears, she brought her fists to her forehead. "I would die first!" she cried and turned away.

"Perhaps that can be arranged, my dear," a voice rang out.

Conor raised his hand, and for a moment time stood suspended. He nodded, then imperiously waved the men outside. They left like grumbling children. Next he drew Cagney aside. And Cagney braced his feet apart and crossed his arms to assume the position of greater power.

"The maiden speaks well. Perhaps we should honor her request," Conor began, sensing unformed questions edging his warlord's tongue.

"It is written that a leader of our people must be perfect, is it not?" Conor intoned and waited until Cagney, uneasily, nodded assent.

"The head of Gawain of the Deformed Eye now hangs upon the longpole, mighty Cagney the Brave. The valley lies quiet. Yours for the taking."

Now Cagney was at full attention; the abalone necklace sent a splash of color across his already ruddy face. His lowered brows did not conceal his consuming greed as he calculated his right to seize king's power. Conor's darting eyes missed nothing and, feigning humility, turned away to hide his tight-lipped smile.

"Say on," Cagney demanded.

"It is said that for a life taken, a life must be given, is it not?" Conor waited. Warily Cagney nodded assent.

"We have been led to this sacred place by Crom himself, and lo, his sacrificial stone awaits. Do we dare turn our back on such a great omen?" Conor made an expansive gesture to indicate the fields beyond. There, sacred stones burst through the earth with power from the hidden realm, guarding the monument of death.

"If Gawain's life was taken, then Brigianna's life shall be given. Then there is balance and the gods be pleased, for if Lord Gawain has found happiness beyond the seventh wave, how fitting his young lover should follow."

"No!" Brigianna cried out. "I am not Lord Gawain's lover. I am Brigianna McColym, virgin daughter to the Chieftain Tormaigh."

"Virgin?" Conor said, whirling around. "That I seriously doubt!"

But then beady eyes quizzed secretive chambers deep, and delight danced a glimmering trail as his smile widened. Turning back to Cagney the Brave, he erupted into canting ecstasy.

"Gods be praised! Bless the earth, for soon comes the harvest! What better time to pour blood in gratitude for earth's bounty and win back favor from an angry god . . . a god who turned his blessings from a forgotten people . . . a people who denied perfection and balance by demeaning themselves . . . and honoring . . . a king deformed."

Fervor quickly spent, he leaned forward to whisper, "And for deliverance, who will the people honor but Cagney the Brave? Not Cagney, common outlaw and father killer, oh, nay I say, but Cagney, hero to the homeless, who unified the central valley and brought peace. Ah, m'lord, you think on it. How dare the people question eternal wisdom that has brought us to this place where we may spiritually purge ourselves in sacrifice by the offering of one so fair?"

Cagney looked at Brigianna. She was listening to them, chin resting upon her knees, thick hair covering her, cheeks no longer radiant, and eyes no longer canny or vibrant.

Slowly the weight of Conor's words registered.

"Lady!" he cried in gushing rush and fell again to her side. "Say ye would be mine and spare your life! If ye would . . . I would even give ye my love . . . I would not even ask . . . more than . . . " he stammered, and the rest of his words caught in his throat.

"I would die first—father killer, fiend!"

But he grabbed her by the shoulders and pleaded. "No! No! Listen to me. Say ye will be mine. Let me spare your life!"

Stonily Brigianna looked right through him.

"Unhand me, knave," she said bitterly.

Soon Yvonia entered, carrying a gleaming bronze tray bearing a wooden bowl and a silver knife. Her manner was calm, almost serene, as with stately grace she set the tray down.

"Yvonia!" Brigianna cried, overjoyed to see her. Relief sent tears to her cheeks as she thrust her bound wrists forward.

"Quick. Set me free, for we must hurry and I've much to tell ye," she said with trusting eyes.

"Hush, hush, m'lady," Yvonia crooned condescendingly and with dazed calm held out the bowl. "First drink this. It will give ye strength."

Brigianna made a helpless gesture, and Yvonia murmured, "Of course, how foolish of me," as she set the bowl down and dropped to the pallet beside Brigianna with knife in hand. A grunt of satisfaction escaped Brigianna's lips when her hands were free, and she quickly worked them against each other to get the circulation back.

"Oh, how glad I am to see ye!" she cried, falling against Yvonia's wide shoulders and comforting breasts, thinking them haven, and burying herself in luxuriant, flaming tresses, aromatic with honey and woodruff.

Instinctively Yvonia put her arms around Brigianna and stroked her hair in crooning lullaby. But when a long nail caught in a snarl, she held the heavy shock and shook her head in dismay. Her finger traced the welts left there by Cagney's knuckles. Green eyes focused and then unfocused. A disturbed look crossed her brow, caused by a love of beauty and demanding faith that upheld symmetry and perfection in all things. Still glazed, she thrust the bowl in front of Brigianna.

"Bitter as last year's vinegar!" Brigianna announced after she had thirstily drunk the half of it and pointed to her ankles.

"I know, I know, but first, ye must drink all of this." Again, Yvonia pressed the bowl to Brigianna's lips in firm demand. Only after it was empty did she cut the cords binding Brigianna's ankles.

Brigianna smacked her lips, surprised by the metallic aftertaste of the deliciously sweet brew. Gratefully, she wriggled her toes, delighting in their movements, and like an entranced child, her thoughts became engrossed. Giggling, she splayed her toes wide, then contracted them tightly. Soon a horridly dull expression crossed her face.

"Yvonia?" she moaned, shaking a head that felt full of water, and turned, heavy-headed, to fit her spine into the pallet as if it were her coffin cot.

Shadows grew long; no longer were they timed to the torch. Turning slowly, like dark-robed dancing maidens, these shadows now bore faces. As she glanced away to stare at the torch, its fire seemed to slowly envelop her until it became a red coal glowing inside of her. She tried to raise a leaden hand, but could not. Sweat beads formed an opal band across her brow, and she whimpered in pain.

"Hush! The draft will make ye sleep, and if ye sleep, the woading will be easier, believe me." Yvonia's words reached her from beyond the seventh wave, and frowning, she tried to fathom their meaning.

Sadly Yvonia traced the welts upon Brigianna's cheeks. "Ye should not have fought him, m'lady. I would have shared him."

"Shared him?" The brew made her tongue as fuzzy as the white caterpillar and just as slow in turning. "I do na ken."

Yvonia's green eyes flickered like fireflies. She raised her head proudly, a satisfied smile crystalizing her porcelain features. "Why, Brigianna dear, Cagney has said I am to be his queen. Did ye not know? And for shame ye have marred that pretty face of yours and must go to the gods blemished." She let a long nail skim the length of her swanlike throat. "I would not have minded sharing my bed, if that be Cagney's wish. As long as I remain queen, of course."

"Yvonia! Ye would betray me so? No, it cannot be!"

Brigianna's outcry was but a plaintive whimper as she fell down the timeless tunnel of drugged slumber where darkness pressed against her.

She floated in and out of consciousness as a soul imprisoned in time, staring back at life as an expressionless haunting.

Her pupils were like minute specks of dust centered in bright blue rings. But at times her spirit escaped its granite prison, wafting in and out of the recesses of the tent, like a simmering summer breeze.

In her waking dreams ravens flew overhead, and one especially had brilliant, searching yellow eyes. Once it came very near, cocking its head with a questioning look.

At times she felt those ravens were perching upon an invisible limb, hovering over the still, darkened form of a creature once known as Brigianna McColym. At other times the ravens flew far ahead of her, circling in and out of a golden sun like dark ribbons embroidering the hem of a festival garment. Always this golden sun shone high above her. When she opened her eyes, it blotted out somber figures that moved like waking shadows in the background. When she closed her eyes, the sun remained bright and all-encompassing. She longed to enter this sun and soar with the ravens, for she thought, sure now, they must know the place gods go to drink, dance, make love, and create new worlds.

But cold granite bones pulled her back. In torment she cried out, and always her cawing thirst was slaked. She ignored its galling aftertaste, craving only the honeyed first taste that sent her soaring.

Catriona came in, followed by a procession of women burdened down with bowls, rags, rabbit skins, bog wadding, and an abundant supply of splayed hazel branches. Fermented, crushed woad leaves were mixed with limewater to form a blue paste that matched Brigianna's eyes. But when mixed with congealed blood, it became a sanguinary purple. Dressed in coarse garments, colorless as the hinterlands of winter, they worked in an orderliness born of ancient ritual. Ages had passed since Cafferty women had done this, yet under the sway of priestpower, they hummed as they went about their work as if sacrifice were an everyday event.

In drugged slumber Brigianna felt, rather than heard, their mensural incantations.

From her invisible perch above them, Brigianna's spirit watched as they ripped her tattered shift and cast it aside. Washing her down with absorbent rabbit skins soft as sponges, they buffed her skin with scratchy rags. Hazel splays made the dye run on her roughened skin at first, but as the paste thickened, colors held and designs began to take form. Blessings and cursings, history and madness; laughter and folly of a people were drawn upon her parchment skin. Cafferty women spared no mercy, observed no restraint. What was drawn upon her skin was accurate; obscene as it was inspirational. For them her flesh became the burning scroll that bore human agony and human hope to the gods.

Yvonia dipped her thumbs into the vial of blood and smeared a red trail upon Brigianna's welt-ridged cheeks. This she covered with woad, which, when removed, would heal the welts but leave a purple banner. With a frown born of honest dismay, she went to work on Brigianna's hair. Patiently she plaited it into tiny braids secured by bright bead baubles, as she had the evening Brigianna was presented to Lord Gawain. But now that hair was sadly matted and had to be combed, strand by strand, else there would not be balance, else there would not be perfection.

Yvonia worked patiently, determined that her artistry be worthy of gods' grace. Secretly Cagney had promised her the crown. With cunning grace she worked her powers over the women and brought them into line. For Cagney's sake. And hers.

Brigianna cried out as the women turned her over. Her thirst was immediately slaked and she sailed back to her invisible perch. Grania held the leather kilt that was to be her only garment, and Brigianna was twisted like a rag doll as Catriona and Maire tied it around her.

When Catriona reached for her boots, Brigianna's spirit cried deep within. Kevin's comb, her father's brooch, the silver knife, and the ravenfeather were tucked safely inside. They composed her cache of life, and she must take them on her journey through the netherworld.

Catriona stopped suddenly and looked up. The women ceased their chanting. A baffled expression crossed their faces. After a moment Catriona shrugged her shoulders and went back to work. When her expert fingers felt the bulges in the boots, they drew back, as if treading upon sacred ground.

In the dark of night when the others were gone, Grania came to whisper in her ear. "My lord, Gawain, has gone to his other world while I be forced to walk this earth in living death." She leaned forward, her words harsh, her unchecked jealousy crackling the edges of her voice. "Ye go. Ye go to him and not me! Tell the gods my punishment is long enough. Tell my lord, Gawain, he must send my fetch." Her nostrils flared in exasperation. "Ye cannot rob me of this final right, Lady, for I have been set aside too long. Do ye not ken?"

Brigianna did not hear: she saw only the hunched form of an old woman bending over a young girl woaded and waiting. Yet when her spirit-self cried out, "Reach for your knife!" she discovered her arm lying like molten lead at her side, impervious to her command.

Later, Cagney came to stand by her side. He put a trembling hand to her neck and in the process smudged the sacred mural beneath his greasy palm. Coarse features, traced with sadness, lay feral as a hungry animal watching the pack feast at the waterhole. Brigianna reached out to him and she experienced firsthand the depth of his utter, cawing loneliness.

Anguish ripped free from Cagney's gut, and he slumped to the ground beside her. With knuckles turning white against clenched fists, he held his rage in check. Like a man filled with sour vomit that refuses to budge, he kept constant vigil and endured his torment in private. Twice he reached out with upturned palms to implore the gods, but they, also, were beyond his reach.

Yvonia sidled to his side. Cagney commanded his rage be still. He averted his eyes as he pulled himself to his feet and, in so doing, missed the knowing glance in hers. Instinctively she reached out to him and their eyes met.

A hungering sob escaped his lips, forcing him to reach out and cup the weight of her pendulous breasts in his hands. Seeking succor in her silken hair, he buried his face in the nape of her neck. In response she stared forward, eyes ablaze as emeralds in the flickering light.

Outside, the funeral pyre was being built, a long, stone slab at its center. This sacrificial altar lay at the north end of the valley near a copse of woods livened by dark shadows that moved within, cunning and silent as the wind.

As the moon's glow gave sanction to the boding night, Conor stood vigilant by his chosen altar. "If the gods have been displeased, blood will warm them to life, and now they will smile, honored by such devotion. In doing this, you shall be blessed," Conor piously intoned.

What wood they found was green and bending, filled with the rich sap of summer. Carefully they laid the foundation of rock and debris, raising it to the level of the cromlech's longstone. All the while they walked softly and spoke not. Conor said they must ready themselves for the great sacrifice. Conor said they must be worthy of this great honor. Deep in the sway of priestpower, they obeyed without question.

At high moon Eric faced Conor with his heart determined.

"I cannot be party to this. I cannot take innocent life for a people who are not." He spat his words like raining arrows from between clenched teeth. His eyes were hardened like the shield used to defray those arrows in the sting of battle. Midnight wind whipped golden hair into angry froth, but with warrior's readiness he stood resolute.

"You cannot be party to this?" Conor screeched. "You cannot condone what gods have decreed?" He flailed his arms at his sides in angry flurry. "Hah! What mockery! Do you dare ask the gods to protect you when you wander the woods homeless and clanless, then?" He batted his arms about, threatening to cast the spell of banishment.

With a quick twist of Conor's hand Eric Cafferty would become a faceless and nameless being whose life would soon echo the hollow of the wind. His sweet Ainne would die in poverty; her sons, with neither home nor honor price, would have to put her up for charity.

Eric glanced at Donny, standing by his side, and lowered his shield. Like one who slowly moves away from a maddened dog, he backed up, step by step, with glinting eyes steady on his quarry.

Meanwhile, Cagney's patrol monitored the Finucane camp, relaying news back as the sound of the thrush or the grohen chucking in the grass.

And Yvonia dutifully tended to Brigianna's needs. The bitter brew was never far from her side. Her nights became days; and day became night once again.

On the opposite side of the valley a lone warrior waited out the night. Squatting on his haunches, he reached into his duffel and pulled out a small leather pouch. Mounding its contents onto a leather disk, he poked a hole in center, then slowly added water to the powdered lime. Patiently he worked the splayed hazel twig in a circular motion until the paste turned the right consistency.

In the dark of night, with only the waning moon as guide, he worked the paste through his golden hair so that each roiling curl held stiffly in place. Twisting the strands of his long mustache around his finger, he slipped the finger free, and let the sculpted curl rest. As the limepaste hardened, it bleached his already flaxen hair white, sufficiently luminescent to rival darting moonbeams. He had no mirror, not even the small bronze oval he usually carried, yet, as the limepaste hardened, his practiced hand swept his mane into a fierce tumble of frenzied curls that halted in motion.

Soon he stood, confident that his countenance was inspiring and terrible. Next he took off his clothes. With arms stretched overhead and palms pleading supplication, he let the moon bathe his naked body in silvery glow until he felt the absence of all conscious thought. In deep meditation and totally yielding his will, he awaited the resurging regeneration of superhuman power.

Suddenly he whirled around and, with a deep-throated growl, slammed a hardened fist into the pit of his gut. His jaw jerked upward, and a look of measured pride set the contours of his well-planed features. "Hard as iron, tough as shield leather," he said with pride.

He dropped back to the ground and began picking at the edges of his wide leather girdle, examining arm loops and pinnings, checking for weak spots or frayed edges. Satisfied, he looped the belt around his waist, and tested the holdings by slamming the hilt.

It snapped as he pulled the sword from its sheath. A thin red trail caused by the heat of friction etched his live weapon's pewter edge as he raised it above his head in sweeping arc.

"Ban," he said in simple homage to the dark-minded god who forged such weapons from the passionate heart of earth's warm fire. Ban, the god who lived and breathed within his creation and, when called upon, stood ready to godbolt the enemy with deadly force.

That aside, he sheathed his sword and sat down to wait out the night . . . wishing for all the world he had a cup of warm beer.

* * *

In another part of the encampment, and just as much alone, Lochobar removed his cup of warmed beer from the hearth. Even as he stood over the fire, his icy fingers refused to cooperate. They trembled as they poured the vial of distillate into the brew, threatening to spill the last of this precious liquid. Jaded eyes turned golden as he lifted the cup and drank the bitter brew without grimace. After setting it down, he hobbled to his pallet, casting a brief but annoyed glance at the throbbing blue vein that threaded a knotty trail from ankle to knee, and lay down.

Soon his body became as rigid as the board upon which he lay.

Chapter 25

Death had come. Darkness invaded her senses with crushing force. She felt herself mystically shunted into the bowels of earth, where her bones would grow cold and where passage from one life to the next would take place.

But first must come darkness; first must come despair. Then must come the courage to challenge death and demand that life which lies beyond the grave. Life did not come for those who did not fight for it, she had been told, even as a child.

With haunting trepidation, she hovered upon the brink of the unknown. Lightning flashed inside her head to lead her way. Her brow was furrowed, her pupils remained widely dilated, and she became irritated by common things, especially light.

Like a hound nosing across the floor, dawn's blue-gray trail nipped at the heels of night.

Her eyelids opened quickly, shut, then tentatively raised a protective curtain. Acute awareness spread over her like sunshafts streaming into the portals of galley graves. Death had played a cheating game! She was not in her tomb waiting to be borne across the pale, to where winds lie still beyond the seventh wave. A voice came to her, floating like zephyrs on the morning air. "It's time, m'lady, they be waiting."

Yvonia stepped inside. She had discarded her somber

deerskin for a gossamer shift. It was bound with golden chains that twined her waist and rounded her hips. Her long nails grasped the edge of the wooden bowl as she thrust it forward and demanded, "Drink, for 'tis no simple summer feast today, Lady. Begods, nay. A grand feast this is, the feast of a lifetime."

"Midsummer is past; Lughnasa's already come?" Brigianna asked, squinting at the intruding light but finding no relief from it.

As Yvonia tossed her head in a trail of mocking laughter, wildflowers buried in coppery curls cascaded like hedgerunners to spread across her shoulders. "Lughnasa's feast came and went when we were in the heat of battle, and us none the wiser."

Brigianna's puzzled look slowly changed to horror as her eyes traveled down her body to witness the obscene story so cruelly etched in blue woad upon her naked flesh. Vaguely she remembered the dark-robed women, the splayed hazel fronds beating upon her body, the dark blue dye telling their wretchedly wicked tale, the throbbing, mensural chant. Now, dressed in ragged deerskin and smeared with dye and blood, she had by their hands become a haunting, a ravening creature of darkness, forced to walk the cavernous underworld in search of prey.

Yvonia dropped to the ground and held out the bowl. Like a water lily atop a muddied pond, her silken flesh pressed against Brigianna's dark woaded arm. Fervor made her voice waver and color rouged her cheeks.

"Drink all of this," she commanded.

Brigianna stiffened, acutely aware of the cold. Her eyes darted wildly about; perspiration ridged her lips. She glanced warily at the waiting brew. Lips naysayed her struggle, but mesmerized by Yvonia's green-eyed calm, shaking fingers slowly reached for it.

She slaked her thirst and returned the bowl with a trace of sadness when it was empty. Smacking her lips at its cloying sweetness, she ignored the bitter aftertaste. Eagerly she awaited the shimmering ecstasy that came before craven madness, which made her cry out in torture and demand more.

Yvonia set the bowl aside and made Brigianna stand. Brigianna felt firm earth beneath her feet and noticed with a drunken smile that she still had her boots.

Like a lazy giant turning in slumber, morning peeped a jaundiced eye over the horizon. As she was led outside, Brigianna stared at this crimson orb with dilated eyes that refused to contract. Tensing in pain, she batted her hands wildly against the obscene intrusion.

"Heavens be!" Grania cried as she and Catriona rushed to her side. Between the two of them they forced Brigianna in line. "Lady! Get hold of yourself," Grania hissed, pulling Brigianna's wrists down.

Dark cobwebs clouded her thinking, and she jerked back, ready to sweep Grania away as she would a scuttling brown spider, when Catriona's sharp nails nicked blood at her wrist. She cried out and stumbled forward, only to have her foot crumble beneath her.

As she did so, her hand brushed the side of her boot and dislodged the ravenfeather hidden there. In desperation she clutched it tight, knowing that it held the secrets of eternity for her.

When Brigianna stumbled, there was an astonished gasp of apprehension from dark-robed Caffertys gathered there. For months surrounding clans had been terrorized by the Pig Man, yet the Pig Man never attacked the Caffertys. And those who fled his wrath joined rank with the Cafferty ranks. Now they understood why: it was a mighty army Cagney had raised, a mighty hero he would become when he led them to victory.

To assure this, and to assuage their guilt, Conor convinced them that sacrifice must be made. "You have heard it said from the beginning: For a life taken, a life must be given. It is law," he said.

In her hurry to save face Yvonia rudely pushed Grania

aside and, with Catriona's help, forced Brigianna back to her feet. Bracing her between them, they marched her forward. Dressed in the white of vestal virginity, and with flowers streaming from their hair, they turned their discarded queen into an insignificant shadow.

Droplets of dew acted like miniature shields, defraying prismatic sunbeams and spattering them into an aurora of blinding light. Again, Brigianna winced and drew back, but slowly, through this blurring haze, she began to make out both face and form of her accusors.

The Caffertys groveled the dirt, drugged, like Brigianna, into somnolent obeisance by the ploy of their high priest. Faces smeared with mud blended with hide robes as they wormed their way backward to create a pathway.

Conor waited by the slaying stone dressed in white like Yvonia and Catriona. Leather thongs, held between clenched teeth, etched a mustache trail down the sides of his mouth. His greasy face radiated the morning sun as he fingered the silver sickle hanging at his belt. It caught a sunbeam that went askance in lustrous light, nearly blinding Brigianna as she stumbled forward.

Her thoughts ran amok, her penchant for Sight gone. Caffertys prostrated themselves before her like a thousand head of cattle, crouching together to wait out the coming storm, yet ready to stampede when lightning struck.

Confused, she whirled around, knocking both Yvonia and Catriona aside, and fitfully brushed her palms on her deerhide kilt, as if to brush her filthiness aside. But her feet were too heavy to run.

Conor held out his hand. And a low murmur threaded its way through the Cafferty camp as Cagney stepped forward, dressed in leather that was dyed black by onion. With both hands he lifted his helmet into the air, its horns dark on the horizon in glutting defiance.

Pig Man.

The mensural chant quickened its pulsating rhythm. Brigianna, with her chin up, took one tentative step. Cagney

Cafferty loomed as dark shadow to her vision. Once more, in searching silence, he begged, Be mine.

I would die first! she cried without words. And in scorching disdain she turned her face away. Cagney slammed the mask down over his face.

She walked with regal assurance, as if born for this moment, as if queen en route to her crowning. Eyes rolled back and stared forth through unseeing whites. Conor gallantly helped her to her bower.

Next he whipped the leather cords from between his teeth to tie her wrists to iron rings. The shadowy shapes etched upon her arms became a passing blur of wombic signs and phallic jest as he laid one palm over the other, ignorant of the ravenfeather lying there.

In sweeping gesture he stretched his arms overhead to match the circle of earth, then slowly, clenching his fists into hard knots that turned skeletal white, drew them down and pressed them against his stomach as he bent forward in fetal crouch.

Then, with retching cry, he shot his fists upward as if bursting from the womb, drew down the power and leapt off the stone.

Immediately three dark-robed men standing to his side threw torches into the waiting bramble. Darting tongues tested tinder before taking hold, and tentative whispered murmurings soon turned to a throaty roar.

The fire quickly sprang to life, and just as quickly smoldered. Willow and hazel matted together in stubborn resistance and, burgeoning with the surging sap of summer, turned to smoke instead. Smoke rose upward, a billowing gray cloud thick with steam. Beneath it fire, rapacious and cunning, lapped its licking tongues, slowly eroding the withes and setting up a well-banked ring of heat at ground level.

Nestled within the cloud of smoke and lying upon cool stone, Brigianna awaited death in calm repose, seeing it from above, as if it had already happened. Cafferty chants became drumbeat in her veins and drowned out the fire's voracious roar.

She caressed the ravenfeather, thinking how comfortable the stone slab felt. Sure, it had been used many times before, for it curved at the round of her shoulders, fit well into the small of her back, and turned her hips slightly to one side. It was as if this stone had been set aside for her from eternity's first dawning. Now it would bear her safely across the sea of nether.

Her nostrils twitched, irritated at the rising smoke, and she tried to raise her hands to wipe away tears streaming like river backwash, but could not. Instead, her hands lay heavy upon her stomach, bound by cords anchored to iron rings. And when her benumbed mind told her foot to move, it responded like one already dead. She seemed to be one with the stone, a graven image supine upon the litter of death.

Soon the temporal world would become shimmering memory, she thought. Life had ended before it had begun, and was just happenstance after all, an insignificant and chance thing.

Trying to rid herself of the incessant tears, she turned her head to the side and coughed. Irritated by the lack of air, she tottered on the brink of death with strangely ambivalent feelings. At each panting gasp for air she rallied, but as the smoke invaded her senses, she yielded to its numbing power, all too eager to be cosseted in comforting darkness.

Had the fire taken quick hold, she would have been cremated by now, purged by fire and sent to the gods. As it was, the drug wore off and she began to remember:

Death must be challenged. Searching through the hazy labyrinth of waning thought, she fought to find the charm.

She had memorized it as a child, waiting the coming day, knowing from the moment she was seized from her mother's arms and set to walk her own course, that death was but a passing. She must be ready to challenge the gods, plead her case, and be found worthy to laugh and love with the selected few who followed the sun beyond its aurora and knew what mystery lay beyond the seventh wave.

Irritated by the oppressive air and irked that the incantation had turned to vapor upon her lips, she tossed her head from side to side. Around her, tambours beat their steady rhythm, and slowly flame licked its tongue around the cool stone slab.

Hovering darkness now turned to desperation: Soon the hall of heroes would be opened for her and her place at table set; soon she would be given invitation to join the boisterous, bawdy banquet.

But what glorious deeds had she done? When it came her turn at the table, of what could she boast? What did she have to say that would make the gods laugh in drunken madness, honor her with foot-stomping frenzy, and shout, "Yah! Glad it is that ye have lived! A thousand welcomes to the Land of the Eternally Young, Fair Brigianna."

Smoke trailed its deadly stream around her; lethal vapors did their treacherous dance. She choked in despair. Earth would not have her, and the heroes' hall would be closed to her forever. Where would she go?

Above her, gray trails of smoke became two large circles that glowed green at the center and then burned rich amber.

"Learning does not always make one wise," Lochobar whispered to her. Compelled to her side by her insistent need, he lingered momentarily before fading away on shadowy wings. She watched him go, knowing he meant that eternities held no more promises than the present, for even there the same mistakes were made over again, and the only reprieve gods got was the simple grace to forgive themselves.

"But for Kevin I would live!" she cried out after him. "Lochobar, hear me! Beg my plea! Demand the gods grant me life. I command it."

Her breath caught in her throat, a rich, round bauble of pure air. Its sudden sweetness filled her numbed brain with dazzling brightness, fresh and zesty as a mountain stream.

"But for Kevin I would live!" she screamed.

Her eyes flew open, reality set in, and with it, terror.

She jerked her hands upward, the thongs pulled tight against the iron rings, and jerked them back down. She tossed her head from side to side, frantically searching for air.

Smoke raked her throat, searing her senses, scorching them raw. But it was heavy with steam from unyielding sap and rising dew, and hung above her like a thin coat of fleece to become her saving grace.

Ripping spasms racked her body as terror took hold. She tried to keep her face to the side, breathing the small pocket of cool air between herself and the stone. She clawed the ravenfeather and gritted her teeth as she pulled against the leather thongs. They sliced her delicate skin, and she felt the bathing warmth of blood. Death smiled in skeletal whiteness, but she screamed back at it.

Her screams were pitched into the wailing of the wind, and the Caffertys matched that wail with their vibrant keening. Chanting turned to bedlam and din rose to an earsplitting pitch as they beat tambours and leather hides, trying to drown her out.

With one pitiable, soul-splitting cry, she slumped back, exhausted.

Morning crested the horizon to bathe the earth in molten splendor. Smoke billowed up around the stone, blocking out everything but a shining sea of gold.

Then she saw them. Two ravens floating in a golden sun. In that sea two ravens flew, wings outspread and barely touching, in steady course and beckoning her to follow.

With a choking sob she yielded to the ravens. Their will had become her destiny; she was now ready to obey.

Suddenly the sky darkened. Ravenwings blotted out the golden sun, sending the smoke into churning, swirling trails, as flapping wings beat the air. They came in endless horde: roiling, raucous, railing, dark, deadly wings. Smoke billowed back, and beneath their flurry, flames were battened down.

One raven in particular had gleaming yellow eyes. Taking the lead, it swooped down to skim over her. Its yellow eyes became green slits before it circled back, banked its turn, and took flight.

Once more the sky became a golden pond. Air turned still: Brigianna held her breath. When she looked up, a tiny smile graced her mouth.

Her heart had met its destiny, her heart had yielded to the will of the ravens. And they had answered her prayer.

Kevin, she breathed in joyous surrender as she saw him.

He stood transformed into the magical beauty of a young god: shining eyes, bluer than the sea, sparkled with the fiery heat of sapphires; golden skin had been burnished bronze and sculpted to perfection by the capricious delight of the gods; hair, stunning as the moon's glow, held each curl in place as if chiseled in alabaster.

In death he had come to her.

Chapter 26

Kevin's war cry cut through bloodlust like a double-bladed ax and sliced it to silence.

With riveting force obeisant Caffertys were yanked back from trance and into reality. Stunned, they groped about, like milling cattle before the stampede, and staggered clumsily to their feet, staring open-mouthed from behind mud-smeared faces. In quiet dread and with delayed reactions they fished inside their robes for weapons.

Above them dawn darkened to night as ravens of war swarmed the horizon and blotted out the sun.

Certain the Great Raven had unleashed a horde of charioteers from the otherworld to ride roughshod over them, they threw themselves back to the ground. Trembling in fear beneath the whirr of a thousand wings, they clenched dark-veined fists. Forefingers searched tremulant thumbs to make the circle and ward off evil. Shaking, and with eyes closed, they waved their magic charm.

Startled by Kevin's cry, Cagney reached for his short-sword and, squinting, put a meaty palm to his brow, trying to see through the smoke.

He thought he saw a shadow standing statue-still, gleaming like molten bronze. He saw Brigianna rise. Then he saw two shadows standing as one on top of the stone. They stood as apparitions inside the smoldering caldron of death and within seconds vanished like vapor before his eyes.

"AIEEEEEEYAY!" he roared, certain he had seen a fey, and charged through the melee. Leaping over his men with sword in hand, he ran to the stone slab and got there just as smoldering coals burst into flame. He yelled again, but this time in terror as he aborted his run midair to doggedly run the other way.

Hot ash exploded like a fountain, spewing red cinders into the sky. Embers returned to earth in a crimson cloudburst, flaming ribbons falling cometlike through thick, dark smoke.

"Rollieeeeee!" Maire screamed and dived into the short, stubby form, knocking him to the ground. "Mam . . . Mam . . . Mam . . . " he sobbed between choking breaths as Maire scuttled sod with him beneath her. Using her elbows to gain ground instead of her hands, she shielded him with her belly and crawled away to safety like a beaten animal.

"Begods, oh, oh, begods a more," Grania babbled and threw herself to Maire's side to grovel ground in lumbering shadow. Just as they reached the edge of the copse, she looked over her shoulder to see Catriona's white-clad form fall in a red-streaked heap.

"Me husband and now me babies, too? Gods, have ye no heart?" she moaned and humped over to rock back and forth, hoarding consolation to herself like a child hoarding its tit rag.

Caffertys who sprang to life were soon turned into human torches by the falling cinders. Screaming, wailing, and flailing the air in frantic confusion, these torches burned brighter by the sudden whip of wind, until death consumed them and they lay in ashen stillness.

Horses shrieked their terror and broke their tether to run rampant into the open fields. Goaded further into madness by the crimson rain, they trampled people and equipment alike.

"YAH—HAY!" Eric cried as he whipped his sword from its sheath and threw his mantle back to uncover his naked body and fight as Fian. Ripcords knotted at his neck. He whirled around with a high kick that sent the man next to him sprawling, and landed on both feet with his raised sword ready for the next man.

"YAH—HAY!" he cried again with gnashing teeth and turned in glistening nakedness to face the enemy. "For Kevin and for honor!"

The ring of metal met agonizing cries of swift and sudden death as Caffertys and Pig Men rallied into action. Too late they realized that more than half of the men standing there were Finucanes.

Like the wolf, padding through the forest, Kevin had returned to the edge of the copse to wait out the night in silent stealth. Moonbeams, falling upon the leaves, dappled his silvery-streaked shadow. His naked body was heavily oiled to keep warmth in but repel the cold, and by morning he was covered with dew like the leaves of the forest. That dew sparkled in the coming dawn like tiny platelets of mica and alabaster, so he crept farther back into the shadows to wait out the time with watchful eyes.

He wore both the Finucane medallion and McColym amulet around his neck. As Lochobar had instructed, he soothed the amber pendant between his thumb and forefinger until it became warm, and it softened to his touch. Well hidden by rock and fern, he squatted on the forest floor with his back braced against a thick ash, working the stone with the patient resolve of one born to long hours of waiting. As night passed, he could feel the heat of it on his chest when he let go, and see it glow with latent fire from within.

As he realized Brigianna was drugged, he breathed a sigh of relief, knowing her ordeal was better this way. He had surmised the spot where she was held prisoner by her absence elsewhere, and by the continual comings and goings from this tent throughout the night. But a double ring of armed men stood guard.

In order to allow enough time for Eric's men to get through the front lines, Kevin had to put aside the temptation of slitting the guard's throat and spiriting her away. From their tipsy slumber he could tell the guards were drugged and knew that one wrong move on his part would only double the danger to Brigianna.

Eric ran the gauntlet of double treachery: by agreement he was to strip naked to fight as Fian; cut the horses from their tether; and then appear in the dark robe of the drugged worshipper to bow and scrape before the altar of sacrifice.

Kevin vowed that if he survived this day, he would think of nothing but Brigianna's happiness forevermore. Even now he would, if he could, spare her this pain. In the nakedness of his soul he knew he was prepared to die at her side if necessary, even forfeit his place in the heroes' hall of eternity if it meant she would live.

In the brief moment before his battle cry, he allowed himself the luxury of suspended time and, with the candor of a man facing death, searched the hidden valleys of his heart. Like the young stallion in the buck of spring, his mind raced back to the day he first saw Brigianna. Newly blooded and now Fian, he went on his first summer mission, and at Colym's Cuirnen surrounding the McColym clanhold, he saw a pubescent butterfly of winsome mirth, walking the wood with her priest and clutching his garments like an adoring child.

Her delicate beauty had burned his brow, and after two summertimes passed he returned to see her again walking the scarp that shielded her father's stronghold. This time as she turned at the spine of the hillock, a whipping wind flattened her shift tight against her nubile body to outline gently rising breasts and softly rounding hips. His heart leaped its cage, for he knew the time had come. When she turned to go, she walked with the hip-swaying grace of a beckoning woman, and Kevin had been able to think of nothing but those swaying hips since.

Yet he did not approach her father's camp.

Instead, he preened and strutted, blatantly prow, and won all the challenges at the triannual clan gathering held on Lughnasa at Uisnech. "Yah, tanist!" clansmen shouted, and Lord Gawain beamed, boldly proud of his foster son. They fell on each other in roisterous, body-hugging tumble, ignoring Cagney's insolent barbs. Kevin won the golden rings but went away disappointed, for that year the McColyms had not made a showing. His cockery was for nothing; a maiden's heart he had not won.

He was given Yvonia shortly after his blooding, and when he returned home, he buried his face in her coppery curls and licked her waiting breasts until she sidled her rocking hips down over him and buried him deep in musk and laughter. But even there he could not forget the ravenhaired maiden whose spritely step was as spirited as the wind.

It was a hard day when Kevin and Yvonia faced each other with eyes held steady, for to look away would be unseemly. Finally eyes once passionate with green fire jaded, and Yvonia was the first to look away. With pride fierce as any warrior's, she refused Brehonic sanction as wife of third or even fourth station. By rights, she could force him to claim honor over her for living with her beyond the first year's mark, but she did not. Instead, by mutual agreement Yvonia marched back to the women's quarters and Kevin took up residence in the warriors' denizen.

He formalized his marriage plea and set it before his foster father, Lord Gawain, who then sent runners back to Erin Finucane. Eternity passed and new worlds were born, it seemed, before Gawain Cafferty came to him. With both hands braced on Kevin's shoulders, he said, "Your father, Lord Erin, has accepted your pledge. Ten prized breeding cows are offered, and the Finucane will spread cloak over clan McColym and protect them as sept. Go. Claim Brigianna the Fair, and make her your woman."

Like a foolish young cock, he went alone, laying bivouac outside the McColym clanhold and waiting for the right moment to storm the lodge and steal his bride. While he was waiting, heaven opened wide, gods smiled in vindictive glee, and took matters into their own hands.

To his utter astonishment, the maiden came running directly to him, right in the dark of night, flustered as a banty hen, declaring that under no circumstances would she bed the likes of him! Well, what could he do but ply his beguiling charms and lure her back to his father's stronghold?

Thinking to what end this folly had cost him, the amulet fell from his hand to lie on his chest like a sheath of ice. He picked it up. Clearing his thoughts, he resolved to face the battle ahead.

Kevin traced the thin white seam of his blooding that threaded a single line from arm bend to wrist.

Cagney had given him that. And Cagney stood before him now.

Crouching, Kevin's wary eyes darted back and forth over the scene before him. Carefully he assessed his strengths and calculated each pressing vantage. The amber talisman glowed warm beneath his touch. As it did, furor rose within. He blotted out the din of Cafferty wailing; he voided himself of all thought. He saw nothing, he heard nothing, he thought of nothing but the matter at hand.

Once Conor moved aside and the bramble was lit, the pathway between him and the stone bier where Brigianna lay was cleared. Caffertys ringed around their altar, hunching over to press their foreheads to the dirt in humble submission.

The rising sun had not yet warmed the earth; the last of the dew clung to rocks and leaves, chilling the air. Caffertys showed no signs of shivering from the chill or huddling together for warmth, but instead, obeyed Conor's every command.

Ungainly actions let Kevin know they were still well tranced; there were no bored worshippers or distracted children this day.

Expecting the tinder to take blaze, he sucked in his breath when the torches fell, fretting for the arrival of Eric's men and fearing his own run ill-timed.

For one brief moment Kevin mourned Brigianna's possible death.

He stood as one man alone on the face of all the earth. If he failed, he would spend the rest of his days imprisoned in inexorable loneliness.

But when he saw dark-robed creatures move like creeping shadows to fatten out Cafferty ranks, he whispered the prayer of one delivered out from among the dead. Nervous whinnies coming from restless horses told him Eric's men had gotten through. Only those Caffertys Eric could persuade not to remain Pig Men were there. Finucanes closed in, with Niall and Hugh at their lead. And they all moved in a purposefully lumbering gait, so that they appeared drugged as the rest.

Now smoke thickened in mass above the altar. Unable to see Brigianna because of it, Kevin shook. Fearing her already dead, he feverishly fingered the golden amulet.

Just as the sun streamed its golden arrows across the plain, a rising horde of black-winged ravens filled the sky. Kevin felt his spirit soar, borne aloft as if he had become the wings of the mighty Raven.

Knowing he must leap over fire and through smoke—and that he would die if he failed—he spread his arms wide and, glistening and naked, uttered his curdling war cry. Ravens skirted his trail, giving wing to his flight. They filled the sky to blight it in darkness as if Lochobar had spread his enormous black cloak over them.

Kevin blotted out everything but the memory of his blooding and, as then, covered the ground swift as the wind to become the triumphant stag. As he leaped upon the altar, he gulped the last full measure of breath ever to be his if he failed. His toes splayed out as his bare feet clung to the smooth stone, gripping balance. With one well-calculated sweep, he whipped the knife from between his teeth and sliced the leather thongs.

For one brief moment he stood stock still. Beneath the veil of flapping ravenwings and through the smoky haze, he heard astonished cries turn quickly into agonizing horror. Around him was the unmistakable clang of metal, and the crunching, slopping thud of broken bone and spilt blood.

He smiled, ever so slightly, knowing Caffertys and Finucanes had united to fight the common enemy.

"Kevin! We are alive!"

Brigianna gulped air and stared at him in amazement. But a retching, deep cough immediately set in. She recoiled in racking spasm, and he hurriedly bent down to gather her into his arms.

"We'll not be alive for long if we don't hurry!" he shouted, gripping her tightly to still her racking cough. He scooped her up and just as he shouldered in for the run, the embers burst into flame.

Butting her face into his chest to give her an air pocket, he leaped off the slaying stone and crashed through the flaming wall of cinders. He whirled around, swaggering in the throes of trying to gain balance and steady her weight in his arms, and Brigianna's feet knocked an angry Cafferty in their wake and sent him reeling.

"Remember Rathdun!" he yelled as he swayed to veer his course. "We lived then and we will live now!"

He zigzagged through the skirmish, knocking awed and panicked attackers aside before they had time to react. Eric saw him and immediately ran guard at his back. Finucanes closed in to stave off the Cafferty swell and give Kevin chance to run at full speed. Leaping a ragged course, he reached the edge of the copse, and both he and Brigianna fell to the ground, panting.

"Keep running, Brigianna." His words tumbled over themselves in hot blasts. "Hide in the trees, for 'tis now as it was the night of the Pig Man." Rushing words choked back on themselves for what he must say.

"Dearest Brigianna, I would give ye my love and my

life. Pray with all that be in ye 'tis me who comes back." His eyes softened, to inscribe her features indelibly upon the memory of his heart and take them there to death, if to death now he must go. Then, with grim resolution, he braced himself, took in a deep lung-burning breath, and with wrenching reluctance pulled away.

"No!" Her fingers gripped the scar on his foream and her nails dug into his skin as she clawed to pull him back. Tears splashed her face like floodwaters breaking bank, blurring the drawings and washing bloodstains away, and try as she might, she couldn't stop them. Looking beyond him, to the bloody field and back again, her eyes grew deep and luminous. "I will die first. I swear it. Oh, Kevin . . . if 'tis not ye who comes . . . I will die. My voice will haunt this wood and become a cree of aching sadness. If ye die, I'll follow. If gods do not send my fetch, my spirit will haunt them, and I will beg them and vex them until they hear my plea. All the world will know of my broken heart . . . if ye . . . do not come back for me."

Words she had so carefully kept imprisoned came tumbling out. "Here me well, for I'll not be clanbound or manbound if not by ye. If I take pleasure, I do it by my own will, and if I choose to have a child I'll stand before the judges to claim it mine. But I swear"—she stopped to heave in air, and her voice turned starkly sober—"no man will lay claim over me 'less 'tis ye, Kevin McErin. Do ye not think I can fend for meself? 'Twas only for the likes of ye I came to Cafferty clanhold a'tall."

"Begods. Ye mean that, Brigianna? Ye would foreswear it in spit?"

"Ye forget I am split clean of honor? I have only what little ye give me." She waved her hands wildly, then broke off, shamed by her outburst.

"But were I still in my father's clanhold, and with brideprice, and were ye to court claim, I would come with honor. I would warm your bed and suckle your babies and your heart would be full to overflowing.

"But I will haunt this wood as the walking dead if it is not for ye I lie." She paused, and her voice fell to the barest whisper. She bared her soul, naked as her body. "I love ye, and ye are a pompous fool not to have seen it from the start."

Kevin looked like he had just been clubbed with a mace. "Aye? Ye do?" he marveled, and his smile tumbled free from its hiding place.

"Then this folly is well worth the trouble ye've caused me," he needled as he slipped his arms around her and gently brushed her lips.

A tenderness filler her soul: a deep, exquisite ache, a joy that brinked the edge of sorrow, touchingly poignant, a beauty so perfect it hurt. She stared at him in hushed wonder, blissfully ignorant of the raging battle surrounding them, blindly ignorant of anything but Kevin.

A timorous giggle rippled through her, and she shyly pressed her lips against his again. "But . . . I did not think ye would have me."

"Hah! Ye are a bigger fool than I!"

Heart's fire flashed in shining eyes as she tumbled back into his outstretched arms.

Brigianna ni Colym was Kevin's woman.

Kneeling, their naked bodies ached for each other's touch. Wanting fingers searched for flowing tresses, but when he reached for a handhold, he got instead, a mass of tangled braids. Coiling fingers through them, his arm muscles knotted up, and his hungry kiss seared her passions like hot flame. In sweating eagerness they writhed against each other and dark shapes painted upon her body smudged onto his. As his splayed fingers pocketed a firm breast, then cupped to gently cradle it, a sword bolt seared her belly and made her quiver in its wake.

Searching out his lips with tender, licking tongue, her arm slid over a rounded shoulder, then drew back from stiffly matted hair to caress pliant, shammy skin. She clung to him, ready to spread her legs willingly and let him fill her belly and her soul with life. "For this passion I would die!" she cried, for him and for him alone.

"No, for this passion we must live, and for that I must fight."

With one last powerful, crushing kiss, he reluctantly pulled away to dig into a cache of arms barely covered by brush. He retrieved his shield and fitted his swords, then turned to face the fray. As he stood, she leaned her naked, dark-woaded body against his back, feeling excitement course through her as erect nipples etched a loving trail across his back, and feeling him tense and stiffen beneath her touch as she did so.

Her cheek brushed his skin, unmindful of the tear that fell there, and as one soul, they sighed deeply and did not move, daring to hold, however fleeting and uncertain, the wonder of this moment.

Then Lord Kevin, who ran wind with Fianna, stepped forward and lifted blade to mighty Ban, god of sword and of might, and drew down the power.

Brigianna leaped forward to reach out and hold the lingering warmth, but there was only cold, biting air where warm flesh had once been.

"Pray gods it be Kevin who returns," she whispered.

Chapter 27

Kevin was Fian, forged by the smithy's fire. He did not bear the sword. He was the sword.

Humming bloodlust's vibrant timbre, the god Ban called him, forcing him to rise up from the miry clay and message death with gleaming blade.

Furor, red hot, grew deep within. The amber talisman resting upon his glowing chest awakened with stirring heat to proclaim its lusting love of life. Even as he tested the knife at his side, even as he raised broadsword and took shield, his appearance changed.

Naked, he ran into battle. In him, fury rode the wind; at his coming, the sea withheld its breath. Granite eyes narrowed to sight his quarry. He beat upon his chest: fierce reverberation demanding revenge. His war cry echoed through the field like drumroll upon a thousand hides.

He was the god incarnate.

In sweeping strides he covered ground: bare feet scarcely skimming its surface; naked body, a silver streak; hair stiffened by limepaste, a bristling halo; brows, mere slashes of white.

Above him the dirge of ravens swelled the horizon in swarming plague, blotting out sunstreams and turning sky dark in sudden squall. Beneath that winging cloud Caffertys and Pig Men cowered in fear.

They had seen Kevin run through dark smoke to rescue

the maiden, fire explode to engulf two bodies, the sky blacken to become the stormy sea of death. Now they saw him again, returned from the fire and bearing the terrible face of an angry god. Fear gripped their souls, as in wretched guilt they fell to the ground, circling thumb and forefinger and cursing the evil eye to stave off torment.

Kevin brandished his broadsword, hacking and cutting and slicing a bloody path. At his first kill he stopped and straddled the Cafferty. Knuckles turned white as they gripped the gleaming hilt. The air, split clean behind the blade's wake, sang shrill until it crunched bone.

He yanked the head by its once proud mane and held it high in trophy. He thumped his chest in the gurgling roar of bloodlust and once again tambours beat a thousand hides. Ravens of war came from the four corners of heaven to blanket the earth in death's shroud. Fear reverberated through the Cafferty camp. Each man stood alone in the arena of death, steeped in his own bloodbath and mired in confusion, seeing his enemy as brother and brother as enemy.

Lord Eric had rallied his men, brought them to their senses, and split Cafferty loyalties. Finucane forces in disguise had crept in behind him. When they showed their faces at the Cafferty front with Eric in command, they were let through without question, and the first ambush happened easily, as attention was diverted.

They had waited, as drugged and staggering, Brigianna was led to her stone altar. Around her, Caffertys wormed the ground, and when the torch fell and the smoke rose, they pulled dark hoods over their faces to nose the down of morning dew, their only protection against rising smoke. Meanwhile, Caffertys and Pig Men at sentry, unwittingly engrossed in the spectacle of ceremony, fell in dull heaps at Eric's club. Eric's men quickly traded mantles, stripped the dead of extra weapons, then slowly crept close to the smoking pyre. Like their fellow communicants, they now wore the somber garments reserved for holy days. As the sun's rays tipped the earth, they waited like death shadows, ready to execute their macabre duty without mercy. There were no longplaids for this final battle, no colors to decry fealty, no clanbadges to claim honor.

Dark-robed Pig Men, Caffertys, Finucanes, and Mc-Colyms looked alike. And for that each man stood alone.

Kevin flung the gory head of his first kill aside and retrieved his sword. He raised it high: the cry for blood that ripped from his throat became their call to arms.

Finucane warriors and Cafferty loyalists tossed off their darkened cloaks and rose with naked bodies gleaming. Well planted within the enemy camp now, they would face death with honor. For Kevin they would fight as Fian. They had to forfeit limepaste because it would have betrayed them. But even without fiery manes they mirrored the furor of their leader. Bodies glowed with generated heat from within, and their roar of death echoed the bellows of Ban burning for blood.

"AAAAAAAYAY!"

Kevin's cry met clanging metal and crunching bone. Finucanes and Caffertys both challenged Pig Men to death's duel: this time without benefit of honor or gainsay; this time on Pig Men terms. Caffertys wrestled Finucanes for land and honor. Caffertys stood divided among themselves, wrestling with liege and loyalty, but with no time to make a thinking choice and with breath hanging in the balance, they were forced to let might of the sword decide right. At first, McColyms shadowed Finucanes, then, when the battle erupted into a caldron at full boil, turned to fight for life and breath on their own terms.

Women and children skirted the edge of the field, raising the din of battle to a feverish pitch by drumming hides and banging kettles. The battle burgeoned to a swelling tide, and when it got too close, they bared their teeth like maddened dogs and reined mighty warriors back in rank with a shower of rocks. Pipers wailed death's dirge. And when they grew breathless, the frenetic clatter of the women picked up pitch and outdid the horde of cawing ravens overhead.

Out in the far field Conor stood alone. Singing madly he battled ravens, not knowing if they were real or imagined.

Kevin ran two standing men to the ground, trampling them face down in the mud as he hurried on. He attacked the next Cafferty from the back, straddling him as he would a horse and yanking a blond mane back to bare the throat. With swift blade the man went down. Kevin rode him as he batted ground on all fours. Too soon the Cafferty fell out from beneath him, pooled in his own gurgle of blood. Kevin's heel butted the next assailant's chin as he flung his leg over, ready to run.

Two men rushed him. He rammed his bodyweight into the first attacker and braced his thigh against him and rivved his sword arm upward. The man grabbed his stomach. He fell forward, gripping his entrails. His guts burst in his hand and he stared at Kevin in disbelief.

Kevin spun around, ready for the second man, who faced him with indignant eyes. A sword tip protruded through his belly to splash his undyed tunic dark with blood. He fell against the warrior who had impaled him, forcing the both of them to the ground. The backup rolled free, and realizing he had killed his brother, beat the ground in despair. Kevin brought his blade down swiftly. Servering the cord at the base of the skull, he split the head clean of its misery.

"Behind ye!"

Kevin made the half-circle in midair, landing with his feet wide and his sword arm ready. Four footmen ringed a net around him, leather shields protecting them from knee-cap to brow bone. Neck muscles knotted into thick cords as Kevin checked the distance. His stomach muscles pressed in and out like bellows as he panted short puffs of air, then drew in like iron grating, as he took one long breath and faced four raised lances.

A high whine filled the air, and the sky rained arrows. Two men fell. The other two stationed Kevin between them and, like a vise, closed in.

"Sow-sucking pig bellies!" he cursed, hurtling foaming spittle at a Cafferty foot. Eyes darkened like iron as the taller Cafferty raised his lance, the blade of it a double handspan. Just as he turned his torso to throw, his shield lifted, exposing raw belly. Kevin was under him before he could throw, screaming bloodlust as his broadsword sliced the man in two. The force of the blow spun Kevin round again in its momentum before he came to a swaggering halt. In a blur of motion he saw Tormaigh's men hedge his right flank like a windbreak.

The Cafferty fell, slumped to the ground just as Tormaigh's arrow pierced his back. "Save your arrows for the live ones," Kevin taunted as he plunged iron into the second Cafferty's shield. Leather, hard as stone, snapped Kevin's borrowed blade in two. The barrel-chested man came down hard on top of him. Kevin gnashed his teeth as he grabbed the shield's rim. He slid into a wide vee and braced his legs like well-rooted tree stumps. Now, with shoulders hunched upward, he heaved forward to push the warrior back. The Cafferty's nostrils flared, and he hunkered shoulder mass forward and braced his hands on the wooden crossbar backing the shield. Legs slid farther apart and were uprooted. Kevin fell, and the Cafferty fell upon him.

Drool slathered across Kevin's shoulder as the Cafferty brought his shield down. With a malicious grin, he slowly forced Kevin's air out. Blood gushed through Kevin's temples, his eyes bulged out, the whites turned red from strain. The hilt, jutting from the shield with its death blow aborted, pressed against Kevin's rib and armpit. He clawed for the broken blade that lay just beyond his reach.

Pain branded him, his face grew ashen, his eyes closed. Blood-gushing dizziness overwhelmed him, and he nearly welcomed death.

But slowly, with cunning stealth, he brought his knee up.

He slammed Cafferty balls with ramrod force.

The warrior pitched forward, sniveling in pain. Kevin was right on top of him. He gripped the shield-bed at its rim and turned it with the jammed hilt outward and smashed it into the Cafferty's face. The Cafferty screamed as his face caved in. He twisted in spastic jolts beneath Kevin: he drowned in gurgle and was still.

Kevin tossed the broken blade aside, reached into his leather girdle for his shortsword and fumbled his side to check other weapons.

Beside him, McColyms crouched with drawn bows. The air rained death even as Kevin got to his feet. At such close range sharp arrows nagged heavy shields, ripping them and defacing their protection. Those arrows that found mark brought slow agony. Men fell, only to watch the battle burn around them, helplessly awaiting death. In their final moments they almost welcomed snagging, sharp-beaked scavengers come for carrion. When one raven boldly tore into living flesh, its owner only stared at it with grisly gratitude, watching his own death fetch.

"HAAAAAAAYAH, TORMAIGH!" Kevin yelled. And Tormaigh tracked his run like a shadow, his banty legs churning dirt to keep up with Kevin's stride. His graying curls clung to his skull, a matted helmet of sweat. Even as he ran, his hand eeled its way to his quiver, fitting an arrow to the gut. His men followed, squatting suddenly in small rounds, then rising in unison with a quick "HAYYAAH" to splatter air with starbursts of death and fit the arrow on the run for the next kill.

The battle showed no signs of weakening. The call to arms had produced a maddened scramble as benumbed worshippers dived for caches of weaponry and hastily strapped leather and tightened buckles. Lances became cudgels at close range, and the mace shared honors with rock and wood as everything within reach was enlisted for protection.

Unlike the Caffertys, Finucanes fought with premeditated

furor, bodies radiant with inner heat. Finucane weapons found home with deadly accuracy. The more men they killed, the madder they became. Bloodlust blotted out reason. The throbbing rhythm of battle became drumsong. Soon it became heartbeat, and they no longer lifted swords in vain.

Instead, they became the living sword of judgment: Ban incarnate. Dark shapes inchwormed the edge of battle and dragged the bodies of wounded men to safety, perhaps to life, even if only to assure them in the arms of death that they had lived happily and died valiantly.

"Grania, my Grania."

Kevin's heart wrenched in pain as at fleeting glance he saw her hovering over her dead. With no male kin to secure her honor, she was now homeless and unprotected as a wayward creature of the forest. His soul split within, when for the briefest second he heard her voice crooning in darkness and felt her patting his dampened hair as the pox attacked him. He was only seven, and because of her sweet balm and sweet voice, he had no scars that showed. Only scar tissue, he realized. He saw, in a flashing vision, the regal calm of Erin Finucane and the haunting yet tender eye of Gawain Cafferty, his two fathers, now gone.

His cry cost him. The shaving sound of an ax, which would have stilled his misery forever, missed him by a hairbreadth. The man that threw it lunged forward, but was killed before he could retrieve it.

Kevin turned to see Yvonia swinging broadsword above her head in swishing arc and dancing in violent circles beneath it. Her long red hair flung out from her skull in lashing tongues of fire. Shrieking her war cry with throat-splitting terror, she brought the blade down. She killed the short man standing next to her instantly.

Two others closed in, tall as she, and well armed.

"Go back, go back!" Kevin shouted, running ragged trail to come to her aid. He stepped on a dead Cafferty's wrist to release his grip on a pike. Tossing the weapon into the air, he held his palm up with fingers and thumb ready, so the shaft fell, evenly balanced, into his hand. He lifted his spear arm back over his shoulder, twisted his torso slightly, and ran behind his well-aimed blade.

Dark iron carved a blue trail, and a Finucane fell at Yvonia's feet. Green eyes crackled like cold glass under boiling water. She bared her teeth, and her frantic cry became inhuman. Those eyes narrowed into savage slits, and her cry turned to the low growling of the she-wolf before attack. Now she flung wild feet into the air, dancing with wide kicks in high arc, as she brandished broadsword in a whirling silver streak overhead.

"No! No!" Kevin yelled as he fell to the ground near her flailing feet. With one hand over his head to protect it, he groveled forward like a newly beaten dog. With the other hand he beat the air behind him, and the Finucane brigand turned on better quarry.

Yvonia shrieked her madness; Kevin crouched below her, with flinching, faltering movements, slowly inching forward. Then, cat quick, he was upon her. His hand shot up to knock the sword from her grip. It cried a metallic insult as it crashed against jutting rock.

Her dazed eyes flickered with momentary recognition as he knocked her backward and fell on top. Instantly she reached forward to claw him.

"Beg ye forgive me, oh, beg ye do someday," he whispered hoarsely.

His fist met her chin with a sharp crack. Her head jerked sideways from the blow, and her body slumped beneath his.

As if they were one flesh, air heaved out of him and he gave in to momentary reprieve, cradling himself upon her softly yielding flesh. His blood-smeared, war-grimed hand reached forward to tenderly smooth a hair away from her cheek.

With eyes closed his lips searched her face. His lingering kiss, poignantly gentle, dared only briefly to remember soft summer days bursting in the passion of youth. Slowly he brought his face down to rest upon her bosom and cry:

"Have I hurt ye that badly . . . that ye could betray me so?"

Chapter 28

Bearing the shield of Black Dhurmod, Cagney the Brave raced across the battlefield trampling dead bodies in his wake. Behind him his Pig Men poured from the wood to emissary death. In their wake Finucanes, Caffertys, and McColyms scrambled over one another, running for cover.

Fat-bellied ravens took off in cowardly disgrace, rising in a single queue, leaving the sky blue, leaving death to shadow fields in blood.

Hoofbeats reverberated through the ground, up Kevin's spine, and bludgeoned the base of his skull. "TOR-MAAAAAIGH! EEEEEEERIC! DONNEEEEEEE!" he yelled as he dived for a spiked metal mace.

Pig Men came to the end of their run at the far end of the field. Dhurmod raised a gloved hand, and midst roiling horseflesh, metal hit leather as men repositioned weapons and adjusted helmets.

Without lowering his gloved hand Cagney thrust spiked greaves forward. Black hide fit him like a second skin; a thickly padded hauberk protected his barrellike chest, and his oiled cape whipped against his animal's rump. Leather strappings strained beneath his weight as he leaned against the waist-high saddleback.

Anger pulsated through Pig Men as through one thumping auricle. Finally horns like the curved tusks of maddened boar darkened the sky as the Pig Man lowered his helmet and brought the gauntlet down.

Kevin ran a dry tongue over lips that were as scratchy as pumice, knowing that a footman is no match for a war horse, but knowing also that if he stepped aside, he would die a coward. Fear of that made his feet stand firm.

This same fear coursed through his men, binding them together as brothers in blood. Facing outward, they stood stolidly sentinel, to live or to die.

Dhurmod's black steed bore down, a dark iron ball whipping the air above its head. The Pig Man adjusted the long chain keeping the iron ball in check so that his arm circled in pattern as part of the weapon. He came at a dead run; his war cry echoed through the field and tumbled the hollows, where, in turning, it gained force to trumpet his coming.

Kevin's hide flickered. Soon the animal's hot breath would be upon him. He kept his eyes on the swirling ball so that the horse became a black blur in his line of vision.

Just as Cagney closed in, the horse hit bog hollow and the force of its run made the ball suddenly jerk forward. It hit slack on the chain to vault back over the animal's ears and snap in the backswing. Vicious spikes clipped the Pig Man's shoulder and knocked him forward. Cagney's splayed hand shouted his surprise, and the ball and chain tore free.

It sang its own death song as it fell to earth with an impotent thud—just missing the interception of Kevin's mace as it turned end over end. Cagney swore motherblood as he ducked the flying weapon and quickly grabbed the horse's mane to keep his balance. With ears battened to its skull the horse picked up speed, and the mace missed them both.

The Pig Man reached forward to retrieve the reins and jerked them backward, forcing his mount to spread its hind legs and dance ground. Hocks bent, head lashing upward, it tried to rear. Again Cagney jerked the reins back, then gored its tender underbelly with the studded bosses of his greaves and, by brute force, cursed the animal into submission.

A preyer at hunt now, Kevin calculated his chances of survival. Battle din raged around him, and at that moment a creamy blur of flesh crossed his vision. It erupted into red cascade, followed by black shadow. Sightless eyes toppled at his feet. Behind it a dull but faithful horse awaited its fallen master.

Eyes steady, Kevin fumbled at his belt. He was down to knives, useless weapons on horseback. Instinctively a hand went to his thigh. The blade strapped there was as long as his shinbone.

"Steady. Easy. Hush, m'lady, 'tis only me," he whispered, cursing himself for not knowing animals as Cagney did. The mare, more intent on heather than on battle, stared at him. He brought his hand down gently so not to startle it, grabbed the knotted rein, and in the split of a moment was on her back digging bare feet into warm underbelly.

"Bastard!" Cagney yelled as he came down upon him. The animals buckled aside as they rammed into each other. Whooping war cries surrounded them as Pig Men thundered into the fray. Then a barrage of arrows fell like cloudburst.

With shields over their heads Pig Men banked their animals' backs and ran them in all directions, to defray attack. Cursing threats and hatred, Pig Men reined their horses back and turned to trammel. But their greed found no match for the threatened honor of Cafferty and Finucane.

Naked and fighting as Fian, loyalists ran with the swiftness of the mount, running shadow to it, and a Pig Man fell as the double-bladed ax clove his back in two.

Cagney bolted across the field; Kevin bit wind and charged after him. Plying his torso flat to his animal's back, he tested its head pull, then whipped the ends of the reins around the saddlebuck and gave the horse its head.

Trained in maneuvers it would run straight ahead until it dropped, and now Kevin could slip from side-to-side at full gallop.

Feeling the mare's undulating pull and instinctively matching his breathing to it, Kevin gripped its mane. Below him the field became a bloodstained blur. Forcing headway against the wind, he put a steady hand on the saddlebuck and drew his legs underneath him so that he now crouched on his haunches. Teetering, his balance fatally precarious, he attempted to stand. Wind whipped around him, blinding his vision. To keep balance, he concentrated on the round metal bosses decorating Cagney's shin and cautiously released a hand.

Thundering at full run beside him, Dhurmod turned a dark face around. His gloved hand grasped the ax handle firmly. Fingers caressed the sharp blade. "Welcome, Brother," he spit, "welcome to death's door."

Kevin flinched as he saw the blade, a quick reflex that toppled him instantly. He fell forward with a resounding thud, again straddling the running horse.

Side by side the war horses plowed the earth, churning up mud and gore. Heavy heads lunged forward, each nosing for victory. As they butted into each other, pain ran a jagged streak up Kevin's naked thigh.

"Ho, Brother, ye faint at that?" Cagney jeered. His gloved hand slipped down the ax handle to turn the blade sideways. "How long I have awaited this moment. So long, I hate to see it pass before I fully savor it." The whites of his eyes mocked Kevin from behind the mask. His arm shot out, and the whirring ax sang its siren's song.

Kevin yanked his mare's head back, twisting her neck in convoluting motion. The gleaming comet came at them, and the blade sank into the mare's fleshy neck. Her scream ran shrill as blood gushed from her in fountain.

Doubling a leg beneath him as the horse went down, he braced a flat foot against its warm flank and shoved as if he were diving off a riverbank. He catapulted through the air and lammed into Cagney. Cagney jerked in epileptic fit as Kevin hit.

Kevin's fingers clawed Cagney's slippery skin without finding handhold, and he was flipped over the running animal's side. As his own weight pulled him down, he grabbed on to Cagney's thigh. Cursing, he bore down and, by using the Pig Man as ballast, tried to fling his legs back over the animal's back. But he couldn't, and the soles of his feet burned fire as they were dragged along the ground.

Cagney raised a hand and chopped him. Pain cracked Kevin's shoulders.

Suddenly the horse veered left to avoid a rock, pitching Cagney to the side. Both men clung to each other as they rolled clear.

"Ye die," Cagney growled, grabbing Kevin's plastered hair.

"No, ye die," Kevin growled as he gnashed into the soft spot of neck between sark and mask. There was a spurt of blood and vile cursing.

Keening hit the wind as survivors from both camps ran forward to rally behind their champions.

Hearing it, Brigianna cautiously inched out of her hiding place at the edge of the copse.

In a flash of black lightning the Pig Man was on his feet and running toward him. Kevin lifted his longknife to Ban and prayed for swift resolution. He must face death in the public arena, he must outwit Cagney, and he must not die a coward.

Cagney stopped a handspan from Kevin's outstretched blade and discharged a wad of spittle at Kevin's feet. "Paugh!" he cried, tossing helmet, mask, and cape aside. "I fight ye not as Black Dhurmod, but as Cagney the Brave, rightful heir to Cafferty crown. I challenge ye, Kevin, son of Erin and pretender to my claim. Fight me now as brother."

A hush fell over the field, weapons slid to the ground, women began to nudge their way into the circle. Pig Men, Finucanes, McColyms, and Caffertys ringed around their champions to await their fate. Woaded and still nearly naked, Brigianna slipped in among them just as Fianna of both clans stepped forward to guard the lines.

"Gainsay, Brother," Cagney demanded. "Fight like a man."

"Ye are no brother of mine," Kevin growled. "Filthy pig sucker. I be no kin to ye or your kind."

"Pig sucker?" Cagney jeered. "Why, ye milk-sucking little shit. Come to Cafferty hearth to become Grania's little darling, taking treacle tits right from my own mouth. Then comes Father. 'Be good to little Kevin,' he says. 'Look at what Kevin's done now. What a fine warrior! What a fine music maker! What a noble king he will be someday!' " Red blotched his face, and sweat ran rivers into his leathers. He beat his chest with clenched fists, and it thundered resonant through padded hauberk. "I am firstborn, in case ye forgot. I will be king! I will rule both Cafferty and Finucane."

"Cafferty and Finucane?" Kevin yelped, and his stern features were set as hard as his limepaste mane. Fury left him as dawning crept in.

"Why . . . 'twas ye that slit cattle to stage this battle—to make Finucanes seethe for Cafferty blood and Caffertys call for Finucane."

Cagney patted sword hilt and snorted. "My, such a clever fox! But your boasting days are over, for it's now I aim to claim your pelt."

"Ye flushed us into ambush—haunting sea and guarding derries by baileywithing at Rathdun. That was your cache in arms at the smith's shop, was it not?" Kevin's brows evened to tawny lines, and his jaw set firm beneath sculpted mustache. "With headquarters there, ye drove us north, all the while pretending to vanguard Cafferty honor. Your sorties, your nightly rides, it was as Pig Man ye rode. 'Defend me or spend me!' they cried to Lord Gawain . . . after they had pledged secret honor to ye as Black Dhurmod, of course."

"Balls a-bursting, ye are a spiny pod, Brother! But what do I have to fear? I am Gawain's own, my claim is good, and now I aim to cleave your chestnuts clean. Ho! Then ye'll keen shrill with the best of them." He threw his head back and laughed so hard his hauberk shook.

Kevin clenched his teeth tight to stay calm, for he knew that a hot temper never won a gainsay. "Uncle Eric? Did ye bribe him to goad his brother to war?"

"Bah—I would claim dear Uncle Eric and sweet pudding Ainne innocent as babes—but now I see Uncle fighting Fian for Finucane honor." He stopped to stroke the sweat-matted beard. "How did ye persuade him? I've right to know if he's to serve on my council."

"When warriors patrol common territory looking for common enemy—warriors talk. It became clear ye had turned traitor."

"Traitor! Ye dare call me traitor? Who was it, I ask, who wore the scarlet hood and stood ready to champion Finucane cause?"

"Enough of this foolish talk!" Lord Eric yelled as he and Donny crashed through the line. "Avenge Lord Gawain!" he cried, slamming his blade into the sod. "I call for blood."

Warriors, who had not yet had their fill of blood, hunkered forward, clamoring to fight. But before they could attack, Hugh and Niall's men fenced them off with crossed halberds.

"Halt, I say. Justice must be met with honor," Lochobar screeched, jumping into the arena wagging a spindly, dark-veined arm. Eric drew back in shock; he had never before seen eyes that burned golden fire.

But when Angus the Wise arrived, the blood-hungry crowd drew back. "We will hear all of this," Angus declared with authority and sat down upon his portable one-legged stool. "All claims and grievances must be brought before the people. It is the law."

"Oh, bitter my cup of dredges!" Cagney cried in a baleful bawl while keeping a careful eye on the ancient Angus. "How I hated watching ye belch the victor's cut. Having your way with women and giving me used dainties. Parrying your sorties into war parties worthy of the Heroes' Hall while ye yet live." As he wailed, septic rage slowly oozed into his voice. Catching himself, he faced the crowd and wheedled, "Lady Brigianna. Do ye not want to know of her?"

"Not from ye I don't," Kevin snapped.

Clansmen drew back, eyes well to the ground, not certain which way priests' favor would turn or if they stood united or divided. In tense concentration heat emanated from them and seared their souls in fiery judgment. Seeing Conor among them, Cagney took courage.

"Raise arms, son of Erin. No Finucane pits crown against Cafferty and lives to tell of it. Father's not around to give ye trinkets for your trouble. Let's see what a fine and brave warrior ye are now."

Raging blood rush spread scarlet over Kevin's golden skin as he could control his anger no longer. "Murderer. Ye killed my father!"

Laughter cracked Cagney's facade, and he made an obscene gesture.

"Aye," he chortled, "but which one? The deformed one who committed sacrilege by continuing as king when he should have stepped down long ago? Or the deceiver who thought to betray us by sending a stand-in beneath the scarlet hood?"

"Enough! I call for blood. Avenge!" Kevin yelled, and Angus jumped off the stool with an agility that surprised everyone.

Kevin's first lunge knicked Cagney's padded hauberk. Cagney tossed his head back; mocking laughter became puffing blasts of wind. Kevin drew back, parrying his knife upward and twirling it in front of him with a fast-spinning wrist movement. His blade became a sinuous extension of the scarline on his forearm given to him by Cagney. His feet danced turf, ready to follow this scarline to the kill.

With careful cunning Cagney lowered his eyes and made much ado over examining his blade. When he spun around, he caught Kevin by surprise. In spite of his bulk he was quick. At Kevin's punting hesitation Cagney rushed Kevin's side but, instead of plunging the blade in, yanked him off his feet by his hair and slammed him on his back.

Kevin's blade shot up. It went in, just above the armpit and below the wide leather shoulder strap, slicing striated pectoral, but not cutting deeply. He pulled it back, ready to stab again. Cagney toppled backward, and his boot knocked the knife from Kevin's hand. It skidded on the grass to spin a dizzying circle before lying still.

Caffertys, Finucanes, McColyms, and Pig Men shouted and jeered at each other as they closed in the circle once more.

Cagney staggered to his feet, sword in hand. Kevin feinted sideways and dived for his knife, rolling in the slick, bloodied grass before careening to a jolting halt. Cagney veered around and shouldered forward, both hands gripping bronze, ready to kill on impact.

But Kevin leaped over him, landing on his feet, and flew at Cagney from behind. Cagney turned in momentary confusion. Then flesh hit flesh, bone hit bone. Cagney's blade angled above Kevin's head, ready to break flesh at the hard round muscle over his left shoulder. Kevin's right arm turned slowly. With painstaking effort he brought his own blade around so that its aim was directed at the soft spot of flesh behind Cagney's collarbone.

At the same time he felt gripping fingers closing around his sword arm, Kevin's free arm shot out, clamping his death hold on Cagney's wrist. He gritted his teeth, calling on the brute force that would bring his arm down and end Cagney's days. The intended death blow met iron resistance as Cagney's knotted biceps forced it back. Kevin's cheek pit against Cagney's beard, and the smell of his own blood filled his nostrils.

Seeing their champions locked in macabre dance, each gripping the wrist of the other's sword arm, each with pointed blade gleaming death to the other's back, clansmen watched in fear-filled silence. Keening stopped and tympans turned silent. Brigianna clung to the shadows, afraid to look, yet afraid not to.

Locked like rutting stags, neither could wrest free. One must die.

Kevin's eyes never strayed from Cagney's blade as Cagney's sweat-greased cheek slid across his own and the heavy head came down to rest in the slippery curve of his neck. Cagney's blade slowly gained quarter: razor hot, it cut clean across the back of Kevin's shoulder.

Blood filled the seeping crack, then slowly dribbled warm down his back. His scream churned inside like vomit; he would not cry out. Instead, his fingers tightened their paralyzing grip on Cagney's wrist.

With a steady gaze on his own blade, now only inches from his eye, Kevin sensed Cagney's flicker of preemptory triumph. It eddied through his bloodstream in silent signal; it reached into the deep well where hope had ceased to exist. It burst within and shouted:

"Kill!"

Bloodlust engorged muscles hard. Hatred became the rod of vengeance.

Cagney's sweat-filled hauberk shifted slightly. Kevin's blade came down swiftly. The tip of it pierced the spongy triangle of flesh, which nestled collarbone to shoulder blade. It sliced the edge of the windpipe and ran into the heart, dividing its chamber wall. It tipped the lungs before its hilt braked hard against the breastbone.

With a wild cry Kevin was jolted backward.

Cagney's head flew back. Darkened eyes clouded in surprise. When he opened his mouth to speak, a river of blood trickled forth.

"Brother," he gurgled as, with trembling hands, he slid down the full length of Kevin's body to crumble at his feet, his outstretched hand turned over in a final act of obeisance.

The cry that ripped from Kevin's throat scattered the birds from the treetops and quieted the animals of the forest. It stilled only when Brigianna McColym ran to him and fell down to his side.

"Lord Kevin and the crown of a double kingdom," rang a familiar voice. Still crouching, Brigianna looked up and cried, "Lochobar!"

Lochobar and Tormaigh hurried up to them, the smaller man still grimy with the stench of battle. He gave his daughter a brief but longing glance, then turned his head away. Brigianna immediately clasped her breasts and lowered her eyes in shame, painfully aware of her disgrace.

"Please, would someone explain?" she begged.

"Very simple, my dear Brigianna," Lochobar began with pontifical resonance. But Kevin shot a hand upward, and to Brigianna's utter amazement, Lochobar shut up.

"I am Lord Finucane, the son of Erin, the man ye are to marry," he began, still flat on his back and rasping for breath.

Seeing the look on Brigianna's face, Lochobar cut in again. "Lord Kevin was chosen for Fian at Uisnech on Lughnasa's feast when he was but seven and given as foster son to Lord Gawain, king of the Caffertys. Lord Gawain accepted the responsibility and groomed him for the crown, yet let him keep his rights as Fian. When he came of legal age, he was free to return to his natural father, Erin Finucane, or remain Cafferty. He chose to remain and that's when complications set in." Brigianna leaned forward, determined brows crooked like ravenwings.

Battle heat was beginning to subside, and Kevin's skin glowed golden again, but under her scrutiny, his face became inordinately red.

"I knew ye as a child. I mean . . . I watched ye from afar . . . on one of my missions," Kevin confessed. "When I came to fetch ye . . . ye fell into my hand declaring a Finucane ye would not wed!" Shrugging his shoulders, he turned his palms up in helpless plea.

"What could I do, m'lady, but lure ye to my father's

camp and see to your safety till ye changed your mind? For there was trouble afoot, as ye well know, and I had to bell warning of my suspicions."

Brigianna heard nothing but the first part. "Fetch me?" she stammered. "The night of Beltaine ye had come to fetch me?"

"That I did," he said firmly, finally catching his wind and, rallying his strength, got to his feet. When he spoke, his piercing blue eyes bore right through her.

"Brigianna McColym, come to fetch ye I did, and now by all that is right and proper, I intend to claim ye."

Chapter 29

"I claim Brigianna ni Colym as my woman!" Lord Kevin shouted.

He stood in front of the women's quarters, dressed in undyed wool, kirtled and bound by a wide leather belt; he bore no arms, no shield, no wide-bannered cloak of kingship. Except for his medallion, he could have come as common man. For he was clean-shaven, like any man. The long, curling mustache, the mark of his rank, was now gone.

As wagging women and clansmen gathered around, Angus barged through the crowd to demand: "My Lord Kevin, what is the meaning of this? On the morrow the lady will be your queen—surely you can wait until then?"

"When I become king, what woman I take, I take as king, not as man."

"Aaaah," Angus murmured now that understanding nudged his side. He whipped his pegstool out from his knapsack and, when settled on his seat of judgment, retrieved his crozier and wrapped swollen knuckles around it. Lochobar stepped forward, but Angus waved him back. Kevin had called court. He must face his own druid alone.

"As Fian, I'm foresworn to uphold the law of Eirinn. Yet when I become king, my wish becomes law, does it not?" he said, choosing his words carefully. "Even if it supersedes the law of the land?"

Angus wiped his neck where it chaffed red from his napping woolens. "You dare play word games with me?" he said evenly.

Kevin focused his gaze just over the Wise One's head, for to look at Angus directly would be deemed impolite. "As Fian I cannot force a maiden against her will."

"Of course, of course!" Annoyed, the ancient, liver-spotted hand waved him aside. But Kevin shouldered in for his gainsay.

"As king, I must provide the pot's fair share for all who are hungry; take into my clan all who beg protection; bind honorprice without letting any man gamble his living away; provide common green; divide bounty fairly among my warriors; meet no man as foe until he first lays hand against me; harm no woman; abandon no child."

"Well said. You will rule wisely," Angus said sarcastically. But the old man turned rigid with intensity as he searched inward.

"The king calls war; the king lays down his life for his people; the king goes hungry, yet the people eat. But it is the Fian who defends his cause, and yet the Fian cannot be avenged! How dare ye say I play games!" Kevin cried with crackling anguish. "I have no games to play."

Angus kept his eyes closed, still ruminating the darkened labyrinth of intricate law: Those who serve public office have no rights to personal happiness. Both king and Fian are honor-bound to marry within station and uphold that pledge for a lifetime. Simple, secure law. Yet here stands a future High Lord calling for his woman as a common man calls for common rabble.

"When proposed, this marriage was seen as benefit to both clans. For that, not for me, it was sealed in spit. But when I went to fetch her, Black Dhurmod was afoot. And I have yet to court my woman. All that a young maid dreams of will be lost, for on the morrow my bride will come to our marriage bed as queen, never knowing.

"One day . . . that is all I ask."

Behind old, closed lids, a shaft of golden light exploded. Angus's first woman was a nut-brown creature from the deep wood; his first plunge into her warm, waiting body a dizzying expulsion of gripping ecstasy. Wizened lips pulled smooth, thinking how long ago that day was, and how fast the time between.

For all the lofty things gods have in store for us, we would, all of us, trade them in for one burning moment, he mused. With grandiose generosity, he brought his staff down and with it a shield of protection that rendered Kevin invisible. Clansmen turned away, suddenly intent upon the mundane, and Kevin jolted in surprise. Never before had he seen the old man smile.

"I come to claim ye as my woman; will ye come?"

Kevin filled the doorframe of the women's quarters, his wide smile no longer hidden by his curling mustache, his golden hair stripped of limepaste, his flashing blue eyes demanding answer.

"Kevin, why now? Why like this?" Brigianna whispered. Only moments ago when Yvonia was combing Brigianna's hair did Brigianna dare to ask: "Were ye lovers then?"

The comb, raised in mid-air, froze. "Aye."

"Tell me about it."

"On the day of his blooding, when he was thrown into the testing pit and had to face the throw of ten javelins, Cagney's throw came down on him. Blood gushed like a waterfall as Kevin fell. I ran to him, smothering the wound with my hair, trying to stop the bleeding, forgetting my station in my eagerness. Later, when he was made Fian, he called for me." There was a break in her voice, a dismissal of words that were still, to her, unutterably private. "Though we lived away from camp, he remained faithful to Lord Gawain and ran with the Fianna. For two years he was mine! Kevin McErin, the strongest and bravest of them all. I walked tall then, Lady. Then . . . one day, he left me. 'Twas over calmly as it had begun."

"Why did ye not plea before the council and demand station rights?" Brigianna asked, hands folded and sapphire eyes remaining guileless.

"Only a noblewoman marries for life. Ye should know that," Yvonia snapped, her green eyes afire.

Brigianna felt the sting, bit her tongue, then pressed the matter.

"Ye loved him?"

"One does not forget a man like Kevin McErin, Lady."

Now that same man stood before her, ready to nullify her betrothal alliance by suspending law. If perchance she did not please him, he could discard her easily as he had Yvonia. If she came by consent, she could bear the same consequences.

Once queen he could spurn her, entertain himself with other women, or relegate her to the women's quarters, but not discard her. For all that hung in the balances, if she spurned him now, she would never be queen. In despair she fingered the embroidery snugging the cleft of her breasts, and her mother's voice whispered in her ear.

"Do you let a crown stand in the way of love, Brigianna?"

"No!" she cried and flew into his arms.

Erin's white mare waited for them; its mane and tail festooned with woodroses, its tack embellished with long tassels. Corm handed Kevin his sword and cape. They mounted, she with a knee wrapped around the saddlebuck and he resting against its strong wooden back.

Petals fell like rain as clanswomen ran along their path to wish them well. Little children toddled forward to pat the mare, or to touch the golden threads of Brigianna's bridal garment. She leaned against him, and warm breasts nestled against his arm as he brought the reins slack.

"Where are ye taking me?" she asked when the sounds of piping and dance were far behind them and they seemed idled in the land of forever.

"Home," he said quietly and spoke no more until the sun

began to cool and the world about them dripped a dancing rainbow of shimmering color.

They rode deep into the darkening forest, where fading light sifted through trees in prismatic splendor. Dusk-darkened foxglove stood in purple shadow, and the air burst sweet with woodbine. Soon rowan and hazel gave way to marshgrass, and they left the copse to make their way toward a large willow guarding the headland of a gurgling river. He reined the white mare beneath it, slipped down, and toppled her into his arms, his lips blazoning sword fire against hers.

The night encased the willow canopy in soft cocoon. Only as she looked up to see the greenish glimmer tenting them did she notice a fire burning well away from trailing branches. Set with glowing turf and ringed with small stones, it looked as hearth for kith and kin, birthings and deathings, laughter and pain; the kind of fire shared by a man and his woman.

"Home," he said without apology. "And I've a hen roasting. But it's not for food I hunger. Perhaps after."

He pulled her to him with such force her tender breasts felt the cold metal edge of the medallion through her many layers of spun gold and wool. His eyes welcomed her presence, and in them he stood as a man stands, naked before his woman.

"In heart I'll always be Fian, and here I would come, spear a fish from the river, gouge the roe, say to meself that life is good, for this is the best there is. But I've never brought a woman here. When I live alone, 'tis proper bed I make; tenderest of green boughs, covered with green moss, and laid with green rush. A good bed, too, fit to cool ye in summer and warm ye in winter; a time-honored bed and one to give a man strength. But on the road I had no time to make a proper bed nor treat ye as Lady."

His cheeks rudded up as any bashful swain's. "I made ye a proper bough . . . so that in our knowing, ye would know me as I am and not as I must be in the days to come."

Brigianna turned to see that behind her, nestled in the fecund hollow of the spreading willow, a bower had been made. It was so at one with the earth, she had not even recognized it. "Lady," he said simply and backed away.

Brigianna stared at the bed and then at the man. "Why did ye not tell me from the beginning ye were the Finucane? I would have gladly come."

"When I came to fetch ye . . . ye were not exactly willing. Foresworn to return to Lord Gawain, in my private ponderings I thought to make a maid a widow before she is bedded is not such a grand thing."

"Ye could have despoiled me for pleasure. . . . "

"Ye jest! No Fian takes a woman against her will."

Firelight caught the macabre trail of his wound: a dark, clotted seam that ran the full length of his back. A vulnerable trail that made him less than a god, exposed itself in the stitched and clotted edge of raw-grained back muscle. Brigianna followed that line with loving eyes, drinking in the sinewy lithe of runner's legs. Firelight seeped through the withy willow curtain, filling the gracious dome of sweeping branches with mellow glow. Beside the Fian's bough the warrior's sword lay resting, and upon it the pageantry of royalty lay begging.

She glanced at his regnal cape, covering a bed more silken and sensuous, she knew, than any that could be offered her at Tighmohr. No woman comes to the Fian's bough: it is sacred and forbidden. No woman crawls beneath a king's cape, except it be given as hers to wear.

In fumbling search her fingers found the opening to her dress, and the gown fell to her feet. Yearning breasts teased his skin, her heart beat against his back, and the pressure of her stomach pressing against him filled her with pleasure. Her cheek fell against the crippling scarline, and she tenderly traced its path.

He stiffened. "It will heal," he said sharply.

"Not without a woman's touch," she said, as she traced the outline of his mouth with the tip of her finger, delighting in the curve of his now naked mouth.

"Brigianna, Brigianna," he murmured as if it were the sweetest sound in the whole wild world, and fire passed between them like a bolt from heaven.

She felt herself thrust rock hard against him, felt passion press upon her belly, even through his woolen kirtle. Aching to have him naked, her nimble fingers searched for passage. His lips formed a molten trail down the swanlike curve of her neck. His precious pearl comb fell unnoticed, making her hair cascade down over the both of them, and peeping nipples, eager and erect, parted the silken strands. His mouth covered one breast, stretching and pulling the nipple with taunting, tickling tongue. As her lips parted in soundless joy, her hips wiggled, trembling and eager for his touch.

Determined, she searched the belt for fasteners, but a firm hand drew it away. His warm kiss fell full upon her belly. When his hot breath found way through the furzing ruff of her maiden covering, she uttered the mixed ring of agony and ecstasy only a woman could make: the sound that spoke to man in the heat of passion, one that came without reason, but one that lived there, indelibly, forever after.

With a wild cry she fell over him, and fingertips gouged deep into hard-hewn muscle. Her legs curved weak and splayed apart.

They tumbled down between the raised rootline of the willow, and she slipped down into the hollow of his arms. She looked down, to behold the eager, straining, rounding head, seeping with pearly dew and the shattering reality of the moment ahead.

What Kevin McErin had spent a lifetime waiting for, he spent no time in getting. Penetration hit Brigianna like searing fire as the maidenhead broke.

She cried out in breathless anguish as she jerked her face away, her features torqued in fright and pain. Her nails gouged his shoulders, and her body went rigid.

He stopped: their eyes met in naked truth.

But the pent-up discipline of the warrior's mettle unleashed itself, and he could hold back no more.

The young stag stood proudly erect, his freshly molted horns etched darkly against the rising sun. Sensing danger, the dark hide trembled. He drew his noseskin tight, then stood still.

Brigianna, just waking to warmth and goodness, saw him standing and gingerly nudged Kevin. The honed hunter marshaled his senses to action, but she quickly put a finger to her mouth. When he saw the deer, his smile matched the golden radiance of morning. The deer, sensing danger past, moved a munching trail away.

"The stag comes here often, and as long as I be here, he is free," Kevin mused, just as the whispering breeze kissed Brigianna's bare shoulder, and she snuggled deeper in the nesting nakedness of rich body heat. Her stirrings were matched by the chuckering burr of the grouse, and Kevin instinctively fingered the ground beside him for a smooth pebble. But Brigianna staid his hand.

"The stag is free, but the hen is not?"

"Not when I'm hungry," he countered, pulling her beneath him in the juicy, scampering kisses of morning. Their frolic ended in laughter, with him on his back panting. She sat cross-legged by his side, as if they had always been naked together, and her rosy cheeks gave the glow of the sun fair competition.

"Soon I make ye mine. I crush the seed of my clanbadge above your head, and ye become my woman," he said, reaching into a pocket of clumpgrass and procuring the woodrose hidden there the night before.

Blue eyes took delight in the tiny veined woodrose, then looked up. "I am not yet your woman?"

"Not until ye are claimed before the people. What a man does on his own time remains his own business."

"Oh, so ye drag the maiden into the wood for a good plow after all?"

"Can ye give me better reason to drag the maid into the wood?" he teased. "And of all things, I will remember last night. But I was not gentle, was I?"

Brigianna's fluttering lashes provided her protective covering.

"I thought not. I've not had to be gentle before. Oh, love, love, how can a man tell how much he needs his woman? How can he even begin?"

She hesitated, making sport of thinking the matter over. "Well, ye said, of all things, ye would remember most last night. So I have but one request," she purred and scuttled closer to knee crinkly folds of soft dugham that suddenly hardened at her gentle prodding to stretch ten lengths of its former self.

"Someday, when we are old and gray . . . " she murmured, pressing him gently backward to fit her naked body, silken and glovelike, over his.

Fire blazoned her belly. Eyes widened in shock as the supine bow of her back snapped like the rippling crack of the whip. Head and shoulders ribboned backward, only to bow forward and lean into the wind. A thousand horses galloped beneath her; a thundering herd pounded between her legs.

When it was over, she tumbled off him in a sweating heap.

"When we are old and gray, ye must tell me which it be ye remember most . . . last night . . . or this morning."

Chapter 30

"Ride proudly as queen, m'lady, and look not to the prisoners. Their fate is no concern of yours," Kevin commanded Brigianna as they rode Erin's white horse into Tighmohr. A runner came bearing Erin's lance and shield. Kevin slammed the butt of it in its holster and with his arm braced, angled it outward to rip the sky's belly. He slipped his left arm into his shield grip, and secured Brigianna tightly against him.

Clansmen from sea to boggy flatlands thronged the hillside, eager to pay homage to the Fian who had freed them. Pig Men who still refused to accept Kevin's kingship were tethered together and forced to remain standing.

Kevin reined his mare throughout the entire encampment, stopping only long enough to exchange brow greeting with each chieftain. Finally, they reached the McColyms' campfire.

Fiona huddled in the crook of Tormaigh's protective arm. Silver wingtips against her dark hair set off the hard lines of her tear-stained face. Amabel stood behind them, eyes lowered and laugh lines gone.

"Your mother and grandmother have just learned of Doughall. Until now, they did not ken all that has happened," Tormaigh said quietly.

"Father!" Brigianna cried and shouldered forward.

Immediately, Kevin's shield slapped hard against her. "Speak but do not reach out. Ye must not be seen condescending to a lower chieftain, even if that chieftain be your own father. Only after ye are crowned can ye afford to be gracious. Do as I say," Kevin barked.

Like warp and woof, Brigianna's heart tore against itself. Keeping her eyes straight ahead, she explained to them all that had happened.

Slowly, Tormaigh reached up, removed his coronet, then dropped to one knee. "The McColym's come in sept to pledge fealty to Lord Finucane, his Lady, and now, my queen," he said.

Brigianna whipped her faced around. "Ye would call me queen? Me? The daughter who disobeyed?"

Tormaigh's voice came to her like the whisper of the wind and set at ease the aching within. "Sons I have to fill my soul. Another girlchild graces my table. Yet, of all my children, Brigianna my Fair, ye be the one my heart has loved."

"Womanhood becomes you, my dear," Lochobar called, yanking her from the dutybound business of wedding preparations. Seeing the calm of his deep-green eyes, she held out a jeweled hand and led him to her private courtyard. There urns filled with fresh flowers adorned the otherwise packed-dirt yard, and a lone wooden bench waited.

"I feared we could walk to nether and back and still not find time to talk. But I feared more that I would come to my queen's crowning, and we not be given the chance!"

He glanced awkwardly at the bench and, instead of sitting down, braced a sandaled foot at its edge and leaned forward. Garish station colors, draped in bulky folds over his frail frame, pulled back to reveal the throbbing vein in his skinny calf. Lanky bones stuck out, appearing much too big for themselves. Pained, Brigianna turned her face away, realizing perhaps for the first time how old he really was.

"You love this man?" Lochobar asked without preamble.

"McErin or Finucane, I'll have none other."

Lochobar's smile turned inward. "Erin was a fine man. Bards will long sing of him. Niall and Hugh both testified that once convinced of Kevin's true love, Lord Erin made provisions for your safe passage. So your prophecy was not amiss; you were, uh, pledged to a Finucane. Yet Balfe refuses to sing of it."

His words were simple, their import thunderous: no chieftain can walk tall if the bards refuse to sing his prow. How could she have done this? How could she not have trusted?

Lochobar's hand, lost in the drape of his great plaids, still rested upon his knee. Even though he did not look up, he knew her thoughts.

"Those who remain true to themselves never apologize for things they do not regret," he said calmly.

"Then ye do understand!" she blurted out. "I had to run. Yet I did not run. 'Twas as if my feet bid me come."

"It was I who bid you go, for if I could not have you for myself, I had to turn against you," he admitted, straightening up and listening to old bones creak as he did. "Truth is, I loved you too much. Too much for my own good, that is. Ah, bonny Brigianna, what a child we could have made, the most beautiful child ever created."

He slipped a weightless arm around her; her gown of teasled wool caressed them like a kiss. Bone pressed upon bone and heart beat upon heartbeat. A finger danced the circumlinear filigree surrounding the sapphire pendant that hung from her swan-like neck. Holding her tight for one delicious unbegotten moment, he crooned, "Oh, what a child."

With dawning smile she drew back and reached into her boot to procure the ravenfeather hidden there. "Will ye be needing this?"

"Not where I am going," he replied, and in the even tone of his voice, an ice-burr nipped her heart.

"They be calling, then?"

Lochobar stiffened, for Brigianna spoke to him now as no one dared to speak, not even one druid to another, and certainly not a woman. "I fear it will not be long. My blood is cold as springwater."

"No! Lochobar, ye cannot go!" she cried and threw herself against him again. Fumbling through the folds of his heavy robe, she hugged him to her in childlike fury, unable to deny her innocent faith once held in trust and the spirit of the man who placed it there. "Ye belong here forever. Tell them ye are not ready! Oh, Lochobar, I love ye so."

"To love and yet not be lovers, that is a treasured thing, rare between man and woman. At least I have never seen it. When you were a child, I loved you as the woman you would become, even turning aside those who would warm my bed. In the hovering flights of my soul, I longed to be near only you. I gave you honor that no man gives a woman."

"I called you Friend."

Tracing the adored, yet feared, planes of his precious face, she shook in suffering confusion. "I'll not see ye again."

"You will see me," he said, quiet as the whispering glen. "You have the ability to See what others cannot. I will never be far from you."

When he lifted her chin with the crook of his finger, poignant pain burrowed her brow, and she knew that even though queen, her heart would always belong to the little girl who walked by his side.

"On Beltaine ye knew that Kevin was waiting?"

"I knew a Finucane was awaiting. But after that my visions blurred, for after all, I never knew what had taken place beyond my Sight. You must never think I led you to your death, dear Brigianna. Never."

"Yet ye go there now."

"They say death holds no fear, that it is but a crossing over, a sleeping time between two realms," he canted, aching to ask what druids were supposed to know. "When the flames came, did you fear?"

In her mind's eye Brigianna's freshly scrubbed skin still bore the marks of woading. Even now mordant stains darkened her boots, yet she refused to part with them: indelibly, they were a part of her.

"No, Father, I did not fear. I was disappointed instead."

As that realization took hold, her spirit soared with the ravens, taking heart in the certain knowledge that she did not wing alone. Lochobar had found Kevin for her, and Kevin had taken her to the forest glen and shared with her what no warrior dares to share with a woman.

That knowledge burst like a fountain deep within her, making her words tumble down upon themselves, each clamoring for preeminence. "Why, 'twas not disappointment a'tall . . . nor was it fear of dying. But I had not lived! Oh, dear Lochobar, I must live, I must."

His smile was older than the birth of Eirinn. "I was younger even than you when I was sent into the forest to face my death. It is an awesome thing, Brigianna, to pit yourself against the cavernous night. I stood at my threshold of crossing and did not leap; I stood at the edge of my world and held back in steady defiance, because like you, I cried out to the gods and demanded my rights. 'No! You cannot have me!' I shouted. 'First, I must live!' "

For one lingering moment Lochobar gently pressed the shivering coldness in his bones against her beating heart, seeking refuge in her fertile warmth, and with deep sigh said: "I have lived long upon this earth, and my time of crossing has come. I go now, with peace in my heart. You were not afraid to die, my child. Do not be afraid to live."

Clansmen from sea to central valley gathered upon Tighmohr's green to pay homage to Lord and Lady Finucane. When the golden crown was laid upon Kevin's head, cow horns trumpeted, pipers wailed, and Angus raised his hands to still the tempest. Brigianna stepped forward and listened proudly while Rory recited Kevin's genealogies. But when her youngest brother recited hers, she wished it were Doughall standing there.

Kevin crushed the hip of woodrose above her head, and the Colym became Finucane. Its seed fell into ravenlocks, where, according to tradition, it could not, for this day at least, be brushed aside. Once more voice swelled its cacophony of praise, and Lord Kevin led her to her throne.

"I offer provision and protection for Cafferty and Finucane alike. The valley will remain common green between us," Kevin announced. Limepaste had bleached the hair around his temples and turned golden strands completely white. His cloak, embroidered with seven station colors, billowed behind him.

"Were the father who fostered me still alive, I would fall to my knee. Were the father that bore me still alive, I would claim my birthright." He thumped his knotted fist against his chest. "But they do not live. I do."

His clansmen had expected rounding rhetoric, a brandishing braggadocio, a grandiose gainsay. This simple statement stunned them.

Lord Eric and Lady Ainne were the first to bow in obeisance. Their sons followed. There was a searing grate of metal as a sword was unsheathed. Niall bent his knee and pressed his blade to his forehead. Hugh did likewise. Then, like grain laid flat by the wind, clansmen fell. Among them, Pig Men stood out like blight.

"Lying, deceitful swine!" Kevin shouted in full timbre. "Ye slept in my father's house, ye ate of my father's food, ye turned my father's people against him. Kingkillers! Traitors! Ye honored Swine Cagney, and like swine ye should die!"

With a flash of his wrist, he unsheathed his sword and swiped it against his leather gird, so that the straining of metal against leather sounded like the cracking of a man's neck. "But I am a fair man. I try ye as Cafferty. So if it's Cafferty ye are, cry—defend me or spend me—or die!"

Pig Men fell to the ground quick as a rain of arrows. But not all of them. The rest of them thought the matter over seriously, then, fully conscious of what they were doing, fell to claim Kevin as king.

"Bah," Kevin cried. "Those too quick to bend their knee know no master but self. Cowards all. Let those live who know the moment's hesitation. The man who thinks twice about the master he serves, serves with loyalty."

He pointed his sword to those men first to fall who, upon hearing his words, squirmed like maggots. "Kill them," he commanded.

Stunned, Brigianna jumped to her feet. "No!" she cried.

Kevin's face paled. "Begods, Brigianna! Stand back!"

His arm flew out to halt her, planting her footfall behind his. Had even her toe crossed that line, her days would be over.

"Am I to come to the throne to see my bride's head roll in the dust?" he said between clenched teeth and with features hard as stone. "Stay your hand against mine and by king's rights, my sword must fall to your neck."

Conor, Angus, and Lochobar rushed forward. Conor's hands clawed at her like waiting talons. Brigianna froze. One look at her clansmen and she knew that at their druids' command, they would leap forward and rip her apart.

"No! I beg ye, hear me all. I do not stay my hand against my Lord. I stand by his side. Our land and our peoples cannot be divided, the McErin must stand as king of all."

Slowly, Kevin brought his arm down. Just as slowly, Brigianna moved to his side. Then Kevin addressed his people.

"The king lays down his life for his people; the Fian defends their cause. The king calls war; the Fian cannot be avenged. I am King. I am Fian. But I do not live or die for cowards. Kill them."

Now Conor leaped forward, curved fingernails clawing the air. "Stop this outrage! It is I, your druid, who claims judgment over life and death. I divide spoils of war. I decide what the king can and cannot do."

Kevin's nostril's flared. He grabbed his father's lance from Corm, who was standing nearby, and raised his arm to throw it.

Angus and Lochobar exchanged quick glances. What happened next was born of time immemorial and of a knowledge buried so deep in ancient memory it mystified even them. Without thinking, they acted as one. Crossing bony arms, they ringed thumbs and forefingers together, and in a unified arc, cursed Conor to the land of the living dead.

Fright blazed in Conor's eyes. Gnashing his teeth in stubborn defiance, he crashed through the cursing barrier and landed on all fours in front of Kevin.

"Save me!" he cried, grabbing his throat. "Get them away from me. I am your druid. Do you hear me? I challenge the sacredness of life, not you."

Words were to no avail. He faced the killing point of Kevin's lance and his eyes bulged out in ebon horror. Kevin threw it. It sliced into the earth and stuck there, quivering, a mere handspan from Conor's nose and just between his outstretched hands.

He scrambled to his feet, and ran from clansman to clansman, shouting their names and demanding that they recognize him. But they stared right through him as if he wasn't there. For to them, he wasn't. To them, he was no more than an animal who must forage and fend for itself.

Slowly, his face became the straightfaced mask of stark realization. He screamed his raven madness, and ran into the fields, tearing at his clothes and batting at the air.

When the crowd had settled down, Kevin called his court to order. His first decision was to make Lord Eric king of the Caffertys in sept to him. And, in the course of making certain all his people would be well cared for, he called Yvonia to him.

"My Grania's spirit has left her, I fear, for she wanders aimlessly from cooking pot to cooking pot and does not even know her name." Kevin paused, holding the depth of his pain within. For what he asked now was a request, not an order. "Care for her, I beg, and by that, all ill will be forgotten."

Statuesque in her summer-green gown, Yvonia's normally smooth brow raised in question and cat-quick eyes grew intense. In them was the unabashed reflection of the love they shared so long ago, and just as unabashed, the honest regret that she had not spoken up for herself on the day he had left her. Trembling, she started to kneel, but Kevin caught her.

"For all we are and have been, I beg ye, never cower in my presence."

His resonant voice put years of spurning to rest. She looked up, and a bright smile broke through her veil of tears.

Brigianna needed no special sight to fathom beckoning green shadows. Her blue eyes flashed fire, and her chin jutted up in dark determination.

"Lady Brigianna?" he said, puzzled.

"'Tis custom at king's crowning for a true king to give away some portion of himself, is it not?" she said as she stood back up.

"Aye, a true king gives his people a portion of what has been given him, by honor and without question," Kevin recited by rote but cast a nervous eye to where prisoners awaited slaughter, then to his warriors-in-arms and druid council. "But of course that honor is double-sided, for no one asks that which cannot be given. Now, say on."

"Upon our first meeting I declared myself a freed woman. Ye spit me clean, granting me power to come and go as I please. And in your great kindliness, ye pledged honor over me, to protect me always. But before ye would take me queen, ye demanded me as common woman. I came to ye in love, and it was by love ye took me.

"But 'twas on chance of being spurned I lay by your side. For ye said in that woodland bower, 'Ye be not my woman till I claim ye before the people,' and later ye declared, 'What a man does on his own time is his own business.' "

"Brigianna!" Kevin cried aghast. "Words spoken between a man and woman are not to be aired publicly."

"To be sure," she demurred, lowering her voice so that the wagging prattle had to quiet in order to hear. "Of that

I be in agreement and did not think to embarrass ye, kind Lord. For a moment ago, in presence of father, priest, and clan, I became your wife. To that I give honor, good husband. But ye stand before me now, not just as man, but as king. For that, Lord, my heart holds a great question."

In spite of the fact that she looked disarmingly helpless, instinct told him to be cautious. "Say on."

"I question, Lord, if first honor still stands."

Hearing this, Lochobar's eyes flashed yellow fire. So! He was not losing Sight after all. The maiden had spit herself clean, coming out from beneath his power. For that his dreams went bad on him, for that he led his people in darkness. Then, at Lord Erin's court, Angus spoke and he found the golden raven once more.

Well, well, dreams were like skeins of yarn, he mused, picked up or raveled from either end. And suddenly, for his eyes alone, the sky turned golden, as two ravens flew overhead.

In the firm voice of royalty Kevin demanded: "Lady, what do ye ask?"

Brigianna looked at her waiting women: for them, as well as for herself, she chose her words carefully. "Ye sang of dear Queen Maeve as freed woman with lands and cattle of her own. . . ."

Flush crept up the back of Kevin's neck. "Aye, that I did."

"Maeve and Ailill were free to come and go as they pleased since they both held crown and lands. But, if that be so, were they not just as free to stay? That is, if they so chose?

"A woman pledges fealty to her man, as much as warrior to liege, for she lays down her life in childbed readily. So it seems the man, if only by sense of fair play, should do the same, should he not?"

Finucane, McColym, and Cafferty men leaned forward slack-jawed, and Angus let out a great gush of wind that was ignored in the tense silence.

Kevin instinctively reached to stroke a mustache that was no longer there.

That her request was unprecedented shone clearly on the face of his council; that his prow was at stake marked the faces of his warriors well.

"Woman, are ye saying that by king's rights and in his travels, there should be no waiting women or dancing maidens?"

"Oh, nay, nay, Lord," she said with earnest shake of her head, "I would say it otherwise. If a woman pledges legs and loyalty to a man, and tends his hearth while he is away, then does it not add sparkle and luster to that trust if the man keep himself thus? Is not that shared by a single woman and a single man like the spit and polish that burnishes gold to a fine sheen? Or the wisdom of a true jewelmaster who sets the single stone in its golden bed?"

He stared at this woman who had faced the wind and run it with him, and all other desire vanished. Yet this was unheard of.

But grousing out his chest he declared, "Fair now! Of a truth, I was thinking the same meself."

He stretched out his hand, and although they were at court, they might well have been on their private balcony by the way she melded to his side. "Ye do not think my request an unkind thing?"

"In breaking clanbadge upon your head I pledged as any man pledges. Prow and provision for ye and our young. But ye tread where no woman dares, fearlessly and without caution. So harken, woman, and listen well." His raised palm quickly quieted the crowd.

"Hear ye all, and let it be so said. On the day of his king's crowning, Kevin Finucane took to wife Brigianna ni Colym as virgin and upon that day did forsake all others who came before her and all who would warm his bed after and, by clan witness and in presence of high druid, did pledge fealty and faithfulness to her and her alone."

In the shouts that followed, the Lady Ainne turned to

Lord Eric with a quizzical look, and he quickly lost himself in the crowd.

Tormaigh embraced his daughter. "Fair, ye have made me a proud man. Twenty cows it is Lord Kevin has given me for your hand."

Brigianna looked as if she had just been slapped across the face. "Ye brought me? After all talk of love and honor, ye bought me?"

"Bought ye?" cried Kevin. "Woman, I could have got you for three. I give ye honor." Indignant, his brows turned into white streaks against his reddened face. "Twenty cows, and from my father's prized strand."

"Ye bought me. Common wench to fetch and bear."

"I did not. I bring ye honor. Twenty cows. That is a good price."

"Ah, there! Ye admit it."

"Never let it be said this Finucane is not a fair man," he harumphed. "Thirty cows, then."

Tormaigh elbowed Fiona, who squinted as she played with her fingers, trying to fathom such a great number. Brigianna's brothers crowded closer, fists and fingers ready in wager. Angus teetered backward on his pegstool, his agile mind busily tallying wager, then looked up in honest surprise as the stakes doubled. Behind him small stones pitched in the ante corners toppled as those stakes grew higher.

"Thirty cows!" Kevin repeated with a slam of his foot.

Brigianna's ire snapped. "Thirty cows? Kevin Finucane, I would not come for fifty."

"Fifty," Tormaigh breathed wordlessly, and Angus put a quick hand to his worried brow. But the commotion upon the dais snapped quiet as Brigianna shouted: "Fifty? Bah. I would not come for a hundred!"

"By my crown, I'll not have ye shangie in front of my men!" Kevin bellowed. "For what will ye come, then?"

A winsome smile toyed with the corners of Brigianna's mouth, and she put a finger to her lip to keep it in check.

"For the likes of ye, Kevin Finucane, only for the likes of ye," she said as her giggles got the best of her. "All ye had to do was ask."

At being twice done in a single day, his hands shot up in surrender.

"Well said, clever Brigianna, well said." His fox fur-lined cape furled behind him, as he pulled her to him with a quick movement. "Which calls to mind another matter to be settled between us."

"Aye, and what would that be?" she parried.

"We would not want it said this Finucane is not a fair man."

"Oh, no, m'lord, no."

"Nor would we want it said the fox came to the Finucane in the guise of a woman and made sport of him on their wedding day," he bandied.

"Lord, we would not." Nervously she fingered her necklace as he scrunched her to him.

"Perchance ye know the other song they sing of the great Queen Maeve? The one sung in warriors' camps and upon the road?"

"Lord?"

"Ah, I thought as much. It seems our beloved queen was quite a wench. And there is only one way to treat a wench. Right, me lords?"

"Right!" they shouted with raised fists as Kevin swooped Brigianna up and over his shoulder like he would a sack of barleymeal. With right arm raised in triumph, he held her well-padded rump securely.

"Put me down, I say!" she screamed indignantly.

Undaunted, but laughing now, he whirled her round and round as he did that day amid swirling sea and sand at the shore.

If her sense of dignity suddenly vanished, so did her balance and bearings in the whirl of vivid colors from sky and land and shining faces blurring into one. "Oh, put me down!" she cried weakly.

"Never!" he shouted in lusty lung for sun and moon and

wind and rain, and the canopy of nether that lies beyond the borealis, to the shimmering aurora of the eternity that comes before and the eternity that comes after, and finally to that magical, mystical, marvelous place, where gods live and laugh and make love forever and, in foot-stomping revelry, lift their horns and shout with gladsome song:

"Yah! Glad it is that ye have lived!"

To them, and to all mortals everywhere, Kevin shouted: "Put ye down, Brigianna Finucane? Never!"

Epilogue

"We have done well for ourselves, Tormaigh, my friend. Brigianna's sons will come kicking from her womb ready for battle," Lochobar said, chuckling in spite of himself, then turned to Angus. "You are not staying? You are moving on?"

"I have never failed to appear where I am needed," Angus replied calmly. And Lochobar looked into lively blue eyes, continuously churning like the welling sea, and just as vast in knowledge.

"The long night calls?" Angus asked, and Lochobar nodded. Already the throbbing in his vein had begun; thinking of the long journey ahead only reminded him of his frailty.

"Then, go in peace, Brother, and I shall be waiting."

Lochobar looked at the wizened, bent body, with pegstool secured in the knapsack and gourd as drinking cup dangling from his belt. He had looked that way when Lochobar first met him—the day he beggared entrance into druid council and was forced to face the ravens. Angus was an old man even then.

But now . . . the Wise One called him Brother.

Tormaigh, understanding none of this, bobbed back and forth, first on one leg, then the other, anxious to return home. As the lines parted, he turned to his priest and confidant and, with a look of unabashed adoration exclaimed:

"One hundred cows. Imagine that!"

If you enjoyed this book, take advantage of this special offer. Subscribe now and...

GET A *FREE*

NO OBLIGATION (a $3.95 value)

If you enjoy reading the very best historical romances, you'll want to subscribe to the True Value Historical Romance Home Subscription Service. Now that you have read one of the best historical romances around today, we're sure you'll want more of the same fiery passion, intimate romance and historical settings that set these books apart from all others.

Each month the editors of True Value will select the four very best historical romance novels from America's leading publishers of romantic fiction. Arrangements have been made for you to preview them in your home Free for 10 days. And with the first four books you receive, we'll send you a FREE book as our introductory gift. No obligation.

───── *free home delivery* ─────

We will send you the four best and newest historical romances as soon as they are published to preview Free for 10 days. If for any reason you decide not to keep them, just return them and owe nothing. But if you like them as much as we think you will, you'll pay *just* $3.50 each and save at least $.45 each off the cover price. (Your savings are a minimum of $1.80 a month. There is *no* postage and handling – or other hidden charges. There are no minimum number of books to buy and you may cancel at any time.

HISTORICAL ROMANCE –

—*send in the coupon below*—

To get your FREE historical romance and start saving, fill out the coupon below and mail it today. As soon as we receive it we'll send you your FREE book along with your first month's selections.

Mail to: 55773-489-5
True Value Home Subscription Services, Inc.
P.O. Box 5235
120 Brighton Road
Clifton, New Jersey 07015-5235

YES! I want to start previewing the very best historical romances being published today. Send me my FREE book along with the first month's selections. I understand that I may look them over FREE for 10 days. If I'm not absolutely delighted I may return them and owe nothing. Otherwise I will pay the low price of just $3.50 each; a total of $14.00 (at least a $15.80 value) and save at least $1.80. Then each month I will receive four brand new novels to preview as soon as they are published for the same low price. I can always return a shipment and I may cancel this subscription at any time with no obligation to buy even a single book. In any event the FREE book is mine to keep regardless.

Name _____

Address _____ Apt. _____

City _____ State _____ Zip _____

Signature _____
            (if under 18 parent or guardian must sign)
Terms and prices subject to change.

*A NEW DIAMOND NOVEL ON
SALE IN MAY*

LOVER'S GOLD

By Bestselling author of Captain's Bride
KAT MARTIN

"The best young historical writer I've read in a decade. Bravo." —Fern Michaels, author of
Texas Rich

When a hired gunman came to her small Pennsylvania town, Elaina McAllister knew with one look at his glinting blue eyes that she could never love this insolent stranger. But against her will, she found herself aching for his touch... Hiding behind deception, Ren Daniels felt his heart become captured by this tender beauty. Destiny tears them apart, leading Elaina to the glittering world of San Francisco's high society. But she yearns for the burning touch of her lover, and for the fire of their everlasting passion.

_LOVER'S GOLD 1-55773-505-0/$4.50

For Visa, MasterCard and American Express orders call: **1-800-631-8571**

FOR MAIL ORDERS: CHECK BOOK(S). FILL OUT COUPON. SEND TO:	**POSTAGE AND HANDLING:** $1.00 for one book, 25¢ for each additional. Do not exceed $3.50.
BERKLEY PUBLISHING GROUP 390 Murray Hill Pkwy., Dept. B East Rutherford, NJ 07073	**BOOK TOTAL** $ ____
	POSTAGE & HANDLING $ ____
NAME_____	**APPLICABLE SALES TAX** $ ____
ADDRESS_____	(CA, NJ, NY, PA)
CITY_____	**TOTAL AMOUNT DUE** $ ____
STATE_____ ZIP_____	**PAYABLE IN US FUNDS.** (No cash orders accepted.)
PLEASE ALLOW 6 WEEKS FOR DELIVERY. **PRICES ARE SUBJECT TO CHANGE WITHOUT NOTICE.**	D591